Ben Alderson

A BETRAYAL OF STORMS

REALM OF FEY BOOK ONE

ANGRY
ROBOT

ANGRY ROBOT
An imprint of Watkins Media Ltd

Unit 11, Shepperton House
89 Shepperton Road
London N1 3DF
UK

angryrobotbooks.com
twitter.com/angryrobotbooks
A Fey As Old as Time

An Angry Robot paperback original, 2024

Cover by Sarah O'Flaherty
Edited by Eleanor Teasdale and Shona Kinsella
Set in Meridien

ISBN 978 1 91599 868 2
Ebook ISBN 978 1 91599 876 7

Printed and bound in the United Kingdom by CPI Group (UK) Ltd, Croydon CR0 4YY.

9 8 7 6 5 4 3 2 1

To my husband, my guard, my love, my duty and my pleasure.
Harry, this is for you, and for our future.

CHAPTER 1

I woke to the uncaring kiss of a dagger at my throat. My eyes didn't need to open to confirm it, not when the familiar sting cut into my skin or the smell of a rusted blade teased my nose. It was strange, I would've never thought a dagger had a scent, but I supposed that having one in such close proximity unveiled such secrets.

"You've got him?" a rough voice asked, but the question wasn't for me.

"Shut it, you idiot!" Another, slightly deeper voice responded. "Let the bastard go, and you'll be paying with your own blood."

I risked opening my eyes, the only movement that wouldn't end with my blood spilled across my nightshirt and bedsheets. It was close to impossible to think straight, but I had to. There was no room for haste, not with my potential end a mere slice of a blade away.

It was still dark, and my room was without drapes, so it must still be the dead of night, or at least the hours surrounding it. My room was washed in a blanket of shadow, for the moon's glow gave only enough to focus on the looming shapes above me as my sight struggled to take in meaningful details.

It seemed, when in a life-threatening situation, one's mind calculated as many specifics as possible. And right now, my mind whirled as I put together what was happening.

The first speaker was a man, his voice rough from years dragging from the pipe, and his broad outline only confirmed his gender. If it was still night, it meant Father was hours into his night shift at the King's Head tavern in town. He wouldn't return until after dawn, which could be a handful of hours away.

I was alone with the assailants.

My dog, Winston, hadn't barked at their arrival. So, he was either dead or just shit at his job. I really hoped for the latter.

The second speaker was also a man, although his voice was lighter, as though someone had kicked him hard in the balls and they'd never returned to their normal seating. He was the one holding down my legs by my ankles as if I'd dare to kick out. I knew better than to act, now at least.

"I think he's looking at me," the first said again, a faint hint of panic in his voice. He put force behind the blade, and it bit harder into my skin. "I don't want him looking at me!"

The second's hands fumbled around my ankles before letting go, but the tightness of touch didn't release. No. He'd bound my legs. I watched him join his accomplice at my side, spying the rope he twisted in his hands.

"Then bag his head."

There was another scent to join the rusted blade. A sharp tang that I was all too familiar with. It smelled of Father, at least it was what clung to his worn clothing when I found him sleeping across the armchair in the mornings after a long shift at the tavern. Lush spice and hot flames. The signature dwindling kiss of whiskey. But this scent did not cling to the assailants' clothes but to their breaths. I would've turned my head away from them just to stop inhaling the wretched odour, but I stayed still, cautious of the blade at my throat.

"Nah, doesn't matter if he sees. Let him. His memory of us isn't going to help him where he is going to end up."

They both laughed at that. Deep, snorting cackles like pigs.

"As long as I get the coin promised," the first said again, leaning down over me. I felt the tickle of a touch against my shoulder. Straining my eyes confirmed it was his bulging, ale swollen stomach. "Got anything to say for yourself… *Robin Vale*?"

I began to fish the face of the speaker from my rambling mind. His stout, broad form and husky, smoker-tickled tone invited the rosy-cheeked face of James Campbell into mind. If he knew my name, the likelihood that I knew his was high.

"James," I said, voice husky from sleep. "To what do I owe the pleasure of your… late-night visit?"

"Shit," the second hissed, stepping back away from the bed.

I pouted, forcing a frown as the blade tickled fearfully close for my liking. "Usually, it's your son who provides me with company during such late hours. Did you hear good things and want to try me out for yourself?"

My focus was on his face, now clear as day as he brought it to hover inches from mine. A face bloated from the years of the drink he'd frequently downed at the King's Head. Even now, the stench of whiskey and dried pork crackling told me that he'd likely left the tavern recently.

"Keep him out your thoughts, filth," he hissed, flashing yellowed teeth and the gaps that surrounded them. "I suggest you think carefully about what you say next, or it may be the last thing you utter."

"I don't believe that a second. If you wanted to hurt me, you would've when I was sleeping," I replied, wagering a bet that I was, in fact, right. "Otherwise, that blunt little blade of yours would have already done its worst."

"Bag his head!" the second shouted. I couldn't place his voice to a face, but that didn't matter. What mattered was *what* they were both here for.

"Shut up," James snapped in reply. His calloused, short-fingered hand gripped me by the shoulder and squeezed. I tried everything not to show the discomfort it awarded me. "A little nick won't change the price we are promised for you."

My initial thought that coin was involved had just been confirmed. He had made that clear more than once. I knew it drove those desperate for it to interesting lengths, but this… this was a step too far. More like an immortal leap away from simply calling him desperate.

My mouth parted as yet another retort sprang to mind. But I was quickly silenced as his hand released my shoulder and slapped over my mouth.

"Gobby little shit, think you're better than *us* even now. Even with my *blunt little blade* to your throat." He mocked my voice, softening his own and rounding the hard edges of his tone as he mimicked me. "Bounty has racked up for the likes of you, boy. I'd be a fool to ignore it. Anyone would. So, for the sake of a little spilt blood, what you are going to do is listen and do as we say."

"Yeah," the other chorused, still hiding in the shadows.

James pressed his weight down on me, causing the bed to groan. "If we get this over with soon, we may even have time to return to the tavern and buy your father a drink with the coin we get for you. Hell, it will be enough to buy everyone in that tavern a drink all fucking winter long."

I didn't blink, not as I took in the man's wide, unblinking dark stare. Even in the gloomy room, I could recognise the feral spark looming far within his eyes, as though he was starved and looked down upon a hulking mass of cooked meat.

It was a miracle when he didn't start drooling over me.

With the hand still pressed on my mouth, I couldn't laugh aloud, but in my head, it was all I could hear. If there was any moment to fight back, it was now.

Hard, I bit down on his palm until he spluttered a cry. Warm blood filled my mouth, causing copper to explode across my tongue and inside my cheeks. The taste was vile, but it did what I needed. James released his hold, enough for me to force myself upwards, thrusting my forehead into his with a sickening crack.

The sound was beautiful. Painful but delightful in equal measures. It filled the room as though the thin panes of my windows had shattered. My head hardly throbbed beneath the impact. Father had taught me well, ensuring I knew how to do as little damage to myself as possible when dealing the most to others.

The pressure of the dagger at my throat lessened, likely with the tumbling fool of a man who stumbled backwards with his face in his hands. I didn't wait to be reintroduced to it as I reached for the rope at my ankles and pulled.

Whatever knot they'd rushed together fell away in seconds. Sloppy, which was fitting, considering how this was all going so far. James had clearly drunk a lot, because he wobbled like a fawn on ice. Kicking my legs over the bed, I stood before the two men had a chance to regain their composure.

"What now then?" I asked, shaking my hands at my sides before clenching them into fists. I'd never been so ready to hit someone before in my life. First, they'd woken me from a dreamless sleep – which was rare for me. Secondly, they were in *my* home, uninvited. And that fact alone stoked the embers of aggression inside of me. "Perhaps you want to rethink your plans this evening before you both end up, well, accosted."

"Accosted?" the softer voice asked, honestly confused. If I could see his features clearly, I would've likely seen a peaked brow.

James stepped forward, his thick body blocking most of the moonlight from the window behind him. "We haven't come this far for you to ruin it, boy. You can either come with us breathing, or we risk ruining our winnings by providing you dead. The choice is yours."

Oh, I wonder what I'll pick.

This was probably the moment to ask who exactly was willing to trade coin for me. But there was no time for questions as James raised the dagger before him, pointing the tip right at me.

"Did no one warn you not to play with sharp things?" I rested my weight on my hip, voice dripping with Father's inherited sarcasm. "Especially not in such... intimate quarters."

My room was small. It was the only room in our ramshackle house that had its own door. Up in the alcoves of the building, there was hardly room to walk, let alone knock two drunkenly stupid men off their feet. But I supposed if there was a will, there was a way.

"I've had enough of your talk."

"Told you to bag his head!" James added before settling hateful eyes on me. "If you want to play games, then let's play."

I smiled, feigning confidence. "If I'm honest, I've never been one for games."

"Good," James muttered. "Nor have I."

I dodged to the side as James lunged towards me with the dagger outstretched, his footing awkward and rushed. Adjusting my stance, I spun, stepping around the man until I was directly behind him. Foot raised, I kicked into his lower back with all my strength until he staggered forward with arms spinning like a pinwheel.

A hand gripped my shoulder, turning my attention before I could watch James falling onto the bed. Instead, I revelled in his cry of surprise before the wooden frame broke beneath his unwanted weight with a snap.

"Pretty bracelet," the second man said. "Will be a waste where you are going. I'll look after it for you, promise."

Long slender fingers reached for my wrist. I panicked. Throwing my arm back, I tried to get some space between me and the man. Seeing him up close still didn't bring a name to mind. But his demeanour was more... put together than James's. I noted strands of thin, blond hair that haloed his thin face, trying to puzzle the details of him into a picture that I'd recognise. He stood straight, his soft hands telling me that he was no fighter.

"Don't fucking touch it," I snarled. The iron looped bracelet was plain and likely worthless to sell, but to me, it was everything, the most precious item I owned. To hell if this man thought he was taking it.

"Now, now. I promise to treasure it. Until I reach the nearest pawn merchant that is."

I punched him, knuckles connecting perfectly with the soft skin of his exposed throat. The man's eyes bulged in his head, mouth open as he gasped for breath. Not wasting another moment, I threw another fist into his gut, doubling the tall man over. His face then greeted my knee with one sharp knock upwards.

He hit the ground like a sack of shit.

I didn't wait for him to get up. Not as the strong urge to run overwhelmed me, and I moved for the door.

"One more try, lad, and I will cut you from innards to fucking ear!" James was already waiting for me, his thick body blocking me from reaching my only way out. His shout shook the very rafters of the house. And as it settled, I heard another noise. The faint crunching of feet over the stone gravel beyond the front door.

Someone was outside.

Father.

I would've screamed for him to help, but I wasn't one to cry out for such a thing. If I couldn't deal with two crazed drunkards alone, I'd only face the disappointment on Father's face.

So I changed my stance, bending my knees, which clicked from the movement. I tensed the minimal muscles in my stomach and arms, focusing on the man before me. He wobbled slightly, brandishing the dagger as though it was a sword ten times the length. Behind him was the open door, and beyond that, the narrow stairs which led down to the ground floor. I prayed to whichever god would listen that Winston was still sleeping. Alive. Useless, but alive.

Stretching my neck from left to right, I narrowed my focus on him. "Unfortunately, it would seem you'll be short on coin for ale this winter. I do apologise."

James opened his mouth, spit linking rotten teeth. But before he could utter a word, I ran.

With my body lowered, I rammed my shoulder into his protruding stomach, taking the brunt of the impact first. Down we both went, like falling dominos. I was lucky for his size as it cushioned the fall. I lost my bearings as we tumbled. Closing my eyes, all I heard where his agonised cries, audible over the banging as we fell down the darkened stairwell. Now this hurt. As my body smashed into the narrow walls and connected with the sharp edges of the steps, I could only hope the heavy man beneath me took the majority of the impact.

It took seconds, long, painful seconds, to register that we'd come to a stop. My head was spinning violently. I opened my eyes and could hardly focus. An ache sang above my eyebrow. I lifted a finger to the sensitive spot, only to find they came back red and wet.

"Ugh… fuck," I hissed, arms screaming as I pushed myself from the ground.

"James!" the second man shouted from atop the stairs. I looked up at him and saw double. "Are you alright?"

"Get… him," James drawled, moaning as he wriggled on the floor beside me. The thundering footsteps of the second, as he raced down the stairs, encouraged me to get moving. I used my hands to fumble my way in the direction of the front door. I could hardly focus on my footing, only that I needed to get outside.

Whoever was there – my father, a neighbour or passing local – would help me.

My vision doubled as I trudged forward. My shoulder connected with the hallway's wall, knocking a picture from its hook. Bare feet scraped over shattered glass, but on I fought.

Get out. Get out.

Blood pooled over my eye, blinding me. I wiped it away, only smudging it more.

"Get off me, you fool! Get him now!"

"Don't worry. He won't get far."

I glanced back over my shoulder and spied both men fumbling over one another. The thinner man tried to pull James from the ground, but he swatted away all attempts. It was almost comical, if I wasn't bleeding from my head wound. But even through my haze, I wondered why they didn't follow.

I could hardly register how strange that was. Not as pain vibrated around my skull.

The world began to still as I reached the brass handle of the door. And still, their footsteps of chase did not begin. Turning the knob, I pushed my weight against the door and threw it open. I cringed as it banged against the outer wall, half expecting a scolding shout from Father. Even at my twenty-four years of age, he still had control over my childish fear.

The cold rush of nightly breeze dusted over me, cooling the cut above my brow. Winter was most definitely coming, as it always made the later autumn nights sharp with the first inhale.

I stumbled out into the darkness, ready to force my legs into a run. If I left the door open, Winston would surely follow. And the King's Head was not far to reach.

James was right. I didn't get far.

I slammed into a body of darkness. In the dark, it was impossible to see where the hard mass began and ended. I stumbled backwards, stopped only by an arm that reached from the shadows and gripped me.

"What *do* we have here?" a voice drawled from the shadows.

Squinting, I tried to make sense of what was happening. Then material shifted, a hood lowered, and a face glowered at me with piercing verdant eyes.

The difference between this man and the two others inside was as stark as night and day. He sparked fear inside of me with a single look. There wasn't a need for a dagger to make me stop in my tracks.

It was not the very shadows he wore but armour woven from the blackest leather and cotton. His cloak swished freely in the late autumn winds as though it wanted to show off the silver threading and intricate detailing, the type of fashion we village folk could not dream of owning.

I caught the flash of metal at his waist, distracting me. Behind me, James and his helper were laughing – greedily.

It made sense why they didn't follow me. Because they didn't need to. And the noise I had heard from beyond the window of my room was not Father arriving, but this mysterious figure who had me held in his iron-clad grip.

I tried to pull away, to fight free, but his hold only intensified. Then his voice came again, full of precision and class. He spoke so calmly that, for a moment, I thought I was safe in his hold.

"What's your rush? Do you have somewhere more important to be? *Fey scum.*"

A shudder sent waves of scratching discomfort beneath my skin as a black-gloved fist came out of nowhere and was thrown towards my face. Before his fist connected, I pinched my eyes closed, as if that would help. A burst of light exploded behind my eyelids, snatching me away from reality in an instant. Those final two words echoed through my mind as I fell into the painless darkness.

Fey scum.

CHAPTER 2

In waking hours, I remembered little of my mother. But it seemed her featureless face haunted my dreams more often than not.

Hair so black it gleamed with a subtle blue shine. Thick and wild, even the smallest of breezes seemed to coax the strands into a dance. Her voice was soft, so much so that it would likely lull the loudest child into sleep.

And her ears, twin peaks on either side of her blurry face. Long and proud, never hidden, always peeking through her hair.

That was it. All I could conjure when I dreamed of her.

I supposed my mind clung to those details because they were what Father would remind me of. The same features I'd taken from my mother; obsidian hair, eyes as black as a winter's night, and a gentle-toned voice. And my ears, although not as long as hers, they stood out painfully among the realm of humans.

The dreams of my mother would never last, quickly morphing into nightmares as I longed so desperately to see her eyes. I wished I could remember if her lips parted when she smiled or if her cheeks presented dimples when something amused her. Little details that, to some, would not matter. But to me... well, I would trade the world if I could, just to know.

Just to see her. To remember her eyes or the curve of her mouth. Any other details that were kept from me were secrets I longed for more than I did the very secrets of the world.

But those secrets would never be revealed because she chose to walk away from me. In the shadowed corners of my mind, I often pondered why she didn't return for me. Gods know my father missed her too. I could see it in the quiet moments when he lost himself to a thought, when his own stare was stuck to an unimportant place, his mind whirling with memories.

I dared not ask him about my mother. It had been years since we shared the last, deathly short, conversation about the whys and hows of her disappearance. So, no matter if it was a dream I saw her in or in the muddled mess of my consciousness, I always found myself reaching for the bracelet of iron around my wrist.

It was last thing she gave me. And that made it my most prized possession.

I woke to screams. Distant yells and cries that sounded like cats fighting in the streets of Grove. I pried my eyes open a tad, only to snap them shut beneath the glare of daylight. Raising a hand to cover my gaze, I found my wrists had been tied together by rough knots of rope.

That's when all the events of last night came rushing back to me. Everything that had happened, not a detail spared. James and the black-clothed guard and his strong fist. I lifted a hand to my brow, feeling the tender skin and dried blood. Throwing my eyes open, I blinked away the shock of light to take in my surroundings.

I was in a cage. One that moved. Wheels squeaked beneath me as I registered the cart-like vehicle that rocked violently across a dirt path. Around me were tall bars of obsidian metal that gleamed in the light. Straining my neck upwards, I took in the covering of equally dark material that was connected from one side of the cage to the other.

The late-autumn sun kissed its warmth down upon me but did little to keep the cold winds from nipping at my nose and exposed arms.

Looking down, I gulped as I witnessed the loose trousers and once white tunic that I'd worn to bed. My bare feet were coated in dirt, a handful of cuts left from running over the broken picture frame.

There were mutterings of a conversation coming from the front of the cart. Keeping as quiet as I could, I looked over to find the backs of two guards, each dressed in familiar dark, stained leathers.

"Excuse me!" I shouted, tugging at my wrists. My jaw ached, and my head panged with the echoing of pain, the leftover memory of the punch that had knocked me out cold. "I think there's been a mistake. Whatever you think I've done, I can guarantee I haven't. You've quite obviously got the wrong person."

One of the guards turned their head, only slightly, then focused back on the road ahead. "Hand over those ten coins," he said, nudging the man to his side. "Looks like the bet is mine."

The second guard responded, clicking his tongue in some signal to the horses before him. "You only won if he didn't wake until we arrived at camp... and the horses are still moving, are they not? The winnings are mine, and you owe me coin!"

My insides burned as the Hunters discussed me like I wasn't here. What I'd give to thrust a fist – or two – into unsuspecting noses. But my anger wasn't a reaction solely for that reason. It was that I'd even gotten myself into this situation. My thoughts were full of 'should haves' and 'could haves'. Should've fought harder. Could've made more noise, alerting a neighbour or someone. Anyone. Then again, would they've come to help?

"James Campbell," I dragged the prick's name from the bellows of my mind. "If he... whatever he has done or told you I've done, it's all lies... I promise I am worthless. I wouldn't even bet ten coins on myself, let alone five."

"Any more talk, and we'll gag you," the guard said, his voice registering through my panic as the one who had punched me in the first place. How much time had passed since I'd been knocked out? Daylight beamed upon us now, it had to have been hours.

"Just tell me what you want from me?" I called out, voice cracking as though my balls hadn't yet dropped. I tried standing for a moment before the cart rocked like a ship on violent waves, sending me crashing back on my behind.

"Shut it, lad! Do yourself a favour and keep whatever little plea you have brewing to yourself. Trust me, we've heard it all before. And then some."

It was clear that these men came from money. Or at least they had money behind them. No one in Grove, or any of the surrounding villages, wore such well-threaded clothing or had carts made of metal or owned horses with such perfect, gleaming coats.

"I'm innocent…"

"Your ears suggest otherwise."

Cautious of my ears, which wasn't exactly a new feeling, the tips of them heated.

"Commander Rackley has given word that we will move for the capital by sundown. A few more of our bounty have been captured. Then we cash in and celebrate."

One of the men patted the other on the back, causing the cloak around his shoulders to flatten out for a moment. A symbol etched in silver thread spread across his back. It took up most of the material but soon folded beneath creases as he yanked on the reins once again.

For a moment, it looked like the outline of a hand. Curved lines of thread stood out starkly against the deep black material it adorned.

I opened my mouth again, seeing how far I could get questioning them, when the noise stopped me. It sounded like… crying. Wailing of children and the pleading screams of those much older.

A murder of crows screeched across the skies ahead of us, frightened by the noise that filled the blue, cloudless void.

I craned my neck, looking beyond the thick bars of the cage as the cart turned. Then the smell hit me. Copper. Rich, intense copper that made me scrunch my nose in disgust. Blood. The source of it was not hard to find.

In an open field, a wall of thick trees crowning at its side, was a camp. At first glance, it reminded me of a group of performers that once passed through Grove, putting on a display of drama and entertainment for three nights. But this was nothing of the sort.

Other cages, like the one I sat within, lined up throughout the jumbled camp. Countless bodies filled them with arms reaching outwards as though those within begged for aid. The closer we gained, the more I could see. There were so many other guards, each dressed in the same black armour of those who navigated my cart. Cloaks billowed, flashing the same hand symbol I thought I'd seen.

Some guards prowled the camp, slamming the sharp edges of swords onto the cages, shouting for the silence of those within. Others pushed people ahead of them, chains trailing between their wrists and feet, all linked to a thick band of metal that strangled around their throats.

And no matter the horror I witnessed, it couldn't distract me from the pungent, sickening scent of blood.

We pulled into the camp, the horses slowing to a stop. Before the men could dismount, other guards reached for the back of the cage and pulled open a gate.

"Out!"

I couldn't speak. Fear thickened my tongue and dried my throat. I scrambled backwards until I was in the corner of the cage furthest from them. I readied my legs to kick out as they inevitably reached for me.

"Feisty one…" one of them said, but it was impossible to focus on who.

"The half-born always are," another replied, in the same pompous accent as the others. These were city folk, from Lockinge most likely. The capital the guard had not-long-ago mentioned when he spoke about Commander Rackley's order.

The name felt important to me, I just couldn't place why.

"Going to bite, half-born? Or do we need to fill your mouth with something to stop you?"

Half-born. Hearing it aloud stung. It slapped across my soul as countless eyes glared at me from beyond the cage.

"You look like the type who'd love that," I sneered.

"Careful of this one," the familiar voice of my captor said. "Tricky prick caused some damage on the way to the collection. You should've seen the two that sold him off. One will be bruised terribly for days, I am sure."

"The coin will smother their ailments. It always does."

They talked of James and his accomplice. Knowing that I had caused them pain sparked some pride in me. But that was soon doused out completely as gloved hands reached for my ankles and yanked me forward. The back of my head connected with the floor. I saw stars with each blink, too many to count. A throbbing across my skull joined the rest of my current discomforts as the hands pulled me across the cage floor and towards the exit.

"Where are we putting *him*?"

"He's been tested, and he showed no reaction. So, you can put him with the other, *useless* bunch," my captor replied.

Someone tsked. "Shame, this batch has not been as fruitful as I hoped. If we come back with little stock, it will not go down well with The Hand."

I tried to focus on what others said next, but it was close to impossible as rough hands dragged me away.

"Get your fucking hands off me." I registered how pathetic I sounded, but there was no room to care.

They didn't listen nor care. They hauled me towards the row of larger cages. Each one was as full of wailing, shouting people as the next. We passed one that was beyond crammed. Bodies stuffed together, hardly an inch of room between them as they screamed and shouted.

I saw children hiding between the legs of women and men. Most cried, but some shook the dark bars of the cage with such vigour that I was surprised the bars didn't rip free.

"Keep back, the lot of you!" My captor only had to shout the warning, and those within the cage stilled from fear.

Patrolling guards thrust the points of their swords between the bars. It caused those near to move far away from the blades, giving those who held me enough room to unlock and open a gate. And from one cage to another, I was thrust inside.

One moment I was held in their grip, the next I was on my knees, palms aching as they barely broke my fall. The rope that still bound me rubbed the skin of my wrists raw.

Metal slammed against metal, and the cage was shut once again. With me inside.

This time it was soft hands which reached me, lifting me from the ground as an echoing of worried questioning rocked over me.

I blinked, unable to still the quaking of my mind. Faces looked upon me, each pinched with concern and equally measured fright. And in every face I took in, I noticed something odd. A detail I'd only seen in my own reflection, or the foggy memory of Mother.

Pointed ears.

These people were fey. No matter their height, size or age, they each had points at the tips of their ears.

And besides my reflection and the distant memory of my mother, I hadn't seen another before. Not half-fey like myself, nor full-blooded. And seeing them all before me didn't calm me but urged the storm within to rile wilder.

"Are you alright?" a woman asked. She had close-cropped blonde hair and bright cobalt eyes. Her face and neck were smudged with dirt and grime. Red marks signified a struggle she'd been through. Unlike my nightwear, she wore garments of finery. But hers were just as ripped and dirtied, as though she'd wrestled with a thorn bush and lost miserably.

"Who... who are they?" I asked, looking around at the overwhelming number of faces. "Those guards, why are they doing this?"

The crowd grumbled, and a small chirp of a cry sounded from below me. Looking down, I saw the round face of a child peeking between the woman's legs, similar wide blue eyes bursting with the same fear that all those around me held.

"Hunters." She took my hands in hers, lips drawn into a frown. "Of our kind."

Fey. She meant fey. I parted my mouth, ready to tell her that I was not, in fact, fey. But something in-between. I'd argued it for as long as I could remember.

Opting to play along, hoping to find the answers I needed to get out of this mess, I asked another question. "And what is it they want from... us?"

"Blood." The answer was plain and simple. "But you don't need to worry. We are powerless – useless. Until they find a new need for us, I hope they'll let us go."

I hardly doubted that.

I wanted to pull away from her but didn't. There was something calming about her touch. She looked down to her child and returned her attention back to me with a shake of her head. It was clear that whatever she longed to say was kept quiet due to the listening ears of the child.

"There is no need for these anymore." She began tugging at the ropes, flashing broken nails and blood-covered knuckles. "Let me help you out of them."

No one else here seemed to be tied up. Discarded rope littered the floor of the cage, or what I could see of it.

"Thank you," I said, wincing as she began tugging with shaking hands. I hissed between clenched teeth as the rope pulled away, revealing the red skin.

I had so much to ask. But chaos devoured the camp, making even the slightest word impossible without shouting.

I wanted to question the kind stranger again, but a feral scream lit the sky. We snapped our attention to our left, spotting a handful of the guards pulling another woman through the camp. They dragged her by the hair, mud covering her exposed legs. She batted at their hands and arms, digging nails into the material that covered them. But on they heaved her.

There was a strange drumming in my chest as I watched. As though a bird flapped frantic wings, trying to catch flight but not succeeding. I pressed my free hand to my sternum, trying to still the feeling.

The guards finally threw the fey to the ground near an aged stump of wood. Even from a distance, I could see scars across the wood, jagged lines that burrowed deep into its surface.

She struggled like a butterfly beneath pins, throwing everything she had at the guards. They forced her body to bend unnaturally until her head rested upon its side across the stump. It took three of them to hold her down, because she fought as though her life depended on it.

Which, I could see, it did.

"*Altar*, take her pain," the fey to my side uttered, reaching down for her daughter, who began to cry quietly. I glanced at her, tearing my attention from the scene to watch the woman press a hand over the young girl's eyes. "Count to ten, my darling girl. Count to ten for mummy."

It was the same thing my father used to make me do when I was scared. A distraction technique. A way to make the mind focus on something simple, over the root of the anxiety.

"One." Her small voice broke beneath a cry.

I looked back to the scene as the entire camp of caged fey fell silent.

"Two."

A giant, broad-shouldered man sauntered towards the woman on the stump. He was dressed in the black-leathered uniform the rest of the Hunters wore, but unlike the others, there was a stained, torn apron wrapped around his waist. In his thick, gloved hands, he carried an axe, needing both arms to hold it aloft. The handle was wrapped in ivory material, and the blade was stained black with aged blood.

"Three."

Before he even reached the struggling woman, I understood what was about to happen. Everyone who watched did.

"Four."

My gaze drifted to a shadow that spread through the grass around the tree stump. But it wasn't cast by the fey woman or the Hunter standing above her. Her hands pressed into the ground, unable to do anything else.

"Five."

Blood puddled around the tree stump, soaking trodden grass and mud.

"Six."

My heart thundered in my chest. My hand shook as I pressed down upon it as though it would stop my heart from simply bursting free of the confines of my ribs and flesh.

"Seven."

The fey woman upon the stump no longer screamed. Eyes wide, she gave up her fight. The Hunters who held her down moved her braid of thin, chestnut hair from her shoulders, exposing the length of her pale neck.

"Eight."

I felt the need to shout. To do something, anything, as the Hunter took his place above the woman, his belly casting a shadow down upon her.

"Nine."

Death was imminent. The entire camp silent as they too expected it.

"Keep going, my girl, keep going."

I reached for my wrist, needing to feel the solid, grounding loop of my mother's bracelet. But my fingertips met skin. Breathless, I looked down to see nothing but the new, red bracelets of rope burn.

The bracelet was gone.

Something the reedy man with James said cut across my mind the second I looked up, back to the scene.

I'll look after it for you, promise.

With both hands, the executioner raised the axe, hoisting it above his head with one great swing. A wink of light caught across its sharp edging. It reached the apex then arched downwards through the air. I could hear the wind scream as the curved blade sliced towards her waiting neck.

"Ten."

There was a wet thud. It knocked the breath out of me, but I refused to look away. Not when the axe rested between her head and shoulders, embedded into the stump beneath. It took a moment for the life to leave the woman's eyes. Then her head swayed off the stump and onto the ground, where it seemed to roll in small circles before finally stopping at the executioner's booted feet.

That was when the screams began once again. I didn't join. Not as my blood seemed to freeze entirely, a creeping sensation of familiar cold that exploded from the beating in my chest and spread down my legs and arms in one large web of energy.

I expected to shatter into shards of ice. Melt like snow beneath the beating sun.

But I kept still, staring as the Hunters kicked the rest of her body from the stump, discarded without care upon the ground.

"Look away…" a small voice chirped, followed by the warm, soft hand that fit into mine like a small piece of fruit. "We can count to ten together."

It was the young fey child, her face bright with innocence and trust as she held onto my hand. She was the anchor, a stranger, who kept me tethered to reality as the horror replayed itself in my mind.

"One," she urged softly. "Two…"

I joined in with her soft voice, my own cracking as I fought the urge to turn back and watch the beheaded fey be carted off. The child's bright eyes entrapped my gaze and blocked out the horror as I focused on her, and she focused on me. The explosion of panic in my chest calmed enough for me to focus, as though her voice leashed the storm and kept it at bay.

"Eight, nine and ten."

CHAPTER 3

I took to breathing in and out my mouth when the Hunters lit a pyre sometime in the late morning. It didn't take long for the sickening scent of burning skin to thicken in the air as the body fuelled the flames. Above the bedlam of the camp, I was certain I could hear the popping and crackling of the fey's bones as the fire ate past layers of flesh and muscle, devouring far deeper.

Like twigs in a hearth, her destruction sounded so painfully... mundane. As though something horrific didn't melt away within the fire. Her body turned to ash as though that was what she was meant for.

An overwhelming, guttural pain in my stomach did wonders at smothering the foreign ache in my chest. From frantic beats of a large bird's wings, it shifted to something calmer. Like that of a subtle flutter of an insect. I'd swallowed back gags, whereas a few others in the cramped cage let their guts spill across the floor. Still barefoot, splatters of vomit splashed freely against them, only urging me to empty my already empty stomach. Not to disregard the old, dried puddles of sick that told tales of what had been witnessed before I arrived.

It became clear what would become of the *useless* fey.

Death.

My mind flirted with ideas of escape. Wychwood was so close, a wall of trees that gave way to only shadow beyond. If I could get out, somehow break free and run, then I could find help beyond it.

But thoughts were soon shot down by the arrow of reality. More Hunters flooded through the camp as the hours passed by. Countless horses pulled black metal cages, unloading their cargo just as they had with me upon arrival. Whatever this was, whatever these men and women were doing, was organised perfectly. Convoys of Hunters arrived, unloading cages only to fill them again with others. But the fey they carted into the cage-on-wheels each had the metal cuff around their neck. It was soon obvious that those were of more interest to the Hunters. Kayia, the mother of the small child, said it was to do with their blood, but what was so different about it?

Kayia cleared her dry throat and pointed to a horse and cart that had just been loaded with chained fey and begun to leave the camp. "They keep doing this, taking some but leaving others. Those fey they–" She paused, inhaling a shaky breath and lapsing a hold of her child who held onto her for dear life. "What they did to her will happen to the rest of us. I know it."

"You said it was their blood?" I asked, gripping the cold black bars and squinting to try and see something, anything that would distinguish the fey that left, from us.

"It has been whispered in court about humans who prey on our kind. Hunting for those of us who possess abilities. Magic. I was a fool to think it was only threats to keep us away from this side of Wychwood. But alas, it was not a threat. Did you not hear the same warnings from your court?"

I shook my head, not willing to admit the truth of my heritage. "When I arrived, one of them said something about a test."

"They did the same with me and Lia. But we, like you, seem to be the unlucky ones."

Although my mother was a mystery, I knew much about the fey. It had been required learning during schooling. Teachings of the four courts and their histories, those who ruled them and the power of what it meant to be fey. It had been hundreds of years since the Wychwood Accords were signed by the royal lineage of all courts and the firstborn human king. Since then, the fey had very much kept to their realm and the humans to theirs.

Until now, I guess.

I fought the urge to lift a finger to my own ears. They had usually made me stand out stark against the humans I lived among. But here, in this cage and with those around me, I looked no different.

I belonged.

"Did your... court say anything more about what happens to those with... magic, when they're taken?" I asked, forcing a smile to the small girl who huddled between us. I was cautious as she listened in quietly, and there was something about her wide stare that screamed of intelligence, as though she could see through my illusion of skipping the questions I did not want to answer.

"It is not certain." Kayia's pale brows pinched, causing lines to spread across her forehead. "The humans have longed for power for generations. If it was not for the accords, they would have demanded it long ago."

I remembered one of my teachers saying something similar to Kayia. Even at my young age back then, I clung to the idea that the humans signed the accords to keep their kind safe from the powerful fey. But now I knew the truth. The fey signed for the very same reasons. A two-way mirror, each side of Wychwood and its boundaries.

Questions filled my head, clogging my throat. I had so much to ask. Even now, caged like an animal with the rancid smoke of burned flesh teasing my nose, I wanted to devour the knowledge of this woman. I'd never been with someone like her. Like me. It was unheard of for the fey to pass beyond Wychwood, losing the protection of their kind. So the idea of ever asking the questions that burned deep within me felt like a distant possibility.

"We need to get out of here," I whispered, keeping my voice low as two guards walked past the cage. "There are more of us than them. We could overthrow them if we acted as one –fight our way out."

Kayia huffed in amusement. "I admire your mind, but it seems that you have been reading too many stories. It is not worth the risk. What they did to her, they will do to us."

I looked around the cage to the faces of exhausted fey. To the children, squashed between adults, whose eyes were swollen from crying and cheeks red and raw.

"I have no doubt we will meet that fate whether we do something about it or not. And I would rather go knowing I tried my best to change this forced fate. Kayia." I gripped her cold, stiff hands. "We have to try."

"I told you…" Tears gleamed in her eyes, her lips pursed with tension. She knelt down, hugging her child close to her chest but not once dropping her unblinking stare from mine. "It is not worth the risk. This is our doing, leaving the protection of Wychwood. We would not make it back within its boundaries before an arrow struck our backs. All we can do is wait and hope that our queen sends aid for us."

Looking at the small child, I could understand Kayia's worry. And deep down, I knew she was right. They would not make it. Looking beyond them, I could spy the edges of Wychwood standing like sentinels of bark and thick leaf in the distance, taunting me.

"Then what?" I asked, thinking of my father. I'd tried hard to keep the image of him from infiltrating my mind. But seeing this woman holding her child only stabbed at my heart like a serrated blade.

He would've returned home to find me missing. Or perhaps he wouldn't have checked on me, trusting I slept soundly, not wanting to disturb me. He often fell asleep on his armchair, only for me to wake him in the morning. But today, he would sleep far later than he normally would.

"We wait and pray that *they* send someone to retrieve us." Her gaze flicked in the direction of the woods, and I could only imagine who she must have been referring to. Her queen. Some fey royal from one of the four courts.

Raised voices and shouting distracted us both from the conversation. It was different to the other noises that filled the camp. For this was fuelled by determination and fury.

A young woman, perhaps no older than me, ran from a gaggle of guards. She weaved through cages, leaping over piles of rubble, her fire-red hair trailing behind her. Although it was pointless, because the guards were not chasing. They didn't need to. Not when a long chain trailed from the thick, metal cuff around her neck that ended in one of the Hunters' hands.

Like a dog, she was leashed at the neck. However, it did little to stop her from trying to get free.

A small gasp escaped me as the Hunter tugged hard on the now taut chain. I almost felt the very wind being knocked from her lungs as she flew backwards, slamming her back into the ground.

The entire camp watched on, but not in the same way they had with the execution. This was different. The first time the crowd didn't whimper in defeat. Instead, they began making clamour, shouting threats to the Hunters who toyed with the flame-haired fey.

Lia spoke up and muttered a name.

"Althea."

I didn't look down at her as I witnessed this *Althea* clamber from the ground and face off the Hunters. Waves of poppy-red curls flowed down her back. She was tall; even from a distance, I knew she was likely inches taller than me. And her body was broad and strong. The muscles in her arms flexed the brown material of her shirt, the leather of her breeches bunching as she lowered into a fighting stance, knees bent and fists raised before her face.

She spoke to the guards, but she was far enough away that I couldn't hear her. But whatever she said caused them to howl, throwing their heads back as they laughed to the sky.

The fey around me mumbled again, some snarling and hissing. And again, like Lia had said, I heard her name, clearer this time.

"Althea."

One of the guards was urged forward by the others. He stepped Infront of Althea and raised his fists to greet hers. Then they both moved, Althea a clear step ahead, in strength, speed and precision.

With as little grace as a newborn calf, the Hunter thrust forward and was bested in seconds. It was impossible to see what happened, for in one blink, he was laid out on his back as Althea darted towards the next Hunter.

She leapt over the chain, thrusting a kick towards another one closest to her. A thrill sliced through me at the sound her foot made as it connected perfectly with bone. The entire camp heard the crack and cheered, screaming with glee. Which seemed to encourage her to fight harder, sharper.

By the time she reached the third, no one was laughing. Other Hunters ran from tents and out of carts towards the fight.

Althea moved as though she was a reed in the wind, body twisting out of the way of fists and outstretched legs. One Hunter pulled free a sword from the belt at his waist; stabbing it forward. I was certain it would cut her down, but she spun at the last moment, missing the edge by inches. Dancing around the outstretched blade, she took the slack chain from beneath her and wrapped it around his neck. He dropped the sword and reached for the chain as she pulled hard. His eyes bulged, and a gargled sound broke free from his throat as he tried everything to pull free.

But like a spider, he was fully entrapped in her web.

"She has come for us," Kayia spluttered from my side. She grabbed onto me, tugging excitedly at my arm. "I told you. I told you they would."

"Who would?" I asked, watching as the fey girl shouted at the Hunters around her. She held the strangled Hunter's back to her chest and yanked hard on the chain. She was clearly negotiating with them, lips moving quickly as she got out what she had to say. But it was not working. Slowly they surrounded her, stepping inward to encase her in a circle of their bodies.

"Althea Cedarfall."

Something about her name registered in my memory, but too much was happening for me to latch onto it. I looked back to Althea, unsure how she would help free us. She was seconds from being overtaken by a haul of bodies herself. She snarled, face contorting into a mask of fury, all while the Hunter's face turned blue as the air was kept from him.

The scene soon changed as the tides of her fate went from in her favour to against it. In seconds she was accosted by countless Hunters who bundled her as one. They didn't stop coming until she was overwhelmed completely. I couldn't begin to comprehend how it took more than five to control her.

A wave of black-clothed bodies threw themselves at her until she was unseen among their huddle. All I could hear was the thwacks of fists and boots as they rained them down upon her.

My knuckles turned white as I gripped a hold of the bars before me. The fluttering in my chest intensified one again. I screamed, joining in with the rest of the captured fey. Swept away by the tidal wave of emotion around me, no one stayed silent as they watched on.

"Cowards. Release her. Let her *fucking* go!" I shouted alongside those around me. Even Lia screamed, crying *Althea, Althea, Althea*, as if it was the only word she knew.

I was certain the cage rocked as the bodies threw themselves within it. Althea Cedarfall meant something to these fey. Something grand, for even Kayia shouted, spit flying from her mouth. She'd not long been defeated but now stood with the demeanour of a warrior. They all did.

"Monsters, you monsters! You dare touch the child of Cedarfall."

"Leave her."

"Me, take me! Let her be!"

I couldn't distinguish one plea from the next. It went on, the sky alive with the cries of countless fey. And the shouting soon did something, because the huddle of Hunters dispersed, leaving only two who stood over the very still and *very* quiet body curled in on itself.

The Hunters moved quickly towards each cage, thrusting swords within the bars to keep the chaos at bay. They tried to obtain order with violence, but there was nothing to calm the feeling that poured from the people around me.

It was intoxicating.

I hardly registered the young Hunter who came towards our cage. But Kayia watched and waited. As he closed in on the cage, she thrust two spindly arms out of it and wrapped them around the back of his neck. With a great heave, she pulled him forward, pressing his face between two bars.

"Help!" was all he managed to splutter as nails raked down across his sun-kissed skin, ripping ribbons of flesh from his face.

More fey closed in around us, each trying to throw a fist or cause him pain as Kayia did. A wall of bodies formed between me and the guard, thrusting me backwards as they all rocked forward.

Lia screeched in terror, and I reached for her just as the hulking body of a fey male almost trampled over her.

"It's okay" I said, pulling her into my arms. "I've got you."

"No," a voice sounded above the noise. "It is *I* who have you."

One moment Lia was in my hold, the next, she was not. Pulled free by the gloved hands of a Hunter who'd taken a moment in the bedlam to open the cage door behind me.

Her scream did wonders at slicing through the disorder. Even Kayia stopped her attacking, realisation and horror darkening her eyes.

"No," she gasped, reaching helplessly as Lia was dragged away. "My daughter, no!"

Lia kicked out as she was lifted free of the cage. I sprang forward, reaching for her ankle before another Hunter could slam the door closed.

"Give her back." Spit flew from my mouth as I lost myself to frantic emotion.

"Feisty still?" the Hunter replied, a familiar grin tugging the corners of his thin, pale lips. "Did you not learn your lesson last time, fey scum?"

Somewhere behind me, Kayia screamed again, but I didn't dare look back. No. My focus was on Lia and not letting go.

"You cannot have her," I seethed, hissing through a clenched jaw.

Lia split her mouth in a silent screech, her face pinched with terror and pain. Pain I was causing her. But I couldn't let her go. No matter the marks my fingers left across her small, delicate ankle. At least she would still be alive. At least her head and shoulders would stay connected to one another, and her body would not be thrown into the flames of the burning pyre.

"And if we cannot have her –" He loosened his hold slightly, enough for me to pull hard. Like butter over a flame, she came free from his grasp and fell onto me. Down we tumbled to the ground of the cage, the wind knocked clean from my lungs. "Then we will have you. Someone must act as a reminder as to what happens when you fight back. And I think you are far more deserving."

Gloved hands found my body and tore me out of the cage.

No one stopped me from being taken. Not as I had done for Lia.

No one called my name.

I couldn't fight back, for the agony in my chest was excruciating. The fluttering was now an army of winged beasts, violently flapping to break free from the cage deep in my chest. My breathing hitched as I was dragged across the ground, the sky shifting above me; all my hands could do was uselessly drag alongside me, dirt sinking under my nails.

Above me, the Hunter smiled. The sun haloed behind his head, covering his features with shadows. "Don't worry, lad, they will all meet the same fate as you. A little secret between us, but when we have filled our quota, and your powerless, pathetic kind are not needed, you will all be left as feasts for the crows and wolves. Nothing more."

We came to a stop, and all I could register was the smell of copper. It was stronger here. Forced onto my knees by unkind hands, I could see the permanent shadow of blood that stained the ground beneath me. And the stump, the one the fey woman's head had rested upon, waited before me. Deep, uneven lines scarred the surface. Old and new blood covered all memory of brown and cedar of the wood, leaving only different shades of red across it.

A hand pressed down on the top of my back and slammed my face down upon the stump. I winced, cheek and jaw throbbing beneath the impact. But the pain was nothing like that in my chest.

Was it my heart? Was I going to die long before the inevitable blade was forced down on my neck? I'd heard of older people passing from heart failure. That was what this felt like it could be, that my heart was about to explode within my chest.

The ground seemed to shake as heavy footsteps closed in on me. I could not see the executioner, but I knew he loomed over me.

Unlike the woman, I didn't face the crowd of caged fey. I could not allow myself to see the faces of those who watched on. Instead, I faced the bloodied ground beneath me, chin scraping the hard bark at the edge of the stump.

"Your kind is worthless. Be grateful we waited this long to purge you from this realm."

I pressed my hands before me, fingers splaying across the ground. Cold tickles of grass rubbed beneath my palms as I dug my fingers into the blood-soaked dirt.

The man was speaking again, but the thundering in my chest finally broke free, filling my entire being with a cold, frozen knowing.

I pinched my eyes closed and steadied my breathing. In and out, I breathed. One long shuddering breath after the next, the shiver built beneath my skin. There was no explaining the feeling, beside the desperate need for freedom. An urge to release. There was no holding it back, this torrent inside.

My eyes shot open, and a shout clawed its way out of my throat. Breath fogged before me in a cloud of thick, white smoke that confused me for a moment.

Then I let go. A key turning, unlocking a box I had never recognised before. And the sensation that followed was of pure bliss. It was unexplainable and unimaginable. Euphoric and free.

Beneath my hands, a sheet of pure crystallised ice exploded outwards, spreading in a wave of unstoppable, frozen mist, devouring everything in its path.

CHAPTER 4

Hunched over the earth, I caught my reflection in the sheet of ice spreading out beneath me. Wide eyes, my mouth parted in a silent scream, hair tousled by frozen winds. Magic belonged solely to the fey, but never me.

The fey were naturally stronger, faster, with senses heightened to a point that hearing conversations they weren't a part of was not uncommon.

But only the ruling bloodlines could bring forth storms, alter their bodies into different forms and conjure elements from nothingness. Four families whose magic and power meant more than simply being good listeners or standing taller than the average person.

Although I knew little of my mother, at least I trusted that she was likely nobody special in her realm. As ordinary to those who ruled above her as the humans I was brought up among were.

The pointed tips of my ears seemed to be the only curse of my heritage. I wasn't blessed with the other gifts even the mundane fey possessed. I was privy to the backlash that came with my ears that never stayed hidden within the curls of my dark hair. But magic, no. Never magic.

I'd often wondered that the snide remarks and frowned gazes would've meant less if I had access to magic like the ruling courts. It might've made the years of torment worth it. Not knowing that I was powerful, but being able to burn those who spoke negatively towards me to ash. Yes, that would have been rather wonderful.

Magic was not a human trait, and it also shouldn't have been mine.

But with each exhale, clouds of thick white mist rolled forward, drowning out all sound. It washed across the ground like an angry, living wave. It devoured everything before me. Beneath my palms, the power poured freely, uncontrolled, leaving a diamond layer of ice which formed mountains of pointed spears and peaks.

I followed its progression, with wide, unblinking eyes. The power was unstoppable. And yet, deep down, I knew I could stop it if I wanted to. Ice concealed the two scuffed boots of the executioner, spreading freely up their legs. Craning my neck upwards, I watched the ice turn flesh to crystallised stone.

It was their cry of agonised pain that stopped me. The shock dragged me from the strange, dark pit of my mind and slammed the open box in my chest closed. In a beat of my heart, the magic simply... stopped.

There was no pressure keeping me on the stump anymore. Taking advantage, I pushed myself up, but my hands stung beneath the sudden, breath-taking cold. I looked down to where my fingers had been splayed, only to find the outline of two handprints left upon the ground, surrounded by winter on all sides.

I scrambled backwards, slipping, as I pushed myself away from the wailing figure of the executioner.

My heart dropped like a stone in my chest. A boulder. The man, with the axe raised in the air, released a keening cry. His swollen, toothless face twisted in pain. From the ground to his waist, he was coated in silver shards of ice. Fingers of mist curled from the frosty layers as the midday sun beat down upon it.

I couldn't believe what I saw, the shock so terrible that my mind didn't link that it was I who'd done this, even though all points of logic suggested so.

All I could do was watch as he shrieked, veins bulging in his neck and face. Then his sounds of terror morphed into a gurgled breath. I hadn't heard the whizz of air as the arrow sliced through it, burying itself through the man's mouth.

He coughed, eyes wide, splattering blood over his paling lips. Droplets of deep ruby splashed across the white, ice-covered ground. I cringed as some splattered over me. I blinked, feeling the dreadful warmth along my face as the man's blood dribbled down my cheek and neck.

Another arrow joined the first. This time I heard it slice through the air. With sure and confident aim, it embedded itself into the man's large forehead. If the first hadn't killed him, this surely did.

He dropped the axe, eyes rolling into the back of his head. My bones felt as though they shattered when the metal fell onto the ice that coated his legs. Then he snapped, his heavy body breaking at the waist, his torso separating from his legs. Half of him hit the ground with a sickening thud. The other half stayed in place, legs frozen still with rivulets of blood and gore dribbling down them.

Bile burned up my throat, gagging me.

I pressed a hand to my chest, trying to still the thundering of my heart. My stomach spasmed as another wave of sickness threatened to claw itself up and out of my throat.

I hardly registered when the ground began to tremble beneath me. If it wasn't for the acute instinct to keep myself alive, I might never have taken my eyes off the dead man before me.

Tearing my focus from the corpse, I turned my head in time to watch a miracle. It was a scene pulled directly from the textbooks that I'd devoured as a child.

Fey, a horde of them in gleaming brass armour, exploded into camp. They rode on large stags whose antlers created a shield of interwoven bone. The Hunters stood no chance as they broke beneath the heavy hooves of the creatures. Blades of silver swung freely at the sides of the stags, cutting down any lucky Hunter who hadn't been crushed beneath their weight.

Hunters fell, overwhelmed by thrice the number of warriors. And all without the fey needing to dismount.

I watched as more fey warriors broke free from the distant shadows of the Wychwood boundary, dust clouds blurring the path behind them as they rode with great speed towards us. By the time the final one met the camp, not a single Hunter was left breathing. Bodies littered the camp, blood feeding the earth, so that when the fey finally dismounted, I could hear the boots squelch in gore

Every single fey warrior focused their attention on freeing those in the cages. I watched as those with cloaks, the shape and colouring of autumn leaves, unlocked doors, allowing the streams of captured to flood out into the open.

All the while, I didn't move. I couldn't even if I wanted to. My body was as frozen as the severed corpse of the executioner, just without the ice coating my skin. But it was inside me, uncurling like a serpent, poised and ready.

Kayia and Lia joined the crowds. Free. They were free.

And I was left alone, surrounded by the explosion of ice with the body of a human still bleeding behind me.

A broad form stepped before me, gleaming like molten gold.

"Are you hurt?" the deep voice asked. The fluttering in my chest exploded as the sudden presence cast a shadow across me. I felt the trickling of calming cold spread across my skin as the lid of that box within me began to creep open once again.

Looking up from my perch on the ground, I raised a hand to block out the glare of light that danced over the deep, brass armour of the figure. Up close, I could see it was more golden, with hues of honey and cedar. Squinting against the light, I made some sense of who this person before me was.

His face was covered mostly by the sharp-edged helmet, but there was no denying his eyes. They shone like twin diamonds, so bright they matched the silver of the sword he held up, pointed at me.

"I am going to need you to use your words," he said, kneeling down so the glare of light settled, and I caught my first glimpse of his face. "Are you hurt?"

"Not yet..." I replied, gaze snapping to the sharp point of his weapon. "Unless you plan to use that against me?"

"Precautions, that is all."

"So you don't have a habit of asking such questions, before dealing a deathly blow?" I asked, my father's sarcasm rising to the surface as the shield it always had been.

Slowly the fey warrior lowered the tip of the sword, pressing the end into the ground. I couldn't deny the relief that pooled within me. I watched warily as he leaned on it as though it was a staff or walking stick. "From what I can see, you will deal far greater damage than I could." He offered a hand, the cream material of the glove flexing beneath the tug of his long fingers. "Now, it is not befitting for you to stay on the ground. Stand."

"From what I can see, you are the dangerous one." I hesitated, fingers digging into the dirt at my side. "You killed *them* all."

Them being the Hunters, but clearly this fey warrior didn't need me to explain myself.

"It may sound like an odd request, but I am going to ask you to trust me."

"I don't even know you."

His fingers flexed, impatient as he waited for me to take them. "I have come to save you. Well, not you personally, but all of those who've been captured by these Hunters. And if you are worried about the Hunters, don't be. They would've done far worse if given a chance. And we did not kill them all. You helped with one of them..."

He turned his head, the shape of his helmet emphasising the line of his jaw. I followed his gaze and looked back at the severed body of the executioner. Ice melted beneath the warm blood, which still hissed as it dribbled down the frozen stumps of his legs.

"I... I... didn't mean to." I couldn't explain it. What had happened, what I'd done. None of it made sense. It seemed my mind couldn't even begin to piece the puzzle together.

"This is no conversation to have with you still being on the floor." He looked back to me, eyes a raging storm of silver. "*You* do not belong on the floor. Not ever, not again."

I couldn't ignore the air of respect that softened the edges of his tone. How he kept his gaze upon mine, his hand outstretched, as though I was something important. Delicate, almost. Which normally I'd be the first to say I wasn't, but beneath his gaze, I felt exactly that.

"My arm is beginning to ache," he said. "Please do me the favour of taking it."

There wasn't any point hiding my hesitation. "What if I hurt you?" Looking back at the frozen corpse, I felt dangerous. My touch capable of something I wasn't prepared to justify.

"Then I am going to be in tremendous amounts of discomfort. For my sake, control yourself and take my hand."

If his face was visible, I was certain I would've seen the quirk of a lip.

Slowly, I took his hand. He was warm to the touch, his fingers wasting no time in capturing my wrist and pulling me upwards. With one strong tug, my arse was off the floor, and I was standing before him. The warrior was far taller than me, and I wasn't exactly short by any means. My line of sight stared right into the base of his neck, with the overlapping brass-metal folded on itself in intricate patterns of vine and leaf.

Reluctantly I looked up, not wanting to reveal my unease. "Is this when I thank you for saving me?"

"I wouldn't stop you." He released my hand, flexing his fingers at his sides. For a moment I thought I'd hurt him, but I saw no frost or ice. "However, I am merely finishing the job you started. Perhaps I should thank you."

Strapped over his armoured shoulder was a quiver full of arrows, the feathered ends identical to those that were buried through the mouth and head of the executioner.

"Well, thanks. But I should really go," I added quickly, realising I actually had no idea where I was in comparison to home. There were a few of the Hunter's horses left. I could take one and find the nearest village or town, someone would point me in the right direction.

"So soon?" he questioned, his eyes never leaving me. There was something about his touch that'd grounded me, and without it, I found the serpent inside me coil in discomfort. "Pray tell, where do you have to go in such a rush?"

"Home," I said, aware that the crowds of fey behind him had all been removed from their cages. This was new chaos. A lighter, hopeful atmosphere, as the armoured fey helped the hordes and comforted them.

"And where is home for you?" The man's gaze dulled as though I was a puzzle that he could not piece together.

"Grove."

"Hm. Interesting." To my surprise, he reached out and took my arm in his hand. The grip was gentle, yet firm. "As much as I would care to aid you on your return, I am afraid I cannot allow that."

The whirling panic returned in an instant. Snatching my hand from his, I stumbled backwards, putting space between us. "And who are you to tell me what I can or can't do?"

"My name is Erix, and I *am* a friend."

"Well, Erix." My face scrunched in confusion. "Do you hold swords to your friends, and prevent them from leaving when they want to?"

"Depends on the situation. And since you now know my name, may I ask yours?" Erix questioned calmly, the camp behind him bustling with noise.

Names were powerful, he was a fool to give his up so freely. "What would it matter?"

"How about I propose you a deal. Tell me your name, and in exchange, I will assist with returning you *home* myself."

I hardly believed he'd change his tune that easily. But it was worth a shot. I huffed, lip curling upwards in frustration over this stranger. Erix. "I don't believe you're in any position to be making a trade."

"Am I not?"

"No!" I spluttered, aware that he had not stopped looking into my eyes this entire time. "You're not."

"I trust you likely do not know where you are and where your home is in relation to this camp. I saw you look at those horses, the hint of stress in your eyes. Unless you have a map stuffed in that… rather interesting choice of sleeping attire, then I think you will need my help returning back to your home. So, give me your name, and I will keep my word."

His persistence was infuriating. Perhaps it wouldn't have bothered me if I wasn't exhausted. Even now, my knees quivered, wanting to give out, and my head throbbed from lack of sleep or energy, it was hard to distinguish.

Reading my body language, Erix reached to his belt. I thought he was going to withdraw another blade, but it was a skin of what had to be water, he offered. "To sweeten the deal, drink this. And no, before you ask, it's not poisoned."

My brow inched up. "I didn't think it would be, but now I am."

I was many things, but a fool wasn't one of them. Well, most of the time. If I wanted to make it back to Grove, I'd need energy. And water would help. So, I took it. Uncorking the skin and downing the contents into my mouth.

As the cool, fresh water rushed down my dried throat, the feeling was close to euphoric. I must've moaned, because as I came back gasping for air, Erix was grinning from ear to pointed ear.

"Thanks," I said, clearing dribbles from the side of my mouth.

"Name?" he persisted, his warm fingers brushing my knuckles as he took back the water skin.

"Robin," I said, giving in to the idea of assistance. "My name is Robin."

Erix pondered me for a moment, head tilting slightly to the side. He pulled his sword free from the ground, then slipped it back into the leather sheath at his side, all without a word.

What he did next surprised me far greater than any interactions that had come before. He knelt, hands pulling the helmet from his head and resting it on the ground before my feet. Erix bowed, flashing the top of his closely shaven head beneath me. Part of me longed to tell him to look at me, so I could see what he'd hid beneath the helmet. Instead, I drank in the features I *could* see. Sun-kissed skin glowed, his hair so short and fair that I knew it would tickle my palm if I reached out and touched him.

"What are you doing?" I gasped, noticing that a lot of people were watching. Embarrassment crept over my face, staining my neck and cheeks crimson.

Erix loosed a breath, armour singing as he shifted his weight and looked up at me. Thick, dark lashes surrounded his bright, silver eyes, making them stand out like snow amongst coal. Matching the colouring of his hair, his jaw was covered in the light stubble of a beard, his cheekbones so strong that they carved sharp lines into his face.

I'd learned about the fey and their ethereal stature. But Erix, he was far more deserving than being described as ethereal. He was –

Smiling at me. His full, pink lips turned upwards at each side. The vision snatched any ability to think from my grasp.

"It would be my honour to return you home, for it's been a long time since it was even believed possible that your *home* would ever be reclaimed. But here you are... unknowing of what you mean to those behind me." I looked over his shoulder again, unaware that everything had gone quiet. Across the camp, every fey who watched on, knelt. With their heads bowed to the ground, not a single one was left standing. I scanned the crowd of downturned heads, unable to truly understand what I witnessed.

"You're not making any sense," I spluttered, almost laughing from deep embarrassment at what happened before me. Waving at him with a forced smile, I commanded, "Are you taking the piss out of me? Stand up!"

"I am most certainly not." Erix stood slowly, his stare latched onto mine as he pushed himself from the ground. There wasn't an ounce of emotion that took away from his serious gaze. "I would not, Robin."

I nodded, fixing my eyes on him so I didn't have to look at the kneeling crowd. "Take me home, as you promised."

"I will. It would be my honour."

"As you've already said." I nodded, conjuring an image of my father and Winston. "I suppose the guidance would help."

Even now, the crowd looked to me, then to the layering of dwindling ice that I still refused to admit I'd caused.

Erix straightened, offered the crook of his arm and said, "Then let us not waste another moment... *little bird.*"

CHAPTER 5

There was little conversation as I trailed behind Erix. A statue of height, broad shoulders and a straight back, he paved his way through the parting crowd of fey. My mouth dried as we passed, catching a few who still knelt. I wanted to skip forward and ask what was happening, but Erix's long strides always kept him just a step ahead.

The display wasn't for me. It couldn't be. Perhaps Erix was of some importance, or they simply feared what I was capable of. I guessed the first, because Erix certainly presented himself as someone who demanded respect. But as we got further into the sea of bodies, the more I noticed his armour was no different than his fellow warriors'. He just carried himself with an aura of pride or arrogance, I was unsure which. All the fey guards were adorned in brass tones of leather and metal. Cloaks trailed across their shoulders, each a different take on an autumnal leaf.

There was no physical trait that suggested Erix was important. No crown or royal signet. And it wasn't Erix who was being watched. The seemingly never-ending stares were pinned to me, and I felt heavy beneath their weight.

Only once I passed them did they stand. A wave of bodies rising from their knees with faces of placid awe. I watched them as they watched me, risking a glance in hopes of understanding what captured their attention, wondering what pinched mouths into surprised circles and kept eyes wide and unblinking. At the tip of my tongue, I could taste disbelief.

"Steady, little bird."

I turned just in time to stop myself from walking straight into Erix's chest. Heat rose up my neck. It might've been down to the embarrassment or a mixture of the annoyance whenever he referred to me by those words. The first time I'd let it pass over my head, but this time I couldn't help but snap.

"You asked my name, but not once have you called me by it. I don't know what is ruder, being introduced at the end of a blade or that."

"My apologies, Robin." He bowed his head slightly. "How terribly rude of me."

There was a hint of sarcasm in his tone. I'd recognise it anywhere. I couldn't help but risk a smile, if only for a moment, even though my insides burned as hot flames.

Now I had his attention, I wasn't going to give up on getting some answers.

"What are they all staring at?" I asked, cautious enough to keep my voice down.

"You," Erix replied plainly.

I gaped back at him, at least expecting him to sugarcoat the reply.

"Was it something I've done?" I shrugged, fisting my hands at my sides. Up until now, I'd feared to look at my hands, expecting to see blades of ice or curls of mist. If I didn't look, I didn't acknowledge it. And I wasn't prepared to justify what'd happened at the chopping block.

"No. Well actually, maybe some of them are looking at you with trepidation. But the rest of them, the majority, are interested because *you* are somewhat of a marvel. To them, to me, to us all."

The lack of answers only fuelled the irritation within me. Not wanting to put off my return home, I elected to swallow my next comments. "More reason to rush out of here then. I preferred my life when I wasn't considered a marvel."

"As you wish. Have you ridden before?" Erix gestured a hand to a large stag who grazed in the empty space before us. Unlike the others, this one had a mottled coat of black and white. Erix was rather tall, but beside the creature, he looked unimportant and small. I trusted that if the stag reared up on its hind legs, it could compete with the fictional giants that filled children's bedtime stories.

"A horse, yes. This beast, no."

Erix widened his eyes, pressing a gloved finger to his pouted lips but hardly hiding the smirk beneath it. "My recommendation is not to offend my steed before riding him. *He* moves far greater than any horse. This beauty is more arrogant than even I am."

"Is that possible?" I said, unable to stop myself.

Erix chuckled back, the sound tickling over my skin. "We shall see. Now, I would feel more comfortable with you sitting before me."

"And I'd feel more comfortable walking."

"With bootless feet, you won't make it far," Erix said, gesturing towards the stag as if to hurry me up. "Tell me if you need assistance clambering on."

"I'm more than capable," I replied, stepping forward with my hand outstretched in greeting. Frightening but beautiful, my fingers brushed over the stag's coarse hair. It huffed in what I hoped was acceptance. It snapped its teeth and I jolted backwards, unable to stop my pathetic gasp. "He just tried to bite me!"

"Of course he didn't, Robin." Erix used my name as if proving a point. "You're not exactly his… taste." He leaned into me. I stiffened as he gently pressed a hand on my lower back. His words came out in a whisper. "Just keep your touch gentle, and he will not be forced to throw you off. And if he does… I will be here to catch you."

"Thanks, that makes me feel *so* much better." I pulled away from Erix, reaching ahead of the saddle and hoisting myself up. With one large sweep, I swung my leg over its side and gripped tightly as the world beneath me rocked slightly. "I think I'll be just fine."

Erix didn't say another word to me. Instead, he looked back to a huddle of similarly dressed warriors and tipped his head in a nod. It was clearly some unspoken signal, for they each moved forward, shouting commands towards the watching crowd.

Out of the corner of my eye, I caught Kayia and Lia. They were being directed into a group, the bustling horde around them alive with relief. I wanted to ask after them but knew they were safe now, surrounded by armed and highly dangerous fey. Hunters stupid enough to surge wouldn't stand a chance.

"Something concerns you," Erix said from the ground, his undershirt flexing beneath his armour as he hoisted himself upon the stag. I expected his added weight would've been noticeable, but the stag showed no signs of struggle. "If you are worried about them, don't be. We have dealt with many camps like this and will certainly deal with many more."

I winced at his comment. If Erix noticed, he didn't care. Instead, he rested his arms on my waist, reaching for the stag's reins.

"How did you find us?" I asked, trying to relax myself as my body hardened between his arms.

"Althea found you. She was leading this mission and went missing two days ago. By 'missing' I mean it was pretty much planned, down to the minute. We were just waiting for our signal. But that didn't happen, because you came along and ruined all those plans."

I glanced down at my hands, palms turned skyward. There was nothing amiss with them. No sign that powerful waves of frozen mist had spread beyond them.

I raised one of my hands and pressed the back of it to my cheek. Sure, it felt cold. But nothing out of the ordinary. As cold as I'd expect for such a late day in autumn. I could've passed it off as a nightmare. But one glance behind me, and

I'd still see the damage left across the ground. Ruin of my creation. A blanket of ice that'd reached further than I believed possible. And still erect, the two legs encased in ice, with no body attached from the waist upwards.

"Is she alright. Althea, I mean?" I asked, not remembering if I'd seen her poppy-red hair in the crowd. The last I remembered seeing was her seemingly broken body left discarded on the ground after the huddle of Hunters attacked.

"Althea is resilient and has been through far worse. Don't be fooled, she no doubt enjoyed a sparring match with the humans. She is stronger than any other person I know – although if your distraction did not come when it had, then perhaps I would be answering differently. Princess Cedarfall will be fine."

Princess. An unimaginable word for an unimaginable day. "She's from the Cedarfall Court clearly. Are you?"

"She is the daughter of the Cedarfall Court. Althea doesn't simply come from those lands, but embody them. The only member of the ruling family who is willing to risk her life saving those less fortunate from the human scu–"

"Please," I snapped, interrupting him before he could finish. "Don't say those words to me."

Human scum. Fey scum. Two sides of the same coin – a coin that I embodied just as Althea did for her court.

Erix was silent for a moment as the stag began to trot forward. "I fear I am making a habit of apologising to you, Robin. Ask me a question, any question, and I will do my best to answer. Consider it my attempt to make it up to you."

So many questions speared through my mind. Words filled my mouth, making it impossible to latch onto just one. I closed my eyes, inhaling through my nose as I took in a scent of fresh cinnamon and handfuls of dried leaves. It was Erix. His scent familiar and calming.

I kept my voice low, not wanting to give this next bit of information away. "I did that... to the executioner? It came from me, didn't it?"

"You get one question to ask, and you ask that one. Of course, it was you. You seem surprised?"

Surprised was an understatement. A royally large and undeniable understatement.

"It's never happened before," I said, thinking back to something the Hunters had said when I arrived at camp. "They even said they tested me and mentioned I was useless. Powerless like the fey I was put with."

"I cannot sit here and explain to you why humans are highly stupid beings. You were presented before them, and they told you that you were useless. When that is far, *far* from the truth."

"Then what am I?"

The question was for Erix, for myself, for anyone who could answer it honestly.

"A miracle. A marvel." My blood chilled as he replied. "A possibility those within Wychwood would never have believed possible. Some might even call you a saviour. I suppose that would depend on whom you asked. But what you are, Robin, is unique. Literally, one of a kind in all senses of the phrase. It has been years since the courts have looked for any surviving heir to the Icethorn bloodline, yet you have been hiding among the humans all this time. Believe me when I say your return is going to shock many."

"*Icethorn*?" I asked, eyes wide as a rushed drawing of a kingdom covered in snow appeared in my mind. An image I had looked over numerous times during our lessons on the fey. "What have I got to do with the winter court?"

"Everything."

"You sound confident." I almost laughed. The idea was a ridiculous notion to grasp. Almost hysterical to suggest. Me being, in any shape or form, tied to one of the four fey courts was ridiculous. And yet, there was no denying the look Erix gave me. Or the way those we passed spared glances at me.

"I suppose I am confident, little bird." His voice was flat when he replied. "You have strayed far from your nest, and it will be my honour to return you home, just as I promised."

A cold chill passed down my spine. In a second, it became clear that my version of home was very different to what Erix believed. Although I didn't know where the Hunters had taken me, I was never more confident that the looming boundary of Wychwood was *not* in the right direction to Grove.

And it was Wychwood where Erix guided his stag.

Panicked, I reached for the reins myself, trying to tug them free from Erix. He clicked his tongue, and the world sprang forward. The stag picked up an impossible pace. The wind whistled past my ears, joining in with the song of sudden entrapment I felt in his hold.

"Let me down," I warned, eyes streaming with tears beneath the sting of cold air.

"I'm afraid I am unable to do that, so it seems I must apologise again."

I attempted to take control for a second time, digging my nails into the gloved hands that snapped the reins, urging the stag to ride harder – faster.

Something Father had said years ago sprung to mind. I remembered it clearly as it was the last time we had spoken freely of Mother. Father had broken beneath the barrage of questions I threw at him regarding her. It was the first time I remembered him truly losing his temper with me. He'd said something sharp, with eyes rimmed red and heavy with shadows, his voice steady yet coated with thick, painful heartbreak.

"If you ever have the displeasure of meeting the fey-folk, do yourself a favour and turn the other way. They are never to be trusted, not ever. The only language they speak is lies."

CHAPTER 6

I'd passed through the Wychwood barrier only a handful of times, and each time was as strange as the one before. It was silly, my reasoning, but I thought that I could go searching for my mother alone. A foolish thought that I'd simply walk blindly into the realm of the fey and find her as though it was fate, or at least, some instinctual family bond that would reunite us.

But I never got more than a few feet into the darkness amongst the forest before turning back. As though I lost all desire to find her the moment I inhaled the air that lingered beyond the Wychwood border.

For all those years, there was nothing stopping her from coming back for me. Yet she'd kept away for a reason. And it was her reasoning that frightened me, not the fear of what I would find. Would she embrace me as I longed she would? Or would she send me back – turn her back on me, just as she had for, well, all my life?

I supposed it was the fear of such raw rejection that always made me return home to Father.

Now the choice had been taken from me, and I was furious. Erix guided us beneath the shadowed canopy of trees. Looking up, entrapped within the hold of his arms, I watched the thick foliage block out any sunlight. The dense green barely let small glitters of light through, but some stubborn beams exposed themselves like stars in a dark sea of green.

The chill of the late-autumn wind stopped as we passed through the trees. But the shiver across my arms didn't cease. Mist danced in waves of silver across the wild bed of the forest. It twisted over giant roots and around moss-covered boulders we passed, fingers of smoke that reached no further than the belly of the stag we rode upon.

"You will be safer in Wychwood," Erix said. Up until now, he had kept quiet, stopping me from pulling free. Beside the apple he'd offered me, likely because my stomach growled like a feral beast, it'd been over an hour since he last uttered a word. There was not an ounce of frustration in his tone but a dash of humour that was impossible to disregard.

"Coming from the man who has kidnapped me!" I'd long given up trying to fight free. Even if I did now, I really had no idea how to get back. Plus, there was something unmoving and hard about Erix's posture. I wasn't weak, but I also knew my limitations, and Erix blew those out of the water. "And if you are suggesting that there is danger returning home, then that is all the more reason for me to go. I can't just leave my father if that's a risk."

Erix released a tempered breath. "That is not a decision for me to make."

"Or me, because I'm your prisoner," I stated, cautious of moving too much because I was pressed so close into Erix's chest. I would've leaned forward to put space between us, but his warmth was welcome against the shadowy cool of the forest. The dirtied and ripped nightshirt was doing very little to keep away the chill.

"You're not a prisoner, but a guest."

"That suggests that you've presented me with an invitation. One that asked for me to come with you. One that I *should* have the right to decline. The only thing I want is to return home."

"As you have said, ten times now? And I have told you, I am taking you home."

I had to swallow a sudden lump that filled my throat. Now was not the time to show weakness.

"Do you even know where your home is, little bird?"

I wanted to snap at him for calling me by that nickname, but I sensed some hint of knowing as he spoke. And as much as he irritated me, I didn't want to ruin my chances of finding out what information he teased me with.

"I imagine the journey back to it would have been confusing, but yes, I do know where my home is. *Grove*. Shithole, potholes in the roads, but home none-the-less. Which even a hound without a nose would know that *this* is the wrong direction."

"You truly believe that?" Erix said, voice piquing with intrigue.

I crossed my arms over my chest, noticing the shift of his body as he closed both of his arms in at my sides, to keep me from slipping off. "Enlighten me, captor." I quipped. "I can tell you want to argue my point."

"*Captor*... that is not a name or title that's been given to me before," he replied, voice thick with mockery.

"What would you prefer?" I scoffed. "Dickhead–"

"I just can't bloody believe it," a softer voice sounded from behind us. I didn't need to turn to find the speaker, as the trotting of hooves picked up, and a body suddenly rode beside us.

Loose red curls flowed in the breeze, revealing skin covered in marks of black and blue. I imagined the green of her eyes would rival that of any natural gem or stone. I'd last seen her at a distance, body broken. But now she rode, chin held high, as she side-eyed me from her mount.

Althea Cedarfall.

"Returning this fool-mouthed heir is, at least, going to smooth the edge of mother's displeasure when I get home looking like this."

"His name is Robin," Erix added, flashing Althea a look of warning. "He'd prefer we used it."

"Well, Robin." Althea's eyes flashed with what could only be wonder. "My name's–"

"Althea," I answered for her.

Her face was dusted with dirt amongst the bruising. A cut had already begun to heal across her lower lip, but the red curves of her mouth still seemed swollen. I expected far worse after what I had witnessed.

She raised a brow as she regarded me. "How's it fair that you know my name, but I know nothing of you?"

It was as impossible that I was speaking with a fey within the boundaries of their realm as it was that she was royalty. Daughter of Cedarfall, the fey realm of autumn. Besides the light and elegant tone of her voice, there was nothing noticeably regal about her. No crown or neck covered in elaborate jewels. If anything, in her plain brown tunic and formfitting black leggings, she looked much like those I had grown up with in the farming district of Grove.

"I'm starting to think I don't know much about myself either, to be honest." I fisted my hands, burying nails into my palms.

Noticing my change in demeanour, Althea offered kind words as a distraction. "What you did back there, for that child. It was… valiant."

"Thank you, my lady… no, sorry, your highness." I felt heat rise up in my cheeks at my lack of knowledge on decorum.

Althea raised a hand, and I found myself silenced. Then she laughed, silky and smooth like melted caramel that the vendors would serve poured over sliced apple. "Gods, Erix, tell me this is a joke!"

"Far from it," he replied. "He is a fish out of water, quite literally."

"Clearly." Althea clicked her tongue, urging her stag ahead of us slightly. Unlike the one we rode upon, hers matched the auburn tones of her red hair. "Robin, how did you get so far without the need of a collar?" She raised the tips of her nails to her neck and pressed it there for a moment. It dragged a memory of the iron shackle she wore across her neck during her scrap with the Hunters and that of the other fey, those being carted away from camp throughout the day. "They test for those with power, it's what is most valuable to the Hunters. Except they were willing to murder someone so precious to them." Her eyes narrowed, darkening to the point I noticed swirls of honey amongst the green. "That is what I can't wrap my head around the most. Well, that and the fact I am actually looking at... well, *you*."

"They said they tested me. But I was not conscious during it." *Likely happened once I was knocked out cold before they carted me to the camp.* "I don't have power, at least not any I'd been aware of before."

"That much was clear," she replied quickly, lips upturned into a grin that stretched the cut across them. "I have never seen such reckless and uncontrolled use of magic before. Powerful though. We all felt that. And it did the job, I suppose. But if you didn't stop when you did, it would've destroyed the entire camp. Those in the cages, as well as out."

"It was not my intention to hurt anyone." I had to keep my tone in check, but I felt the bubbling need to stand up for myself. "Nor is it my intention to go where *he* is taking me. But I fear I'd no control in either outcome."

Althea pouted, brows furrowing. "Do not blame Erix, he is only doing what is required." Then her expression changed, softened enough that it almost seemed empathetic. "Unfortunately, it is not possible for you to return to... well, wherever you came from. But if it makes you feel more at ease, we will collect what you require."

Collect what I require? The offer was genuine but only spurred me into a warmer sense of annoyance, solidifying the feeling that I wasn't going back to Grove anytime soon.

To my shock, it was Erix who butted in, silencing me before I could throw the prisoner word around again. "It would seem that Robin holds concern for his... father's wellbeing."

"The human?" Althea laughed but caught my narrowed gaze and swallowed what she was going to say next. Pausing with an exhale, I could almost see the turning of wheels in her brain as she worded her response better. "Robin, you likely have worked out that humans are not welcome beyond Wychwood. It hasn't stopped them from trying to enter before, but most of the time, the Mists of Deyalnar are sure to keep any wandering mortal from getting far. As soon as a human enters, they'll find themselves turning back around without question or thought."

"Unless invited," Erix added, coughing into a closed fist.

Althea rolled her eyes at his comment, telling me that she would not have revealed the option if he had not brought it up. "You should try staying silent like the other loyal guards to my family, Erix. You may find that it gets you further in your career."

"If I did, how would you be kept entertained?" he muttered back.

"Then invite him," I said, interrupting them sharply. "If that's all it takes, then do it. I will go with you to collect him."

"I hate to be the one to remind you, I really am. But you will be coming with us," Althea retorted. "Returning to Durmain isn't an option."

Heat flooded my cheeks, but for the sake of Father, I kept my composure. Instead, I forced out a word that did not come naturally to me. *"Please."*

"As much as I would like to accept your request, it is not my decision to make. We will present the proposal at court for my mother and father to decide," Althea said.

A small shuddering spark of hope lit in my chest, mixing among the cold of the closed box that I now sensed as though it'd always been there.

"Entertain me, Robin. How was it you came to be captured by the Hunters? I am not complaining that they found you, *Altar* no. They accomplished something our people have long believed impossible. But I have infiltrated camps for months and not once have they bothered with a... well, they usually search for full-blooded fey."

I almost choked on her question as I tried to discern if she meant offence or not. During the hours caged with the others, I'd pondered what had driven James and his accomplice into selling me, and I could only link it to one thing.

Desperation.

"The people who turned me in needed the coin. To them I was no different to a piece of meat sold at the market. Winter is fast approaching, and coin will be what keeps someone alive during the long months, or not."

Althea mulled over what I said for a brief moment before diving further into her questioning. "And you said the Hunters tested you?"

I nodded. "I wasn't aware of when or how. But that's what they said when they brought me into camp."

She was contemplating my reply, gaze lifting to the thick foliage above us as her mind whirled. "You possess an undiluted bloodline of pure power, Robin. I do not believe for a moment that their test simply *skimmed* over it. Luckily for us, it did, I suppose, otherwise, you would have been shipped off before we arrived. But what I can't explain is how you slipped through their net."

I was likely focusing on the wrong parts of her commentary, which was causing this conversation to flip from topic to topic. "My bloodline? You are talking about my half side... my mother?" My heart skipped a beat as Althea looked back to Erix, who stiffened around me. "Erix said something about the Icethorn Court?"

Althea shot Erix a look of pure fury. "Erix has a habit of opening his mouth far too often. When we arrive at court, you will be subject to a barrage of questioning. I should hold back my own intrigue and wait for it to begin. But I sense that you're genuine about your lack of knowledge regarding your power. I just do not know if that will fill my family with much confidence upon your arrival."

There was concern in her expression. It was so obvious I could almost taste it, like the sour bite of unripe berries. Erix's silence didn't help the matter either. He, like Althea, was a stranger, but even I couldn't deny the familiarity of their shared worry.

"Do you know who my mother is?" I asked, almost a whisper as though I couldn't believe I was saying it aloud. It'd been a long while since Father answered one of my questions. There'd always been a faint shadow of a forbidden nature surrounding the topic of my mother.

Althea bowed her head, so her eyes no longer met mine.

"I deserve to know." I drudged up the name of the court that Erix had mentioned not that long ago. "What've I got to do with the Icethorn Court?"

With a snap of her head, she stared at Erix with glowing eyes. Power gleamed in them as though a blaze had been lit deep within. "That remark I said about your career and keeping quiet? I am contemplating changing it to keeping your life instead of career."

Erix released one hand off the reins and raised it to our side. "I thought he knew."

"Do not expect me to believe that."

"So, it is true?" A new feeling jolted in my chest, booming like thunder. "My mother is in that court?"

Althea answered my question with one of her own. "How old are you, Robin?"

"Uh… twenty-four."

"Interesting." She sucked her tongue against her teeth.

"Is that a bad, thing?"

"No. I'm just shy of my twenty-sixth year. I'm only asking, because your birth date makes a lot of sense. It was around the time she–"

Althea stopped herself, lips practically forging together.

"She what?" I questioned when she trailed off, feeling as though answers were close but were slipping away from me by the second.

Althea raked a hand through her red curls, tugging strands away from her face to expose the point of an ear and glistening, ivory skin. "There is no denying that your power is linked to that of the Icethorn Court. Only those within the bloodline can call upon frozen winds and conjure ice from the very moisture in the air. Some – the most powerful of those in the long lineage – could bring down dreadful storms that brought a time of eternal winter for all who were unlucky enough to cause anger to the family. I suppose you look like her too. Any fey, old or young, who would look into your eyes would not be able to refuse the blizzard that brews within them, dark and cold like the night."

I zoned out, my mind and body numbing as Althea spoke. Years of wanting answers seemed to come all at once in the form of someone I didn't know. Part of me expected this information from Father himself. But I'd question if he even knew her. Was that why he didn't tell me details of Mother and his time with her? No. I couldn't believe that. Because his face scrunched beneath the phantom lingering pain of heartbreak whenever I'd brought her up. A person's eyes didn't dull, nor would their body hunch over, at the mention of someone they didn't care deeply about.

I looked down at my hands, wiggling my fingers slightly as though they were freshly sharpened knives that required the handle of care. The red burn marks around my wrists had already faded, far greater than any cut or wound I had experienced before; only the faint pink band was left in the place where Mother's bracelet should have been sitting. I lifted a hand to the wound over my brow, but felt nothing but fresh, unmarked skin.

Odd.

Something clicked in my head as my mind contemplated the missing piece of jewellery. I looked up to Althea, who waited patiently, with peaked brows, for me to break the silence. "Why did the Hunters place a collar around your throat when they left me and the others without?"

Althea hadn't been the only one wearing the uncaring collar.

"To nullify my abilities. It is fey blood which is potent with magic we have learned the Hunters are looking for. Iron is the only way they can keep us... unthreatening."

I cupped my empty, naked wrist. The bracelet had been iron – the one Mother had left for me. And at some point, it'd gone missing, likely in the sticky hands of the reedy man who had threatened to take it. Perhaps it'd been removed *after* my testing? A sloppy mistake the Hunter had clearly made.

I couldn't wrap my head around it. Not entirely. The bracelet hadn't left my wrist for years, not since it was presented to me. And if I'd taken it off, it had only been for short moments. Having it on made me feel close to her. To Mother. That was why I kept it around my wrist all these years.

"Before I was taken, I wore something that my... my mother had left for me. It was a bracelet made from iron. When I woke in the back of the caged cart, I no longer had it on me. Could that have prevented me from passing whatever test the Hunters did on me?"

Althea's lips parted, but then they turned up into a brimming smile. One that raised more on one side than the other. The kind of smile I expected a cat to present after it scratched you for no reason.

"How devious," she cooed. "Keeping you smothered for all these years."

I took that as a yes to my question.

She'd confirmed my suspicions with her somewhat vague reply.

Althea's face had cleared of all emotion. "I am going to ride ahead, warn them of our arrival. Keep him close and well watched until you get to us. If the other courts catch word of *his* return, we will likely be put on the back foot. You know what I need of you?"

"I do." Erix's arm walled in closer to my sides. "I'll consider him my most precious possession."

There were few things I liked less than being talked about as though I wasn't there. It irked me, irritating me beyond comprehension.

"Robin, you are in good hands. We will speak further on this matter soon, but I assure you I will petition for your father's invitation." With that, Althea nodded, clicking her tongue in signal and digging her heels into the side of the stag.

Like wind, she blurred forward, hair rushing behind her in waves of blood as she rode off into the distance. In her wake, I was left with more questions than I had before, all of them filling my mouth and threatening to choke me.

Erix leaned in, armoured chest pressing into my back. His lips dusted so close to my ear that I froze in one spot, just like the executioner had beneath my foreign power. "Where were we... little bird?"

Unable to hold my tongue anymore, I bit back. "Call me that one more time, and I will... I will push you off."

My threat was pathetic, I knew that. Erix seemed to think so too, evident as his smoky laugh sounded back. "If I go down, you come with me. And did you not hear what I said to Althea? You are my most precious possessi–"

"Okay, I get it!" I rolled my eyes, huffing out a shuddering breath of annoyance. "And did you not hear what she said about staying silent? I suggest you give it a go, for both your life's and career's sake."

Erix leaned back, and I was suddenly aware of the lack of warmth. With the tug of the reins, the stag beneath us jolted forward again, all without him uttering another word. I quickly discovered that his silence was far more irritating than his voice.

CHAPTER 7

The last thing I wanted was to fall asleep, but the rhythmic trot of the stag made it impossible to keep my eyes open. Between Erix's persistent silence and the night and day I'd just had, sleep came naturally.

Until I woke abruptly to a deep chortle. My mouth was dry, likely from having it hung open like an unattractive flytrap. My neck and shoulder shared an ache from the awkward angle I'd fallen asleep in.

But the worst feeling of all was knowing how close I'd pressed myself into the hard torso of Erix's frame, as though I'd fallen asleep with my back against a wall. And his arms, those two statuesque arms, seemed to be closer now. They held me in place, preventing me from tumbling from the saddle.

"Now, I am not confident if it was your own snoring that woke you or something I may have done," Erix said, his laugh thumping through my back. "If it was the latter, I do apologise."

My heart dropped like a rock in a lake, embarrassment heating the tips of my ears.

I was acutely aware of my arm, which hung to the side of the stag, and my hand, which rested upon the muscular thigh of the fey man. Snatching it away, I wiped the back of my hand against my mouth to clear any spit that dared dribble down my chin.

"I don't snore," I said.

"Not that it matters, or proving you wrong means anything to me... But you do, in fact, snore." I felt the shift of his torso as he laughed beneath his breath.

I inhaled, and his scent of spiced cinnamon seemed to be all I could register.

"How long have I been out for?" I asked. I was still tired, and scolding myself would not change that I'd let my guard down enough to actually sleep. Even though I'd woken untouched, unharmed and with the whispering feeling of safety.

"A few hours. I thought it best to give you a moment to gain some energy *and* gift myself with a lack of questioning."

Was that why my head ached? Because the sleep had done little to give me reprieve? Choosing not to respond to Erix, I distracted myself by taking in my surroundings. The view around me had changed dramatically in such a short time.

We were deeper into Wychwood, which meant further away from Father. But I clung to Althea's promise of his invitation. Worrying about it wouldn't change the outcome. And I was far from actioning anything to aid in providing his invite. Pushing that thought away, I focused on the view around me.

The trees were no longer thick with different shades of green. The many branches were sparse. Only a few amber leaves clung to them as the rest fluttered to the forest bed like falling golden flecks of snow.

At first, the stag's footfalls had been muffled by moss, grass and mud. Now each step responded with the crunch of leaves beneath it. Peering towards the ground, it was covered in a bed of amber- and ruddy-coloured leaves, a blanket of autumn that stretched out in all directions for as far as I could see.

I also noticed the lack of a convoy. The crowd of fey who'd walked among us, and the many mounted warriors, had thinned. I could've counted the number that remained, but Erix spoke again, snatching my attention.

"You woke in time for our arrival to Aurelia."

"Aurelia?"

Erix had said it as though it was no more than a passing comment. A name without meaning. But what he must've known was I, and others beyond Wychwood, had little understanding of the lands. The place was mostly a mystery. No human cartographer had depicted what lay beyond the Wychwood barrier. Across any human map, the space was a shadowed mark, with a known beginning but an unimaginable end. All the maps revealed were the four court's names and boundary lines.

"Aurelia is the southernmost, and second-largest, dwelling in Cedarfall. *The Golden City*. A message arrived whilst you snored – I mean, slept. Instructions regarding our change of course. It seems news of *you* has reached the capital before Althea, which was not what was intended."

His comments only added to the ache in my head. I pressed a finger to my temple, massaging in small circles in hopes of easing the pain. "How's that possible?"

"Anything is possible, but I do not know who the informant, in this case, has been. I am sure Althea will find out who it was. She has a way of getting answers that others cannot obtain."

"What happens when we reach Aurelia?" I felt a small buzz of excitement at the thought of seeing a city and a fey one at that.

"You eat and drink, even rest on a bed with considerably more cushioning than me."

As my eyes widened in shock, I was thankful that no one travelled beside us. That wave of embarrassment rolled back over me just as I believed its original tide had dispersed.

"A bed that is considerably less sarcastic as well, I hope?" I snapped back, fighting the tug of my lip.

Before he could respond with yet another witty remark, a thundering of hooves interrupted him. Looking towards the sound, we both watched as we were greeted by a party of armoured fey. Instead of stags, they rode horses, and I couldn't help but enjoy the mundane nature of their arrival.

"We have arrived, and just in time too," Erix whispered, his voice harder than it had been before. He spoke to me as though it was a chore. Had I offended him? It shouldn't have worried me, not with everything else that had happened, but it did.

A clear difference, besides the mounts, was the armour the arriving fey wore. They were women whose hair had been braided into a whip down their backs. Their armour was shades of deep brown, with threading of gold that spun in swirls and shapes across their torsos and shoulders. The closer I got, the more I could see that those details looked like twisting, golden branches with small, carefully sewn leaves which seemed more like the scales of a gilded, scaled beast.

The stag we rode huffed with my shared excitement, raising his antlered crown as though he wanted to show off to them.

"Erix. We have been instructed to escort you to the manor," the lead fey spoke. They didn't wear obscuring helmets like Erix had, exposing faces equally mature and beautiful. Lines of experience wrinkled the corners of their lips, but their brown skin glowed with life and warmth. "By request of the Cedarfall Court."

"Then we shall follow your lead," Erix responded, his tone still void of emotion. He'd become the stoic warrior I'd expected from a fey of his build and demeanour. It *almost* matched what the female warriors exuded – but they had an air about them that presumed power that even Erix didn't have.

I kept silent, highly aware that they did everything not to look at me. Without sparing another word, we began to move forward again. The new arrivals spread themselves around the small convoy, equally spaced as the main lead at the front.

And all the while, I couldn't ignore that they each had a hand hovering above a sheathed weapon, all whilst studying the forest around them as well as the path ahead.

The forest soon gave way to a view of open fields. I couldn't believe how bright the late afternoon light was as we had been under cover of trees for so long. But it wasn't the sudden open space that snatched my breath away, or the fact that the forest actually did have an end.

It was what was nestled in the valley before me that had my stomach jolting wildly.

Wind swiped at my face, whipping my clothes across my chest as I stared down the decline towards the city. In amongst a sea of deep, golden-leaved trees was a maze of stone. From our perch, it looked as though I could sweep my hand through the air and pick up the city in my palm. *Aurelia. The Golden City.* It was clear why it had that title as it was surrounded by the monstrous trees that confirmed its namesake.

Trees of literal gold-leaf. Hundreds of them.

I soon realised that Erix had slowed our mount to allow me to take it all in. Only when the leading fey woman noticed we had fallen back did he knock his boots into the stag to urge it forward.

"It looks so small up here," I said, voice soft with awe.

"You are looking at the exposed heart of the city. The majority of it is hidden beneath the ancient trees you see, and I can assure you Aurelia is *far* from small."

I couldn't help but smile at the view before me.

My stomach jumped as we began our descent towards it. I felt like a child, looking upon a place I had often wondered about, but this, what waited before me, was far more than I could have dreamt up.

Erix was right, Aurelia was certainly not small. In fact, beneath the impressive golden forest, I was the one who felt tiny. Everything did.

The city was a blend of stone and wood. Buildings similar to those I was used to seeing back home lined the streets we passed through. Wide, cobbled roads broke off in different directions, exposing more pathways. A maze – an endless, beautiful maze. One that didn't solely belong on ground level. I lifted my head up, staring up into the bottom of gold-leaf trees, unable to comprehend what I saw. Wooden pathways that wrapped around the hulking trunks of trees, linking them together. Among the shadows far above, buildings of dark wood had been built onto the sides of the giant trunks, connected by walkways and bridges that glowed in the dark belly of foliage thanks to the numerous golden-flamed lanterns. Without them, I could only imagine how dark it must be to dwell far up in the reaches of the ancient trees and their thick, dense twisting of branches and leaves.

Similar lanterns had been lit along the main pathway we rode upon; they separated the road from the walkways on either side, walkways that were filled with countless bodies of people – *fey* – going about their daily lives in this incredible city.

I'd never seen so many people in one place before. Grove was well populated for such a small village, but nothing like this. Aurelia was large, bigger than large, and the streets were full. Likely more complex than Lockinge, the human capital.

Fey flooded in and out of buildings, threading around markets and open-aired taverns. We passed many who sat at tables, food and drink lifted to their mouths as they conversed with one another.

Life. That was what this place was riddled with. Life. A hub of it. More people than I had likely seen in my complete existence.

No one paid much mind as our convoy passed through the main street. If the king had a parade of his soldiers through Grove, it would've captured everyone's attention. But this seemed like a normal part of day-to-day life.

There was a scent to the city, one that couldn't be ignored. It seemed to come from the golden trees themselves, because it started the moment we reached the bottom of the valley and entered beneath them. It coated the back of my tongue with each inhale, reminding me of the sweet and fresh aftertaste of maple. It wasn't unpleasant, but the further we got, the more I believed I'd never rid my skin of the smell. I could no longer pick up the spiced scent of Erix, who still pressed close behind me, even though a part of me wanted to.

"Welcome to my favourite place in all of Wychwood," Erix said from behind me, awe filling his voice.

So even a local was enamoured by this place.

"It's unlike anything I could've imagined," I answered.

When he spoke again, I got the impression he wasn't speaking about the city. "That is a sentiment I certainly understand well today."

The cobbled road we travelled began to slope upwards slightly towards a large building which sat waiting for us at the end. It was a blend of both stone and wood, mixing the architecture I'd seen so far into one place. It'd been built around the old trees, some even looking as though they had grown straight through the middle. Its grey stone walls rose up tall, covered in countless glass windows that glowed with inside light. A shiver of anticipation coursed over my exposed arms at the thought of getting off the stag and seeing what awaited within.

This must have been the manor the fey guard had mentioned when she greeted us. The word had originally conjured an image of a rather large home, but this was like a castle, with towering walls and a pitched roof that connected to the impressive linking of paths that went up and up into the ceiling of foliage above it. In some way, this manor was connected to every part of Aurelia, as though every road, path and floating walkway led directly to it.

Without audible command or signal, the stag slowed to a stop. Erix cooed his thanks and praise to his mount. He slid effortlessly from its side, then offered his hand to me. "It is by foot from here."

I hesitated, staring down at my bare feet as though I'd forgotten how to use them. Still in my nightclothes, I could only imagine what I looked like, especially as Erix stared up at me, his silver gaze the only thing exposed behind the helmet he'd put back on.

I didn't take his hand, instead using my little remaining strength to lower myself to the ground. The cobbled road wasn't cold to the touch, but my feet did tingle as though I stood on a bed of pins.

My focus on the city had resulted in me not realising that it was only Erix and I left, among the party of guards. No longer did the crowd of fey follow. For someone who praised himself on remembering details, I was doing a terrible job at it now.

"Lady Kelsey is honoured to welcome you to her home, Robin," one of the fey-guards announced, making me jump slightly at her sudden appearance. Until now, she'd acted like I didn't exist.

She was shorter than Erix, like me. I recognised her as the leader of the escort who greeted us in the forest. Her dark brown skin glowed beneath the uniform she wore, the gold threading across her breastplate matching that of her gaze. However, I couldn't help but notice that the length of her ears didn't extend as far as Erix's or the other guards around me. They were shorter, curved and covered in earrings of brass and silver.

"Where is our host?" Erix asked, looking to the empty stairwell that led up to the castle's entrance.

"Lady Kelsey sends her apologies for she has yet to return from her trip. Although I am sure you understand your arrival was untimely and unexpected. Lady Kelsey assures you that her home is yours and can be for as long as the court requires."

There was something inquisitive in the woman's honey-gold stare as she spoke to me. Her eyes bored into mine, looking for something. Searching.

"What of Althea?" Erix questioned, voice steady and full of authority.

"Althea Cedarfall will return shortly, but until then, you are invited to rest. I am certain you require it."

Erix spoke for me. "Thank you for your hospitality... and as you have expressed, rest is exactly what Robin requires."

The woman's lip pursed at Erix but then softened when she looked back at me. "If you require anything, please only ask. My name is Gyah, but any of my comrades would be happy to aid you during your stay. It has been many years since we last hosted the Icethorn Court, and it is our pleasure to do so again."

I fought the sudden urge to laugh. Gyah looked at me as though she knew me with more certainty than I knew myself. And that thrilled me. Because that meant she likely knew my mother. Opting not to be rude, for Father brought me up far better than that, I bowed my head as I replied. "Thank you, Gyah."

When I looked up, my throat tightened at the sadness that glazed over her golden-hued eyes. It was there only for a moment, but it was unforgettable. It halted me from saying another thing. And she seemed to catch herself, because she spun on her heel and beckoned us to follow.

I paused only until Erix's guiding hand found the small of my back and urged me forward. He didn't say anything. Had he also seen the tears that clung to her eyes?

The lingering feeling sent a great rush of unease through me. But, with the rest of my discomfort, I swallowed it and promised myself to deal with it when my world was not entirely turned upside down.

CHAPTER 8

I saw little of the castle as Gyah led us, on quick feet, through long, endless corridors and up so many stairs it should've been a crime. The muscles in my already tired legs burned with each step. Whereas Gyah and Erix breathed with ease, I huffed and coughed, my body rejecting this level of exercise.

I wasn't exactly a stranger to hard labour. I'd spent the last three years working alongside Father at the tavern on nights when it was so busy people opted to stand rather than sit. My body was lean, with subtle lumps across my stomach that whispered the possibility of muscle.

Perhaps my inability to catch my breath and hold my composure was the human half of me coming through. In fact, I'd never felt so human. So very, obviously different from those who seemed to glide around me with grace, heads held high and broad statures carved from hands of the fey god, Altar.

I usually felt taller around other humans, even Father stood several inches beneath me. But with Erix, Gyah and the many shadows of female warriors who separated from walls to join our journey, I felt small.

By the time we reached the closed door, which Gyah had announced as my chambers, there were countless stern faces around us. They lined the walls beyond the door, silent guards who showed no emotion, so tranquil that they could've been mistaken for statues of stone instead of flesh and blood. Each fey warrior was covered in weapons strapped around strong waists, across shoulders and dangling by sides. I could only imagine the number of blades hidden on their bodies, but I didn't dare stare long enough to investigate.

It was Gyah who instructed me to enter, promising a freshly filled bath and to return with food and drink shortly. My stomach grumbled at the thought. The water and apple Erix had given me had barely touched the sides.

Erix hadn't said a word, mainly taking orders from Gyah, who instructed him with short commands. He simply nodded, joining the many fey to stand guard beyond the door. I watched him leave, almost calling out to stop him.

Alas, I bite my tongue and focused on Gyah.

"The room is yours to rest within." Gyah's voice was rough when she spoke, deep and full of authority that made Erix seem like an unsure boy in comparison. "If you require anything before Althea's return, then please ask."

I forced a smile, holding back the urge to look for Erix a final time as Gyah slipped through the door and closed me inside.

Then there was a click and then the turn of a key from the other side. I didn't need to reach for the brass knob to know I'd been locked in. A knife of discomfort sliced down from the base of my skull to the bottom of my spine; in a single moment, I'd gone from feeling like a guest to a prisoner.

The chamber was enormous, undeniably the most comfortable of prison cells in both Wychwood or Durmain. There were the living quarters which I'd first entered, with dark oak furniture, plush chairs and an unnecessarily large number of gilded mirrors hanging from the cream papered walls. Three alternative doorways waited on the far walls of the room, each leading to yet another incredibly decorated room.

I felt ridiculous being here, standing with dirtied feet in the ripped nightclothes. A light breeze lingered in through an open window, and I suddenly noticed just how terrible they smelt. The room had a scent of vanilla and something fresh, like a field just after a downpour of rain. Raising an arm, I sniffed the odour that seeped from me and fought back a cough.

My first instinct was that Erix must've noticed. Forcing him from my mind *again*, I decided that washing was my most pressing priority.

Moving through glass double doors at the back of the living quarters, I entered a bedroom which was equal in size. I kept my hands to myself; I didn't want to dirty the elegant, shifting curtains of lace that draped from each of the four posts of the large bed, with a mattress big enough to fit a number of bodies and still have room to stretch.

Entire walls, if not taken up with ornate windows, were lined with wardrobes that reached far up into the high ceilings. A small ladder was connected to the nearest wardrobe to me, with wooden wheels at the base. I gave it a push, and it slid soundlessly across the many wardrobes.

I found the bathing chamber with little effort. Steam flowed beyond an open door, beckoning me to enter with fingers of curling mist. There wasn't a moment wasted as I unclothed and walked across the bedroom towards the doorway. By the time I entered, there was only the cold dusting of air across my bare body.

I slipped into the warmth of the brass tub that was, as promised, filled with water. Time wasn't a concept I could grasp as I let the warmth wash away the day's events. The cage, the deaths I'd witnessed, all of it. I thought of Father and our home, which conjured an ache in my chest, a longing that flirted with the closed box deep within me, tickling a finger of consciousness across the lid as a reminder that it could open if I wished for it to.

The angry marks across my wrists were so faint now that they were almost impossible to see. But they *had* been there, and my skin had healed far quicker than I'd ever experienced before.

The comments Althea had made about Mother's bracelet and the effects of iron trickled into my mind. Had that suppressed far more of me than I could understand? Even in the familiar, comforting cuddle of water, I knew that it was Althea who'd answer that question when she returned.

After what could've been hours, I climbed out of the brass tub, the water cold and discoloured. Wrapped in a towel as soft as snow, I trailed wet footprints into the bedchamber, in search for new clothes.

But with each step, my mind clawed at the thought of my mother, making my stomach jolt with anxiety.

That possibility of seeing her was all that kept me stable. She'd have answers for me, I knew she would. A path, or guidance, wasn't that what mothers offered? Again, I wouldn't know – never had one.

Twenty-four years old, and I relied on a mother I didn't even remember.

I found clothes hanging within one of the many wardrobes. Not caring what I wore, I pulled on a pair of dark brown trousers and a fitted, long-sleeved green shirt that had swirling gold thread across the shoulders. Turning before the mirror, I noticed how the design flowed down the back of the shirt like wings across the material, wings the shape of fallen autumn leaves outlined in gold, much like the design across Erix's cloak when I'd first seen him.

"And I was beginning to think you had drowned," a familiar voice sounded from the living quarters beyond the bedroom. "A few more minutes and I would come to check."

I followed the soft voice to find Althea, who sat with her feet up, resting across the low table before her. Her back was towards me, but her face turned slightly that I caught the lift of her sharp lips, which tugged into a smile.

"I didn't hear you come in," I said, fists relaxing slightly but not before she had noticed. "Is knocking not a custom in Wychwood?"

"Hold on, whose home are you in? Oh yes, mine." She spied my balled fists, and chuckled. "What good will they do?"

"Not that I have anything to prove, but they can do some harm." My arms snapped to my sides, and I tried to relax my posture. Althea turned back to whatever she focused on before her, which I soon saw was a pastry of some kind that she picked apart, pieces flaking across her lap.

"I'm at least pleased to see you have some fight in you. Here." She took her heels from the table and sat forward, gesturing to a plate piled high with similar pastries and cakes that she devoured. "You should eat something. An expenditure of power can have a draining effect on a fey, and the food will help. So will the sugar."

I got the impression, from her erudite tone, that she knew I needed insight into the fey. It was unspoken between us, only adding to how different I felt. How human I was in comparison. Althea was right, though, I was hungry. And I didn't realise just how much until the scent of warmed, sweet cake enticed me to pick one from the plate. Taking a seat in a plush chair opposite her, I began stuffing my cheeks with food. An explosion of sweetness filled me with a hint of stewed apples as I soon found the pale, green filling in the middle of the bun.

"The cooks will love you," Althea chortled, picking at the honey-dipped bun in her hand.

"Mmhm," I mumbled through full cheeks.

Althea studied me now, hardly bothering with her own pastry that she toyed with on her lap. Then she shook her head as though she broke herself out of a trance. "Sorry, I should not stare so much. I just can hardly believe that I am actually sitting here with you."

I smiled, swallowing the lump of pastry audibly. "The feeling is mutual. I don't know much about Wychwood, if I'm honest. Or what is going on. Although these certainly sweeten the situation, you can imagine I still have many questions."

"That much is clear, Robin." A shadow of concern passed behind her stare for a moment before dissipating as though I had imagined it. "I thought you'd want to know that your father has been granted an invitation by the court. It's far from custom, but a convoy has already been sent for him. I expect him to arrive by the morning, if he accepts, of course."

A ringing filled my ears. I leaned forward, heart thumping at the back of my throat, so intense that my thanks almost didn't come out. "Thank you."

"You do not understand what your return means to... us." Althea's stare widened, and her jaw tensed. She was both parts beautiful and dangerous. Even her lips were sharp like a blade, and her stare full of untold threats. But I didn't sense her desire to hurt me, in fact, it was the opposite.

"Is that why there are untold guards outside my door?"

Her brow pitched upwards. "It is."

"And the locked door?"

Her eyes narrowed on me. "That was just a precaution. As much as you're a guest, the idea of your trapsing around the castle isn't exactly one that makes me feel comfortable."

"Am I in danger?" I asked, finding that it was the most important question to follow her comments."

Althea rocked back, returned her focus on the honey-coated bun and replied. "Now, that would depend."

Depend on what? Did I even want to know the answer to that?

"And if I ask why I mean a lot to you, would you tell me?"

Althea paused before replying, looking away as she contemplated her response. "What do you know of the Icethorn Court?"

"Is it a trait of your kind to answer a question with a question?"

"You tell me... Robin." Althea shot me a look. "You're one of us, after all."

I sighed, pulling at the pathetic threads of knowledge I held of the fey and their kind from the depths of my memory. "Icethorn is the fey court of winter. And, from reading between the lines, you believe it's where my mother comes from?"

There it was again, the concern in her stare, but this time joined with sadness; it was identical to the emotions that I'd seen from Gyah and Erix, so palpable that it tugged down her lips at the corners and furrowed her brow until lines cut across her freckled forehead.

"I *do* believe your lineage is that of the Icethorn Court." Althea's voice was thick and quiet as though she feared the very walls listened in. "But your mother is far more than *from* the court. She was the–"

The chamber door opened with a bang, interrupting Althea. Before I could see who'd arrived, Althea had unsheathed twin axes, holding them steady at her sides. The honey bun was squashed beneath her foot.

"We've got some trouble heading our way," Erix said, practically growling. Seeing him in such a state of worry made the panic inside me build. He'd seemed like such a controlled person, but I was beginning to think otherwise.

"What trouble?" she questioned Erix, who filled the doorway with his broad frame. His silver eyes met mine, and even behind his helmet, I could sense his alarm; it darkened his eyes, turning them into a storm of grey skies.

"Gryvern," Erix answered, his voice as sharp as the sword he pulled free from its sheath. The metal sang as he held it before him with two hands.

"How many?" Althea ran to the window that overlooked Aurelia, leaving me like a fool to sit numb in the chair.

"Unsure." Erix closed the door, not before I noticed the hallway beyond was empty of armoured guards. Where had they gone? There was no time to answer as Erix booted the door closed.

"That is not helpful, Erix, give me a number."

"A handful, potentially more to follow."

"What's going on?" I asked, standing up, tense and highly aware that I was without a weapon. Once again my fists balled, but they really did feel pathetic in the face of the tension around me.

Althea ignored me, instead barking an order at Erix. "Get him into the back rooms and barricade the door. Do *not* open it, or assist, unless I request it. Am I clear?"

"Very." Erix nodded, moving towards me.

I took steps back, my voice hardening with demand as I asked again, "Someone tell me what is going on. Now."

An inhumane screech sounded from beyond the window, spurring a hiss from Althea as she fumbled back. "Shit. Shit. *Shit.*"

Erix reached for me with his gloved hands, but I pulled away. Using the chair as a barrier, I danced around it, enough to sidestep him and run for the window. Althea didn't bother to reprimand me for joining her, and I could see why.

Her attention was forged on the monsters filling the sky.

Large humanoid figures flew through the air outside the manor. I counted three with wings so wide that they caused shadows to pass over the ground far below.

The streets were full of chaos as people ran for shelter. Their cries of terror itched at my skin, muffled only slightly by the thick pane of glass separating us from the creatures that filled the skies.

Erix had called them gryvern, a name I wasn't familiar with. As they drew closer, I saw they were made up of melted-grey flesh, blotches of red and yellow as though their skin dripped from their bodies. Their wings were leather and hairless but equally as pale as the rest of them. Horns protruded from their deformed skulls. Then I focused on their faces, and my heart slowed. Dark, empty sockets hollowed their visages – where eyes should've been, were instead pits of shadow that seemed to never end. Mouths split from round ear to round ear, flashing rows of stained, pointed teeth.

Their strangled screams would haunt me for an eternity.

"Room!" Althea shouted at me as though she'd only just realised I stood beside her. "Now!"

This time I didn't refuse. Erix was behind me, wrapping a large arm around my shoulder as he guided me away. The box in my chest creaked open, bringing forth a rush of cold, icy wind. The power trembled from my skin, sending the lace curtains around the bed to shift violently.

"What are those things?" I asked, voice cracking. I wasn't one for running and hiding, but I also had never been faced with creatures like those beyond the castle.

"Unnatural demons, conjured from the lust for fey flesh and bone," Erix said, his voice without fear. There was something shielding about the way he put himself between me and the door.

The screeching beyond the manor stopped abruptly, and for several moments there was nothing but silence.

I pressed a hand to my chest, trying to still the whirling of pressure within it.

"I'm beginning to think that I would've been safer back at the Hunter's camp," I blurted out, wincing as my ribs ached and lungs burned as each intake of breath was ice cold. I then thought of Father and what he'd be exposed to if he accepted the fey's invitation. For the first time, I felt a creeping slither of dread at the idea of him passing the Wychwood border.

"Those creatures – the gryvern have not been seen in almost a decade." Erix lifted the sword before him, the tip inches from the closed door to the living quarters.

"Why now then?" I listened out, trying to stretch my hearing to catch if the creatures still filled the skies or if they had retreated.

Erix peered over his shoulder, gaze dark and lips pursed white. "Because your return has already reached the ears of those who see you as a threat. They are here for you, Robin."

Dread pooled like a pit of ruin at the base of my spine.

Before I could respond, the shattering of glass exploded from the living quarters, and the high pitched, scratching screech sounded the arrival of the monsters.

Monsters who'd come for me.

CHAPTER 9

All I could do was listen as inhuman screams filled the living room beyond the closed door. The noise was terrible. A symphony of horror and dread which made my skin crawl. My conscience screamed for me to help Althea, but Erix guarded the door, stopping anyone or anything from entering as much as he kept me from leaving.

Amongst the sounds, I tried to locate Althea, but it proved impossible over the thudding, crashing and smashing that occurred within the room.

"We have to help her," I stuttered, finding it hard to speak over the turmoil of pressure in my chest.

Erix was as silent as a statue and equally unmoving, showing no signs of racing forward to help with whatever was happening between Althea and the gryvern.

When he finally replied, it didn't help the burning desire to ignore the command and run back for Althea. "The only thing that needs help is the monster stupid enough to attack. Althea will be fine. It would be a far graver mistake to underestimate her. And she gave me my command, one I take seriously."

A small, gargled shout of terror burst from me as something heavy thudded into the doors. Even Erix flinched, lifting the steady sword higher before him as though the doors would soon be ripped free from their hinges.

My heart thundered in my chest, ribs hardly able to

contain it. Discomfort was my friend, a building of pressure that clawed itself up my throat, ready to burst free across the room.

It was Erix who startled next when a long blade sliced through the wooden door like a knife through melted butter. He stepped back, waving for me to keep away as a spreading of obsidian blood dripped from the blade's tip. The silver of the steel seemed to repel the gore, for it hardly left a smudge, only staining the white wood of the door where it dribbled into a puddle onto the floor.

He looked at me with his eyes full of confidence. "What did I tell you?"

There wasn't any more screeching or screaming. And it was clear that the gryvern pinned between the door and the blade was dead. Or dying – like a butterfly pinned to a corkboard.

The door swung wide, exposing Althea, who looked unharmed and unbothered, only a strand of red hair covered her gaze, which she blew away with one great huff. A splatter of dark gore was plastered over her tunic and skirt, but it didn't belong to her.

"The rest of the gryvern are retreating," she explained, breathless. I hardly took notice of her as I stared at the creature before me. It was, in fact, dying, but the blade that had pierced through its skinless neck kept it from making much noise. Thick, oily black blood popped and bubbled from the wound. Grey-leathered wings hung limp at its side, its unnaturally long fingers and thin bent legs spasmed like a fish out of water.

And the stench that reached me almost had me doubling over with my hands on my knees. It was rotten, the sweet and sickly smell of death, as if the creature before me represented it, even without the sword piercing its neck.

Holding a hand to my nose, I struggled to breathe, eyes watering and pain clenching my stomach.

This… this *thing* would fill my nightmares for a long while, that I was confident about. Not only because of the dark blood or grotesque figure, but because there was something so honestly… *human* about the creature. Looking at the gryvern, ignoring the wings and horns, it could've been someone I knew. With features familiar, round ears and the shadows of a nose, mouth and hollowed spaces for eyes. It was just stretched and long and wrong. So very wrong.

"Robin, are you okay?" Erix stood before me and the dying creature, blocking my view.

What kind of question was that?

"No," I barked, blinking rapidly to rid the image from my mind. Commotion before the living room told me those fey warriors who'd been missing had suddenly entered, assessing the damage.

"Where were you?" Erix demanded, his fury laced in his tone.

"There was another attack in the north wing," one of the guard's replied, fumbling nervously over his words. "Our order is to protect Lady Kelsey–"

Erix didn't let them finish. Fury radiated from every pour. He stood rigid, an air of danger lingering in the pinch of his mouth, and the furrow of his brow. "I want guards stationed alongside Robin at all times."

"But sir–"

"At – all – times."

My chest warmed at the way Erix spoke for me. Part of me wanted to say I'd deal with this alone, but there was something oddly comforting in having a stranger looking out for me. And then I saw why. Because I finally got a good look at the damage, and it was *bad*. The window was now a gaping hole of stone and shattered glass, leading out to Aurelia. Dustings of gold leaves fell like snow beyond it, dancing in the light wind that now filled the room.

"Erix, take it easy," Althea added, her hesitant stare speaking a thousand words. Like the guards, she was frightened of him. Or of what he *could* do.

There was something terrifying about the silent stillness of Erix's demeanour. I might not have known him well, but that didn't stop me from reaching out and laying a hand on his arm. "I'm fine – everything is fine."

"But you might not have been," Erix replied, eyes flicking to me as he slowly broke out of whatever rage-induced trance he'd found himself in.

"Look at me," I found myself saying, which was stupid, because all Erix was doing was looking at me. "I'm safe."

"It won't happen again," he replied, voice low and calm. "I can assure you."

"Would one of you care to explain what exactly has happened?" I asked no one in particular. Althea broke away from a hushed conversation with a fey warrior. "They were here for me... Erix said as much, but why? If this is the type of danger that dwells on this side of the Wychwood border..."

"Then what?" she asked, gaze narrowing. "You would have returned to your father and the mundane, normal, likely boring life you have left behind? You do not understand what you have exposed, using your abilities in front of so many. The gryvern would have come for you either here or back in whatever dwelling you found yourself in. At least with us, you have come away in one piece. I do not imagine the outcome would have been the same if you were not so protected." Althea spoke with furious speed, hardly stopping for a breath. "So, I think what you meant to say was *thank you*. Thank you for saving my arse and damaging a very expensive room!"

Defence bubbled within me, but there was something about her demeanour that had me thinking carefully about my reply.

"Thank you," I started, highly aware that it was not what I wanted to say, but it was what I needed to say. "But you must understand that I've got no idea what's going on here. Any of this. I'm thanking you for saving my life for reasons unbeknownst to me. But that makes giving thanks slightly difficult."

Althea paused, lips pursing as she regarded me from the ground up. "I was certainly hoping we would have had more time before news of your return spread, but it would seem that was wishful thinking." Her expression melted into something softer, but I was not fooled, for I still caught the sharp edges she hid – powerful and regal edges for someone with clear authority. "The gryvern are like bloodhounds, fixated on a target and not satisfied until their target is eliminated. You, Robin, you are why they came. Likely why they will return shortly to attempt to kill you again. And again, until their appetite is sated."

"Why?" I muttered, aware of how still the creature had grown behind me. The gargling and spluttering had ceased, and its body stiffened as true death took hold of it. "Please, help me understand what I'm facing."

Althea drank me in, the sadness creeping back into her green-brown eyes.

"Everyone out," Althea commanded to the room, authority rippling from her in powerful waves. Those two words were all that was required for the many fey to leave, Erix included, who paused as though wishing the command was not for him. Althea simply signalled with a gaze that he was not required, and he left with a bowed head. "Erix, see that fresh food and water is brought to us."

"I'm not hungry." I mean, how could I possibly be? But one sharp look from Althea and it was clear that 'being hungry' wasn't an option.

"I suggest you have a drink or eat something whilst we discuss, well, you. But it would seem the uninvited guests have ruined the options."

I followed her stare to the table that was smashed into pieces. Among the rubble, I made out the mounds of cakes and pastries, but they were covered in glass and debris.

It took a moment for the room to empty. This time I knew the guards wouldn't leave the corridor again, not for fear of

Erix's wrath. Once the door was closed, Althea settled her eyes on me and that sadness had only intensified.

"What do you know of your mother?" Althea asked, breaking the silence of the ruined room.

"Not a lot," I replied, pulling a face at her reference. "Sorry, it's odd hearing someone actually refer to her as my mother."

"If there is another title you would prefer I used..."

I couldn't ignore the cold expression that clung to her beautiful, deadly face. It was as though she fought hard not to express it, but her eyes gave view to the emotion that swirled deep within her.

"Mother is fine," I said with a pathetic smile.

Althea waved her hand, encouraging me to actually answer her question.

"Truthfully, I hardly remember her. What I can, only comes in pieces," I admitted, knowing it was the first time I'd said such aloud before, to anyone beyond Father, at least. "I know she is fey, and that was the reason she never came back for me. My father once told me that there was a time she stayed with us, but I was only a baby. By the time she left, I wouldn't have had the ability to remember her."

Althea winced. "Do you even remember her name? Where she came from? Did you not care to ask?"

Infuriation as a result of her accusations riled through me, urging that closed box in my chest to jiggle slightly. I wanted to snap at her again. "Of course I asked."

I didn't want or care to explain it further, and Althea could sense that as she moved the conversation onto a different path.

"I only ever met her once." Althea looked to an unimportant place on the wall, not at me. "Your mother, I mean. I was young, and it was many years ago, but her face, *your* face, is one I could never forget. Even if you didn't reveal your magic, my people would be fools to ignore how closely you resemble her. Dark hair and equally black eyes – the physical traits of an Icethorn. When I was younger, I never could understand how they glowed both black and blue, as though her eyes did not care to choose a single colour."

My heart swelled at her comments, so much so that I almost raised a hand and touched my own face in disbelief at what she said. But dread crept up my neck like the scratching of a clawed hand; the feeling was so real I thought, for a moment, that the gryvern had come back to life and reached to touch me.

"When you speak about my mother, it's in the past tense."

I hoped she'd tell me she'd been wrong to use certain words.

She didn't.

"Robin, I am so sorry." Althea's eyes filled with tears, and my chest cracked wide before she spoke further. "It was not intended to tell you this. Not like this... but it is clear you know little of the fey's history." There was a great and terrible pause as I waited for my dreaded fear to be made a reality. "Your mother was killed years ago, alongside her husband and children, and it has been long believed that the Icethorn Court would never be reclaimed by the royal bloodline... Until you."

I wasn't unfamiliar with grief. It was a feeling that troubled me when I was old enough to name the pain. It was a horrible, twisting sensation my heart felt when I saw other children with their mothers. It always found a way to internally devour me. Even over the years, when I glanced at the bracelet she'd left for me, I'd contemplated ripping it off, throwing it far into the belly of a lake or fire, anything to break the ties to the woman who'd left me. *Left us.* I grieved her, the idea of her. But even in that feeling, there was hope buried beneath it.

Having grief towards the living was only the tip of a blade in my heart. Knowing that she was dead felt as though that blade had finally been buried to the hilt within me.

The cracking in my chest turned into a deep, dark split that carved across the lid of building pressure. The box didn't simply open. It was ripped in two by the revelation exposed between us.

Magic exploded beyond me. An intense chill filled the air. It whipped at my skin, snatching tears from my cheeks.

Althea was speaking, repeating two words over and over. But I couldn't hear her, or make sense of what she said from the movement of her lips. A storm of power filled my head and threatened to smash my skull beneath the unwanted pressure. Ice crept from beneath my feet, oozing from me and spreading across the floor. Even the air seemed to harden around me, thickening in clouds of mist that whirled across the room.

I thought the gryvern had ruined the room, but I would tear it apart brick by brick.

I clamped my eyes shut, squeezing them so tight as I willed the image of my mother to fill my mind.

A flash of dark black hair. The melody of her soft, calming voice. Her featureless face, one I'd wished to put together like the pieces of a puzzle. Now those pieces would never be reachable. Just when I had believed there was a chance to see her, even if she didn't wish to see me, it was taken away like a toy from a child.

The worst feeling of all was the small, relentless possibility that she'd never come for me because she'd been dead all along. Not because she didn't want to see me, but because the choice was taken from her. And that didn't only create more sadness. No. It fuelled a storm of desperate anger which materialised in a power around me.

Winter. Pure, destructive winter devoured the room.

It coated the walls in jagged spears of ice, causing icicles with deadly points to drip from the ceiling. I'd lost track of Althea but cared little as the storm of grief took hold of me. In truth, there wasn't much room for thinking – only feeling.

And I felt it all.

Years of buried emotions exploded from me in power that was strange to me. A power that seemed to be endless now that it was completely out of its box. A power that I never believed possible. I didn't control it – it controlled me. And I would never be able to put away again.

A sudden flare of light and heat ahead of me pulsed to life. I flinched as I saw the flicker among the shadows of the storm that rushed between me and where Althea had stood.

Another flash and I felt heat singe my skin. It warmed the flesh of my arms, jaw and chest. It was close now, a rose of orange and ruby that danced between two delicate hands.

Althea stepped forward against the wind, skin paled and hair whipping in strong gusts. She lowered her head against the waves of power, body leaning forward as she fought to be closer. And that rose – the bud of warmth and light – pulsed between her hands.

Fire.

"Robin, you have to – calm – down." Althea struggled, her cheeks and nose a horrible red, a coating of ice spreading across her eyebrows. "If you do not, you *will* hurt a lot of people."

It was as though I listened from a dark cavern at the back of my mind. Her voice was an echo as I watched her fight against the force that rolled from my very being. But it never let up.

She spread her hands wider, encouraging the fire between them to grow and spread in an orb that floated above her palm. The heat was… welcome. It soothed my skin and mind.

"I understand your pain." She winced, forcing more of herself into the fire she commanded. But her power, unlike mine, seemed limited. I couldn't explain the feeling, but I'd never been more sure of something. It was as though I could see the leash that connected her to it. Whereas my power, this part of me, was without a leash and collar.

It was free.

"I understand, but you must calm yourself. Breathe, focus on breathing, and it will get better. Lighter."

Anger quickly melted into panic, a barrelling realisation that I had no control, and that was a feeling I didn't like.

The change in my own emotions only seemed to fuel the power to grow stronger. Althea's voice lost all its soft, calm tones as she commanded me this time. "Stop now." The glow of fire between her hands darkened, and it conjured shadows to dance across the lower part of her face. It made her cheekbones stand out like horns, and her eyes morphed into dark pits like that of the gryvern. "Or I will stop you myself, and I really don't want to hurt you, Robin. Trust me."

I focused on her eyes and tried to do as she said. Breathing deep, in and out, I focused on calling in the power to the barren, broken box in my chest where I tried to put it back. In my mind, I imagined it like threads, glowing silver as I tugged them back and stuffed them into the box.

Time seemed to go on as I focused, urged by the intensifying heat of Althea and her commanding power. I'd pinched my eyes closed, unsure if it was working, until her voice became clearer and the warmth of her flame stronger.

"Good... keep breathing, and you will be alright," she sang. Although she was close to me in age, as she spoke, I felt as though she was an older sister; at least, that was what I imagined this supporting aura felt like.

When I opened my eyes, I was confident that control was back in my grasp. Cold wind no longer ripped wildly through the room. My breath didn't fog with each hulking exhale. And I felt warmer, not entirely, but enough for the panic to subside.

Furniture had been blown against the outer walls of the room. The elaborate wallpaper was hidden beneath a layer of ice, the floor coated in frost and snow.

"I didn't mean to–" I started but was silenced by Althea as she threw her arms around me. For a moment, I expected to feel the burn of fire, but that had extinguished alongside my own power. Instead, her arms tightened, holding me close as her scent of sun-warmed cedar and roasted nuts over a crackling bonfire enveloped me.

"Do not apologise," she whispered, her hold strong. It felt silly to stand here with my arms by my side but equally wrong to return the hug. "It has been a long day and one full of answers I realise you never expected to uncover." She pulled back, holding me at arm's reach as she studied me intently. "I think we should find you a new room and allow you to get some rest. Burn-out can be terrible to a fey's body. And I can't promise that tomorrow will not be an equally tumultuous day."

My heart beat in my throat, the symphony broken and fleeting.

"I never got to see her…" I murmured, almost admiring the destruction I had caused around me. It should have unnerved me, this strange power, but it was likely the only thing that felt right to me. "I'd allowed myself to forget it was ever a possibility, and now I feel like a fool for daring to wish it was."

"Never be afraid to wish, Robin," Althea said, expression hard but stare gentle. "Because many people in Wychwood also gave up wishing for Icethorn's return. But like both edges of a blade, one always seems more terrible than the other. I understand what I have told you seems like the sharper side, but to the people out in that city and beyond, you mean a lot more."

Erix forced his way into the room, ruining the moment as the door cracked over the ice-hardened floor and slammed into the wall. A few icicles broke from the ceiling and fell onto the ground, shattering into countless shards of diamond upon impact.

"I was gone for a few minutes–" He drank in the scene before him, settling his silver eyes on the pain written over my face. Sympathy flashed over him, lasting but a second. "Lady Kelsey will not be pleased to see that you have chosen to redecorate her room."

I still hadn't met this Lady Kelsey, not knowing her beyond being the owner of the manor. Truthfully, I didn't really care about what I'd done to the room. I cared that my mother was dead, and I'd never meet her.

And the underlying knowledge that someone had murdered her.

"The room was already fucked, Erix." Althea stood close to my side, warmth flooding from her very being. "My aunt will hardly mind. It gives her something to gossip about at court, and more reason to spend court's money to redecorate. She'll thank Robin, if anything."

"That she will," Erix said, studying the damage around him. I wondered if Althea noticed his smirk of approval as his eyes found me. He didn't ask me if I was alright, because the question would clearly be wasted. Instead, he settled his entire attention on me, lips parting as he added a final statement. "I have a feeling you are going to be a handful, little bird."

CHAPTER 10

I slept well, considering the events of the day. It'd likely been the longest day I'd ever lived through. One I never wished to revisit again. For the first time in a long time, I'd woken in my own time, swaddled in heavy, stiff blankets as though I was a baby in a crib, the feathered pillow so pregnant that my head drowned in it, blocking out all sound around me. When I'd closed my eyes, it was as if I floated in a sea of nothingness.

The new room was smaller than the first, windowless and buried deep in the pits of the manor. It seemed to be far below ground where natural light didn't reach it. Undying flames burned in lamps throughout the modest room, reflecting a halo of burnt orange light across the chunky, mundane oak furniture that filled the room. Not that I was complaining, for it was far more comfortable than the room I'd left behind. Small, like the bedroom I left behind in Grove.

I loved the seclusion, mainly for the quiet but also for the added fact that no windows meant no flying demons smashing through to get me. And as I blinked the sleep from my eyes, the vision of the gryvern still seemed as prevalent in my mind as it had before I'd fallen into sleep.

A young, nervous-looking girl entered after knocking on the closed door. For a moment, before she came in, I stared at the door as though my silence would succumb to an answer. Did she wait for my invitation or signal that I was awake? But soon enough, she slipped into the room, and the door opened enough for me to catch the glint of armour beyond it.

I was still being guarded, whether from the gryvern or something else, I wasn't entirely certain. But nevertheless, fey warriors, each decorated with weapons that I couldn't name, were close.

That gave me a sense of comfort.

After what Althea had explained about my suggested heritage, I understood I was highly important. And that caused a sickening yet thrilling bubbling to fill my empty stomach.

The Icethorn Court. My mother was dead.

As though sleep had muffled the grief, it all came flooding back at once, popping the bubbles of thrill in my stomach, leaving me only feeling sick.

I snapped out of the daze as the clinking of silverware rattled before me. The young girl lowered a tray across the crumpled bedding, bowing her ginger-haired head low. I tugged the blanket up to my chin, covering my chest, and forced a smile of appreciation.

"Thank you," I said, trying to lighten the obvious tension. "I'm so hungry I could eat an entire horse."

She reacted as though I'd screamed bloody murder. The young girl suddenly turned, her little feet pattering across the slabbed floor as she exited in a rush, still careful not to slam the door on the way out.

"It's a figure of speech… I don't really want to eat a horse," I called after her, swallowing my shout towards the end as a guard caught my line of sight before the door closed again.

Strange, that was the only way I could sum up the interaction. How she couldn't look at me in the eyes, or how her hands shook as she presented me with the tray of food.

She was scared, or at least uneased by my presence. Had she seen what I'd done to the first room? Or was she more frightened that if she lingered too close to me, the gryvern would return and take her too?

One thing was clear, I was starving.

I wasted no time checking on the food she left. My mouth watering with anticipation. I ate the warmed sausage, toasted bread and cheese without leaving a scrap behind. It hardly filled the void, but it would do. Once the plate was empty, I clambered from bed and changed back into the clothing I'd worn when Althea and Erix had escorted me into this secluded room. The only difference was the creased material, caused by leaving them in a forgotten heap on the floor.

Father would scold me if he saw, and that thought made me smile. For a man with little to his name, he taught me to take pride in what we did have. Keeping him in mind, I brushed my hands over the shirt and trousers to ease the creases out.

Did he know she'd died? The thought came so suddenly, it almost made me spew the contents of my full stomach over the bedsheet.

"A horse?" Erix asked as he slipped through the door, unannounced. I couldn't tell if it was my audible shout of surprise or the way I held my fists up before my face that had him grinning from ear to ear. His smile lit the room, teeth white and straight with the smallest gap between his front two. "You've got the entire serving quarters alight with rumours that humans actually eat horses... I hope you understand what damage you have caused."

My cheeks burned hot as the weight of his sudden, overwhelmingly chipper mood bored down on me. "It was a..." I shook my head, silencing the attempt at an excuse. "Do any of you know how to knock on a door?"

Erix stepped back, lips pouting as he pressed a hand to his chest. "How devilishly rude of me. Here, let me try again."

Before I could contest, he opened the door and left, closing it softly in his wake. There was a pause – only brief – followed by a rap of knuckles on the other side. "May I come in?"

"Was that necessary?" I felt even embarrassed as I caught glimpses of the armoured, stern-faced guards who likely wondered what was going on between us.

"I only did as you asked." Erix nodded his head, the skin around his silver eyes scrunching in lines at their corners. "I'm sorry for my unannounced appearance this afternoon. I will do my best to remember it going forward."

"Afternoon?" I spluttered.

Amused, he carried on. "You have been sleeping for a long while, and your body must have required it, for the guards were instructed not to wake you. I was beginning to think you would never wake, but when the snoring ceased, I knew it was only a matter of moments until hunger brought you back to the land of the living."

"I – do – not – snore," I retorted, turning away from him so he could not see the shadow of red creeping up the skin of my neck.

"Of course, little bird," Erix drawled, and I was thankful for him shifting the conversation.

"Robin," I corrected, balling the bedsheets in my fists.

Erix ignored me, but from the look of amusement brightening his eyes, I knew he'd enjoyed playing this little game with me. "Althea has given me orders to keep you occupied whilst she is busy dealing with the arrival of the Cedarfall family. I had an entire morning and afternoon planned out, but we hardly have a few hours left until you are expected at dinner."

Was that why he was stripped of his armour, leaving him in black trousers that hugged the thick swell of his thighs and the off-white tunic that exposed the defined line delineating his chest? It was close to impossible to keep my eyes everywhere above the nape of his neck.

There were no men like Erix in Grove. Not in the fey sense, but in the way that the men back home seemed to have fewer teeth and more... desperation. Erix was incredible in his armour. I would've been a fool not to notice. But seeing him so casual sent a shiver across my skin.

"What… what did you have in mind?" I didn't refuse, for a conversation with Erix would lead to more answers, and it was rather more pleasing than sitting here alone. I was never one for sitting still.

"Since we do not have long, and you have only just eaten breakfast, how about a stroll around the city? It would be my honour to give you the grand tour. That way, you can see some sights and prepare your stomach for the feast that is to come this eve."

A flash of melted flesh, gaunt hollow eyes and ripped, leathered wings filled the shadows of my mind. "Is it safe? What with the flesh-starved monster that ripped a room apart to get to me… did you forget about that when drafting up your plans?"

Erix shifted his imposing frame and leaned on his hip, crossing both arms across his chest and threatening the very existence of the threading across the seams. "First, I am offended you think I could not handle myself against the gryvern."

"Well, you did hide behind a door," I reminded him.

He winced. "Good point. And secondly, we will, of course, be shadowed by a great number of guards who would be ready to cull anyone or anything that got too close to you."

I wanted to question him on the *anyone* part of his comment but chose ignorant bliss.

"Come on. Aurelia is most beautiful during the late evenings when the sleepy sun's beams lay their final light through the leaves of the city's namesake." He extended an arm, the crook of it presented as an invitation. I stared at his arm as though it was the most peculiar thing I'd seen. Erix must've noticed my hesitation, as he soon lowered it, lips lined with disappointment, before he motioned for the door. "It is time for you to spread your wings, little bird, before it is determined if they will be clipped by the council."

I almost corrected him again, but the nickname was starting to not bother me as much.

* * *

The council, Erix explained as we left the manor shadowed by the promised guards, was no more than a glorified family meeting over wine and dinner. In fact, he called it a ball. I hoped he didn't notice the colour drain from my face as he explained the entire Cedarfall Court was currently travelling to Aurelia to see me. And from his description, there were *many* family members of the Cedarfall bloodline. Even Erix couldn't answer my question with a number, only waving off the comment with a rough estimation of between twenty and thirty.

It was common knowledge to humans that the *fey* lived far longer lifespans than them. Not immortal, but not mortal either. Something in between. However, I couldn't imagine how ancient the ruling king and queen must have been to have so many children and grandchildren.

"I get the impression I'm about to be paraded before a crowd who fear me – or at least what I stand for," I said, wrapping my arms over my chest as the chill of the late autumn breeze flitted around me. We soon began our incline up a twisting wooden path that was erected upon one of the great trees the city was nestled beneath. It wrapped around the hulking trunk but didn't seem awfully secure as the wind shook it beneath each footfall.

"The feast will be brief, meant more as a celebration for the city. If the occupants of Aurelia see the arrival of the Cedarfall Court and a feast is not put on, they will gossip that something is amiss. It will cause unease, which is not what they need at this time. First, we will celebrate, and then the Council will begin behind more private doors."

I could hardly imagine what the feast would be like. Far different from the drunken *May Day* celebrations in Grove when we danced and drank and… partook in other events beneath the clear, spring evenings. No one wore grand garments as we didn't have that sort of money to spend having them made. Being one of the furthest villages from the capital of Durmain, it meant clothing and finery weren't as easily obtainable.

Yet, among this city, I knew it would be far different. Perhaps the complete opposite. Already the occupants of Aurelia we'd passed by were decorating the exteriors of their homes and shops. Across the leaf-covered streets, fey strung banners between buildings and lit glowing lanterns made from brown-, red- and orange-stained papers.

"All this because I said I would eat a horse?" I joked, dealing with the nerves with humour.

Erix walked beside me, sparing me a quick glance, the corners of his lips tugging into a smile. "That may or may not get brought up tonight. However, I do wish to see your face turn red if it does."

Even as he spoke, I felt the disobedient wave of warmth flood up my neck. Turning away, I looked backwards, glimpsing the sea of guards who trailed behind us. Perhaps I should've felt more uneasy, knowing what creatures longed for my slaughter. But I didn't. It had much to do with the weapons they held and the hilt of Erix's sword that his hand seemed to linger on without much thought.

"I admit, I am fascinated with you," Erix announced as we continued our climb, leaving the ground level of Aurelia far beneath us.

"How so?" I said, thankful my voice did not crack. Boys had said similar things to me, but never a man. Never one like Erix.

"Just how little you know of your potential."

"Well, I'm glad I take up so much of your mental space." I regretted saying it the second the last word was out my mouth.

Erix didn't tell me I was wrong with my assumption.

"Tell me, what it was like growing up among the humans?"

"It was…" I began, mind swirling to visions of my past. "All I knew. Normal. My hometown was plain and dull, but somewhere I've always felt, somewhat, welcome. I imagine you would scoff at it, having grown up in Cedarfall."

"You take me for someone who peers down the tip of their nose?" he asked, a hint of surprise melting beneath his tone of offence.

"I don't know you well enough to answer that," I replied quickly.

"You're not wrong there. But since you are being so open with me, I will share a fact about myself. Consider it a trade. I did not grow up in Cedarfall, but in another court. I came here when I was a young boy, young enough that I should have not come alone, but old enough to know it was the right decision."

There was a further story there, but I did not feel comfortable enough to pry.

"Which court do you belong to?" I questioned.

"Ah-ah," he said, wagging a long finger before me as he studied me through a narrowed stare. "It is my time to ask you a question. Something personal."

"Like what?"

Erix ran his fingers down his jaw in contemplation. "What do you fear the most?"

"*That* is what you care to know?"

Erix's finger trailed down his neck, catching in the collar of his shirt. I followed it down, drinking in the shadowing of a beard that accentuated the sharp line of his jaw, to the fine hairs caught over his chest. "If I am to be your personal guard for the foreseeable future, I think I should be privy to this type of information."

"Personal guard!" I didn't know what was worse. Having two shadows, or one of them being Erix with his sheepish smile and lingering, intense gaze.

"Unless you petition that you think you will be fine without one, that is." Erix leaned in, whispering through the corner of his mouth. "Although between you and me, until you get some proper training of your abilities and what it means to be an Icethorn, I think someone with extra... steel would come in rather handy."

A blush crept from my thickening throat to my cheeks. Although Erix's sarcastic nature was grating, I couldn't ignore the way his comments conjured a grin across my face.

"The dark," I answered.

"Say that again?" He peaked a single brow.

"I'm frightened of the dark," I replied, staring ahead. "That's what you wanted to know. Now it's your turn, Erix. What're you going to do as my personal guard to combat that? Brandish your... extra steel and keep it back with your rather intoxicating nature?"

He paused in his response, and I did not look at him to see how my sharp comment affected his expression. But the long sigh that followed had me gritting my teeth in preparation for his retort. "I can't answer that question, but the next time you find yourself in a dark room, little bird, just call for me. Then we will see how I react."

There was no controlling the blush that erupted over my face. I skipped a step ahead so Erix didn't see.

I was never more thankful for the twisting, continuous walkway to change into a flat podium. It was made from wood, much like the swaying path, but it was not moving with each step. Fixed to the large body of the tree, it was static and gave way to the most wonderous of views.

We were so high up that I could almost reach out and pluck one of the golden leaves from the branches above. Some fell like gilded ash, landing on my head, shoulders and around my feet. I plucked one from my shoulder, noticing the golden dust that was left behind. Rubbing my finger and thumb across its smooth surface, it left its glittering remnants beneath my touch.

"It is said that when Altar first died, the great trees of Aurelia grew in mourning. They grew and grew, far past what was normal, only stopping when the tears of the fey of Wychwood dried up."

"I've never heard much about Altar." The humans believed in another god. The Creator, who birthed the world and waited in the ether for the day when he returned to destroy it. And he was far from described as dead. He was simply… sleeping. Waiting for a time when we grew lazy and forgetful of him. But never had we learned about Altar – perhaps strategically, to almost pretend the fey and their god didn't exist. None of the books I had read or stories that had been shared ever told of such things.

"And I do not expect for you to have known either," Erix said, reaching for my face. I closed my eyes in anticipation, and then the subtle shift of my hair followed as he took a leaf from it. I opened my eyes to see him pull back, studying the leaf with intense concentration.

"I am intrigued by you, but I too hold some level of pity. Brought up in a world whose people hunt our kind for coin. The humans are terrible, hateful and full of unkind beliefs. Yet here you are, seemingly normal but with a mind that is still closed off from us; I can see that in those dark, unending eyes of yours. You know nothing of your lineage, let alone what it means to be fey. Yet you will be thrust into a world where much is expected of you. Robin, forgive us for what you will soon uncover. We do not all share the same visions of the future, and to some, you present a new possibility of a future that many will not welcome so willingly. Remember that. And if you ever require reminding, as your personal guard, I will only be a short distance away."

At first, his words felt like a slap to my cheek, but the phantom touch soon melted to something softer, kinder, as he held my gaze.

I dropped the now rumpled leaf to the ground, where it fell without grace. Shaking my head, I looked down and broke the heavy silence. "Not that I am keeping count, but I believe it's my time to ask you a question."

When I peered up through my lashes at the giant of a man, I noticed how the smile he presented didn't quite reach his eyes. They seemed darker, haunted by something that lingered in his mind unseen. "Perhaps my story is one best left for another day. And we will have many of those ahead."

"Closing the book before I even have the chance to turn the first page?" I said, lifting the corner of my lip upwards.

"We should return to the manor and prepare for the night's events."

"You cannot get out of it that easy..." I said, stepping before him, blocking the pathway back down to the city.

"What if I told you your father has likely arrived and will be wondering where you are?"

I stuttered, heart leaping in my chest so that I had to press a hand atop it. "Already?"

He nodded, peering over my shoulder. "Only one way to find out."

My question for him died on the tip of my tongue, forgotten. Without hesitation, we turned back to the castle, trailing down the swaying pathway with quicker footsteps, and all my storming mind could think about was Father.

But somewhere, in the depths of my mind, I couldn't help but feeling like Erix and I had left something unspoken on the podium far above us. And the thought of returning to him to uncover it didn't disturb me as much as it likely would have hours before.

CHAPTER 11

Father waited for me in my room, sitting on the edge of the bed with his head buried in his hands. He looked up as the door clicked shut behind me. Dark rings hung beneath his eyes, which seemed dull and empty. His posture was hunched as though he carried the world on his shoulders.

"Robin," he murmured, deep voice hoarse. "I thought I'd lost you."

As he studied me from his perch, I could see some of his worry bleed away from his face. His forehead softened, and his russet eyes widened. He stood, the bed creaking in thanks for the lack of his weight, and crossed the space towards where I stood completely still.

"Are you alright?"

I hated feeling like this, but it was like looking at a stranger. Someone who kept answers from me, purposefully leaving me in the dark.

No wonder the dark was my fear.

"I suppose. Are you?" I asked back, allowing him to take me in his arms. In rare moments like this, when he held me close, I felt like a child again, protected by him entirely, as though nothing in the world could ever harm me; gryvern, Hunter or fey.

"Worried sick," he replied, pressing a breathy kiss to my forehead. Pulling away, he held me at arm's reach and searched me entirely. "When I got home and found you missing, I never imagined for a moment it was the fey who had you."

"They didn't take me," I added quickly. "Not in the way you may think."

"I know that, son. But I'm still uncomfortable knowing we must have a conversation on *this* side of the Wychwood border." He turned his back on me, not before I noticed the wetness in his aged eyes.

"Is Winston…" I asked, sickness twisting like waves of a rough sea within me.

"He's fine. It was Winston who got me out of work earlier. When he turned up at the tavern barking, I knew something was wrong. By the time we got home, it was too late."

Relief washed over me, and a weight I didn't realise I still held onto lifted from my shoulders. Winston, our golden-furred hound, was unharmed. I longed for his familiar, comforting lick to cover my face just so I could hold him.

"I tried to fight them." I felt the need to shed light that I had attempted to get away. "I was so close to getting away. If the Hunter was not waiting for me out of the front door, I would have made it to the tavern."

A strong hand gripped my shoulder and squeezed. "Don't explain yourself to me, my boy. I'm just thankful you are still – that you're okay."

He was going to say alive. I knew it.

I blinked away tears, swallowing a lump in my throat as hot, striking anger lit through me. "I know who it was that sold me off."

"I know who it was too." Father's lips were pulled tight in a line. I caught the tension in his expression before he turned his back on me as he carried on. "Silly pricks didn't know what to do with the payment but return to the pub and whisper what they'd done to the other patrons. I got wind of it." When he turned back around to face me, his hands were balled into fists at his sides. That was when I noticed his bruised and bloodied knuckles, and swollen skin that told the truth of a brawl he'd not yet revealed. "They'll need far more coin than what they got for you, to pay for any healer skilled enough with a needle and thread. Even then, I don't believe that there is enough coin in all of Durmain to replace bone in a nose. James can wear the damage I gifted him like a badge of dishonour for the rest of his life. He should be thankful I left him with a life at all."

His words told enough of what he'd done to James and his accomplice, and his bloodied fist only proved as much.

I spluttered a laugh through a nervous smile. "They deserved it. God willing, I'd like the chance to seek my own revenge."

"They deserved far more than what I did. But revenge isn't always the revealing thing you think it would be. I knew beating them into a pulp wouldn't bring you back. I panicked, believed you were lost because no one returns from the Hunters. I was preparing to find them myself when the fey arrived at our home and told me what'd occurred. I'd never felt more ready to enter a place I've fought hard for years to keep from my mind."

This was it. I could feel the walls Father had built around himself crumble as he looked at me.

"Did you know?" I asked. "That my mother was dead?"

He bowed his head, chin to his chest, and even his entire posture seemed to hunch forward. "I had my suspicions."

"Then why didn't you tell me about her? About the Icethorn Court and what it means for me?" I spoke quickly, getting my words out as though time was running out and Father would throw those damn walls back up around him.

"I was trying to protect you."

Resentment burned within me, only joined by the guilt of harbouring the emotion. "From what?"

"Responsibility." He looked at me, really looked at me, as though he searched for something deep within my soul. "And equal parts selfishness on my part. When she left *us*, I thought my world had come to an end. You were so young. And I was so pathetic. But then I watched you grow and change into a version of your mother. You've always been a vision of her, with your dark hair and eyes, that it sometimes caught me off guard. I didn't want to lose you, just as I'd lost her."

My heart felt as though it was made from glass, and Father's words were like stones that crashed into it. I wanted to comfort him, but I feared that I was only capable of sobbing if I gave myself the chance to open my mouth.

"This was never how I wished for this to happen," Father said. "*But*, in some strange sense, I'm relieved that you are now aware. I longed to talk to you about her and share stories of our time before you came along. But I knew the memories would be too painful to go through. After thinking I'd lost you, I knew that the pain I expected would be nothing compared to what I felt when I came back to our home and found you missing. Please, don't hate me for it."

I reached for my father, holding him up by his elbows as if the weight of his words was far too great to bear alone. "I... understand what you had to do. It's hard, but I understand. I could never hate you, Father, not ever."

He didn't seem to believe me, from the way he winced. But that emotion faded, and Father forced a smile whilst a single tear raced down his aged face. "They told me what you did. How you used your mother's magic against the Hunters."

Mother's magic. My chest warmed, and that box filled with untapped energy didn't seem so frightening. Having something else that belonged to Mother first, like the bracelet, felt like a gift more than a curse.

There was comfort in the knowledge.

"They were as shocked as I was," I admitted, conjuring the image of the executioner and the frozen stumps of legs.

"I often wondered if you'd share in her gifts, or if your human side would become more dominant. Then again, she explained that magic is in blood, and hers was far more potent than mine would ever be."

I hugged Father again, clasping my hands together behind his back. "I feel as though I should apologise for being such a painful reminder all these years."

"Never apologise for being you, my son. No matter how others make you feel. That was a lesson your mother taught me, and I feel as though you should take heed of it."

"Thank you for being honest with me, finally anyway," I murmured, pulling away from him as a fresh warmth spread from my chest and across my entire being. "Although I've so many things I want to ask you. I hope you will be willing to tell me."

He smiled, looking at me as though I was his most prized possession. "And we can discuss everything it is that you wish to know. But perhaps later? It has been a long... couple of days, and I feel as though I will be able to sleep soundly knowing you are in safe hands. And you have duties now, ones you can't hide from. Let me rest whilst you go and learn to be you. I've been informed that the evening festivities are important and shouldn't be missed by their guest of honour."

"Come with me," I said, unaware of how much time had passed since Erix had left me at the door. "Did your invitation not extend to cover tonight's events?"

Father shook his head. "Even if it had, I wouldn't go. The interactions between fey do not involve humans, and I care little to see you being paraded around. I loved your mother more than words can explain. But even she had stories to tell of her kind, and I care little to involve myself with them now. What I care about, Robin, is *you*. I'm here for *you*."

I wanted to correct him by reminding him that I, too, was fey, but it was not the time to spoil the atmosphere.

A knock sounded at the door to the room, and it was Althea who popped her head around as it opened.

At least they were knocking now.

"I do hope I am interrupting," Althea said.

It took me a moment to understand what she said.

"You are," I confirmed dryly.

"Good," Althea said through a grin. "Because I, unfortunately, must whisk Robin away to prepare for the evening. There is much to do and even more to prepare for. We are quickly running out of time. Robin, if you would follow me."

There was no room to do anything but agree.

"I will see you soon after," Father said, patting me twice on the back. "Tomorrow. Bright and early."

I beamed at him, feeling more confident to deal with the evening's events knowing he was nearby if I required. "What do you say to sharing stories over breakfast? There is one, in particular, I have always longed to know."

How they met. Countless versions of that story had played out in my head, and now, with Father's willingness to be open, I'd finally discover how it came to be.

"Tomorrow," Father promised with a nod of agreement. "Now, don't keep them waiting. Have I not brought you up understanding the importance of haste?" He knocked a fist playfully into my shoulder.

"Listen to the human," Althea called, souring the mood. "It is high time we get you ready for the feast. There are many expecting to see you, Robin Icethorn. Judgement time awaits."

That name, my name, repeated over and over as I was scrubbed, measured and dressed by the army of staff who had flooded my rooms. Even though there wasn't any ignoring the way they seemed to flinch as they touched me.

Their discomfort and fear didn't bother me much as it should have.

I paid them no mind because I finally had something I had longed for.

A name. One that linked me to my mother, whoever she would have been.

I felt a little lighter after my conversation with Father, so much that I believed if I jumped high enough, I would've floated back down to the ground slowly.

For a while, I was poked and pulled in some other grand room, only adding to the many I'd seen. Like the first apartment quarters I'd been taken to before the gryvern and my uncontrolled magic ruined it, this was made from many interconnecting chambers; like pockets in honeycomb, it was expansive and never-ending.

I'd been bathed in warmed water soaked with so much lavender that even after I'd climbed out of the tub, my skin still sang with the remnants of the scent. Then members of the serving staff had cut my hair, mainly trimming the sides and back as Althea described that a fey never hid their ears behind anything. Especially not hair. Still, the length of slight waves fell across my forehead, yet I couldn't help but notice the chill where the rest of my hair had been cut short. I felt the wisps fall around me as the snip of sharp shears nipped close to my ears, but the noise was drowned out as my name continued its loop in my mind.

Robin Icethorn. Robin Icethorn.

Once the friendly-faced woman finished, she gave way to another wave of servants to take over. It was a game of give and take, one group completing a task, whether it be bathing, or cutting my hair, then giving way for others to do what was required of them.

This time the floor was given to three men, each reedy and slim. It was hard to sit and do nothing as they stepped into the ample-spaced room, hauling in a closed trunk between them. They struggled to carry it between themselves but waved me off with scoffs and huffs when I offered to help. The tallest, who had similar dark hair to my own and bright emerald eyes, ordered me to stay on my chair. He tutted, clapping as the other two dropped the trunk before me, as though he was the one who had lugged it all by himself.

"Tiresome work," he announced, voice light and full of song. "But the real work is only about to begin. Let me see you... ah, thinner than I thought. I may need to tailor some material, but it is workable. It's not like I was given measurements nor time to prepare. I can only do the best with what I am given, which isn't a lot."

I forced a grin towards him, sensing how very familiar his persona was. He was older than me, evident from the peppering of silver strands that shimmered among his obsidian hair. He was also the first to speak to me directly, enough to snatch me from the continuous loop of my name that I repeated internally.

"I'm sorry," I said, trying to keep in the sarcastic tone that longed to lace my words. "It's not like I was given much time to prepare for all of this either."

"Never mind that!" He waved it off, closing his eyes and scrunching his face. "This is a miracle. Never did I think to see the day when the Icethorn bloodline returned, let alone have one of them offer me an apology. If only my mam and dad would see me now. Oh, how it may have made them proud." He put a hand on his narrow hip and leaned on one leg. "Suppose they would never have believed me if I told them."

He looked at me, really looked at me, as though I was a lump of clay and he was the sculptor, searching for the statue that he'd soon carve out. Then his sharp gaze softened, and a cloud of sadness passed behind his stare. I was getting tired of seeing that emotion in everyone.

He clutched at his chest, legs giving way dramatically as he plonked himself on the lid of the trunk at his feet.

"Are you alright?" I asked as he began to sob. He flung a hand to his head, holding it there as he cried a tearless cry.

"Altar, I am *more* than alright. Weak in the knees, but fine."

"Eroan thinks the world is his stage," one of the other men said, his voice equally soft around the edges but full of annoyance. "One for the dramatics, he is."

"Hush now," the crying man – Eroan – snapped, eyes wide with shock as though he had been slapped across the face. "I pay you to pick materials, not question my emotions."

"You do *not* pay me."

Eroan forced a laugh, eyes flicking between me and his helpers. There was nothing malicious about Eroan, that was clear. But there was everything dramatic and explosive, which made me like him.

"We do not have the time to waste. Chop, chop." Eroan leaned forward as though his emotions had been disconnected in a heartbeat. "The last time I dressed someone from Icethorn was so many years ago... and before you say it, I know I have aged well. When Lady Kelsey sent word that a garment was required for the heir of the lost court, I swear my heart nearly imploded that moment. I almost refused, believing the letter to be a cruel joke. But now, looking upon you, there is no denying that you are Julianne's son. Her very bloodline."

Julianne, a name I'd heard Father murmur a number of times. I'd guessed it was my mother's, but hearing it from Eroan only added to the confirmation of it as truth.

"Julianne," I said it aloud, feeling how it rolled off my tongue so naturally. "You saw her?"

"Darling, I *dressed* her. Clothed her in the luxury gowns and costumes that impressed most and blossomed jealously for others. She was my finest model, my most daring and honest muse." He reached for me, clasping my hands in his and holding them tight. "And it is an honour to do so again, for you."

Gone was his flamboyant flair as he spoke his final words. They were honest and real.

He reached out a thumb and cleared a tear from my cheek before I'd even realised it was there. Whispering, he said, "Do not ruin my hard work with tears, dear boy."

I spluttered a laugh and a cry, smiling as Eroan pulled back and stood abruptly from the chest.

"If Princess Cedarfall sees you with red cheeks, she would have my fingers chopped off."

I wiped the tears with the back of my hand. "I wouldn't let her."

"I believe that. Now, shall we unveil what I have crafted just for you?"

"We," the third man added, rolling his eyes, which only made me laugh more.

"What *we* made for you, yes, thank you, Davern."

I nodded, clearing my throat, and reining my emotions in. It was unspoken, but Eroan must have been from the Icethorn Court. I wanted to ask him why he'd left, but swallowed my curiosity. Because somehow, I knew the answer would lead to Mother's death, and that was a topic so raw that I was willing to leave the reasoning in the dark.

For now, anyway.

"I'd love to see what you have made," I announced, straightening my back as my focus shifted to the trunk.

"It is rushed and sincerely not my best work. But I believe it will make a statement, and that is the most important rule which you should follow. Davern and Jaymie will be here to nip and cut, stitch and tighten the garments, so by the time they call for you, you shall be ready."

I nodded, warmth spreading across my chest as I looked upon three grinning faces. "I trust you. If my… my mother did, I do too."

Eroan clapped again, springing to action by unlatching the trunk and throwing the lid open with a bang. "Sweet Julianne had a saying whenever we prepared for events, no matter how large or small they seemed."

"What was that?" I asked, overwhelmed with this insight into the stranger who still kept my heart.

"Doors of possibility open when one commands attention, but it is the confidence you wear that demands for those very doors to close again."

CHAPTER 12

I stood before double doors, Althea by my side and Erix standing a step behind. He was taking his role as my shadow seriously, once again dressed in silver metal and worn leather. As we waited for the doors to open, I fussed with the smooth silk of my tunic, flattening out non-existent creases. I'd never dressed in such finery, and I was far from confident in it. I felt more like a clown – an imposter just trying to fit in but failing miserably at it.

It didn't help that Erix's gaze had hardly left me. Whenever I looked at him, he was looking at me. If I passed the shimmering reflection in windows or mirrors as we paraded towards our destination, his focus never wavered.

Perhaps he could see through the cracks of this forced illusion. In the small glimpses I had risked, it was hard to read his emotions. He was stern with an expression straight and void of his usual grin.

Eroan had almost cried as he studied me in front of the mirror back in the room. His nimble hands brushed over the outfit's blend of a storm-grey silk tunic, charcoal leather belting, and the tufts of white fur that rested over both my shoulders which draped into a deep navy cloak that trailed behind me. The boots he'd laced came up to my knees, hiding the form-fitting leggings that matched the same storm-cloud hue of my tunic.

This clothing was a far reach from the worn and usually

ripped options that sat crumpled in a drawer back home. The dull and moody tones that Eroan had dressed me in made the darks of my hair and eyes stand out. Eroan had explained his choosing was very much inspired by the fashion of the Icethorn Court, a colour palette taken from the snow-tipped mountains and storm-pregnant skies of the court. Even the silvered arm bracers blended into the outfit, separated from my long-sleeved tunic by the hem of fur beneath it. The colours were a statement. I'd understood it more when Althea collected me, dressed in an elegant gown of rust browns and deep, burnt orange. She, like the others I'd seen during our walk, all looked like they belonged in the court entrapped by eternal autumn. Whereas I would've survived during the gale of winter winds or just the storm of strangers I was about to find myself surrounded by.

It was clear that I was dressed to embody the Icethorn Court of my heritage.

Right up until we stood before the doors, listening to the muffled chatter of countless fey beyond it, I had to stop myself from turning and fleeing back to Father.

But it was too late to turn back now.

"Remind me again of what I have to do if it all becomes too much?" I asked, looking out the corner of my eye at Althea. Her flaming locks of red hair were scraped back from her face, showing the sharp-bladed curves of her jaw. A thin circlet of brass wiring which glittered from the dark rubies carefully placed around it held her hair from her face, not a strand out of place, unlike mine, which seemed to fall over one eye no matter how many times I pushed it out of the way.

"You will quickly come to know that someone of *our* prestige never has the opportunity to escape an awkward conversation," Althea said, raising her chin as she stared ahead. "But for now, Erix will remove you from the festivities if required. At least until the council meeting begins after this charade. There's no getting out of that, I am afraid."

I nodded, swallowing audibly as I waited for the doors to finally open. Clenching my hands into fists, I felt nothing but nerves; they filled my lungs with each shuddering inhale.

"I have no idea what I'm supposed to say, let alone *do*," I admitted. "What if they ask me questions that I can't answer? Actually, I'm starting to think this is a bad idea. I could just–"

"No one is going to ask you anything," Althea interrupted, releasing a sigh of frustration. "You are the heir to the Icethorn Court. They will only speak to you when you address them. If you would rather not engage in conversation, then simply keep your mouth closed."

"Encouraging," I muttered under my breath as a shuffling of footsteps behind the door caught our attention. Someone spoke atop them all, and the noise of the crowd beyond stilled to silence.

"Do not leave Erix's line of sight," Althea warned, voice full of tension. Something was bothering her, but I'd no time to ask as the doors swung open and her face split with the most enchanting of smiles.

Before us waited a balcony which overlooked a grand room, one so large that I couldn't see where the walls and ceiling came to their end.

My lips parted in awe as the scene before me blew away the cobwebs of nerves with one strong breath. Althea stepped forward first, and I quickly followed. Around the balcony was a bannister, posts of interwoven wood. On either side a staircase flowed down like the rivers of a waterfall, carpeted by a runner of deep red material that complimented the polished wood of the flooring beneath it. It was all so... expensive.

I overlooked the bannister to the room far below, and the scene turned my stomach inside out.

Countless faces looked upwards, each a mirror of my own bewilderment. And they all looked at me. Not a single pair of eyes flirted with the notion of looking at anyone else. Not even Althea, who glowed brighter than I did.

I commanded the crowd's attention – their awe. Disbelief rolled off them in gargantuan waves, so much so that I could almost taste it across my dry tongue.

Creator, I needed a drink.

The crowd of fey were dressed like a bed of resting autumn leaves. From my height, it was as though I looked down upon the bed of foliage, where reds, oranges, golds and brass tones melted together as one.

I gripped the bannister, catching a glimpse of the grey of my shirt, and felt even more like a thorn among roses.

"Robin," Althea whispered through a smile, eyes widening as she flicked them towards the stairway. It was as though my name was the loudest noise I'd ever heard, as the silent crowd still watched on. She extended a hand, her skin shimmering beneath the sheer gloves that went up to her elbows. "Take my hand. We'll do this together."

I did as she commanded, slipping my shaking fingers into her warm hold. Althea gripped onto me with support, so grounding that I felt she could've held me up by that one hand alone. Then she guided me towards the staircase, and we began our descent.

I hardly looked down to make sure I didn't miss a step as I studied the guards waiting for us at the bottom. They'd formed a path of such through the gathering fey. And with each step downwards, the conversations and murmurings began to grow until the crowd no longer stared in silence.

In a single breath, it was like I was no longer here. Instead, they stared out the corners of their eyes as they forced conversation with those around them. Hiding their interest. Concealing their thoughts in hushed murmurs to one another.

"Not so bad, was it?" Althea said.

"Was it not?" I asked, a nervous grin tugging at my lips.

"Nothing wrong with a little attention. You are going to have to get used to it. And quickly for that matter."

My mouth was dry, and my mind a whirlwind of thoughts. "I need a strong drink."

"You *deserve* a drink." Althea looked over my shoulder to where Erix waited. I didn't need to turn to confirm it. He was taking the personal guard claim very... well, personally.

"Think you can handle the hungry looks alone?" Althea asked. "I've got some awkward conversation to have myself. Then I will return with that drink you deserve."

"He won't be alone," Erix said from behind me, as if I needed the reminder.

A shiver spread up my spine and across my neck. I was trying my best not to engage with anyone's eye contact, focusing solely on Althea. It was exhausting. Whereas she seemed so at ease among the bustling crowd, which set me at ease, somewhat at least.

"I'll be fine," I replied. "But Althea, make sure the drink is strong!"

Althea smiled, and for a moment, I believed it to be genuine. "That will be the gravest of mistakes you have ever made. I will be back in a moment unless I am swarmed by my family. I know they are lurking around here somewhere."

Her comment actually made me look away from her, scanning the dense forest of bodies for a glimpse of red hair, trying to spot one of her siblings.

"Are they..." I began, trailing off when I noticed she had disappeared.

The space she left was soon filled with bodies connected to smiling faces and outstretched hands. Discomfort riled through me, but I held my wince in and kept my chin raised.

"Hello... thank you... excuse me."

I spoke in a string of short, precise words as I fought my way through the crowd. Althea's warning about keeping quiet was forgotten and put to the wayside. It was impossible to simply stand and wait for Althea's return for fear I'd be suffocated by the many waiting faces of those who longed for me to engage with them.

A few times, Erix had to clear his throat, stopping a seemingly harmless fey's attempt to get close. I smiled and muttered my apologies, pushing forward to some unknown destination.

It'd barely been a few minutes, and I needed some space.

My mind went back to Erix's enquiry to find out what I feared. I felt like I was adding another answer to my list. *Being buried alive by bodies.* Yes, that thought was frightening and felt too much like a possibility.

This place was miles different from being at the tavern, surrounded by the swaying, singing bodies of drunkards as we welcomed the first day of spring after a long winter. Even with sticky arms and the beat of thick ale breath upon me, it never bothered me.

I would've chosen the tavern if I could've swapped places. Without question.

Ahead of me, a member of the serving staff carried a round tray of thin, delicately stemmed glasses filled with a golden liquid. I didn't care what was inside, only that whatever bubbly concoction it was took some edge off my overwhelming anxiety. I grabbed two glasses, swiping them from the tray with each hand. I should've taken my time, but hindsight was only helpful after the mistake was made. So, two glasses would be just fine.

"Wait," Erix called out behind me, voice a gasp.

In seconds I'd downed each glass, long before the shocked girl even noticed. Erix was before me in a blink, tearing the glasses from my hands with such furious speed I was certain they'd break under his grip.

"What is wrong with you," I hissed out of surprise, catching the attention of the crowd around me once again.

Erix's face was pinched with anger, but as he spoke, he did so calmly, even though his lips were pulled taut, and his eyes practically bulged from his head. "You can't just drink or eat anything you so desire!"

"Who do you... think you are?" I slurred, pushing an awkward hand into his chest. The drink had been sweet and light, filled with bubbles that seemed to pop and burst, revealing more flavour as it traversed my insides. I'd a strong stomach for alcohol, having started at a young age when I would steal goblets at the tavern and drink them beneath the tables with the friends who'd dared me. But – only two glasses in – I felt as though I'd drunk far more than two.

"It is not safe for you. You are permitted to eat and drink only when your Taster has done so first."

"Taster?" I questioned, flashing the girl a grin of apology before picking up my pace and walking away from Erix. I blinked, lids heavy, as I stumbled through the crowd, no longer offering apology to those I bumped in to.

"Where do you think you are rushing off to?" I heard the click of glass as Erix forced the empty glasses back onto the tray, then the thundering of footsteps as he chased after me.

"I can handle myself." I hiccupped, breathless. "Just give me some space – I need some space"

"What you need is water and fresh air."

"What I don't need is a fucking Taster."

"Yes, you do. Or have you forgotten that you are the only living heir to the Icethorn Court? Your life is more precious than all these fine men and women combined. It is a precaution for your food and drink to be tested."

I waved him off, feet feeling as though I had lead at the bottom of my boots. "I was thirsty, and Althea has not returned with the promised goods. Call me... resourceful."

I should've probably worried about the threat of harm, so much so that someone had to taste my food or drink. But the bubbling, sweet and frankly *moreish* liquid I'd downed kept that worry, as well as others, at bay.

"You are not listening to me." Erix caught up to me, reaching for my arm. "Robin, stop."

And I did stop, dead in my tracks, as though what he had said was the most offensive thing I had heard. "Why did you call me that?"

"Call you what?"

My chest warmed; words slightly slurred. "Robin. You just called me by my name."

"That is what names are for." He glared at me with those large, bright silver eyes. His brows furrowed inward, causing lines to crease his forehead.

"Then you should use it more often."

Erix grinned slightly, relaxing his annoyed expression. His full lips parted, and his eyes filled with an emotion I could not place. "If you desire, little bird."

"Urgh." I could hardly string words together now. The world seemed to spin, so I leaned against the wall closest to me for support.

"Althea will have my guts for supper if she knows you have been exposed to that drink. Again, I suggest you are in need of some fresh air to help clear your head."

I blinked, and for a moment too long, keeping my eyes closed. A bubble of a laugh traced up my throat, only stopped by my fingers that pressed against my lips. "Fresh air sounds... nice."

It did – sweat was beading over my brow and beneath the tight outfit. The sensible part of me – the part that the drink had imprisoned at the back of my mind – longed for cool air. Not only to clear my head but to get me away from the many people who watched on, likely judging my every move.

Erix stepped closer to me, his body shielding me from the many stares.

I craned my neck upwards, keeping my stare fixed on his.

"Follow me closely," he said, voice full of quiet command.

Erix's hand found the curve of my lower back, and he applied a gentle amount of pressure.

Soon enough, the crowd thinned out the further we travelled to the outer edges of the room. Then a wall, towering and endless, reached up to shadowed heights before us. Curved, windowless archways gave way to the gentle breeze of evening beyond. The decorated guards nodded to Erix, who urged me outside into the illuminated night.

Lanterns glowed across the stone bannister, reminiscent of the one that I'd not long looked over. Beyond it was a painted scene of a sleeping city, likely because most of its occupants now prowled in the room we had just left.

I took a breath in, filling my lungs with the evening breeze. Instantly I relaxed, noticing that not a single person was out here.

Only Erix and me. We were alone.

"Your cluelessness is not as endearing as you think it is," Erix said, finally releasing his hand from me.

"I don't remember caring about your opinion," I replied, closing my eyes as the breeze cooled the skin around my neck. Already the immediate effects of the liquid were easing, as though the very air snatched it away. Instead, I was left with a faint headache behind my eyes, but nothing that another sip wouldn't cure.

"Next time let me do what I have been tasked to do. It will make keeping you safe less of a challenge."

"What is the worst that could happen?" I snapped, leaning back against the stone barrier. "Is a gryvern going to poison my food and drink?"

"You are a fool to believe the gryvern are the only beings wishing you harm. There is much you do not yet know, so until you do, be cautious, for your sake as well as mine."

I glared at him, gripping the cold stone. "Since you wanted to learn so much about me earlier, let me give you another lesson. Don't treat me as a child. Even my own father does not, so you also have no right. Perhaps you, Althea, and everyone else should simply sit me down and lay all the secrets out on the table. I don't appreciate being kept in the dark at all times."

The dark – a place I fear – just as I'd revealed to Erix.

"It is not my place to counsel you," he murmured, mouth pulled into a frown. "It is to keep you safe."

"I can look after myself," I snapped.

"Can you?" he said, moving towards me in a single, long step. "Do you really believe that? Perhaps you were stronger than the humans you grew up with, faster and luckier. But here, you're weak. Untrained, uncontrolled and a complete liability."

His words, and the alcohol, only made me want to prove him wrong.

"Would you like to test me?" I asked him, knuckles white as my nails dug into stone. A punch would not hurt him, but the swirling of cold that rattled in the chest inside my body would do some damage. That I was certain of.

"Do it then." Erix was inches before me, shadows cast across his strong face from the lanterns around us. "Show me that you can look after yourself, and maybe I will believe you."

"There is nothing I need to prove," I replied through gritted teeth. "Especially not to you."

Erix breathed deeply, the tips of his boots touching mine. "There is something entirely infuriating about you... little bird."

"Back to nicknames?" I asked, jaw tense. "I feel like I should have one for you." I pushed off the bannister. "Any suggestions? For you seem to have a lot to say tonight."

Erix didn't move, not even flinch, as I lifted myself up as far as I could to get in his face. If anyone looked at us, they would likely think I looked pathetic as I leaned up on my tiptoes, contesting the hulking giant of a fey who leaned down over me.

"Suddenly so silent?" I mocked, voice no more than a whisper as the final dregs of liquid courage dissolved.

"Your eyes are endless and beautiful. I can see the storm within you."

My mouth parted, breath hitching as his words settled over me. Erix's hands brushed over my own, tickling upwards on each of my arms; his touch left a trail of fire in its wake, melting away the cold of night.

"I have never known someone so equally…" He paused, lips pursing as he contemplated his next words carefully. And I longed for him to say them, speak them aloud before he changed his mind. "Striking yet intoxicating."

A blush spread up my neck and filled my cheeks with warmth, only urged on as Erix's gentle touch moved over the ridges of my shoulders and stopped only when he cupped my face.

"Erix…" I breathed, unsure if I wanted him to release me or if I wanted to urge his touch to deepen.

"Yes?" he asked, head tilting as though he regarded me as a dog would a bone.

What I did next shocked me. Perhaps the strong, fey spirits hadn't entirely left my body, because I reached up, wrapped my frozen fingers over his hands and held him in place. I didn't pull them down. I didn't tug them from my skin, or urge him to release me. I just held them, pressing upon the gloves and keeping him in place.

I risked a glance at the curve of his lips as they lifted into a smile. They parted ever so slightly, and my stomach jolted as the pink tip of his tongue escaped and trailed a line of glistening moisture across his lower lip.

The world no longer mattered as that subtle movement entrapped me in a charm.

"Erix," Althea's voice sounded, shattering the moment of frozen clarity.

That single word had him pulling away from me, letting my own hands drop awkwardly to my sides as he stepped back.

I glanced to Althea, recognising a familiar stemmed glass in each hand, then back to Erix, who rubbed a hand over his chin in embarrassed contemplation.

"Perhaps *I* should take over your... duties for the remainder of the evening. Next time you will be the one to fetch the drinks." She glared at Erix, powerful eyes raging with the ember of fire I knew she could conjure. "Robin, do you care to join me for a toast?"

I looked at Erix a final time, wondering why he refused to meet my gaze. He looked everywhere but at me.

Annoyed, and frankly desperate to clear my head of him, I joined Althea, leaving him behind.

"Has that wine been tasted?" I asked as I plucked the glass from her hand, my voice void of everything but accusation. "Wouldn't want to risk the chance of being poisoned this early in the evening."

Taking a small sip, I started to walk away from them.

"We will discuss this later," Althea hissed back towards the dark balcony where Erix clearly lingered, and then the click of her heeled shoes sang across the ground as she chased after me.

I was sure to keep ahead of her as we lost ourselves back into the crowd, not because I worried about how I was going to explain what she'd walked in on; I cared little to try and unwrap that. I was more concerned she could see the lingering warmth of Erix's touch where he had held me. And the truth that it was a feeling I didn't wish to forget.

CHAPTER 13

No one danced all evening. Not that I'd been to a ball before, but I was more than confident that dancing was a main factor during one.

Perhaps that wasn't what occurred at balls, I had nothing else to compare it to. I, at least, expected swaying crowds, music and frolicking. Instead, it was just a sea of people who spoke to one another, although not entirely focusing on the conversation they shared, especially not when I passed them, anyway.

Althea hadn't said a word to me about what she interrupted on the balcony, and I was thankful for that. If she questioned what'd happened between Erix and me, I feared I wouldn't have been able to provide an answer. Just thinking back to his strong touch and hungry gaze made me uneasy; at least that was what I thought the sensation was – a jolting flip of my stomach and the strange chilling in my chest, two feelings that did well to distract me from the many who bowed heads and smiled as I walked by them.

Erix didn't return to his station as my shadow, not even when a plainly dressed man called from the podium and instructed for the evening's events to cease and the council to begin.

I clutched at the half-empty glass as the crowd moved like a wave of flesh towards the exit. It was close to impossible not to be pulled along by the movement, but Althea stood beside me with an arm hooked around my own. Her hold was an anchor, and I was thankful for it, even if her silence or blatantly ignoring what'd happened made me feel just as awkward as I had when she interrupted us on the balcony.

As the crowd thinned, I noticed others who didn't leave. Men and women, young and old, waited back as those around them dispersed, exiting up the grand staircase and leaving the hall.

I focused on them, realising quickly that they all shared the deep tones of red and orange hair. Like Althea, they stood with pride, faces sharp with beauty and authority, a littering of statues that'd been hidden among the patrons of the ball. I didn't remember noticing them before, but one glance told me all I needed to know about who they were.

The Cedarfall Court.

Members of Althea's family, and there were many of them. I was left stunned and embarrassed at the thought that they'd overheard mine and Erix's initial argument, or seen me drunk on fey wine. I swallowed the hard lump of discomfort, forcing my expression to be neutral as each and every one of them turned to face me.

Some smiled, others tried to keep their faces empty of any exposing emotion. When the grand doors finally closed after the remaining stragglers were ushered out, the Cedarfall family sprang into action.

"Whilst they prepare the supper, I will introduce you." Althea tightened her grip on my arm as an older woman stepped forward first. She wore her auburn hair in a messy bun atop her head. It reminded me of a nest; it was disappointing not to see birds among it. Lines crowed the sides of her eyes, but that was all that signified that she was far older than Althea. She carried herself with graceful steps, her golden gown trailing behind her like silken water.

"So, you are the dear boy who ruined my favourite guest quarters." She smiled, closing her eyes as her face morphed into a dramatic grin.

Althea curtsied quickly, prompting me to bow. "Lady Kelsey, it is my honour to introduce you to Robin Icethorn."

"Stand, my dear," Lady Kelsey said, barely dropping my gaze. She reached a golden painted nail and lifted Althea up by the chin. "You of all people do not need to bow to me."

I felt the need to apologise as the blur of ice and smashed bricks flooded my mind. "About the room, I'm really sorry."

She laughed, pressing a jewelled hand to the taut skin of her chest. "I refuse to accept your apology as well, dear boy. For your little mishap has given me the most perfect stories to brag about during the dullest of events, such as the one we have just had to be privy to. Who else can say they hosted the return of the Icethorn Court?"

"My aunt," Althea added, gesturing with rolling eyes towards the woman, "will talk about it for years to come."

"As many years as I am blessed to have left," Lady Kelsey said with a genuine smile.

Even tipsy, I knew that she was the type of person I could warm to instantly.

"Thank you for letting me stay and for allowing my father to join me. It makes this... unexpected transition a little more manageable."

She waved away my comment as though it was a fly. "It is unbecoming of someone of your stature to apologise or provide thanks for anything. My dear sister would never dream of it, let alone her husband. I admit I was going to question just how much you knew about your heritage, but one look at you and it answers all my queries. You truly knew nothing, did you, my dear?"

I nodded, flicking my gaze to Althea. "Not who my mother was, nor what it meant to be her son. Although I'm slowly grasping it, I guess."

"Then you will learn, in time," Lady Kelsey said. "I do *hope* you enjoy the feast and the conversation that comes with it. As I have already said, my sister is not one for apologies, so let me do it on her behalf. The conversations that follow this evening will heavily revolve around you. If at all you feel as though you are a ghost haunting a room full of people who discuss you as though you are not here... they do not mean it. And also, remember that you are as important as they are. Do not be afraid to remind them of such."

Althea drained her glass, tipping the contents into her mouth until not a single drop was left. Pulling it away with a breath, she finalised the conversation with a single sentence. "I should introduce him to the rest of the family before we are called in for the council, it may soften the inevitable tension."

Just like that, the conversation was over, and Lady Kelsey knew it.

"My dear, it was a pleasure to meet you," Lady Kelsey said, soft hands grasping my own. She leaned in, whispering to me as if her niece could not hear. "I can see a confidence in your eyes. Do not let my family throw you with their comments or expressions. The Cedarfall family are historically known for their severe nature. At least some of us are not as... sharpened as others. But we have always been the Icethorn's greatest allies, I do hope that continues."

"Thank you," I replied, ignoring the tsking of Althea at my side.

"And some are historically known for chewing the ears off of those too polite to end a conversation," Althea added, to Lady Kelsey's amusement.

With that, Lady Kelsey left in a cloud of light giggles, sweeping off to claim a full glass of darker red liquid from a member of the serving staff.

"She was nice," I said to Althea as she urged me forward.

"She was intense," Althea grumbled. "My aunt means well and is more comparable to a magpie. But instead of shiny objects, she likes pretty boys and glittering jewels. My mother named her as Lady of Aurelia just to keep her busy and out of trouble. She is kind, but you will soon grow tired of her insistent parties and parades. Believe me."

Lady Kelsey didn't seem that bad, but Althea seemed to paint a picture of somebody completely different to whom I'd just met. "I sense some unresolved family tension."

"When you have a family of my size and... intensity, there will always be issues. Come, let me introduce you to my siblings. Oh, you are going to just *love* them."

Somehow, I didn't believe her.

Althea ran me through the introductions to the countless people that followed after Lady Kelsey. Her brothers and sister each looked like older and younger versions of one another. Almost perfect mirror images. Some regarded me with kindness, but some held wary gazes and closed off postures. I just smiled, cheeks hurting, and opted to not say much. With each person I met, I wondered more about what they thought about me. I was never one to care, but it seemed that I'd changed entirely the moment I passed the Wychwood border. It was that or the strong wine continuously sipped.

"Exactly how many siblings do you have?" I asked Althea out the corner of my mouth. I believed the next crowd we moved towards must have been other relations, but each time I was proven wrong. It was hard to count those I met, not whilst I was busy failing at remembering the many names.

"Twenty-three," she said through gritted teeth. "And believe me, what you are thinking, I'm also thinking, but three times worse."

It was almost impossible to believe, but the more fey I met, the more obvious it was that they were related, from the deep, auburn hair to the freckles and sharpened features.

"Where do you fall among the ranking?" I asked, fighting the urge to raise a hand and massage the apples of my cheeks where they ached.

"I am lucky number seven. Not that I dare dwell on it, but it was said that my mother and father spent a century entwined in love, resulting in the rabble you see before you. The thought only makes my skin crawl, but it is somewhat nice to know they care about each other so much that they want to see themselves running around in miniature forms."

"And all the work that comes with it..." I said, ignoring the pang of my heart, which always occurred when others shared stories about their families.

I didn't hear what she said next as I caught the blur of a form out of the corner of my eye.

Erix. He was back.

I studied him, but it seemed he did everything in his power to find a reason to look elsewhere. His obvious disregard irked me as if I'd done something to cause his coldness. I hardly knew the man; he was as much a stranger as the rest of the people around me. And it was he who had touched me first.

This awkwardness between us was his doing, not mine.

"If I need to change him out for another," Althea said above the rim of her glass, "I can. Gyah has already offered herself as another suitable guard for you."

It took a moment for me to realise that she was speaking to me. Shaking off the annoyance, I tried to push the thoughts of him to the back of my head. "It was nothing. Plus, sending him off would only make me feel like I've lost to whatever game he is playing."

"Nothing looks an awful lot like something," she retorted. "I've never been one for games."

"Me neither," I said, just as the grand double doors opened.

A servant stood between them, hands clasped before him as he addressed us. "The council will begin shortly. Please take your seats for its commencement."

Now it was my turn to down the remaining bubbling liquid

in the glass I held. After the last drinks I'd devoured, leading to the strange encounter with Erix, I'd taken my time sipping this one. But the uncertainty of what waited beyond those doors set my nerves ablaze.

"A tip for you," Althea whispered as we joined the river of her family, who moved towards the next room. "Speak when it is your turn. You may be the heir to the Icethorn Court, but you are on Cedarfall land, and that requires you to show respect to the court."

"I know how to handle myself," I reminded her, voice slurring.

Althea raised a brow as if to say *'Yes, okay, Robin. Whatever you say, Robin'*.

"Then this is the time to prove that, to me, yourself and those who wait in that room. The answers you demand may soon be revealed, and I hope that brings you some clarity. But you must remember that not everyone – even my own blood – may be as quick to welcome the *idea* of your return."

"What do you mean idea?" I said, almost tripping over my feet as Althea finally let go of my arm.

"To some, in this court and in others, you represent the excuse to prevent unrequired bloodshed." A chill spread down my neck and made my limbs heavy. "But to others, you will only be seen as an obstacle stopping something we have planned endlessly for. A thorn in the rosebush of plans drafted over years... plans that many will not wish to see ruined."

"I don't understand what you mean," I muttered, stopping dead in my tracks.

"There is a war coming, Robin, and I hope you have returned in time to prevent it. But not everyone will think the same as me. This meeting will be important for many reasons, one being that it will shed some light onto who of my family I can trust and who I cannot."

* * *

The Queen of Cedarfall, head and ruling crown of the court, refused to take her amber eyes off me, not when we entered the room, nor when Althea guided me to a chair which'd been pulled back on a long table that took up most of the room. Her gaze was burning, itching at my skin in two points as she studied my every move.

Althea's mother was the spitting image of her, except older and more intimidating. Her thick red hair had been pulled over her shoulders, revealing the exposed sharpness of her collarbone and narrow frame. White strands of hair hid among the deep red, which made it seem that a seamstress had woven them deliberately throughout; it gave her added wisdom and age, which only intensified her aura of authority. She didn't look old enough to have sired twenty-three children, nor did the man who sat beside her.

The King of Cedarfall. He shared similar facial features to Althea, more so than her mother, such as the point of his nose and thick dark brows; there was no denying they shared blood.

Both the king and the queen at his side wore crowns of golden roots and autumn leaves which glittered underneath the grand, burning chandelier. Authority and grace rolled off them in waves of pungent power that I could feel even over the distance from their table to the one I now sat at.

"They keep looking at me like I'm a serpent about to strike," I whispered to Althea, who hardly cared to notice.

She waved a folded napkin, resting it upon her knees. "Did you expect to be ignored?" Althea said, sparing me a glance.

"What would you think if I admitted that being ignored was exactly what I hoped for?"

Althea nudged a shoulder into mine, and I could tell she was trying to calm my nerves, but, at this point, they were an uncontrollable storm. Especially after what Althea had last said about a war – something I'd never have dreamed was a possibility.

"I would tell you to grow a pair and sit up straight like you are meant to be here."

I swallowed audibly, taking Althea's friendly hint and sitting up straight in my chair.

"All rise for Queen Lyra and King Thallan Cedarfall."

I couldn't see who had spoken, but the screech of chairs sounded down the long table I had found myself in the middle of. Stumbling to catch up, I stood alongside Althea and the rest of her family who'd been seated on either side of us.

The only two who remained seated were Althea's parents, who watched us carefully. It was Queen Lyra who raised a hand slowly, interrupting the silence. "Thank you, my dear court and family, who heeded my invitation for this meeting at such short notice. And to my darling sister Kelsey, for hosting."

There was a rustle as heads turned to Lady Kelsey, who stood towards the end of the line. She bowed her head, a grin plastered across her face. "Always a pleasure, never a chore, sister."

"Please, sit." Queen Lyra clapped jewelled hands. "We have much to discuss, and a meal has been prepared to keep us going."

Everyone in the room shifted in unison. Everyone but me. I was likely the last whose bottom touched their seat.

Lyra's stare found mine once again, but this time she didn't stare in silence. "You cannot imagine the… disturbance your appearance has caused, Robin Icethorn."

"Mother," Althea warned softly. "Play nice."

"It's fine," I replied, voice cracking as I forced too much false authority into it. I could have done with another drink as I held the powerful stare of a queen. "I believe I've somewhat of an understanding, although it's not a clear picture. Although, I am confident it will be by the end of this meeting."

Out the corner of my eye, I watched as King Thallan placed a hand upon his wife's and held it on the table before them. "When my daughter brought me news of what had happened, I was convinced it could not be true, but you have since displayed abilities that are only possible for Julianne's bloodline. With that fact, combined with the gryvern's recent attack, I believe it strongly supports the claim to your lineage."

"What have those creatures got to do with it?" I asked, the echo of my voice reflecting the slight shake in it.

"Because the gryvern have not been seen *since* they slaughtered your dear family." Queen Lyra paused, a muscle in her jaw feathering as she contemplated her next words. "Then they turn up at our doorstep not even hours after you arrive. Do you believe it to be coincidence, or do you claim to be the heir of a court long believed to be lost to the past?"

"Coincidence?" I said calmly, even though it was far from what I felt. "I don't believe in such things. And if you are trying to ask if I knew about my heritage before this all occurred... I knew nothing until I came here."

"*Nothing* at all?" she requested again, her voice laced with distrust.

I nodded, biting the inside of my cheeks to stop myself from saying something I would regret. "Yes. I gain nothing from lying."

"Well, there is no denying you certainly look the part. And every member of the court can sense the power that riles through you, so I do not deny that you are, in fact, Julianne's child. That much, I understand. But what I do not understand is how Julianne had a child without it ever being known. It is not something that can be hidden lightly nor overlooked. And trust me, I would know."

I was aware of Althea and her many siblings who sat around us, each likely looking at me, waiting to see what I would say back to their mother.

"With all due respect, Queen Lyra, I know no more than you do." If they could sense the power in me, perhaps they would also feel my honesty.

"Hmm. I'm interested as to why your father decided to keep such knowledge from you. I suppose that is a question you can ask him yourself, now he is comfortably taking lodging in my court." Lyra studied me for another moment of silence, carefully watching for how I would respond.

I did my best to bite my tongue, but that was never a skill I was adept at. And the glasses of wine certainly stopped it from working. "With all due respect, the insight into my father's mind and reasonings isn't why I'm here."

If I expected my retort to displease Lyra, her subtle smile proved me wrong.

"Robin, you're right. There are other pressing matters that need discussing, which do not include your father's incredible skills of lying." Before I could respond, Queen Lyra spoke up again. "Matters such as what Robin Icethorn's life will mean for Wychwood going forward. As a court, it seems that we must be the first to decide on the stance we wish to proceed with. As you are aware, and so is our treasury, a lot of time and coin has been funded into preparing for our one-sided war. With the Passing mere weeks away, it is not long until Wychwood's preparations are put into motion. Now, it would seem, we have come across a bump in our perfectly drawn-out plans, and we must determine if we carry on over it or turn our backs on the path entirely."

Thallan cleared his throat before he spoke, voice deep. "Perhaps, before we begin this feast, we can come to a decision. This way the food will not be spoiled. Both the Elmdew and Oakstorm Courts will be receiving word of the Icethorn's return, and they will visit to see him for themselves. When they arrive, we must be in a *joint* understanding."

"If I may speak." A younger man stood from the table we sat at; all attention turned to him as he regarded his parents with a straight back. "I have something I feel that needs to be said before we continue."

"Please, Orion, share your thoughts," the king requested.

Orion – who Althea had already introduced me to – hardly regarded me now just as he had back in the hall, even though this time his words were meant for me to hear. "We should not allow the years of preparation go to waste. If we go back on our plans, it will not only upset our people, but the courts we have spent twenty-years securing peace with. And it is far more concerning having enemies this side of Wychwood than it is the humans."

"Oh, brother, do the other courts frighten you?" Althea said, leaning back in her chair as she spoke.

"War between our people–"

"There will be no war between the fey," Althea interrupted him. "Just admit to the crowd that you want to see bloodshed and be done with it. There is nothing wrong declaring you are an evil sadist who enjoys the concept of war."

"Althea, that is enough," Queen Lyra snapped. "Your brother has his views, as you have your own. This council meeting is an open conversation and open it *shall* be."

"If he can provide me with a valid reason as to why he would choose war over peace, then let him speak it," Althea said, stiffening in her chair. "I am all ears."

"The humans have been taking our kind, harvesting their blood for whatever plans they have."

"Wrong," Althea interrupted again. "Not all humans are involved in the abductions of our kind. You cannot accuse them all of a crime most do not know is committed."

"Well someone has to pay." Orion slammed his palms on the table. "How long have you been working to locate the Hunters' leader? The Hand has evaded your attempts for years. All that time wasted, and still, you return without their head."

"If you were so concerned, you would join our missions in retrieving the stolen, not sit here hoping for everyone else to enter the realm and kill the humans for you. If the cause is that close to your heart, then help me. Join my legion in finding those taken and see that they are brought home. But do not sit here and use that as the excuse for why you would allow war even though we have the perfect reason to prevent it sitting with us."

Orion's freckled face burned red, but so did the cloth beneath his palms; smoke twisted across the table, and the rancid smell of burning soon reached me.

"Rein yourself in," King Thallan ordered. "And sit yourself down, Orion."

I could see in the shaking of his face and body that he wanted to say something more, but Orion kept quiet, sitting back with a thud. His palms had burned marks into the table from the fire that spread from his skin, a fire I'd seen blossoming between Althea's hands not long ago.

"It is clear Althea is in favour of preventing war. Does anyone else believe as much?" Queen Lyra asked, eyes scanning the row of her court.

Another stood, this time a girl likely younger than Althea. Her hair was darker like her father's, but her amber eyes glowed like a jewelled flame, matching those of her mother. "If we have a chance of preventing the release of the Icethorn Court's power across the human realm, we should take it. What is to say it will not affect us in years to come?"

"Our barriers are strong. The labradorite stones are left unturned."

"The Wychwood barrier should have been secure, but it has cracked like the shell of an empty egg year by year. There is no saying the power, after devouring the human realm, will not turn back on us. No one understands it. We should not pretend that we do," Althea added.

I couldn't begin to fathom what they spoke of.

"Dear, would you let another speak for once?" Lyra said, smiling, as though Althea was a source of entertainment or pride; it was hard to tell which.

"Sorry, Eleanora," Althea said, winking at the younger girl who still stood and smiled in return. Eleanora was so young her mouth held gaps where teeth had fallen out, as mundane as a human growing.

"I stand with Althea. Robin is the perfect excuse for us to pull out of support of the siege on Durmain."

"Think of the waste of coin!" Orion shouted from his seat, stamping his feet beneath the table. "The time and resources we have put in!"

"What of the lives that will be wasted?" Althea snapped at her brother again. "Do you not think the fey will suffer greatly if we follow through with our plans?"

My head was bouncing back and forth, following the conversation and building tension.

"Robin, you have stayed awfully quiet… do you care to share your thoughts? These are your people's fates we discuss," Lyra said, looking at me. "You have lived among the humans. What are *your* views on the matter?"

I shook my head. As they argued over a war I never knew was a possibility, I could only think of the towns and villages nestled close to the borders of Wychwood, and what would happen when an army of fire-powered fey would trample over them. Yet all I could mutter as a reply was pathetic. "I don't know what to say."

"The humans killed your family," Queen Lyra said. "You should want to see them pay for that, no?"

A spear of anger pierced my lungs. The accusation that it was the humans who killed my mother was shocking to the core.

"You said it was the gryvern who… killed her?"

"Those monsters are nothing but puppets to a master. A master who we believe Althea had been chasing."

"Unsuccessfully," Orion barked. "Of course he would want to see them pay."

Ice cracked beneath my hands, coating the fork beside me. It took considerable effort to keep the magic reigned in as I faced Althea's brother.

"Don't tell me how to feel, or what you believe I should want. You don't know me." My knuckles turned white as I gripped onto the arms of the chair. "Never speak on my behalf."

Althea snickered beside me.

"Speak up then," Lyra said, expression urging me to continue. And speak up I did.

The chair nearly toppled backwards as I stood from the table. "Two days ago, I could not have even imagined that I'd be standing here. And now I'm asked to add my reasoning as to why you should not go to war with my kind." *Humans.* One half of a two-sided coin. "You might as well be speaking in riddles because I don't understand why you would even want war. What good has ever come of it before?"

"Land, power, riches. Three of many other reasons that would entice me to raise an army against the humans," Queen Lyra said, voice stern and sharp. "That and the fact our kind have been going missing for years, more so as the barrier keeping the humans from entering the Icethorn Court has weakened so much that they are able to pass in and out as they please. There has not been an Icethorn to calm the power building in those lands. It has lowered our defences and made our people easy for the picking. Like Orion explained, that is enough reason to raid their lands. To stop them." I opened my mouth to disagree when the tone of her conversation changed. "But I also see Althea's point. With your return and willingness to cooperate, you could claim the wild Icethorn power before the Passing and prevent the enraged magic from breaking the barrier entirely. You could restore the misbalance and petition for our sister courts to lower their blades, as I am contemplating doing."

Pain had claimed a home in my head. It started behind my eyes and made the light of the room hard to take in. I squinted, lowering into my seat once again as Lyra continued speaking.

"Robin, are you willing to claim your heritage and accept the unclaimed court as your own?"

I couldn't answer. It was close to impossible to speak as the pain in my head intensified, that and I didn't *have* an answer.

"Even *he* does not know what he wants." I pinched my eyes closed as Orion called out

No. I didn't know what 'claiming my heritage' entailed. "I need time."

No one seemed to hear me as the argument of my wishes and desires fired around me.

"Robin?" Althea said, placing a hand on my shoulder. "Are you okay?"

I shook my head, forcing my eyes open as a sharp twist of pain ripped open the flesh of my brain. "This is all too much."

"He is right. This isn't a discussion we can expect him to make on the spot," Althea spoke out, hand gripping my shoulder.

"Time is not something we have, my daughter," Lyra cooed. "The Passing is weeks away, and if the court is not claimed, the power shall break free of the barrier and wreak havoc over the human realm whether we want it to or not. Robin can either stop it, or we will ride the storm across the border and into their lands, seeing through our plans."

"What has that got to do with war?" I asked, my heart beating so hard in my chest it ached.

"The storm building in your homeland is simply the first step," Queen Lyra replied, the room growing silent. "It is what follows the storm that will be the war."

What follows the storm?

"I do not believe a decision is required immediately," King Thallan added. "Time may be sparse, but we have not run out of it completely, and we do not need to make any choice this very instant. When our sister courts join us for the Passing, an answer can be provided then."

Lyra regarded her husband for a moment, both entrapped in each other's stares as though they spoke through their minds. Then she nodded in agreement, and the pain in my head subsided, only a little.

"Then it is for Robin to decide the fate of his kind and ours," Lyra announced, taking a seat once again. "You can have as many days as your hesitancy will allow, before a decision is made for you. Until then, we feast, and tomorrow we begin anew with the preparations for the Passing in the capital. Althea, since you have made claim to Robin as your cause, I leave him in your capable hands... I will stipulate what this requires by morning. Now we eat; all this talk of war has really conjured an appetite."

Hunger was far from my mind.

Althea gently squeezed my shoulder again and then lowered her hands upon the table. "If you can survive that, you can survive what comes next."

"How about another strong drink..." I whispered, my own voice affecting the ache in my head.

"You certainly deserve another." Althea's lips turned up at the corner. "I do not want a war, Robin, and a selfish part of me will do everything I can to aid you in making sure it does not happen."

Queen Lyra waved a hand; the signal was not for us but for the servants who stood behind us. "Bring the food. Having something to chew on may give someone else the chance to speak."

Before she had time to finish her last word, a line of servants flooded into the room with trays full of food.

In a single moment, the room went from scentless to bursting with smells so divine that my mouth watered on cue. Each plate was the same, I noticed, as the serving staff placed them on the table before us. Suddenly, hunger was exactly what I felt. A forced feeling, as though the scents were spelled to entrance me.

My hands fidgeted on my lap, wanting nothing more than to reach out and take a handful of the mashed potatoes and stuff them into my mouth. Instead, I followed Althea's lead, who sat patiently, waiting for a command to eat.

Once each person was presented with a plate before them, the servants still didn't leave. Instead, they took their place behind each of our chairs and stood, carefully waiting for a command. I glanced back to see a young woman behind me. Her hair was dark and cut pixie short. Bright, piercing eyes looked ahead, not caring to notice me. And behind her stood Erix. Before I could see if he looked at me or was still ignoring me, I averted my gaze, focusing back on Queen Lyra.

"Tasters, please step forward."

The servant I noticed moved forward until she placed herself between Althea and me. She, as well as the other servants, each revealed a fork from their loose sleeves and moved it towards the plates of cooling food upon the table. It was a dance, each of them moving in sync.

Althea tensed, but not at the man who reached for her food, but to the girl between us. I even noticed her bright gaze flick towards Althea, but the moment was brief, enough for me to understand that they knew each other.

"What are you doing?" I asked, stomach turning as the woman lifted a forkful of potato and meat towards her lips.

She paused long enough to reply. "I am your Taster." Whatever the fuck that means. Then the fork passed between her lips, coming back empty.

I remembered what Erix had said about my drink being tasted before I'd downed it. Had the same girl drunk the bubbly wine that Althea had gone to get for me whilst I was too impatient to wait? Was that how she knew her?

Somehow, I believed it was more personal than that.

Glancing at Lyra and Thallan, they both began to eat as their own Tasters moved away. They spoke between themselves, not once looking my way, which I was thankful for.

"All is fine," the girl announced, stepping back to reveal a relieved look on Althea's face.

Althea caught me looking, so she quickly glanced towards her own plate and spluttered a laugh. "Cannot harm to be cautious during such events as these."

I forced a smile, but it was weak and lasted no more than a second.

A heavy thud sounded behind me as I reached for my own silverware. A crack of something hollow echoed, followed by a gurgling noise that sent a deathly cold shiver down my spine.

It was Althea's gasped cry that had me turning. The girl, my Taster, shook violently upon the floor, a green foam spluttering from her paled lips. Her arms and legs thrashed, kicking out against the legs of my chair. I should've moved – should've done something to stop her head cracking over and over again against the slabbed floor. But I just sat there and watched, unable to make sense of what was happening before me.

"Briar!" Althea shouted, throwing herself from her chair to cradle the girl in her arms. "Briar, stop it! Briar, stop!"

Erix was beside me in a blink, guiding me from the chair and away from the plate of food this Briar had tasted.

"Did you eat anything off your plate?" he demanded, hands grasping my upper arms with such frantic tension. But I did not answer. I could not do anything but watch as Althea held the girl in her arms, snarling at anyone who got close. "Robin, tell me! You need to answer me. Did you touch the food?"

He placed his body in front of the horrific scene, blocking it from view. I looked up to see Queen Lyra, a beautiful face pinched with worry. She spoke in hushed tones as her wide eyes screamed with an honest pleading I had not seen from her thus far. "Take Robin back to his rooms, it is not safe, even here."

"Right away," Erix responded, trying to steer me away by my shoulders.

"The food…" I said, body numb. "There was poison in the food?"

Lyra closed her eyes and bowed her head in confirmation. When she opened her eyes again, they were ablaze with fire so intense the warmth rippled over my skin. "Get him out of here. Now."

CHAPTER 14

Someone had tried to kill me. *Again.*

The thought overwhelmed me as I paced my bedroom, scuffing the floor with my heavy steps.

They'd made an attempt on my life, and it was clear as to why. Orion had made it painfully obvious that I was a threat to stopping a war – one he so dearly wanted to proceed. Had he been the one to poison my food? It was not impossible to believe. Whoever wanted me dead must have a reason, and removing the threat I posed to the war was the only one I could think of.

"Will she survive?" I questioned, hands shaking at my sides. Half-moons had etched themselves into my palms, leaving behind a slight sting as I flexed my fingers.

Erix had sat himself on the edge of my bed in mostly silence, his elbows resting on his outstretched knees. "It is hard to tell. It depends on the poison and how quickly a healer has been deployed to help her."

Guilt stormed within me. Guilt for someone I didn't know but who took the brunt of an attack against me anyway. She'd not asked for this. All I kept seeing in the dark of my mind was her gasping expression, lips coated in the green-foam, how her body convulsed violently, legs and arms kicking out, and her head slamming into the ground over and over again.

"Can you at least go and inquire?" I snapped, unable to fathom how he could sit still during such an event. "Or take me to see her. Anything but sitting here and waiting."

"I will not be leaving you. Not now, not again. Nor is it safe for you to leave this room. Word will reach us soon whether the Taster has survived."

"Her name is Briar." I stopped dead in my tracks, shoulders tense as I glared towards Erix. "I heard Althea call her by it. Don't refer to her as anything but her name again."

Erix regarded me for a long moment, silver eyes looking over every inch of me. The muscles in his jaw feathered as he contemplated his response. "*Briar* was only completing a task set before her. She knew the risks, and she did what was required. Do not bear the guilt I see you harbouring. It will do you no good. Instead, lay the blame on the person who wished to harm you, and in turn, hurt Briar. That is a better use of energy, little bird."

I couldn't even cringe at the use of my nickname.

"Is that it? All you have to say?" My torso ached with the slamming of my heart. The chest, that dreaded, cold box, crept open, letting a trickle of unbridled power out. The release of pressure was incredible, the feeling almost exhilarating. I sighed a heavy breath, watching it cloud before me as the air itself seemed to drop violently in temperature. "Don't think for a moment that your wise words make me feel any better. I didn't ask for a taster, nor do I deserve one. There *is* a world in which her life doesn't need to be a sacrifice for mine. If I had refused to come with you, perhaps she would still be…" I couldn't say it because admitting her potential death was too raw and painful.

"It is clear that your life is at risk, whether at the hands of the humans and their twisted pets, or those of my kind who see you as a wall in their road to war. Regardless of where you are, news of what you did at the Hunter camp would have spread, and your life would still have been in danger. Believe that."

I tried not to blink, for every time I did, I saw Briar cradled in Althea's arms. "Althea knew her. Before she ate the food, I could see her discomfort. And the way Althea reacted…"

A sour taste filled my mouth as I dredged up the haunting memory of Althea's shattering cries.

"I am not one for gossip, but for years rumours of Althea and the Taster – Briar – have spread around court. But it is not for either of us to question it. Not everyone requires their relationships to be open for judgement or questioning. It is why I never brought it up with Althea, even after Briar was demoted from her position as the princess's own Taster. Robin, all that matters is *you* are alright."

"What matters, Erix –" I spoke his name as though it was a weapon, sharp and swift "– is that no one else's life is required to be a safety net for my own. This is so fucked. All of this. I want to know if Briar is alive, then I want to know who would have poisoned the food. Am I not to eat again for fear someone else will make an attempt on my life?"

"We can get you another."

"And leave a trail of bodies in my wake whenever I grow peckish? I will not live in fear. Not against the gryvern, nor a plate of fruit or meat."

I was shouting. Not at Erix, but at the situation. Frustration blew through me in gusts of frozen wind. I felt the magic pique its interest within me, waiting, longing for me to let it out.

Erix stood suddenly, making me stumble pathetically over my next words. As he stepped closer, I felt the chill of my power retreat as though it feared his presence.

But I didn't fear *him*, far from it.

The phantom brush of his touch raced up my arms, all without him needing to raise a hand. "You are extremely determined. It is hard to believe that you have not always been brought up in a family of authority. Perhaps your power and namesake are not all that was passed down in blood."

I tried to hold his gaze but gave up. He was beautiful in ways which should be impossible for a man of his appearance. It was easier to look away to prevent myself from losing my train of thought in his never-ending stare. I opted to look at the polished black of his boots as he took yet another step forward.

"You know nothing of me," I said, voice quivering. "You've made assumptions, but they're wrong."

"Strange, because I feel as though I am getting a rather good grip on who you are."

"You think I am weak compared to you great and almighty fey." I turned my back on him, facing the dimly lit room instead of feeling small beneath his stare. "I can look after myself. I did a good job of it before you came along, and will after you go."

"Ouch?"

I couldn't stop letting the words flow out of me without thought. "I don't need you to stand guard for me, nor do I need someone eating from my spoon before I do. I was doing rather fine before."

There was no mistaking the low chuckle that followed. "Is that so? Because the whole 'stuck in a cage with fey-hunters' suggested otherwise."

It was stupid, this argument, but I wasn't going to back down. Stepping in, toe to toe, I glowered up at him. "I was *outside* the cage by the time you showed up."

Erix's chuckle turned into a full belly laugh.

"Are you fucking laughing at me!" I snapped back around to glare at Erix, who didn't attempt to hide the smile spreading across his handsome face.

He regarded me, running his forefinger and thumb over his prickly beard as his large hand framed his grin. "I am."

He was testing me; I could sense it. How his face burned with mischief as he spoke, tilting his head to the side like an innocent puppy, whereas the gleam in his eyes was far from innocent.

"Give me your dagger, and I will show you." I pointed to the dark metal hilt that protruded from a sheath at his side. Without looking down, his hand moved over it, resting his fingers tentatively on the handle.

"If you are trying to prove a point, come and get it. Or do you usually ask those you duel for their weapon before starting?"

My gut flipped as my eyes moved from the dagger to his irritating smile, a smile I wished nothing more than to wipe clean from his face.

I took a step forward, slowly, one foot before the other, as I closed the space between us.

"Did you think I would simply forget to bring up what happened on the balcony?" I asked him, hands steady at my side.

That bastard's smile faltered, flattening into a straight, plump line. "Care to remind me?"

"Do you treat all the helpless boys like that?" There were no more than a few inches between us now. I kept my eyes on his, noticing the slight parting of his mouth as his pink tongue trailed between his teeth. "Or is there something you wish to share with me?"

"Trust me, little bird, you do not want insight into my thoughts at this moment." The intensity in his tone had my readying hand pause.

"What would have transpired if Althea had not interrupted?" I asked, forcing my voice into a soft lilt.

Erix ran his thumb across his lower lip, heaving a large sigh before replying. But there was no chance for him to utter a word.

He was distracted by the concept, which was exactly what I wanted.

I shot my hand out, gripping the warm hilt of the dagger and pulling it free from the sheath; the blade sang as metal sliced along the leather. I raised the weapon through the chilled air, stopping only when the sharp side introduced itself to the underside of Erix's chin. Beneath the glint of the blade, the lump in his throat bobbed; I could hear the tickling of his hairs as the blade moved over them.

"How devious you are," Erix purred, barely flinching.

"Do *not* underestimate me again." I scowled, applying a sensible amount of pressure that was both threatening but safe.

Erix lifted two fingers and pressed them to the sharp side of the blade. With force I did not expect, he pushed back, effortlessly moving it away from him. "Allow me to share a secret with you. Not for a moment have I believed you didn't have it in you to cause some damage, little bird."

"Stop... calling me that."

Erix ignored me, which only infuriated me more. I thrust the blade upwards again, causing him to throw his hand out of the way. This time the blade pressed into his throat with careless pressure until he hissed out.

"You have cut me."

Erix said it as though he could not believe his own words. But he was right. I had. Blood dribbled from the nick and onto the blade. My eyes fixated on the ruby droplet as it spilt down the glistening metal, spreading onto the hilt and warming my skin where it touched me.

I relaxed my hold, breathing out an apology. "I didn't mean to..."

"I have had a number of blades put against me; a little blood is nothing. You are going to need to find something else to create fear in me, I am afraid." He leaned in, teeth flashing beneath his grin as he winked. "But nice try."

I kicked out, forcing my knee between his legs before he could do so much as blink. Erix retaliated as though he saw my attack coming. Faster than I could imagine, his hand gripped my thigh and held it in place before I could connect with that sweet, soft spot between his legs. My skin ached where his fingers gripped hold of me. I tried to pull away but could not.

"Ah, ah, ah. That was not very nice, was it?"

"Believe it or not, I wasn't trying to be... nice." I struggled against his hold. The blade clattered to the floor as I needed both hands to push against the firmness of his chest. Then, all at once, he released me, and I stumbled backwards. I closed my eyes, anticipating the pain as I was not prepared to stop the connection to the floor.

But the pain didn't follow.

Instead, a hand gripped the back of my head, catching it before I connected with stone. I still heard a crunch of bone, but it was not my own. Erix was above me, face wincing in agony that I had not attempted to cause this time. His hand was wedged between the curve of my skull and the floor.

"Erix…" I breathed, lifting my head enough for him to remove his hand. He pulled it out, cradling it to him as he growled in discomfort that pinched his handsome face.

"It seems you proved your point," he said, opening one eye as he released a breathy laugh. "Even if you did not mean to."

I felt the bubbling of a chuckle brew within me, too but swallowed it down before it had a chance to escape.

"Are *you* hurt?" Erix stood, towering above me, where I pushed myself up onto my elbows.

I shook my head, taking the hand he offered me. With a great tug, he pulled me up, stopping me as I pressed into his torso. I stayed like that for a moment, sensing our shared hesitation as his hand brushed down the length of my spine.

It was hard to tell who let go first because there was suddenly space between us, and all I knew was I didn't like it. A fact I wouldn't admit, aloud or to myself.

I ironed out the creases of my jacket, keeping my hands busy as Erix reached down for the discarded dagger.

"You can keep this," he said, offering it to me. "It is clear you work well with a dagger, but it is also painfully obvious you will need some more work on perfecting the craft of dagger play. I would rest better knowing you have something with you when you are alone. Who knows, perhaps the next time you try and attack me, it will be me who hits the ground first."

"Trust me," I said, fighting the urge to smile as I took the blade from him without thanks. "I will get you on your back one way or another–" I swallowed hard, a shiver of embarrassment spreading down my spine.

"Careful, little bird," Erix said softly. "Words like that will get you in far more trouble than brandishing a blade with an untrained hand."

"Is that so?" My cheeks warmed. I wondered if he could see the blush creep into them as a result of his comment.

"It is. You should rest." He swept past me suddenly. "I will be outside if you need me."

"What about Briar?" I asked again, part of me wishing he would not leave so soon. If I asked for his company, would he decline it? Deep down, I knew he wouldn't, but there was also a sudden hesitation from him that made the thought as awkward as our encounter on the balcony.

"If you promise me to try and sleep, I will bring news of her when you wake. And food. I will taste it myself if I have to, but I will see you eat a full meal."

I gripped the dagger with both hands, aware of how warm the hilt was after Erix had held it.

"What if I don't want you to taste it?" I asked him, not wanting to explain it further.

Erix's hand paused as it gripped the handle of the door. His broad shoulders heaved from a sigh, and then he turned his face to look at me. His profile was striking against the glow of the lanterns; a sharp nose, full lips and beard caused his cheeks to dip between high cheekbones and a strong jaw. "I am ordered, as your personal guard, to keep you safe. If you will not let others risk themselves for your sake, then I will take it upon myself to do so."

Ice crept from my fingers, coating the hilt and draining any of his warmth from it. I did not fight to pull the magic back into the chest within me. "But–"

"What is the matter?" His grin returned once again, and all I could smell was cinnamon as he pulled open the door; the breeze in the hallway beyond forced Erix's scent to reach me and fill me entirely with even the smallest of inhales. "Hmm, and I was beginning to believe you wished to see me harmed. How quickly that seems to have changed."

With that, Erix slipped out of the room. As the latch fell into place with a click, I was certain I heard him whisper beneath the sound of the closing door.

Goodnight, little bird.

CHAPTER 15

Once I'd returned from visiting my father, I was greeted to a package of clothes waiting on my bed. I'd spent hours sat with him, dancing around the topic of my mother so much that I left in a storm of annoyed silence.

A note from Eroan sat atop the package, his handwriting a swirl of beautiful lines. The letter explained that he'd missed the evening's feast to prepare the outfit as requested by Althea.

What concerned me was not the fact someone had been in my room whilst I slept, but the reason as to why I required the training leathers in the first place.

Although, with the pent-up frustration from my father's silence, the idea of punching something sounded perfect.

The training leathers that I'd been adorned with weren't like anything I'd worn before. Form-fitting and made from dark material, the outfit clung to *all* parts of my body, making me self-conscious. Despite feeling discomfort in my own appearance, I couldn't deny the physical comfort of the clothing; not much different to a second layer of skin, it allowed for free movement.

To my surprise, it was Lady Kelsey who burst through the doors to the room. Her gown swept behind her as she practically floated inside, a beaming grin yet another countless jewel she held.

"You are awake," Lady Kelsey exclaimed as she joined me. "Although you look, well, terrible."

"Thanks?" I said, shifting from one foot to the other.

She waved me off, flashing her many-jewelled fingers. "Sleep is important for both body and mind. Your skin is pale, and your eyes dull. Is the bed not comfortable enough?"

"I slept fine." I tried to rein in any negative tone, aware that I was sharing the company of the woman who owned this very castle. Offending her was not the brightest of moves, even if she offended me with her off-hand comments.

"I am not convinced." She side-eyed me. "No bother, I will request for you to be excused early this evening to catch up on some much-needed rest. The last thing you need is... late night company to keep you from sleeping."

A blush crept up my cheeks in a wave of warmth. I bit down on my inner cheeks to try and stop the embarrassment from flashing red across my face. "Forgive me if I come across rude, but is there something I can do for you?"

"For me?" She pressed a hand to her chest. "No, dear, it is *I* who can do something for you. Whilst Althea is... occupied, my dear sister Lyra has asked for me to be the one to guide you through some... basic training of your magic. Something even the most inexperienced could follow."

Her last few words felt oddly similar to a slap, but her smile seemed to soften the blow. My mind then went to Althea and Briar, and my heart sank into the pits of my stomach.

"Briar. Is she...?"

Lady Kelsey's face straightened for a moment, bright eyes dulling as something dark passed behind them. "The girl has survived. Just about."

My breathing altered at her revelation.

A weight lifted from my shoulders as Lady Kelsey continued to explain. "It is still too early to understand the lasting effects of the poison, but Althea has commanded the best healers and apothecaries in Aurelia to aid in the investigation."

"Is there anything I can do to help?"

"You can help by becoming less of a hindrance and more of

a threat. My task is to aid in making you independent, in tune with what it means to be an Icethorn." Her eyes scanned me from the tips of my polished, laced boots to the pads on my shoulders. "Eroan has outdone himself. Truly. You look ready, but do you *feel* ready, Robin?"

"For what?" I asked, acutely aware of Erix's dagger, which rested beneath the plush pillow.

"Control." Lady Kelsey stepped forward, slim, golden gown spilling around her feet like a pool of molten lava. With her hands gently clasped before her wiry frame, she regarded me. "Yourself and your magic."

"I guess I am," I said, excited about the concept.

"The first step of control is acceptance of it. So, we are off to a great start. Now, Robin, tell me what you know of magic."

"Not a lot," I admitted, mind wandering to the sealed box in my chest and the cold tendrils of power that it harboured. "I know it belongs solely to the fey and is as dangerous as it is beautiful."

"Wrong, wrong *and* wrong." Lady Kelsey began to pace before me. "Magic belongs to no one. It is the wielder who belongs to the essence of magic. A common misconception. I forgive you for your lack of understanding." I didn't realise I asked for forgiveness. Before I could say as much, Lady Kelsey carried on her speech. "And not all fey are in alignment with magic. As you could imagine, that would be highly chaotic and, frankly, rather disturbing. Only those who harbour the blood of one of the four courts can call upon it. Each power is unique from one another, and never the same."

I watched, mouth agape, as she raised a hand. Snakes of silver smoke lifted from the tips of her fingers, twisting up into the air as though she'd blown a candle out on each one.

"Our family members each share magic of warmth and flame." A flash of Althea cradling a rosebud of fire between her hands came to mind as Lady Kelsey spoke. "Now, I understand you are highly aware of your own abilities since you have used them, perhaps unwillingly, on two occasions."

I raised my own hand before me, toying with the idea of letting that box open and releasing the chill that hid within. No, it was far too dangerous. Fisting my hand, I dropped it like a stone to my side.

"You should not fear it, instead, make it fear you. Think of it as training a wild wolf. You cannot simply leash it and hope it listens to your bidding. You must allow it to trust you as you learn to trust it. Grow familiar. It is the only way you will ever gain some level of control and understanding. And with the amount of power that you possess, control is utterly important, for your sake and those around you."

"That doesn't exactly fill me with great confidence." I laughed awkwardly, waiting for Lady Kelsey's face to show she was exaggerating.

Her expression was nothing but serious, which made me feel worse.

"I am not here to make you comfortable," she admitted, wiggling her fingers until the smoke vanished. "I am here to make you understand your magic, because if these attempts on your life persist, you are going to need something to use as defence or, my favourite choice, offence."

"You think it will happen again?" I asked her, feeling a sense of motherly comfort spilling from her. I did not remember any of her children being introduced at the council meeting. Perhaps she did not have any, but her demeanour seemed to scream with maternal comfort and instinct.

"Of course it will," she said plainly. "I have no doubt about that. But whilst you are in my city, I will be sure to keep you as protected as possible. That means both with the guards I fund and the time I will invest into ensuring you can use your power when required. You may think of me as a tutor, and you're my student."

I smiled at her, the idea not off-putting. "If it makes me less of a liability, then I'll be the best student you've ever had."

"Then let us begin."

* * *

"Slower," Lady Kelsey demanded, teeth chattering as ice clung to her skin and hair. Not an ounce of enjoyment could be found upon her. In fact, a smile hadn't been shared since we began this dance of magic and exhaustion.

It'd not taken much for me to focus on the chest within me and command it to open. Locating the new, strange power was the easy part. It was holding it back that I struggled with.

My hands shook, arms aching as I held them up. It was as though I held a ball between my hands, but the space was empty of the mundane. Instead, a whirling frozen storm spun between both palms, a vortex of magic which lashed out, spilling its hungry, cold presence into the rest of the room.

We'd been at this for what felt like hours. Lady Kelsey's calm attitude had soon melted away as she snapped at me to rein in the power before it destroyed yet another room in her home.

"I am trying…" I said, straining with focus as the ball of pure energy throbbed. It was close to impossible to even breathe normally. My head was growing lighter, my eyes sore against the light of the room, but on I persisted, trying to gain some level of control over such a small amount of power.

With a great splutter, the power winked out, the ball of magic exploding in a puff of ice that fell to the floor in a flurry of perfectly shaped snowflakes.

"Even the most persistent of teachers knows when to call it a day." She swiped a hand over her forehead as though it was herself who had done all the work.

"You look… exhausted, truly," I said through laboured breaths. "How did you cope?"

"Nasty boy." She flicked a hand at me in jest. "It will be harder for you. You are years behind in training, and your limits are far greater than mine or anyone else's in our court."

"Why is that?" My legs wobbled as I stumbled towards a chair I had been longing to fall into this entire time. Lady Kelsey joined me, gown creasing as she plonked herself down in the chair opposite me.

"Since we are *clearly* finished with the practical side of our lesson, we can finish up with some theory. The larger the family of a court, the weaker their ties to their inherent abilities will be, as though the magic in our blood dilutes."

I thought of the power I'd seen from Althea and Lady Kelsey and had – up until this moment – praised their control over it. But it wasn't control that kept their power small, but instead the weakening of it due to the size of their family.

"It is why the history of each of the four courts has some horrific tales of bloodthirsty murders. Siblings killed siblings, and children killed their sires, all to strengthen their own magic. I have limits to what I can do. It was not always this way, but when my sister had her many children, it caused my magic to weaken." I partly expected to see some level of disappointment or resentment as she spoke, but it did not show itself. "I suppose whereas one could look at it as little, whiny brats stealing from you, I just saw it as a fair trade. Magic for family. But there is only one of you, Robin, and that means you house great power within you, something that has not been seen for years."

"The more I learn from you, the more I uncover yet another reason why someone may want to kill me off."

She sighed, shrugging her shoulders. "The Cedarfall Court is the largest of all four. The Elmdew not being far off. Whereas the Oakstorm Court have always believed in smaller families to ensure their power stays... potent. Until now, they have not been rivalled by another court."

I raised my hands in defeat. "I'm really not interested in being a rival to anyone."

She laughed, throwing her head back dramatically. "Oh, dear boy, the Oakstorm Court have other concerns than you."

Oakstorm – the summer court.

"Such as?" I asked, aware there was more to her comment that she was not sharing.

She leaned forward, resting her elbows on her knees and propping her face up in her hands. "The *humans*."

The chill in my chest spread wide like the unfurling of wings. "Dare I ask why?"

"It was believed that the lost Queen Oakstorm and her second-born son were the first to be captured by Hunters beyond Wychwood. Since then, King Doran Oakstorm has been the sole contributor to the pending siege on the human realm. Him and his son, Tarron, have been rather persistent in their goals of taking Durmain by storm – literally. In fact, if memory serves me, they were the first to put forward the idea of war to the courts a few years after your – Julianne was murdered. Oakstorm and Icethorn have always been tense but close allies. The Icethorns' supposed end was the final straw that broke King Oakstorm into petitioning for the war that he spearheads to this day."

I swallowed hard, thinking of Orion, the poison and the gryvern attack. "And they do not see me as a threat? I know what I mean to stopping the war. The Oakstorm Court sound hellbent on making sure it proceeds."

Lady Kelsey reached for my hands and held them in her own. Her warm touch was a stark contrast to the chill that had seemed to bury itself into my skin. "They are as much a threat to you as my own kin are and the humans who likely wait with their beastly pets for you to step out of safety."

"Every time I think of eating, I see Briar convulsing on the floor. Every time I look out a window, I see the gryvern. All I see around me is danger, and I admit I'm not ready to face it."

She squeezed my hands, contemplating something in silence as she dropped her gaze from mine. "The world is a nasty place, that I cannot deny. So, let us sharpen you into a weapon, both mind and magic, then you will be prepared for any opposition you face."

"You are a wise woman," I said. "Has anyone ever told you that?"

"Wise?" She gasped, pulling back as though my touch had burned her. "Owls are wise, and I am no owl."

I laughed, unable to stop myself. "Then what are you?"

"Lady Kelsey Cedarfall, sister to the queen. But to you, I am a weapon forger, and you are my latest creation. A little dull, but soon we will sharpen you until I am confident you can face any threat, no matter which side of the border it comes from."

CHAPTER 16

Briar's chest rasped as though it was filled with water. An awful, slick gargling sound rattled its way out her parted lips. The sound scratched at my skin, turning my empty stomach into knots. Her lips, and the skin around them, were as pale, crusted with the remains of a sticky, green substance that stained the corners. No matter how many times Althea cleared the residue away with a cloth, it only came back.

Althea sat upon a seat beside Briar, dirtied napkin clutched in shaking hands.

Briar was in a deep slumber, uninterrupted. She didn't even wake when the rattling became a hacking cough that convulsed her short body in the bed. Althea would spring forward, hands holding Briar down at her shoulders. Only when the fit would stop did she release her hold, although reluctantly.

"I'm scared she does not have long left," Althea admitted, voice almost void of all emotion as though she was entirely dry of it. I could see it from the bloodshot haze that overwhelmed the whites of her eyes and the red tip at the end of her nose. She'd likely spilled every tear imaginable.

"How long do the healers give her?" Erix asked from beyond my shoulder, his close presence welcome as we stood watch over Briar. It hadn't taken much persisting for Erix to take me to see her. As soon as Lady Kelsey had dismissed herself, he was waiting beyond the door and hardly said a word when I'd asked.

It was strangely easy to force the command into my tone as though it was natural. Had that unlocked itself with the lack of iron wrapped around my wrist? Only another of my mother's traits making itself known?

The infirmary was modest in size. I found it nestled in one of the many winding corridors of the castle. As we stepped inside, the intense brightness of the decoration had me wincing. The walls and floor were covered in pure white tiles, which gave the impression we stood within a never-ending box.

There were many beds set up along a wall, but only Briar's was occupied.

Besides Briar and Althea – who'd hardly regarded us when we entered – the room was almost empty. There was the occasional appearance of a healer who was dressed in cream and brown garments, with a creased apron tied around her stomach. But that was it.

"It is impossible to know. I can't I bear the thought of putting a time limit on her life, so I didn't ask," Althea said, all without taking her eyes off Briar. "Each healer I call upon says another outcome than the one before. I was tired of their careless comments, so I dismissed most of them."

I looked to the older healer, grey hair hidden beneath the shawl, as she shuffled loudly from one side of the room to the other, fussing over bottles and packages of dried herbs. What had made her special enough to stay, I wondered. Perhaps her answer had been less morbid than the other healers Althea had mentioned.

"Do they know what poison was in the food?" I asked, feeling awkwardly out of place in my training leathers in such a sterile room.

I knew little of poisons, but could see from Briar that it attacked her lungs. I'd once seen a boy almost drown after he showed off to his friend, swimming further out across the dark lake that was a short walk from Grove. Turned out he was a shit swimmer. It was my father who dragged him out of the depths, just before his skin had turned blue; another moment and he would've died.

The noise Briar made was similar to the sound the boy made as he coughed up the dirty water of the lake whilst gasping for breath. It was as if she drowned from the inside – lungs filling with the green phlegm that seeped from the corners of her mouth.

Althea dropped the cloth to her lap and reached a hand for Briar's. "Tugwort, at least that is the most common guess. And that is all it is, a guess. It would explain why they cannot heal her. Instead, I am to just sit back and watch her lungs fill until she finally stops breathing."

I winced as Althea snarled her last few words. "Surely there's something that can be done?"

"Maybe," Erix answered. "I have been informed that a messenger hawk has already been sent east for aid." Erix spoke as though he shared information he was not supposed to.

"And? That means nothing. The request will fall upon uncaring ears. What then? Do we wait for someone else to arrive on a white horse and save her? That is supposed to be my task. I should be the one saving her, but all I can do is fucking sit here cleaning up spit and putting all my trust in the hands of…" She choked, unable to finish. Althea angled her body in her seat, so I could only see the back of her head. But I was certain, just for a moment, I caught the glittering of a tear escape her angered stare.

"If news of Robin has reached the shores of Oakstorm, there is no saying Tarron has not already heard. The invitation would be all he requires to come and investigate himself."

"Tarron," Althea sneered, resting her forehead upon the rumpled sheets at Briar's side, "has denied aid for years. I see no reason for him to help now."

Tarron Oakstorm – the heir to the summer court. Information Lady Kelsey had not long shared. What could he do to help?

"The humans might know of something that could help," I said, clearing my throat as I interrupted their conversation. The room was relatively quiet thus far, but after I finished speaking, I could have heard a pin drop. Even Briar's rough breathing seemed to calm.

"Tell me you are joking." Althea did not sound as though she was willing for comic relief, and nor did I want to provide it.

"Althea, if the fey don't know a cure for Tugwort, maybe they do?"

I was confident she would shout at me. Call me stupid and laugh. But she was quiet, so much so that I could almost hear her brain work as it took in what I had to say.

"It is not the best of ideas, but not a terrible one either," Erix added. "I admit I would rather see more humans in these halls than Tarron."

I thanked him with a quick, weak smile. He nodded slightly, jaw clenched as he, too, waited for Althea's retort.

"Each hour that passes I hear more reports of Hunter settlements popping up across the weakening Wychwood borders. What do you expect to do… walk right through them in search of answers? I have more hope for the pompous princeling to accept my invitation than I do finding a human who wishes to help with this. Thanks though."

My cheeks grew warm beneath her judging stare. "I'm only trying to help."

"Have you not helped enough?" she snapped, eyes burning and wide.

"Althea," Erix's deep voice sounded in warning.

"Remember your place, Erix," Althea snapped, turning the full, burning wrath upon him. She was crying now, silent tears cutting down her cheeks as she snarled like a wolf over its wounded pup.

I'd never enquired about Althea and Erix's relationship but could understand that he was comfortable reprimanding a child of the ruling court, and she was just as comfortable snarling back.

"Robin, I think I should take you back to your rooms." Erix turned his back on Althea, putting an arm out until it rested over my stomach. "Leave Althea to have some time alone."

"No," I told him. "I'm not ready to go anywhere." It took little effort to sidestep him and move towards Althea. I joined her at Briar's bedside, where I placed a hand over her trembling shoulder. "It is not my place to know anything about you and Briar, but I can see you care a lot for her. And I would do anything to help return her to full health. If I offended you with my suggestion, I am so sorry–"

"She was always so gentle," Althea interrupted with a whisper, voice breaking like glass across stone. "Seeing her in such a state pains me in a way I would not wish my worst enemy to experience. And what hurts me the most is I had promised her a way out of her task the next time I came to Aurelia. I failed her with that promise. All I brought her was…"

"Me," I finished.

Briar's demise.

"You did not place the poison in the food." Althea's tone darkened. "And when I find out who did, I will ensure they too experience what it is like to drown, except it will be in their own blood."

Briar convulsed upon the bed, drawing Althea's attention away from me. I stepped back, giving Althea room whilst she tried to still her shaking with her own weight.

"Robin, let's go," Erix whispered, his voice barely audible as I watched in horror at Althea clasping Briar as if she'd slip away from her if she let go.

A warm hand slipped into my own, tearing my attention from the scene back to Erix who looked down the length of his strong nose.

"Okay," I said, shocked that he used my name, recognising the power he had on it.

I nodded, unsure if I was to pull away from him or return the gentle squeeze he gave me. I allowed him to guide me from the room, leaving the quiet sobbing of Althea behind us.

It was silently agreed, but she needed space; I only hoped she knew I'd return if she needed me.

Erix didn't let go of my hand. Not when we strode down the corridor beyond the infirmary, passing the many guards who shadowed me, or when we were rooms away, deeper into the castle, as we followed the familiar route back to my chamber.

I was thankful for him anchoring me with his touch and for the way his thumb moved slowly in circles across the back of my hand.

Even if I was too weak to refuse it, his comfort was welcome.

"I fear for the person responsible for Briar's pain," Erix finally said, one hand still gripping mine, the other resting upon the hilt of his sword at his hip.

"And what if they're not found?"

"Nothing can stay hidden forever," Erix replied, the door to my room coming into sight as we rounded the final corridor that sloped into the lower floors of the manor. "You are likely the greatest secret of all, yet you have been revealed. It is only a matter of time before those who cause you harm decide hiding behind poisons is meek, and move onto other means."

"That makes me feel so much better," I said. "*Not.*"

All at once, he dropped my hand, and I found that I forgot what to do with it. It made sense being held by Erix, but without his touch, the hand almost felt pointless.

Erix's silver stare was etched with concern as his brows furrowed and his lips pulled into a thin, tight line.

"Robin." His use of my name was strange. It was not the first time he'd said it today, and it was beginning to irk me more than the nickname he gave me. His strong, handsome face was filled with determination. "I would never let something happen to you again."

"Because you are my personal guard?" I questioned, pressing my back against the cold wood of the door. "And that is the task you have been presented with, just as Briar was tasked with being my Taster?"

"Something you will come to know about me, little bird –" I sagged in relief at the use of the nickname, the one he used more commonly than my name "– I rarely do anything that is asked of me. Regardless of my duty, I will make sure you are safe."

"What is so different now?" I dared to say it aloud as the question was far too loud to keep locked within my head.

"You," Erix said softly. "You are what is different."

CHAPTER 17

Erix's words clung to me like sap on a tree, sticky and resistant to my attempts to forget them; they showed no signs of budging from my consciousness.

I'd expected him to come into my room alongside me, so I couldn't deny the blush of disappointment when he closed me within and remained outside.

For what seemed like hours, I played with the idea of inviting him to join me. But then what? All my mind could think of was his touch and how distracting it was. I wondered about his limitations, where his touch would begin or end. My mind was full of silly thoughts, distracting and unimaginable. Yet I couldn't shake them.

Because a *distraction* was exactly what I craved.

I supposed I could've taken my mind off *him* by thinking of Briar, but the haunting vision of her frail body in the bed was not something I was ready to reimagine.

Instead, I sat myself on the bed, legs crossed before me, as I reached for that strange yet familiar chill that curdled in the box deep in my chest. The power was frightening, but I called for it to heed my invitation. As it had with Lady Kelsey, I almost expected some resistance, but the sudden rush of ice that spread through my veins was a shock. It had me gasping for breath.

The magic slipped out of the box like melted butter, dripping down the dark edges of its confines, filling me with a cool gust of winter wind until each breath caused fog to slip into the room. Relief. That was what it felt like. And the release gave me what I longed for, another vision to replace the one of Erix.

Mother. Her dark hair and melodic voice filled my mind. I closed my eyes, not wanting anything to divert me from it. *Julianne.* Her name echoed in a voice similar to my own, but deeper and aged, like ale left in a casket over summers. It was Father's voice. I could hear him call for her as though it was a memory I'd only now allowed myself to remember.

I didn't need my eyes to open to know that the hungry, devouring ice that longed so deeply for escape crept across the sheets of the bed; had I shifted. I could hear the crackle of material as it snapped beneath my weight.

The cold was what I needed to silence the heat that had blossomed in my core as a result of Erix. His words had sparked the itching fire, but his stare... his knowing, wanting stare, fuelled that feeling.

And I couldn't stop myself from contemplating if I returned that want.

The answer was almost too simple.

What do I want? The thought turned Father's calling into a mere whisper. It was a question I had not allowed myself to face, nor had I the time to think on it. What I wanted was now out of reach, a chance to see my mother. *Julianne.* It was the only thing I had ever truly wanted. But now, even knowing I would never see her, I felt oddly closer to her, more than I had before.

Answers. Another thought replied. *I want answers.* To learn everything I could about her, whether it was Father telling me or not.

I fell into a trance of kinds, allowing my mind to ponder everything that had happened and everything that *was* to happen. The choice I was left with. Accept the Icethorn Court and prevent a war, or turn my back on it and watch as the world beyond Wychwood was devoured beneath the wild power that threatened the humans.

What do you choose? I didn't know.

Then I thought of our home in Grove, and the many who lived around us, even the sprouting of other small villages and slightly larger towns that peppered the lands of Durmain all the way to the northern capital of Lockinge. I couldn't see those I'd grown up with – no matter how they had looked at me – destroyed in the explosion of wild power.

Power I was supposed stop, yet I didn't even understand what that meant or what I had to do.

I snapped out of my trance as the door to my room slammed open. How long had it been? Time was hard to grasp in a room without windows.

Magic surged from me in response. It was instinct to throw out a hand, opening my eyes in time to see five teardrop-sized shards of ice split from the tips of my fingers. Like arrows, they sliced through the air, each thudding into the open door, narrowly missing Althea, who stood beneath its frame.

"Before you say it, there isn't any time to knock," Althea added, eyes unblinking as she regarded one of the shards that embedded inches from her face into the surface behind her.

With a shuddering breath, I recalled the cold back into the box, mentally closing the lid. I was too horrified about what I had almost caused to truly recognise how responsive the magic had been to my command.

"What's happened?" I swung my legs from the bed and stood to greet her.

"Hope. That's what has happened."

"Briar, is she okay?" I asked.

"No. Not yet at least" Her face was straight as she responded, her voice etched with tension. "I have just received word that the Hunters have breached a weakening spot in the barrier and have made it quite far into our lands; all the way up to The Sleeping Depths. Which, as per the second message just received ahead of Tarron's arrival, is exactly where the weed needed to evict the Tugwort out of Briar's system is located."

"The Sleeping Depths," I questioned, reminding Althea that I knew little of the geography of anything north of the Wychwood barrier. "How far is it?"

"It is a loch that covers both the land of Cedarfall and Icethorn. Which means the ballsy fucks have grown confident enough to make it that far from Durmain. And I'm not an idiot to know just how well timed it is that Hunters are in the same fucking place the antidote for Briar is. But I am in the right mood to pay them a visit." Her arrival had happened so quickly that it took a moment to realise she was dressed in the armour of a warrior, steel and leather overlapping one another, not an inch of skin on show from her neck down. Althea's deep red hair had been collected in a braid that rested over her shoulder. "You said you'd do anything to help if you could. So, I want to know if you are coming with me."

"Me?" I asked aloud, almost laughing at the thought. "Is it safe?"

"Yes, you." Erix pushed past Althea, entering the room with arms full of clanking armour and darker material. "The Hunters are currently occupying *your* land. By birthright, it shall be your hand that ushers them from it. That and it is important you actually see what the decision held over you means. Seeing the Icethorn power in person should help you make your decision."

Nerves prickled my skin. "But... what do you expect me to do about it?"

"To be honest with you, Robin, you are accompanying me because I need Erix and his tactics, but by command, he cannot leave your side. I also see the importance of you understanding just what we are up against," Althea said, a sly grin creeping across her striking face. "And nothing will keep my mind off Briar's failing state...better than breaking some bones." She paused, taking a hulking breath in. "That antidote is mine. I'm not returning without it."

Part of me wanted to refuse to join, to stay locked in the room away from the danger beyond it, but then I wanted to slap myself. Swallowing the knot of worry, I nodded. "I will try and help where I can."

Erix's gaze flicked to the melting shards of ice that dribbled down the door. "You may be more help than you could imagine."

Althea clapped, the metal gleam of her armoured chest catching the light. "Then it is done. Robin, get yourself changed. I expected the introduction to the Icethorn Court to be far less bloody, but I suppose we cannot have it our own way."

Realisation settled across me at that moment. *Home*. I was going to see it. The hairs on my arms and neck stood to attention, matching the line of guards waiting silently against the wall beyond the room. "I wouldn't mind throwing a few fists either, if I'm honest."

My magic flexed within me, readying itself for a promised release.

"That is exactly what I like to hear," Erix breathed, his grin flexing the shadow of a beard across his jaw. He held out his arms, offering the pile of clothing and armour towards me. "Then let's see what Eroan has crafted for you, shall we?"

"And whilst you change, I will prepare the party," Althea said, slapping Erix on the back of his shoulder. It was impossible to ignore his wince at her strength. Then she looked my way, thrusting two outstretched fingers to her eyes and then to me. "It is time you see what being an Icethorn means. What the title comes with. I'll give you a hint, it's a shitload of land. And right now, there are Hunters on it. Show them why you deserve your name and what happens when that name is threatened."

Our *small* party left the protection of Aurelia's trees and exposed ourselves to the harsh lashing of rain and wind that battered down upon the world beyond. The thick crown of gold leaves and the monstrous branches kept the weather out of the city, but the land beyond was not so fortunate.

Erix's tall frame behind me sheltered me from the pelting of cold autumn rain, but still the water soaked into the tips of my midnight-black gloves and soaked my hair into dense strands across my head. He must've noticed my shivering as his arms tightened on either side of me as he leaned in. The metal of our armour kept us inches apart, but I liquefied into him in as much as I could.

Eroan's outfit was similar to that of the training leathers he had supplied, except where my arms and chest had been exposed, they were now covered in a flexible, form-fitting metal that was etched with intricate patterns; the armour was as beautiful as it was useful.

The journey was long and made miserable by the unrelenting weather. We were a party of five, far from the size of the one that had galloped into the camp of Hunters all those days ago. This was small for a reason, to be kept unseen, but with enough power to destroy the moderate-sized camp of Hunters that Althea had explained we were to face.

I was surprised to see that Orion had joined us. Adorned in the same armour as his sister, they rode side by side on stags of equal height, then there was Erix and me, followed closely by the fey-warrior Gyah. Her expression was stern and unbothered by the rain, as though it was something she was used to, droplets of water falling from her dark lashes and streaming down the sides of her face.

The sky above had darkened into charcoal grey that smudged for as far as I could see. It was impossible to know how late in the day it had become, for the storm kept any sign of the sun and its placement from view.

I focused deeply on the rolling lands we trailed, studying how forests turned into glades which opened out into vast fields that highlighted the faint outline of mountains far off in the distance. Everything I witnessed was grand, even through the sheet of unrelenting rain. Wychwood was magical in every sense. I was used to farms and hills and fields and lakes. But this… this made the world I'd known feel far more than flat and dull.

Soon enough, the fat droplets of rain softened into a flurry of snow, its appearance taking me by surprise as a large flake landed on the tip of my nose. The change in weather happened so quickly that it was impossible to see it coming. It was first obvious from the lack of noise, the pinging of water against the armour and the thud of hooves into thick, muddy ground silenced entirely.

Then the welcoming burn of colder air filled my lungs, and I felt my shoulders relax for the first time since leaving Aurelia.

"I have not been this close to the border of Icethorn for many years," Erix muttered over my shoulder; the tickle of his breath against my ear had me gripping onto the material of my trousers. "Yet it is painfully clear that the truth of the power weakening the barrier is not fabricated. It does not snow in Cedarfall. At least it *did not.*"

"I have heard much about the power but don't know what it is," I mused, contemplating pulling my back away from his chest but deciding against it.

"Winter. Uncontrolled, wild and frantic. It will make more sense when you see it. Each court rules a season, keeping it in balance for as long as it is required. But without your – without a person to claim the court, the season is left *untamed.* The power has swelled and grown and twisted into an entity of its own destruction. I am surprised the barrier has lasted this long."

"You make it sound like it's a monster," I admitted, staring ahead into the sweeping valley that was blanketed in white.

"Anything left forgotten for long enough becomes a monster. But monsters can always be slain… by the right person."

"And you think I'm that person?" I asked him, unsure if I was ready to hear his answer.

"It doesn't matter what I think, little bird. If *you* believe yourself to be, that is all that counts."

Your opinion matters to me. But I dared not let those words leave my mouth.

"Do you believe so?" I pushed on again, urging him to reveal what I thought he wished to say.

Erix's arms flexed at my sides, tugging on the reins of the stag to slow its pace. "Never rely on what others think of you. It matters not what I think or how I see you. All that truly matters is what you believe."

"That sounds like a polite way of letting me down gently."

"Far from it." I could hear the smile in his voice. Even among the chill of snow and wind, my chest warmed, that spark of fire glowing brighter as he fed it once again. "I believe you can do anything you desire. And I look forward to seeing your face when you finally realise it."

We rode in silence again after that, closing our ranks as the snow grew heavy and the sky darkened as dusk set over Wychwood. I wanted to speak more with Erix, to play with the way his words made me feel. But that would require asking him questions, and with the constant glares Orion had gifted me, I wanted to not bring attention from the princeling, not more than I had to, at least.

By the time our journey came to an end, my arse was numb, and my lower back whined in discomfort. Erix slipped from the stag's side, offering a hand to aid me in clambering down.

I didn't hesitate to take it.

Dusk had settled over Wychwood. The snow had eased slightly, but each of our breaths clouded beyond our lips. It was cold, so cold that Orion's teeth chattered, and even Althea shivered. Gyah was eternally unbothered. Erix joined the Cedarfall siblings, leaving me alone. He might've said something to me, but I couldn't focus. Not as a strange, pulling sensation invaded my body.

It was odd, faint at first, but the moment my booted feet touched the snow-covered ground, it was impossible to ignore. It was as though the very air called my name, but it was more a feeling than a sound, a tugging and pulling at the box in my chest, the cord disappearing far off into the dark distance ahead.

"Do you feel it?" The deep voice of Gyah interrupted my daze. We'd not spoken the entire journey; in fact, I couldn't recall her saying anything to anyone. "The feeling in your gut?"

"There is certainly something I can feel," I replied, feeling slightly detached from reality. I pressed a gloved hand to my chest, over the twisting coil of cord that slithered like a snake. "Do you sense the same thing?"

She shook her head. "I'm not recognised by the Icethorn Court. But you are. It is your home. When I leave the court which I have sworn to, a deep, longing sickness fills my chest. Only when I return does it ease. It is a feeling you grow used to, but the first time is… jarring. From what I remember anyway."

I looked into the distance, squinting to make out the subtle shapes that stood out in the darkness. "It's not the home I've grown up used to. No matter the label, or truth of what this place should mean to me, it's as much a stranger to me as I am to you."

"I suppose you are right," Gyah added, her body stiff as a spire next to me.

I massaged the leather strapping across my chest, trying to ease the ache. "So, are we close to Icethorn land now?"

I knew the answer already, but asked the question anyway.

Gyah snuffed a laugh, voice vibrating in the dark around us. "You don't need me to tell you that, Robin. Can you not *feel* it?"

I did. I felt the energy around me, as though every flake of snow selfishly wanted to land upon my skin, or how the chilled breeze flirted with the skin at my neck and jaw, a finger of ice that kept me looking forward to Icethorn.

"You cannot deny it," Gyah added, "just as it cannot deny you."

"Robin," Althea called out my name, joining us with her brother and my personal guard in tow. "We have reached the furthest point to the Sleeping Depths. Across it, if the message was correct, we should find the Hunter's camp. And with it, Briar's antidote."

There it was again, the hope flashing in her eyes. I tore my attention away from her, looking out to the distance.

I couldn't see the named lake, not through the curtain of white drifts and darkening sky. Nor could I hear the usual lull of water against a muddied bank or sand.

"I can hardly see a thing. How can you be sure?" I asked, moving ahead in search of the promised body of water. A hand struck out, gripping me by my upper arm, halting me.

"It is named The Sleeping Depth for a reason," Erix warned, urging me back with a nervous grin. "It waits in silence for the unexpected to stumble into. It is not a place you would want to find yourself within, even by an inch. Those that go into it, never come out."

His words sent an unnatural chill down my spine, settling at the base where it pooled outwards.

A torrent of questions clattered around my head, but I was far too distracted by a sudden glow of amber that sparked before me. The light was stark against the night, causing the daring flakes of snow to hiss as they fell into it.

The orb of flame hovered above Orion's open palm, casting shadows upon his stern face. "Your promise of him keeping out of the way is proving difficult to keep, *sister*."

"Do not make me regret asking for your assistance, *brother*," Althea snapped.

I looked at him, holding his heated stare. He bared teeth through parting lips as a snarl overtook his round face. "Please, Robin, have a little walk and see if you can locate the lake."

"Careful," Erix warned, voice deep and tempered, his pupils engulfing the silver, even with the light spilling into them.

Orion smiled, brows narrowing in over his haunting stare. "Oh, relax, *Berserker*. It is a joke. I am not stupid enough to harm a hair on his head. Not with you in the way anyway."

Althea raised a hand, stopping Erix from taking a step without a word.

"Are *you* familiar with Tugwort by any chance, Orion?" I asked, feeling the shift of Erix's dagger, which hid in my left boot. Before we'd left Aurelia, I'd slipped it from beneath my pillow, keeping it on me as a precaution.

Erix had his sword strapped around his waist. Althea carried twin axes, both curved like crescent moons with the same silvered metal to match. I cared little for the bow across Orion's back nor the fire he fuelled in his palm.

Although, I'd yet to notice Gyah's weapon of choice.

"If you are suggesting that was my doing, you are greatly mistaken," Orion said, stepping toe to toe with me. Erix didn't stop him, nor did Althea. It was as if they wanted to see what I'd do. "If I wished to see an end to you, it would have been achieved far before now."

"Then why haven't you?" I cocked my head to the side. The thundering pressure eased that box open, ready for me to call upon the magic within to aid me against him.

"I'm not an idiot," Orion replied quickly, his words rushed. "That is why."

"That could be debated," Althea muttered through taut lips.

"Then what are you?" I asked Orion.

"*Patient.*" Orion's arms tensed, a warning of his next move. The flame in his hand recoiled as he lifted his hand over his shoulder, and then he launched it forward, careening it over my head like a falling star of light.

I winced from the sudden appearance of heat as the ball of golden flame careened off into the distance.

That was when I saw it. The Sleeping Depths was uncomfortably close. Erix had been right to stop me, because the water's edge was a short stone's throw away.

Its still, glassy surface stretched out for as far as the ball of fire soared, and even further, I was certain. The obsidian water was unmoving as though it had frozen into a mirror of night, reflecting nothing but the unending shadows beneath it.

When the ball of flame finally fell into the waiting body of water, the black depths devoured it. In a blink, it disappeared without a splash, or hiss of smoke to prove it'd ever been there.

"Understand the need for caution now?" Orion said, his sister pushing him back with a stern arm.

"For fuck's sake, Orion, we do not need to give the Hunters any inkling that we are here. What were you thinking?"

He scoffed, deep voice a whisper to mock his sister's worry. "Let them know we are coming. It would not be a fair fight otherwise."

"If you jeopardise me getting the antidote, I'll kill you myself." Althea stood with her back in the direction of the lake.

"Sounds like fun, sister."

Ignoring her ignorant brother, Althea regarded the group, reciting our plan for the umpteenth time. "The plan is simple. We venture to the far side of the Sleeping Depths in hopes the Hunters have yet to move on. Once we reach them, we kill them, all but one. Get Briar's antidote and then leave. This is the perfect opportunity to gain insight into the Hunters' movements, and as much as I hate to say it, keeping one alive is the only way of obtaining the information we require."

"Not that I question your plans," Erix spoke up, clearing his throat. "If we are to walk the perimeter, it could take us all night. Time is not a luxury we have to waste."

"Who said anything about walking?" Althea's voice was full of mischief. "The quickest way is not to go around."

"But over," Gyah muttered. She was so quiet it was easy to forget she was there.

"Gyah," Erix said coldly. "Are you certain?"

All the warning of the lake made me want to scramble away from it, not venture over its still, haunting surface.

"Erix, tell me that is not fear I hear beneath that husky voice of yours?" Althea asked.

"It is a risk," he retorted, gaze falling upon Gyah. Then I noticed that nearly everyone stared at her. I joined them, noticing how she looked undeterred by the sudden attention.

"Please do not insult me, Erix" Gyah said, dark stare flicking to him. "I have traversed far greater threats than this bastard lake. You are always welcome to wait here if your lack of trust in me is that great?"

I shook my head, unable to grasp the conversation or what it meant.

"Then what are we waiting for?" Althea said impatiently, waving a hand in gesture. "Gyah, if you will."

"Certainly, my princess." Gyah curtsied, but not before I caught a mischievous smile cutting across her face.

What happened next had me rooted to the spot. I watched, unblinking, as Gyah's body folded in on itself. A chorus of snapping bones and ripping flesh filled the vast space around us. My stomach jolted violently, my heart filling my throat. I couldn't speak or take my eyes off her as she… *changed*. Gyah's body grew, elongated and twisted into a hulking form four times her original size.

It was impossible to grasp if the change had happened quickly or not. Her skin melted from her body, revealing a layering of gleaming scales. Wings unfurled from behind her. The air around Gyah twisted in shadows that her new body absorbed, feeding into it as though darkness gave her more size, weight and height.

"Impossible…" I heard my own voice as the creature lifted its long neck, revealing a jaw of sharpened teeth and two glowing yellow eyes.

In the place where Gyah had stood, was now a creature I couldn't name. Graceful, narrow body slick with dark scales. She swung a long neck, thick tail coiling like a viper on the ground. She had two great, claw-tipped wings twitching as she fanned them out at her sides.

"I suppose that is one way to make an entrance," Orion drawled, stepping towards the creature with an outstretched hand. "And all this time, an Eldrae has been hidden under our dear aunt's nose. How long have you known, sister?"

"She was never hidden," Althea added. "Just a well-kept secret."

"And why was I not privy to the knowledge?"

"That conversation is for another time, brother. For now, shall we get a move on? I have a desire to see some blood spilled tonight."

CHAPTER 18

Gyah was a shapeshifter. Erix had whispered the name of her kind, sending a shiver over my skin as his lips practically brushed my ear. *Eldrae*. A fey with the ability to rip, snap and then repair her body into something new. A powerful creature whose wings hardly had to move to keep us aloft as we sailed over The Sleeping Depths.

Gyah's body was long and thick, like a snake made from shards of black glass. She had wings but no other limbs to hold herself from the ground. Her two options for travelling were slithering or flying.

We sat in a row, each clinging to one another for fear of falling from Gyah's slick side. I tensed my thighs, worrying it would cause her discomfort. But nothing seemed to bother her.

Erix, as I was growing all too familiar with, sat close behind me. His own thighs gripped on either side of mine, his hands wrapped around my waist where they comfortably rested on my lap. If we weren't so high up, slicing through the dark sky with a terrifying body of water a sure drop below, I might've allowed myself to enjoy his closeness.

But there was no time for that – at least not yet.

It was a long while before a glow of campfire from below could be seen. A fire, gleaming in tones of red, orange and yellow, haloing its light and keeping the chill of winter away. The Hunters. It had to be them.

Althea shifted before me, pointing to the glow when she noticed it. Then my stomach lifted awkwardly as Gyah began her sudden descent. Soundless, she slipped above the lake's dark waters.

From the heaving rise and fall of Erix's chest at my back, it was clear he was far more nervous of flying. He'd not seemed shocked to see Gyah shift into this form, nor did he hesitate when climbing onto her back. But the tightening of his hold as we dove suggested I'd uncovered a fear of his.

Gyah touched down a distance away from the camp, far enough that we couldn't see the fire among the darkness; moonlight was our only source of light. I watched, in awe and unknowing, as Gyah shifted back to her fey-form in an unravelling of smoke. There she stood, skin ashen from exhaustion, but fully clothed as though she'd never been any different.

Magic was confusing, but equally as impressive.

Althea offered an arm when Gyah stumbled a step forward. "You were fantastic."

"Thank you, my princess." Gyah yawned, holding onto Althea as though she were a pillar keeping her up. "Give me a moment, and I will be ready to proceed. It has been many a month since I last allowed the beast to take over."

I moved to Erix, who was pale and silent. "Are you alright?"

He looked up at me, the lines around his eyes relaxing. "Besides the urge to spill my guts across the ground, I am fine."

"Good," I said. And I meant it. "You knew what she was, didn't you?"

"I did, but only when Althea informed me before leaving. The Eldrae," he whispered, "they're very rare beings. The majority of the surviving lines reside among Elmdew, so I was surprised Gyah claimed Cedarfall as her home."

I regarded her from a distance, noticing the points of her ears and tall, straight frame. "There are others?'

"Of course. They are much like you. Half fey, Gyah is the descendent of a powerful line of beings who could change forms. They were believed to be created directly from Altar, the father of our kind. Like all the Old Gods, Altar was greedy in love and had many partners. Gyah and her kind are the offspring of one of his many relations, or so that is what the stories say. Part fey, part monster."

I wanted to ask him more questions, but they hitched in my throat as I looked up at him. Flakes of snow still fell around us, some catching across his hair and in the dark lashes that outlined his steel-coloured eyes.

"It would seem I've got a lot to learn," I muttered.

Erix wrinkled his nose as a flake landed at its tip. With the back of his glove, he smeared it off, leaving a trail of glistening, cold water in his wake. "That you do."

"Are you both done?" Orion's drawling tone called to us. "Or would you prefer we wait for you to finish up?"

Erix looked over my shoulder towards him, lips curling into a slight snarl. But when he spoke, his voice was nothing but controlled and emotionless. "We are simply waiting for your command, *prince*."

It was obvious that Erix didn't like Orion. I simply put it down to Erix being a good judge of character. Then again, even the dead could recognise that Orion was a prick.

"Then join us over here, and receive it."

I followed at Erix's side as we rejoined our party. Althea gave the command, explaining what would happen next. As she spoke, I listened carefully, wanting to make sure I was equally as prepared, since naturally I was on the back foot.

It wasn't that I was worried I'd be a hinderance in a fight. I knew I could handle myself, and frankly needed the second chance against the Hunters to prove it. I'd never been dreadful in a fight before, and now I came with a new skill set. Something that itched beneath my skin, begging for me to use it.

Magic.

Nervous adrenaline flooded my body, its presence a sickly-sweet taste which lathered my tongue and filled my cheeks.

I tried to focus on Althea as she laid out our plans, but that became impossible when Erix touched me. His large, strong hand rested itself upon my shoulder and squeezed. His touch made the noise drown away, both grounding and distracting.

Orion noticed and smirked to himself. That reaction alone made the urge to reach up and lay my fingers atop Erix's hand almost too delectable an idea.

"Are you certain you want to do this?" Erix whispered as Althea finished up.

I peered over my shoulder, swallowing the small part of me that wanted to admit that I didn't want to help, but the iron resolve and belief in his gaze seemed to clear any remnants of that feeling from me. "The Hunters almost had my head. I feel it is only fair to find out why."

We surrounded the camp in the shroud of darkness. The messenger who tipped Althea in the first place, and whose anonymity she worked hard to keep, had been correct. The camp was small, only six Hunters visible.

Althea had mentioned that the antidote for Tugwort was a thin-stemmed flower with a bulbous violet bud. Turned out Tarron Oakstorm wasn't wrong. Because the closer we gained to the camp, the more of the weed we found. I caught her snapping a few as we went, clearly in case we didn't get the chance when we came face-to-face with the Hunters.

As we approached, footsteps light, I listened in to the drunk singing. It was awkward and loud, grating on my nerves. Two of the Hunters sat with their backs to us, bodies outlined by the glow of the campfire before them. They had their cloaks wrapped around them, the symbol of a hand etched in golden thread across their backs. My nose tickled at the scent of charred meat, before I saw it skewered over the flames. It made my mouth water, as did the welcoming scent of stale ale that filled the tankards in their hands.

It reminded me of home.

Another of the Hunters swayed where he stood, legs apart, stumpy cock in hand. He pissed into the waters of The Sleeping Depths without a care in the world. His head was leaning back, face to the star-filled sky as he sang his raspy song, words slurred due to the sheer amount of ale he'd clearly drunk.

It was Orion who pointed out the huddle of three Hunters on the opposite side of their makeshift camp. From here, it looked as though they rested, large bodies nestled into one another like pieces of a puzzle as they slept on snow-covered mats rolled out on the bank.

They were no threat. These men had no fey in chains. They presented no clear issue.

My grip on Erix's dagger relaxed as I regarded the intoxicated crowd. I'd dealt with others like this before, back at the King's Head. It wasn't uncommon to be throwing out drunkards onto the street who always tried their luck with sloppy punches.

I hardly imagined that this bunch would put up much of a fight.

Orion moved first, listening to the command that Althea had given him. He outstretched a hand, focusing on the campfire. Lines creased over his brow as he pinched his eyes closed in concentration.

Then the flames began to dim, licking tongues of red dwindling and shrinking. It took a moment for the two Hunters to realise, halting their singing, rubbing their eyes as they watched the impossible happen right in front of them.

Orion was undeniably an idiot, but I still admired the control of his blood-given powers. I didn't have to like him to admit to being slightly impressed.

The Hunter next to the obsidian lake dribbled a trail of piss across his boots as he turned around to see what the fuss was about. He barely made much of a noise before the axe in Althea's hand swung wide, embedding itself into his skull with a ferocious crack. She slipped from the cloak of shadows before he hit the ground.

The Hunter crumpled in on himself, hand still gripping his cock, blood spluttering out like a spring of water. Althea burst forward, the twin axe in hand, as she pulled free the other from its place in the man's head. The slick, wet sound that followed dried my throat, but there was no time to react as the camp exploded into chaos.

Something felt wrong about this. Even if I wanted to share my worries, it was too late. Death had arrived in the form of our group, and only one of the humans would survive the night.

Althea stood, chest heaving with a devilish smile sliced across her downturned face as she surveyed the remaining Hunters. "Who is going to be the lucky one tonight, boys?"

Her question spread across the camp of shocked humans, each fumbling for a weapon as they rose to greet her. It could've all been over by now, a quick in and out, but Althea had told us all to wait in the shadows. She didn't need our help, nor did she want it.

Not yet anyway.

Althea surveyed the humans like they were nothing more than her playthings, toys ready to claim and destroy when she was done with them.

"What do you fucking call this?" one of the Hunters shouted, slicing his sword from his sheath, metal singing against leather. Everything about his movements was untrained and awkward, from the ale, or his lack of experience, it was not clear. "You promised us a peaceful welcome–"

It was his comment that caught me off guard. Even Erix spared me a concerned glance where we waited, kneeling on the ground, ready to spring forward when Althea signalled.

The Hunter's comment didn't go unnoticed by Althea either, whose expression faltered. I watched as the words settled over her for a moment of confusion which lasted no more than a single breath.

Then she twisted her wrists, flicking the axes in a wide circle in warning. Like a cat, bored of waiting for its prey, she pounced, a blur of auburn hair and glinting armour as she sped through the group.

I winced as the axes met flesh. Sprays of hot, dark blood filled the air in bursts. Althea's brute strength had her blades pass through bones as though they were constructed of water or mist.

She'd finished with the camp long before my knees began to ache where we waited. Her foot pressed down on the chest of the final living Hunter, who whimpered like a child on the ground beneath her. The bodies of his comrades littered the area in chunks around him.

"Consider yourself blessed tonight," Althea said, barely out of breath. "Do as I say, and you may even make it to morning."

Althea whistled through her teeth, the signal we'd waited for. I followed as Erix and the others stood from their perches and entered the bloodied camp.

"Record timing, sister," Orion said, his sick sense of humour only making the cold touch of dread intensify down the back of my neck. He joined Althea at her side, looking down at the final Hunter with a sneer. "Then I suppose it was rather easy, wasn't it? Are your ventures into Durmain like this?"

"Killing is never easy," Althea responded, her snarling expression splattered with red. I didn't know her well, but I could see from her frantic glances to the shadows around, that something unsettled her. It was a feeling we both shared. "But is necessary in most cases."

Was it? It felt different, watching on in silence as Althea cut her way through the camp, not as it had been during that fateful day when I'd been taken to the Hunter's camp outside of Grove. These were just men. There was not a single sign that captured fey had even been with them.

Not to mention the first's strange comment about being 'welcomed peacefully'.

But it was the noticeable clumsiness about the Hunters. Clearly untrained as they each gripped onto swords with shaking, uncalloused hands. They were dressed in the garb of Hunters but were far from the ones I'd seen before.

Novices, all of them. And even that was an overly kind remark.

"I have some questions for you," Althea sneered to the whimpering Hunter beneath her boot. She rested her axe across a shoulder, stained garnet from the deceased's blood. "And I think it'll be wise to answer them, for you may end up like your friends if you do not cooperate."

The Hunter beneath her was the youngest, his face untouched by bristled hair, his skin peppered with spots and marks of youth. His lips were pure white from tension, chin wet with spit and tears as he stared up at Althea as though she was a harbourer of death come to take him to the next realm.

"Wh – why are you doing this?" he spluttered, tugging at the hiding sympathy that I pushed to the back of my chest.

She cocked a head. "Why what, boy? I will ask you the same. Why do you need fey blood?"

His gaze nervously scanned the group of us as we looked down upon him. I could see the gleam in his ocean-blue eyes, that he forced some sense of bravado. Evident how his jaw tightened, clenching teeth hard until they almost broke in his mouth.

"They told us not to trust you." His voice was as rough as the village he was likely brought up in, accent thick with years on farms, not the precise accent I had heard from the Hunters who had stolen me.

"And it is *they* who I am interested in," Althea said, voice as calm as the lake behind her, it matched in deadliness as well. "Who is funding you? Who gives you your orders?"

"Why would I tell–" Orion jolted forward in a blink. The Hunter was silenced by a fist to the jaw; his head snapped back as knuckles connected with bone.

"Was that necessary?" Althea said, glaring at Orion, who shook his hand out at his side, pride creased across his freckled face.

"Ask again and find out."

Althea simply looked back to the young boy who flinched beneath her stare. Even the slightest of movements had him cowering, as though another fist would rain down upon him. "So, are you going to answer, or would you prefer to be reintroduced to my brother?"

The boy spat blood over her boots, a fat glob not making it further than his chin, turning his teeth black as he snarled. "Fuck – off."

He did well to hold himself in confidence as Orion reached down once again, cracking his head back with another punch.

Erix spoke up, mirroring the internal disagreement I was experiencing. "Not that I care to tell you what to do, but perhaps the aggression is going to hinder the answers you are hoping to achieve."

"Did I ask for your input, Berserker?" Orion seethed at Erix, who held his stare in return. Orion, like I, had to look up at the towering giant of a man. It gave the sense that he was a misbehaving child arguing with their parent. The parent, in this case, being Erix, who was deathly still as he looked down upon the Cedarfall prince. "You are not one to make comments on aggression. Do you care to show us what you are hiding?"

There was that name again, a single word that caused a deep purr to emanate from Erix's chest.

"There *it* is." Orion's skin shimmered with heat.

I was beginning to notice a clear difference between Orion and his sister. Whereas she dealt with anger like a silent assassin capable of control, Orion was a messy toddler, red-faced and chest heaving as though he was the one who'd cut down the group and not his sister.

Erix was mute as he stared down upon the red-faced prince. Then he turned his attention to Althea, expression softening. "Permission to subdue a prince?"

"Denied. Orion, put your fists away before you hurt yourself." Althea barely looked at her brother as she backhanded her disregard towards him. She then focused back on the whimpering boy, removing her foot from his chest. He trembled across the bloodied bank like a worm completely entrapped by fear. "If you tell me what I require, then I will let you live."

"Why should I trust you, trickster fucking fey?" Hot tears rolled down his dirtied face. "I knew we shouldn't have listened to the request. Knew you fucks would trick us."

"What request?" I asked, stepping into his line of sight. His comment echoed something one of them had said before Althea sliced her axe through his neck. "Why are you here?"

The boy laughed as he looked up at me, as though I'd told the funniest of jokes or pulled a face. But his response screamed both delusion and insanity, as though he could see that Althea would ensure he'd meet his end no matter what he answered. "You asked us to come, so we did."

"Say that again," Althea breathed, dragging his narrowed gaze from me to her once again.

"Commander Rackley received a letter of invitation. Sent a guide and everything to take us here. Said we'd be collecting a bounty that the *Hand* wouldn't want to refuse. Couldn't pass up on it, he said."

Commander Rackley was another name I'd heard before, back in the Hunter's camp.

And the mention of a guide? A bounty? My mind raced with what he revealed.

Orion and Althea shared a look, one that mirrored each other's concern and my confusion. "The guide, they brought you here?" Althea pressed on.

I scanned the dark, searching for a sign of someone we had missed.

"I told them not to trust the messenger, but what Commander Rackley says goes. Would have put him in grand favour with the *Hand*..." His eyes were wide and full, brimming with tears even the faintest glow from the campfire caught. Tears of fear I believed.

"It is how they got past the Deyalnar Mist," Gyah added, drinking in every detail with wide golden eyes.

Erix nodded in agreement as though they had already shared a conversation prior.

"*Who* was your guide?" Althea asked calmly, although her arms tensed as she slowly lowered the axe.

"How am I supposed to fucking know that!?" he screamed. "They never told me a thing."

"Then you are no good to us alive," Orion snapped, his reaching hand stopped by Althea.

"If he will not tell us with words, then someone in Aurelia will get it out of him."

"Have you grown soft, Althea?" Orion buzzed with unsettling energy, a coiled snake ready to strike, but at whom I was unsure.

"Silk is soft," Althea replied, "but can still strangle the largest of men. Remember that."

I felt some relief knowing that another life wouldn't end here tonight. The feeling was greatly unsettling, twisting that cord within me into knots. This was Icethorn land and, in some burning sense, I was connected to it. As the blood of the Hunters seeped into the ground, it felt as though it coated my very skin.

"There is a fey working with the Hunters," Gyah said, pulling me from the sickening feeling for a moment of reprieve. "If that is the case, then we have a traitor to uncover."

"What did the invitation promise?" Althea said to the Hunter, agreeing with Gyah through a silent stare.

"Power," he replied willingly, opening up like the pages of a tattered book.

"Power?" Erix echoed the word, hand reaching for the hilt of his sword without thought.

Then the boy's gaze flicked to me, and I felt my feet root to the spot. There was something heavy about his stare as it brimmed with recognition and knowing. "Blood. *His* blood."

Erix pulled free his sword, a growl erupting from his core. He side-stepped me, blocking the boy's frightful stare from reaching me, but even with the broad body between us, I couldn't shift the horror that'd become a tenant in my blood. Peeking around his frame, I refused not to watch, even if Erix longed to hide what occurred next from me.

"We should kill him," Orion said through gritted teeth, the tip of his glistening blade pressed to the Hunter's neck.

"For once, I agree with the prince," Erix growled.

"No. If someone is working alongside the Hunters, we will be able to find out with him alive." Althea's tone had grown tense.

"Who told you about the Hunters, Althea?" There was accusation in Orion's voice. "You knew they were here, sister. What else do you know?"

I looked around Erix's back as Orion's suggestion settled over me. Who *was* Althea's informant? It hadn't been something I'd thought to ask, but clearly it was enough to turn brother against sister.

Tarron had mentioned the location of the antidote, but the message about the camp had come from someone else. Althea had already confirmed as much.

"You dare suggest I was previously aware of this?" Her voice was on fire; I could almost see the flames bursting from her mouth as she spat back at her brother. He flinched as she thrust her fingers into his chest, knocking him back several steps.

The Hunter, no longer pinned beneath her gaze, tried to scramble back, only to be stopped by Gyah.

"Who told you of the Hunters, Althea?" It was Erix who asked now, his tone less suggestive but equally concerned. "I do not believe you would have known, but whoever informed you is likely involved."

Althea turned from her brother, chest rising harshly as her breathing deepened. "It cannot be. She would not have known."

"Althea," I said. "Tell us."

She swallowed something large in her throat, face pinched as though it was sour. Then she revealed a name that thrust open the box in my chest, releasing a billowing torrent of icy winds to pour from my skin.

"Lady Kelsey gave me the information. She was my informant about the Hunters."

CHAPTER 19

When I was a child, my father brought a conch shell back from a visit to the eastern trading port of Ralarn. Alongside the shell, he'd unpacked stories of the crescent-shaped harbours filled with ships, large and small. I'd held the salt-dried, curved body of the shell as though it was my most prized possession. It'd became a habit to run my little fingers over the divots and ridges, imagining the vast waters of the seas of Stafster and the world far beyond them. Father whispered tales that the shells of Stafster held on to secrets of the unknown, only to be heard if held up to one's ear.

So I did just that. Young and naive, prepared to listen to wonders the shell would unveil, but all I heard was a static roaring.

When I grew older, I realised that even a shell from the depths of the Stafster had nothing of importance to reveal, that it was all a lie. It wasn't secrets the shell whispered to me, but the roaring of my own blood echoing back at me.

That was what I heard now as Althea had repeated her aunt's name, a thundering roar of my own blood.

Orion was laughing, nervous eyes unblinking as he waited for the punchline of the joke. "Our aunt is as frail as a feather and as self-absorbed as the peacock the feather comes from. She could hardly organise herself, let alone a ploy of this kind."

"I am not suggesting she planned this, but it was her hand that gave me the note." Althea's stare was lost to a place on the ground before her.

"And what is there to gain from organising this?" Orion's laughter faltered back into his stern snarl. I could see from the shifting of his gaze that he, too, was beginning to realise that this was not a joke.

"It was too easy," Althea muttered, echoing my inner thought. I knew little of court politics, but it seemed pointless arranging this meeting through means of secrecy. "There will be an explanation for it, one I will question when we return to Aurelia. Tie the Hunter up and prepare yourselves. We have got all we require–"

A scream broke the night around us. The noise sliced claws down the spine of my subconscious, turning my body to ice where I stood. We all tensed, Erix loosing a raspy swear as he surveyed the dark surrounding us.

"What's that?" the Hunter spluttered, trying to stand but getting nowhere beneath Gyah's effortless hold.

I knew the answer as clear as I knew that we were in trouble. *Desperate* trouble.

"Gryvern," I answered, chest aching as my heart's patter turned into a thundering canter. Flashes of the monsters filled my mind, making my chest ache from the frantic canter of my heart.

One scream became two. Two became more, until it was impossible to know the number of gryvern or the location they flew from.

They were all around us, that much was clear, but in the dark, I couldn't see a single one of the winged demons. The air pulsed with wretched winds, the dark alight with the song of death.

Suddenly, the flames of the campfire exploded to great heights, the fire fuelled by Orion's power. The orange halo of light burst across the camp, casting heat over my cheeks as it unveiled the mutilated bodies of the Hunters around us. The flames grew so high that even The Sleeping Depths could be seen.

I craned my neck, unable to catch a breath as I surveyed the horror that flocked above. In the dark skies, cast deep navy above the firelight, there where countless shapes of the gryvern as they soared towards us.

The Hunter's scream was a chorus of horror and terror. Erix was shouting, putting his strong body before mine, as if that would do much to stop the gryvern as they dived upon us. Althea and Orion screamed commands, each gripping their weapons as they looked up at the scene above them.

"*This* was her plan..." Althea's panicked voice made it through the chaos. "The gryvern knew we would be here!"

"Bitch!" I didn't care to know who shouted it.

"I don't believe it," I said.

Lady Kelsey, the person who had housed me, gave me insight into my power and was nothing more than a kind, caring woman. She couldn't have been behind the attacks.

"Don't want to, or can't?' Althea questioned, axes drawn and ready.

Unlike when I was younger, I no longer saw the world through the rosy haze of naivety. Lady Kelsey was tied up in this attack – it was the only answer. And the gryvern wanted blood, as they had with my mother and the Icethorn Court.

And they wanted *me*, no matter who commanded them. I was their end goal. And I wasn't going to let them have me willingly.

Fury unspooled in me, filling every vein with a maelstrom of power.

I reached for the dagger, hand steady as I gripped it. My body swelled with the cold power that also filled the winter air around us.

The gryvern flew with perfect synchronicity, a vortex of shadows. I watched and waited for them to break formation.

"I will not let them harm you," Erix snarled through a tense jaw. My eyes darted, for a moment, from the gryvern to my guard, only to witness the granite shadows that darkened his stare. "But, for that, I am going to need you to fight. Fight hard, little bird."

Fight hard, little bird.

I swallowed a lump in my throat, wanting to show him that I was brave and ready. I only hoped he didn't see the tremble in my knees, or the shake as I gripped the dagger. Both minor details giving my fear away. "I will try."

"That's all I could ask for." Erix spared me a glance, his lips refusing to close as though he had something else to say.

The tense silence between us stretched like a taut string, waiting to give way on either side. Instead, he arced the large sword in both hands and held it before him. Before *us*.

We waited for what felt like an eternity.

"How do we kill them?" I asked, eyes flickering between each grey body, unable to keep track.

"Sever a limb," Erix explained, words poised and oddly calm. "A blade through the head or heart will also do."

"Or, Robin, you *burn* them." Orion attacked.

Althea swore at her brother, unable to stop him as he pulled back an arrow in his grand bow until his fingers shook with tension. Through one squinted eye, he angled the arrow towards the night sky, muscles screaming in his arms as he readied himself. Then a spark of light sang to life across the metal tip of the arrow. I had but a moment to notice it before the thwack of the bow signalled the release of the arrow. In to the sky it cut, flying sure and fast, towards the huddle of gryvern.

Like a golden star, it filled the night with fire. No wind or bout of snow was able to snuff out the flame.

It found its mark.

Even from a distance, I could see as the flaming arrow buried itself into a leather wing. The thin membrane exploded in fire, a vicious tongue of heat devouring the limb of the gryvern. Its scream scratched at the night, making the very stars hide behind thickening snow clouds.

Then the gryvern fell, one wing flapping frantically to keep itself airborne, but there was no use. A comet of flesh and fire, it careened towards the camp. The ground shook with the collision, the body exploding beneath the impact.

I felt the biting of sickness at the base of my throat but had no time to dwell on it, not as the army of monsters released a war cry and dived us as one.

We exploded into action.

Erix swung the sword, splitting flesh with ease, cleaving bodies in half. One after the other, each slice of his sword found a target. He hacked a path through the falling claws, wings and teeth, shielding me from danger.

Erix did well to keep them from me, but the nick of claws grew closer and closer, no matter how close I tried to put myself to his back.

I jabbed out with the dagger blindly. It was as though I punched a wall, each thud of the knife embedding itself into sicky flesh to the hilt. Warm, thick blood burst across my hand, wetting my hold on the weapon. It was near impossible to know if the creature at the end of the dagger was dead or not. Stabbing over and over. Some attacks hitting and others missing.

My forearm burned with fire, but I fought through it. Slashing and cutting. I was aware of the dark, warm blood that spread across the hilt and onto my fist. But I didn't care, didn't falter, as I kept thrusting the dagger forward into the swarm of gryvern. Not that it would do any good unless they got close, and that was certainly not what I wanted.

Erix did his best to fend them away from me. Bursts of fire and the slicing of steel could be seen through the storm of bodies. Althea and her brother fought with backs pressed together, Orion focusing more on his power, whereas Althea relied on the axes she swung in a cloud of limbs and sharp edges.

Gyah had disappeared the moment they swarmed, but in the dark, a slithering beast snapped jaws around the gryvern; she was in her Eldrae form.

No matter how many Erix killed, more seemed to join the attack. The wave of unstoppable beasts squawked and screamed in ways that shouldn't be possible. Yet on he battled, not faltering for a moment.

If there was time to gawk at his brute strength and skill, it would have been now, but there was hardly time to think besides keeping the angry rhythm of the thrusting blade in my hand.

My body grew tired quickly. My mind slowed. I longed to fall to the ground and cower beneath my arms as the claws and teeth shredded at my skin. Even Erix's shouting had silenced, conserving his energy into the constant swings of his sword.

Do something. The command came from within me and around me. *Release me.*

Exhaustion. It was exhaustion that conjured the voice.

Let go.

My magic begged for release. But with one look around me, to my friends and allies, I worried what would become of them if I released the uncontrollable power. Which danger was greater? The storm in my blood, or the threat of winged monsters who showed no signs of relenting.

My arm slowed, fingers slipping on the hilt. Something wet and heavy slammed into my forearm, knocking the dagger into the throng of limbs. Erix called my name. But so did the voice.

Robin. Release me. Let me go. Do something.

"Erix…" I called, voice weak and breathless as I dropped out the way of clawed feet. Erix arced his blade, metal glowing like molten stars as it cut right through the beast above me. I closed my eyes against the showering of warm, vile blood that splattered upon me. "My dagger… I've dropped my dagger."

I was blinded from exhaustion and the gryverns' gore.

Gyah released a roar above us. Clearing the blood from my vision, I gazed upon the horror of four beasts upon her, clawed, mangled hands tugging at her wings and body. They had her trapped, teeth deathly close to sinking into her skin. Fingers of red flame lifted from the campfire, reaching for Gyah and the gryvern around her.

Althea and Orion worked together, each now without weapons as they were likely scattered across the grounds. They raised hands, arms moving like the waves of water as they controlled the fire to do their bidding.

I could see – and *feel* – that they were both drained, reaching the limits of their powers. Althea's face was sheet white, covered in grime and soot. Orion's eyes could hardly stay open as he forced more strength and will into the fire, teeth bared in an eternal snarl. No matter how hard they tried, they couldn't help Gyah. They were barely keeping the gryvern back from themselves, as they used the ruby tongues as a barrier of safety.

"We are losing," Erix huffed, his blade no longer silver but black with blood. "We have no chance of seeing this through."

Let me go, Robin.

Time slowed. Erix risked a glance, his eyes a storm of worry and apology. He was giving up. His lips moved, mouthing two words that never made it over the roaring of chaos. But I could read them, taking the words from his dirt-covered lips and piecing them together.

Little bird.

It was a plea. A request for help.

Seeing him – gaze locked on me, hope sparking in the silver of his eyes – my hesitation shattered like glass over stone.

I reached for the box within my chest. This time I didn't invite it to open as I had in my short lesson with Lady Kelsey. Instead, I ripped the lid completely from the hinges and let the cold, frozen power fill my soul.

In a moment, I was aware of every flake of snow that fell around us, joined with the nightly breeze of the Icethorn Court as it stretched across the vast and unexplored land of my heritage.

The power filled me until I was it, and *it* was me.

Instinct took over. I raised my hands wide with fingers splayed, offering the power a gateway to leave its vessel. Every single flake of snow and ice ceased itself midfall, held in the sky, unmoving and patient as it waited for my command.

I felt the sharp edges of the flakes. I saw the beautiful, intricate designs in my mind's eye, and so I shaped them into arrows of ice, points turning in the direction of the gryvern.

I'm free.

My hands clenched shut, and the countless, never-ending, unfathomable number of snowflakes pelted towards the monsters. They sliced through flesh and ripped wings until they were nothing but useless, loose rags around bone frames. A hiss of mist spread from my skin, curling around me and Erix where we stood.

Then the gryvern fell as one, as they'd done when they first attacked. Except, this time, they didn't get up again. Dead. Lifeless. Puppets cut from the strings of their master. Their heavy, ruined bodies slammed into the ground, echoing the pounding in my chest. I almost felt the ground beneath my feet tremble, but that was soon forgotten as I lost myself to the magic.

Winds tore at the camp, snuffing the fire as though it was no more than a candle. Swirls of fresh snow met with old that was ripped from the ground, spinning in vortexes of white around us. The movements of power followed my gaze as it trailed over the darkness before me, or perhaps my focus was its control, the power waiting for my eyes to shift onto something new before following like the proud but loyal dog it was.

I smiled among the throng of the terrifying winds and its brisk, cold bite. I could no longer feel the tip of my nose, or the sodden dampness of my blood-soaked gloves. Teeth bared to the night, I invited the power. Not only had it waited within me, but it seemed to have followed me in the very air and ground the moment I'd stepped foot onto Icethorn Court soil.

This was different to when I'd used the power before. It was endless and without impossibility.

The gryvern were no more. Only the shallow cuts of their desperate touch left across my arms and shoulders remained, a crisscross of stinging marks hidden beneath my ripped jacket and shirt. I glanced down upon my arms as the wind's kiss cooled the discomfort. Torn material flapped violently, and my skin beneath, briefly exposed, was as pale as the moon that no doubt hung beyond the layer of dark storm clouds.

I focused my attention, drunk and slow on power, to see larger hands filling mine. Great, scarred knuckles flexed as fingers wrapped around my own, holding me. An anchor of skin. Warmth among the chill that seeped from my skin. My eyes took a moment, flirting up the arms of muscle beneath torn material, all the way to squared shoulders.

Erix. His jaw tensed, hard-set eyes focused on me.

Ice clung to his skin like a dusting of jewels, snow slapping into the side of his face as my power lashed over him. But steadfast he stood. He gripped onto me with urgency, as though the power would lift me from the ground and take me off into the night.

But I could see in his silver stare, glowing within like a star, that he wouldn't let that happen.

Not now, not ever.

"You are undeniable," Erix mouthed, voice straining over the screaming winter. Tears streamed from his eyes, turning to diamonds before the torrents of air ripped them greedily from his cheeks. "You've saved us."

I couldn't respond, not even if I wanted to. The pressure of this power was turning quickly from thrilling to frantic, as though the leash I held was slipping from my weakening grasp.

"But, little bird. You need to stop this."

I shook my head, wishing for him to see the panic in my eyes.

Where were Althea, Orion, and Gyah? I couldn't see them through the dark, thick storm. Only Erix.

In a world of cold darkness, there was only Erix.

I tried everything I could to push the power back into the box in my chest, but as I reached inside for it, I found myself hollow. Empty. Void. Fear gripped at my soul with sharp, poisonous talons; it spread through my body like a terrible sickness.

What was different this time? What made the magic so unruly – as if it recognised me, but still didn't respect me.

Perhaps it was because I didn't respect it. No, I feared it.

"I…" My voice came out like a child, small and meek. "I can't do it."

Erix pulled me into him, holding my head to his chest. "You destroyed a host of gryvern with a single action. If you can do that, you can do *anything*."

I closed my eyes, inhaling his welcoming scent as his gentle, circling touch stroked the back of my head. His fingers tangled with my dark hair, tugging the knots ever so slightly, and that feeling felt familiar, like a key unlocking a memory once lost.

Robin… A voice of silk filled my head and echoed across the magic of ice and storm around me, my name carried by each flake of snow, each twisting of brisk wind. *Robin*. Then *she* filled the darkness of my mind, flowing black hair and humming a tune that I had replayed in my dreams for years.

My mother.

I let go of the tugging cords of power. It was a risk, but I did it anyway, as though the humming tune had ordered me to do so. Instinct, in the familiar form of Mother. It was her voice that echoed across the magic around me, calling to me, welcoming me home.

The power ripped away from me. On all sides, the winds recoiled as a flame would to the fall of water. Back into the dark, vast expanse of the Icethorn Court it ran away, no longer required for this place – for me.

"Little bird." Erix's voice vibrated through his hard chest. "It is done."

I pried my eyes open just in time for a flare of fire to return to the campfire. On the other side, the two silhouettes of Althea and Orion waited, hunched and torn, from my power and the gryverns who now lay covered in bouts of snow around them.

The world settled, the breath returning to my lungs, still cold but not destructive.

"Is everyone okay?" I asked, voice husk as though I'd screamed for an eternity. I'd the overwhelming urge to lie down, tiredness weighing heavy on my body and mind.

"Frostbitten and bloody, but alive," Erix responded. Then it hit me that I was still holding onto him, his grip as strong and welcoming as my own. "Although it would have been worse if you didn't intervene. We were losing, until you."

Pride glittered within Althea's pinched eyes, her red-curls gathered in clumps of iced moisture. "Well done, Robin Icethorn."

I dropped my arms from around Erix's waist, stepping back even though it was far from what I wanted to do. "I felt it. The power was too much."

"That is because it has been left untamed and unclaimed for years," Erix explained. "No one is expecting you to command it with ease during your first encounter."

"First encounter?" I stared up at him, noticing the thin slice of a cut that separated his thick eyebrow.

"What you've just encountered is pure power, your family's magic left to run wild and uncontrolled. That is a hint of what will destroy the barrier between the realms, and devour Durmain if you do not make your decision."

I blinked and saw it – a world of ice. Grove ruined by the power, trampled beneath its uncaring chill long before the army of fey followed it.

"I do not know whether to slap you on the back in pride or scold you for your decisions, Robin." Althea was before me, hair tangled and gaze still as stern as it was before. Then it melted as she threw her arms around me, whispering something into my ear. "But, for now, I'll thank you."

I didn't know whether to return her hug. Before I could think too hard on it, she pulled away.

"Could have done it sooner," Orion said, looking at his nails. In the glow of his fire, I could see that he too was covered in cuts, some deeper and angrier than the rest. "But thanks, I guess."

There was a shuffling of snow, and we all jumped at a mound that vibrated. My heart sank to the bottom of my stomach, expecting a gryvern to spring out of the ground, but it was Gyah, no longer in her Eldrae form.

She pushed herself up, shaking the relentless snow from her shoulders. Her golden glower boiled like coals over a fire. "Treasonous as it may be, I will tear your aunt's head off for this."

"Not if I beat you to it," Althea replied, voice steady and void of much emotion. "We need to return to Aurelia and present what has happened. I've got the antidote for Briar, and we have the proof of Kelsey's involvement."

"Oh, how I look forward to seeing the look of utter surprise when we return. Scathed, but alive," Orion added, sharing a half-smile with his sister. At least they finally agreed on something besides the outcome of *me* and what I meant to them both.

"Surprise that will soon become disappointment, no doubt." Erix scanned the darkness, concern etched across his brow. "However, it would seem we are one traveller down. Seems the Hunter either got away or is buried alongside the gryvern."

The Hunter had slipped my mind completely.

"Fucking slippery bastard!" Althea kicked at the hard body of a gryvern. "He best be dead, or if I find him, I will make sure he is. Gyah, do you have it in you to return?"

"Give me a moment to rest," Gyah pleaded, hunched over to catch her breath. "My body feels like it's been dragged through a field of thorns."

We were a band of tired, bloodied and torn travellers. Gyah kicked her way out of the mound of snow before quickly dropping to sit on the exposed corpse of a gryvern. Althea dug her axe into the ground and leaned on it, the other lost in the battle as my dagger had been.

"I think we have all earned a short rest," Orion said, stifling a yawn which caused the flames to flicker in response. "Emphasis on short. I am not one for sleeping among the dead–"

Orion never got to finish his sentence. Not as a blade sliced cleanly across his throat in an arc that split skin, causing dark blood to spill and splutter down his chest. The snow at his feet turned pink and scarlet, all before he could finish his final word, the last word he would ever say.

Orion was dead before his body crumpled in on itself and fell to the ground.

Behind him, blade in hand, stood the missing Hunter, chest heaving and eyes glowing with pride. Spit lined his thin lips, tongue panting, hand shaking and stained red.

"I killed a Cedarfall fey," he sang above Althea's haunting cry. "I killed a prince."

CHAPTER 20

My body was frozen in shock, unable to move or speak, as the pool of ruby spread beneath Orion's downturned face, seeping around him in a halo of death.

A shift in the air caught my attention. I looked up to watch Erix lunge forward, sword outstretched for the Hunter. Gyah moved too, hands like claws as she cleared the space, boots barely touching the floor.

They were both screaming, but it was hard to fathom if they made sense with words or just angered noises. All I could think about was the blood, dark and thick, as it spread across the ground towards me.

I looked to Althea, and my heart cracked clean in two. Her eyes were wide, both brows raised high, and her mouth parted in a small, unignorable 'O' shape. Surprise softened her face, whereas the burning of disbelief drained the colour from her cheeks and the glow from her eyes.

Then she snapped out of her daze, swinging an axe while barely making a sound. She caught Erix's blade with the curve of her own weapon, one large twist of her arm, and the momentum tore the sword from his grasp and sent it surging off into the darkness. Gyah was next, stopped dead in her tracks by a flash of burning hot fire that exploded from the skin of Althea's outstretched palm. Both warriors stumbled away, missing the wild swing of the axe, as she spun to meet the Hunter.

He was caught in his own manic laughter, not noticing or caring for the danger sweeping towards him.

Althea's cry broke the night like thunder. The axe was the lightning, warning of what was to come as it turned on the Hunter. The murderer. I winced, expecting to see more blood, deserving blood, spill alongside Orion's, but I was wrong.

In a blink, she'd turned her wrist, angling the flat edge of the axe's body towards the Hunter's head. Metal connected with bone and flesh, the crack deafening as though the very mountains we'd seen on our journey had fractured.

His head snapped back, eyes rolling to whites as a gash poured angrily over his left brow. The dagger, Erix's dagger, fell from his hand, embedding itself to the hilt in the bloodied ground.

The Hunter dropped like a sack of shit, alive but unconscious, evident from the heavy rise and fall of his chest.

"Althea," I croaked, reaching a hand for her shoulder. Her back was to me, facing the Hunter, shoulders moving rapidly beneath her breaths.

What could I say? Words were useless as she glared down at the dead body of her brother, shoulders rising and falling dramatically. I didn't know Orion well, or like him, but death was death, and he was her family. She didn't have to like him, but through blood and time, she had loved him as her kin.

And now, he was gone. Forever.

I wrapped my arms around her. She was warm beneath my touch, or perhaps I was just cold now, having hosted the untamed power of the Icethorn Court.

I waited for her to speak, giving her the time she needed as she regarded the unconscious Hunter beneath her. Her entire focus was on the human boy now as though he held coveted answers to the universe, and he was about to reveal them all.

I noticed a dark mark on his neck, peaking out of the collar of his jacket. It was a symbol of ink on his skin – in the shape of a hand.

The mark of a Hunter, as if that was his only crime.

Althea shrugged out of my hold. When she finally spoke, her voice was rough like that of stormy oceans, harsh like winds through forests. "We need to return to Aurelia. Immediately."

Erix was beside us now, sword back in his hand and the point held upon the unconscious human. "Then we kill him here. Now."

"No." Althea's answer was final, her voice void of negotiation or options. "I will not allow that."

"But he–" I wanted to reach a hand over Erix's mouth, but Althea's retort silenced him before I could waste a second imagining it.

"I am well aware of what has occurred, Erix," Althea snapped, eyes ablaze with the fire she held internally. "If we return with my brother dead, and no proof of what happened, then nothing is stopping Lady Kelsey from suggesting that his blood is on our hands. I do not know what she has planned, or what collateral she has prepared for, but the Hunter comes with us. If Orion's death is questioned, they can rip his mind open and see for themselves what happened here."

Tears ran down her face, but not a single sob broke out her mouth.

"He will be lucky if he lives that long," Gyah muttered, eyes hardly straying from the downturned body of Prince Orion Cedarfall.

"The boy lives as long as I command it," Althea growled. "Only by my hand will he die for what he has done."

I wanted to reach for her again, to comfort her with my touch. Words were useless in this moment, even I knew that.

"It is a long ride back," Erix said, speaking aloud the thought that filled my head. "And the night is even longer. Berrow is a shorter journey. Althea, you need to rest. We all do."

"Do not tell me what I need." She spun on Erix, wild-eyed. "My brother needs to be returned to his court for his body to be dealt with accordingly. The boy needs to face the consequences as urgently as my aunt. I will rest when I choose."

Still, Althea hadn't spared the stiffening corpse of her brother a glance, not even a flick of her gaze. There was restraint there, in the way her neck was tall and sharp, her face angled awkwardly so she couldn't accidentally skim her furious stare across him.

"I am merely advising, as you called me here to do," Erix replied, bowing his head.

"Gyah," Althea said, ignoring Erix. "Can you fly now?"

I studied the Eldrae, whose own stare seemed full of calculation. Her hand became a fist as she placed it above her heart, eyes wet with tears. "I will do my best for you – for Orion."

Althea nodded, huffing in relief as though she expected resistance. "That's all I ask for."

Erix shook his head in frustration or disagreement, it was hard to determine one from the other. "Gyah is strong. But she cannot lie to please you, Althea. Do you truly believe she can take us all to Aurelia? With the added weight of your prisoner and your–"

He couldn't finish his sentence. And it didn't need to be said either, as his attention looked back to the body of the Cedarfall prince.

"We can wait then," I added, voice cracking with desperation to fill the silence before another argument broke out. I held Althea's stare, sensing gnawing sadness within the depths of it. "If it means you can take him home, I will stay back."

"It is not safe for you." Althea spared me concern, eyes darting to Erix, who shadowed me.

"It is safer being here, in… my land." I couldn't explain it, but that power I'd experienced was the only protection I required. If it could ruin realms, it would also destroy anyone who stood in my way. "If Lady Kelsey is behind all of what has occurred, then surely it would be better for me to return once she is accosted? I don't doubt Gyah's strength and ability, but it doesn't feel right asking such a thing of her."

Althea held my gaze, then looked to Erix in silent command.

"I will stay with him," Erix added, in almost a rush, reading Althea's unspoken request. Not that it needed to be said. Erix would never leave me, that much had already been made clear. "I will ensure his security until Gyah returns for us."

My chest warmed. I wanted to look at him, as I knew he looked at me, but I kept my focus on Althea, who pondered the suggestion.

"Fine. I permit you to find shelter in Berrow. No further. Gyah will collect you from there tomorrow."

It was done. Agreed without further contemplation or discussion. I felt both relief and some puckering of discomfort from splitting from the group. But it was the right thing to do, solidified by the physical relaxing of Gyah's shoulders, knowing she had fewer people to carry. Gyah gifted us a smile of thanks, although it hardly reached her golden-eyes. There was a slight limp as she walked to the unconscious Hunter. Erix had noticed it before any of us.

He was right. Gyah was in no position to take us all back.

"Robin. Help me, please," Althea commanded, braving a look at the final body remaining to collect.

Her brother.

I nodded, biting the insides of my cheeks as I watched her acknowledge the dead beneath her.

Althea knelt beside him, hands resting upon her lap and fiddling with the material of her tunic to keep them occupied.

"Tell me what I can do," I said, voice a whisper as though I feared to disturb Orion in his endless slumber.

Althea finally reached out a hand, resting it upon the tousled red hair of his head. "He did not deserve this. His death is my responsibility. I will relive this moment, playing over what has happened, telling my family."

"This isn't your fault, Althea."

"It was my careless lack in judgement that killed Orion."

Just like when Erix told me not to take blame for Briar's poisoning, I gave the same advice to Althea now, hoping it would help her like it helped me.

"Don't harbour this guilt, Althea. It won't do you any good. Instead, lay the blame on the person who planned this. They killed Orion. Focusing on them will a better use of energy."

She looked at me with wide, unblinking eyes; they glistened with tears that she did not dare lose. "I hear you, Robin. But my family are a different matter. They will certainly question how this happened. Why I let a small, insolent boy slit the throat of my own brother when I was inches away. It *is* my fault, and I do not wish to hear you say otherwise again."

"Lady Kelsey may not have held the blade, but she nudged the hand in that direction," I said. "She will pay a far greater price than the Hunter."

"If she is truly the person behind it, that is." Althea blinked, keeping her eyes closed for a paused moment. "Maybe she is, maybe not. And if not, I will find out who is, for *his* sake." She ran her hands down her brother's back, a muscle feathering in her taut jaw. "Robin, more will die, known and nameless, unless you claim what is rightfully yours, Orion will become but a name on a long list of lives wasted."

An overbearing weight rested across my shoulders. Unseen, but there. "Orion wanted war. I don't believe that wish has changed."

"He wanted war, and his life paid for it. So ask yourself what it is you want... and if you will allow anyone else to perish whilst you ponder your decision."

I swallowed hard, unable to conjure words as Althea studied me intently. She was not angry at me, although her comments suggested otherwise. She looked exhausted, eyes rimmed with shadows and shoulders hunched forward, her frame smaller than before. I thought of the Taster, Briar, and now the body lying between us.

Who would be next?

"How do you not hate my existence after what I have caused you to lose so far?"

A lover and then a brother.

"Because the outcome I wish for requires you to be alive. And hating you will not aid my hopes. It would hinder them." Althea levelled her gaze, lifting her chin as she rolled back her shoulders. A single tear fell from her eye, trailing a river across the sharp edge of her cheekbone and down towards her nose. She didn't reach for it to clear it from her face. I did, catching it with the brush of a finger. "He will not be the first, nor the last, to lose a life to this conflict. And who am I to hate you when I see a man who has lost far more than me. Make the choice, Robin. Not only for your sake. Do it for those around you."

I cared little for the ache in my legs, or the stinging of cold winds which ripped across my face. Not when all I could think of was Althea holding the limp body of her brother across her lap as Gyah's wings flapped wildly, before they sliced off into the night.

The vision followed me all the way to Berrow, Erix leading ahead as we battled the thick darkness. I could've walked like that until dawn arrived, lost in a storm of my thoughts. They were so consuming that I hardly noticed as the snow-coated ground smoothed out to old stone, and the outlines of buildings stood guard on either side of us.

It was as if the town of Berrow slept. There wasn't the glow of a fire to be seen in the shattered windows, no noise besides the slamming of doors in the wind, hanging from rusted and forgotten hinges.

There was no life here, only Erix and me.

I don't know what I expected to find, but a place void of any life was certainly not an option.

Looking up, I took in the buildings, crumpled and ruined beneath the weight of winter. Snow layered across concave roofs, walls covered in frost that caught glints of the only light brave enough to be here. The moon had split through the thinning of clouds, a thankful guide, making it bearable to put one foot in front of the other.

"Robin," Erix called, demanding my attention. He'd deviated from the straight and sure path he'd walked. Now he waited beside a cottage-like building to my side. Much like the others, it looked as though one good gust would blow it down. "We going to stop here for the night."

"Not that I don't trust your judgement, but are you certain it will be standing by morning?" I asked, wrapping my arms around my waist in hopes to hold in some body heat.

A weak smile found itself across Erix's face. "I suppose there is only one way to find out."

He reached for the door and wrestled it open. The screech of wood and worn metal had me cringing as it seemed to shatter all silence of the darkened village. Wrapping my arms around my waist, I followed Erix into the shadowed building.

"What happened here?" I asked, following him into a connecting room down the narrow hallway we had entered. Even here, evidence of destruction littered the ground, furniture toppled over, items of clothing and other objects discarded across every inch of flooring.

"Winter happened," Erix said, voice quiet and steps steady as though he expected someone to jump out of the shadows and attack. Not once did his hand leave the warm leather hilt at his waist.

"It's like it's been ransacked." I stepped over a toy bear, seams torn and features distorted by years of neglect.

"Just forgotten," Erix corrected. "When your mother and her court were killed, the magic of the land was left without a person to control it. It took a matter of days for the power to spread. A storm so great that it left homes, towns, villages and hamlets in tatters. Berrow is the furthest west and likely the most well off from the horror. This is nothing in comparison to what ruin has taken tenancy on Icethorn land."

"So this is what'll become of Durmain, if I don't do anything?" My body tensed at the thought, imagining my home like this, trampled by a storm until it was nothing but ruins.

"What *may* become of Durmain." Erix stopped in his tracks, face shrouded in the darkness of the home. He was so close, hands brushing either side of my hips as he urged me before him. "I think we should start by making a fire, then we can talk."

I nodded, wondering if his piercing gaze could see the reddening of my cheeks. "That would be nice."

He breathed out slowly. "Yes, little bird. It would be."

Turned out, the hearth was unusable, piled up with spilling snow which likely filled every inch of the wonky chimney. Instead, beside a bed in the far back room, Erix piled armfuls of forgotten items into a pile before striking flame from a small piece of flint that he had hidden in his breast pocket.

"Always prepared, never surprised," I said.

Erix turned to me, the halo of light casting shapes across the side of his face. "What's that supposed to mean?"

I gestured towards the flint in his hands. "You've come prepared, that's all. It's something my father always tried to drum into me. Not that I listened."

Thinking about him, the distance between us both physically and mentally, stirred an ache in my chest. I battened it down, like a hatch in a storm, leaving that concern for when I wasn't so exhausted.

"Little bird."

I almost held my breath at the suggestion of his tone. "Yes?"

There was a seriousness to his stare, one that flayed my skin from my bones until I was utterly exposed before him.

"You look like you've been pulled through a bush of thorns," Erix said, studying me from his perch on the edge of the bed we had uncovered through our exploration of the home.

The firelight gave me a better look at the countless scratches and cuts across his face as well. "And *you* look as though you lost a fight to one."

"I nearly did, but you saved me." Erix dragged a finger and thumb down the side of his face, barely wincing as he ran over the ridges of the many marks the gryvern had left on him.

"Saying I 'saved you' is a bit of a stretch."

He looked at me, brow raised, not needing to tell me how wrong I was.

"Do they hurt?" Erix asked, eyes trailing over the wounds down the side of my neck.

I shook my head, holding a breath as his finger reached for them. Closing my eyes, I readied myself for it, the warmth of a fingertip as he trailed the line of my jaw. But it didn't arrive. Opening my eyes, I saw his lips, one side curved upwards into a smirk that longed to be wiped clean from his face. "I thought I lost you for a moment."

"You are infuriating," I admitted.

Erix rocked back, resting on both arms which propped him up. The bed frame screamed in protest. I was amazed it was still standing by the time he made himself comfortable.

"You know, I have been called worse."

I rolled my eyes. "I can imagine."

"When we return to Aurelia, I want you to be seen by a healer."

If I was standing, I would've put my hands on my hips as I scolded him. "Not even my dad speaks to me with such demanding tones, you know."

"Well, your father is far from here now, which leaves you in my capable hands."

"Oh, lucky me," I said through a yawn that'd been impossible to keep away. "Remember, even you admitted I saved you. I think I'm pretty capable of looking after myself."

"You have a point, but even you need to sleep." Erix shifted his weight, hands on knees as he pushed himself to stand. "That amount of magic use is exhausting."

I was tired – exhausted, Erix was right – and far greater than I'd ever been before. Even without moving my legs, I knew they wouldn't cooperate even if I willed it. All I wanted to do was lie back on the cold, dusty sheets and let my heavy eyelids close.

But what waited in the dark of my eyes sent a burst of fear through me.

Before Erix took two steps from the bed, I spoke up. "Where are you going?"

He put a hand on his hip and pointed towards the shadowed doorway. "There is another bedroom down the hallway."

I couldn't explain it, not that I wanted to either, but the thought of him leaving me in this place was unnerving.

"Well," I said, looking around me as though the excuse I required was hiding among the messy room. "What's wrong with *this* bed?"

"It is occupied." Erix's stare pinned me to the spot. Then he turned his back again and stepped towards the threshold of the room slower than before. "Only room for one."

"But the fire." I grappled for an excuse for him to stay. "You've only just made it and have barely warmed up. If you go somewhere else, what is to say you'll catch your death from how…"

"Little bird." He turned on his heels slowly. "If you are asking me to stay with you, then ask it."

"I don't–" His body shifted an inch. "Okay, stay."

The smile Erix gave me lit another fire deep within me. I tried not to let the creeping heat add colour to my face, but there was nothing he couldn't notice with those storm-filled eyes.

"Not even a please?"

If there was a pillow to throw at him, I would've jumped at the chance.

Before I could retract my offer, I kicked my boots from my feet, one after the other, and swung my legs over until I was lying down, facing the low ceiling. Erix walked to my side, looking down at me, his back haloed in the firelight. "Infuriating, am I?"

Yes. My mind screamed. But it also wanted a distraction, and I needed that now. With the images of Althea and Orion, the Hunter and the gryvern plaguing my thoughts, I needed a distraction.

And the comfort of his presence.

"Just get in before I change my mind."

His grin told me that he didn't believe a word I said. Erix didn't speak again, not as he tugged at the belt around his waist, pulling it through the loops of his breeches until the sheath and sword were discarded to the floor.

Once Erix clambered onto the bed beside me, I felt *greatly* overdressed. I praised myself for not watching him undress, so much so that I was surprised by the brush of bare skin against my arm. His torso was exposed, skin taut as he lowered himself down. There was no time to count the ridges of muscles that lined his stomach.

My breath hitched as I saw the dark material of his trousers. I looked away quickly before he could notice my wandering gaze.

Here is the distraction I longed for.

"Are you not going to be cold?" I asked, rolling over, so I faced the small bundle of flames in the middle of the room. I shivered, although the fingers of heat reached for me without restraint.

"Do not worry about me," Erix said, breath brushing against the back of my head. On my side, I fit him around me like the piece of a puzzle, his tall, broad body folding around mine, so close that I was certain he saw the shiver of hairs standing to attention across my neck. "It is my job to be concerned about you."

"Well, I give you an order to cease those worries, if but for one night."

"Is that a command, Robin Icethorn? Because it sounds like you are beginning to grow used to your future of demands like a duck to water."

I folded an arm beneath my head like a pillow, trying anything to get comfortable, but failing. "Can we not talk about that?"

"Is that another command I hear?" Erix's voice was riddled with teasing.

"A request, nothing more. I don't want to think of anything right now. Not of tomorrow or what has happened tonight. I just want to sleep."

An arm folded over me, strong and grounding. Erix's fingers trailed close to my stomach, hovering inches away from touching the loose material of my tunic. "Then sleep."

There was no conversation left to be had. I couldn't move beneath his entrapment, and nor did I want to. This was exactly why I didn't want him to sleep away from me. Not because I cared for him being cold. It was my own selfish desire to feel... guarded. We'd seen so much darkness tonight, and I wasn't ready to battle the shadows that waited when I closed my eyes.

Not alone.

So, with Erix pressed close, I shut my eyes, welcoming the flicker of red light, easing me into the darkness. Part of me wondered if my mind would become the next hurdle in keeping me awake. I focused on Erix's breathing, counting in my head each inhale and feeling each warm exhale on the back of my neck.

Before I could reach the count of ten, I was claimed by sleep.

CHAPTER 21

I woke, bolting upright, my heart slamming in my chest like a hammer on an anvil. Not even my hand pressed above it could still the discomfort.

The room was cold and concealed in darkness. No longer did the fire glow proudly. Now it was nothing but cinders across the room's floor. And all I could see was the flashing of claws and yellow-stained teeth beneath empty, endless eyes.

"Robin. You are okay." Erix sat up beside me, hand rubbing my back in wide circles. "It was just a dream. A nightmare. I've got you."

My mouth was dry as I searched the room for the beasts of my nightmare. It took a moment to realise that I'd left the horror in sleep. The gryvern, no matter how real they felt, were not in his room.

Confusion and fear danced in a mixture that put a horrific taste in my mind.

I buried my face in my hands, trying to focus on calming my breathing.

"Talk to me," Erix said, voice rough from sleep. "Tell me what haunts you. Let me help banish it."

I couldn't put it into words. I feared that speaking the nightmare aloud would only make it real again.

My words were muffled as I spoke into my palms. "I'm fine. I just need a moment."

"Take your time. I am not going anywhere."

I was warm, even without the fire beside me. My skin itched beneath the tunic, my forehead damp with sweat. It was close to impossible to latch onto what was real and what was not. So I did what I always had after such intense dreams.

I breathed. In and out, slow, deep inhales to blow the beast of the memory from my body and mind.

Erix's fingers never left my back. He was an anchor, as my anxiety wrestled to keep control. He simply held his hand upon me, feeling the rise and fall of my curved back. It made focusing on calming my breathing easier to manage.

Steeling myself enough to look at him, I peeled my face from my hands and was greeted by a look of pure concern.

"I am sorry if I woke you," I said, voice hoarse with sleep.

Erix's expression was as calm as a lake in spring. The line of his full lips was pulled tight, his eyes heavy with sleep but alive with concern. Completely ignoring my apology, he leaned closer to me, muscles in his taut stomach rippling. His hand dropped from my back and cupped the side of my face, the other joining on the opposite side. "I have got you. Do not concern yourself with how I am feeling right now. Just focus on detaching yourself from whatever visions have haunted you."

His voice was no more than a whisper. Even the hissing of cinders across the stone-slabbed floor demanded more attention than Erix.

In the dim light, I could see every detail of his face. How the faint shadow of a beard connected seamlessly with the short cut of his mousy hair. The silver of an old scar that had nicked his top lip was so pale that it stood out only when he held an expression of such intensity. And from the flickering of his storm-grey gaze, I knew he studied me equally. His eyes traced my body, risking only for a moment to break away from my own gaze.

It could've been my exhaustion from the interrupted sleep or the disorientation the nightmare inflicted on my mind, but a truth seemed to escape my mouth before I had a chance to claw it back. "How is it that I feel so safe every time you touch me?"

Erix's eyes glowed from within, alight as though a bolt of lightning struck in the heavy clouds within. "It is my job."

"Is that all it is – I am to you?" I asked, melting into his touch. "A job?"

Erix released a long sigh, hands moving in tandem from my cheeks to the back of my head. His fingers brushed back the dark strands of my hair, so not a single one obscured my view of him. "No, little bird. You are more than that. Far more."

"Then tell me." *Distract me.* From my thoughts, from the nightmare, from the responsibility that would return to my shoulders when morning came. "I want to know what goes through that mind of yours when you look at me."

"I am not one for words," Erix warned, teeth tugging on his lower lip. "I've never been good with them, so I fear I might answer and say the wrong thing."

"It's okay," I replied, warmth spreading in my chest. "I'm shit at talking as well. I've always been better showing how I feel with... actions."

I regretted my reply for only a second, until Erix's eyes widened in realisation.

My reply was an acceptance of the invitation that'd silently been presented to me. Erix knew it, his pink tongue escaping and trailing his lower lip, leaving a glistening path across it. I lifted a hand, forefinger touching down upon his hard chest first. My hand shook slightly, stilling only when my finger left a print on his skin. I'd lain with men before, enough to count on one hand. But I was left with nothing more than a bad taste in my mouth at their memory.

But Erix was different, and deep down, I'd longed to explore his touch before I actually realised myself. And that was what I needed now. Him. The thought was selfish, I knew that, but as my hand splayed and his muscles tensed in reaction, I knew what was to come.

"If we do this, little bird," Erix started, looking down where my hand pressed against him. "I do not think I will be able to stop myself."

My mouth watered at his truth. I stared at him, deep in his eyes, and replied, "I have not asked for restraint. All I want is for you to do what it is you want to. Be selfish, Erix. That is a command."

"Are you certain that is what you want from me?" He leaned forward almost excitedly.

I chuckled to myself, already letting go of every other thought but *him*. "Take my clothes off."

Erix's hold on the back of my head stilled. "I will take that as a yes."

Not another moment was wasted. Erix's hungry hands reached for the bottom of my tunic and lifted it. I shivered as his knuckles brushed the bare skin of my stomach. The cold air of the room was welcome as it washed over my skin, the tunic now discarded upon the bedroom floor among the mounds of other forgotten items.

I was on my knees on the bed, fingers fumbling with the buttons of my trousers. Erix watched me, leaning upon his arms. There were no words to share, but urgency screamed in the air between us, so thick it made my hands shiver with anticipation. There was no room for comments or remarks, only his silent attention on me as though I was a trophy of gold that was close to his grasp.

Erix must've grown tired of his hesitancy, because his hands overtook mine, tugging with ease until the buttons popped freely. We shared a laugh as I fell back onto the bed, legs raised as Erix guided the trousers from me, exposing the bare skin of my legs.

It was my time to watch him. It seemed as though his stare didn't miss a single detail. He drank me in, brows furrowed as he discarded my trousers without thought.

Erix placed two fingers on my calf, running them upwards slowly. Each inch he grew closer to my groin sent a buzz through my blood. "Have you ever done this before?"

His question was painfully clear.

I nodded, holding his gaze as it found my eyes once again. "I have experience, if that answers your question sufficiently"

"It does." Erix released a tempered breath, mouth parting into a grin. "Although. forgive my brash nature, but no experience will prepare you for me, little bird."

His comment didn't unnerve me. Far from it. An explosion of euphoric thrill filled my body, as if I was made up of it rather than muscle and bone.

I lay still as his touch tickled over the bulge in my briefs, coming to stop over the hard layer of my lower stomach. For a moment, I believed his hand would linger; but when it didn't, a small twinge of disappointment struck.

"I've heard that before," I said. "And every time, I've come away disappointed. What makes you think you will be any different to the others, Erix?"

He lowered himself down upon me, so close I could almost taste the sharp tang of sweat that laced his skin. "I will show you."

"Then do it. Show me…" was all I could muster as a reply when his lips pressed down upon mine.

This connection was soft. My eyes closed as if by instinct, not wanting that sense to distract me from the pure explosion of his physical touch. I didn't need to see him to enjoy him.

His taste, the brush of his tongue, the nip of his teeth.

I loved every bit of it.

My hands reached up, cupping the sides of his face. I was briefly aware of his closed fists propping him up above me, pressed onto either side of the mattress, entrapping me in a cage of his flesh.

It began with just our lips, moving in synchronicity, like a lullaby of waves against sand. Erix moved, and I followed, tugged by his strong current of desire. Then our lips parted further, allowing our tongues to join the dance.

I could taste him, sweet like peaches glazed in honey, but then I would breathe in and smell burning fire and the undertones of spiced cinnamon. He was a glory of any sense I had. Erix fulfilled me in more ways than I could even begin to comprehend.

This was what I desired. A distraction unmatched. The only thought I could grasp onto was *him*. How his tongue moved with trained and experienced flicks, enough yet not too much. I noticed how his tensed arms shook as he held himself up above me, his broad shoulders a layer of protection from the shadows beyond him.

And I wanted *more*.

I rocked upwards, breaking the kiss. Erix didn't resist as I urged him onto his back beside me, my hands so small and smooth against the prickle of his defined chest. His lips were plump and red, the skin around them raw and wet.

"Have you had enough already?" he asked, voice crackling like flames across dry wood.

"Not yet," I muttered, the bed creaking as I moved onto my knees. Erix must have known what was to come as he willingly allowed me access to him, lifting his arms and resting his head in his hands behind him. "Unless you would prefer to stop me?"

"I do not think I have the ability to use that word with you, little bird. Not now. Not tomorrow. Not ever."

My heart seemed to spin for a moment, catching me off guard. "Ever is a long time."

"You are right, it is," he replied.

I wanted to scold him for a moment, to voice that this was a distraction and for him not to put strange and unseen thoughts in my head. So, I punished him in the only way I knew how.

With my mouth.

Tease him.

Erix's stomach muscles tensed as my eyes roved over him; it seemed his skin felt the very path of my gaze.

The size of a partner never bothered me, truly. It was usually how they used their length that mattered. But unravelling what was beneath a man's trousers always seemed like part of the fun, a mystery that I enjoyed unveiling. And as my eyes found the hard outline of Erix's cock – tucked up into the buttoned waist of his under shorts – I knew this was yet another reason as to why Erix deserved my attention.

Erix's confidence had certainly suggested he was well... endowed. But actually seeing his length peeking out the top of his waistband confirmed my suspicions.

The insides of my cheeks pricked with spit, my tongue desperation for connection.

My hand wasted not another moment in reaching beneath the material of his briefs. My grip met with long, thick and hard warmth. I took hold of Erix, spurring a pleasured sigh followed by the suck of tongue against teeth; in my hold, his cock seemed to flinch with its own excitement.

I shifted into a better position, my head further down his body. It took little effort to wriggle the briefs down his thick thighs, exposing every inch of him, and there was much to expose.

Dropping his cock, I let it smack down upon his hard-lined stomach, the tip reaching as far as his belly button, resting just above it. Erix flinched, but not from pain, more in disappointment that I'd released him. But from my angle, a bubble of nerves mixed with the excitement of what was to come sighed from his parted mouth.

Erix was undoubtedly the largest I'd been with, and I barely believed we were both prepared for what was to come. Yet the thought didn't deter me from lowering my mouth to the base of his cock and pressing my tongue to the firmness of his skin.

Erix exhaled a single breath as I laced my tongue from his base, all the way upwards, stopping only to inhale when my lips fit over the perfect curve of his tip. Then I buried him deep in my wet mouth, sparing not an inch.

My jaw ached within moments. Erix was far more than a mouthful, but in the same sense, he was a challenge. And I loved a challenge. Cautious to keep my teeth at bay and my tongue moving, I worked him up and down. Wrist following the dance of my jaw. I felt powerful as he wriggled beneath my touch. Erix didn't care for silence, instead vocalising his enjoyment in groans and moans that lit the night.

"Just your mouth..." he commanded through heavy breaths. The deep rattling of his voice made a moan escape from me.

I took my hand away, looking up at him, my lips glistening with spittle as I removed his length from my mouth. "Who are you to make commands when my teeth are so close to causing discomfort?"

His gaze was so intense that it could have sparked the flames back in the dead fire behind us. "No. Hands." A grin etched across his face. "I am not ready to finish just yet."

But he was close, and that made me smile. Truthfully, I could taste the kiss of his seed lathering my tongue.

He was delicious in every sense of the word.

But I did as Erix wished, thankful for his authority as it only motivated me to perform for him. His cock slipped back between my lips, my hands gripping onto his stomach to keep them from wandering back downwards. I cared little for the ache in my neck, jaw and back, the feeling completely forgotten when a rough hand gripped the hairs at the back of my head and kept up the momentum of my motion.

I tasted his want to release. It trickled into my mouth, sweet and dangerous, urged on by his quicker, more rushed guidance and peaking groans of pleasure.

All of a sudden, it came to a stop.

Erix reached down for me, fingers tangling in my hair, his other hand pulling his cock from my mouth. He urged me up to greet him, tugging at my hair to control me. Our mouths crashed together, it was not soft this time but deep and hard. I latched my teeth onto his lower lip and bit down to assert my dominance, which lasted no time at all, for Erix growled wildly, pushing me down until I was straddled across his lap.

His hips rocked beneath me, the hard, wet rock of flesh rubbing against my behind. I felt it soak into the material of my briefs as he held me down upon him.

Erix's two strong hands gripped either side of my arse and squeezed, pulling them apart to let the outline of his cock slip between. I bit down on his lip again in response, his mouth not once pulling away from mine. Even when he spoke, it was through the muffled press of our lips.

"I want to *fuck* you."

"You do?" A flutter of wings filled my chest. "As if that isn't obvious."

"Oh, I do." He continued rocking beneath me, eyes hungry. "I want to fuck you. To make you feel every inch of what I can offer."

Distract me.

Nerves bubbled in my chest and popped one by one as we lost each other in another passionate kiss.

Not for anything but his size and the lack of less natural lubricant. I couldn't imagine he had prepared a vial for the journey, nor that we would find any in this ruined home.

"Then what is stopping you?" I told him, breaking away breathlessly.

"You. You are so fucking beautiful, I fear hurting you. To end this quickly. When you looked up at me with those midnight, endless eyes, I could have filled your mouth. I do not think I will last long… but I want it. I want you."

For a moment, I faltered, unable to hold his gaze for a moment, fearful I would reveal my deepest and darkest of secrets. "Have me. *Take* me, Erix."

"I do enjoy when you give me commands," Erix said, proving himself as his cock pressed harder into my flesh. "I *want* you, little bird, but what do *you* want?""

"I want you," I replied, mouth salivating.

"Are you sure?" Erix gained closer, his mouth close to grazing skin. "Do you want me, or what I can offer you?"

His questions caught me off guard, but I answered it honestly anyway. There was no point in skirting around the truth now.

"Both," I admitted. "I want it all."

For a moment, I thought I'd ruined it. Exposing the truth felt easy with him. And my reply was the truth. I wanted both. A distraction from reality, but in the form of him. And *only* him.

Erix's entire demeanour softened. Effortlessly he laid me upon my back, tugging my briefs off without dropping my gaze. "Then you can have it. All of it. All of me."

My breath caught in my throat, the sound delicate even to my own ears.

Everything Erix did was practised and thoughtful. He pulled me forward and raised my legs upwards. I watched, heart beating rapidly, as he raised his hand to his mouth and spat; it glistened off his fingertips, caught only for a moment before he moved his hand back down towards his cock.

"If it hurts, I stop." His hand moved back up towards his mouth again, spitting more upon his fingers. "I follow your lead."

It took a few more cupped fingers of saliva to coat himself completely.

"I trust you." My stomach jolted with a thrill, like a bolt of lightning through darkened skies.

Erix spat upon his fingers again, but this time he didn't reach down for his length. Instead, I tensed as fingers rubbed gently across my sensitive entrance. I was like clay beneath his touch, being moulded without complaint as he rubbed his wetness across me.

I'd had sex without lubrication once before. It was rushed and foolish but thrilling all the same. However, the partner I'd claimed for one night and one night only was no match to Erix.

This would be different.

I focused on my breathing as Erix leaned forward over me. He bent down, nuzzling his face into my neck, where his mouth began to nip and suck at the skin. It took my mind off his next move.

I groaned in delight and surprise as his girth pressed against my sensitive entrance and pushed inside. The feeling was a spreading of warmth that moved through each cheek and relaxed my back. I focused on breathing, expecting the sharp discomfort of pain to follow. But it didn't. There was no pain, only pleasure, all the way until he pressed his hips right up against my arse, not a single inch of him left in the cold room.

"You're perfect," Erix breathed into my ear, breath tickling the hairs across my neck. "In every sense of the word."

I gripped onto his back, nails latching into skin, as though to stop him from leaving. My feet were numb with tingles that spread slowly up my legs. I wrapped those around him, too, held up by his hands. All the while, he did not move within me, just kept his length pressed deep inside.

"Do it," I begged as he still kissed deeply into the skin of my neck. "Fuck me, Erix."

I felt the shift of him only slightly, and that was enough for a gasp to erupt from my very soul.

"Forgive me," he said, coming up for breath.

I'd no chance to ask why he wanted my forgiveness. Not when he began to thrust. His strides were long and desperate, as though he pulled himself to an inch of leaving me before pushing back in with force that made words impossible to conjure.

Erix fucked me in all senses of the word. It was bliss incarnate.

Every now and then, he'd slow, looking down at his cock as though it was a prize of glory. He'd spit, letting the lathering fall from his mouth and onto his shaft.

Then Erix would begin again.

Droplets of sweat fell upon me like spring rain. Some trailed down the tip of his broad nose before falling, others laced the entirety of his body, covering old scars from battles long gone and the fresh cuts left over from the gryvern. Although I did little but lie there and let him devour me, my skin dampened too.

Erix had reached for my cock and worked away at it in rhythm with his fucking. It was as though he knew I was ready as much as I could sense he was close.

Storm-grey eyes rolled into the back of his head as his breathing laboured. He snapped his head back, groaning loudly to any god listening, as though they watched down above us, witnessing his grand climax.

I found mine at the same time. We shared the moment. I'd never experienced it before, sometimes leaving unfinished and disappointed. But now, here in this forgotten room, in a forgotten place, we both finished as one.

Silver, cloudy liquid splashed upon my tensed stomach as Erix allowed his to fill me within. It was impossible to know who made what sound as our bodies tensed and shivered.

The feeling was pure paradise and washed through me in a tidal wave that I almost drowned within.

Erix slowed his movements as my body grew sensitive suddenly. When he pulled himself from me, the feeling of his phantom touch lingered long after he lay down beside me, breathless.

"You are incredible," I admitted, eyes growing heavy. "*That* was incredible."

A hand reached for mine, fingers linking with my own where we lay. "I believe that title was made for you, little bird.

Not me." I didn't open my eyes as Erix leaned over and placed one last paused kiss upon my lips. He pulled away, hovering above me by inches. "There are not enough words for me to describe you by," he admitted. "Believe that."

I smiled, squinting to see his colour-blushed face, his eyes fixed to me as though he dared not look elsewhere. "Do you see something of interest?"

"You." My chest blossomed like a rose in summer, heart unfurling petal by petal. "I see you."

His thumb picked up a droplet of sweat that rolled down my cheek. For the first time, I felt a strange sense of embarrassment, as though the realisation of what I had shared and who I had shared it with came crashing down upon me.

I looked down, staring at his length which rested across his lap.

"We should sleep now," Erix said through a yawn.

I felt tiredness too, but the flash of a gryvern filled my mind in warning. "What if I'm not brave enough to close my eyes again?"

"You are brave and know that I will be here to distract you from your next night terror." Erix leaned in, pressing his forehead to my skin. "In a twisted way, I hope you have another. Just so I can do that to you over and over, again and again."

CHAPTER 22

I woke before Erix, and I felt nothing but relief at the knowledge. The moment my eyes crept open and the realisation of what'd happened between us returned to my consciousness, I itched to clamber out of bed and get some fresh air.

Was it my regret, or the worry that he'd wake with second thoughts – I wasn't sure. Either way, I needed to get out.

I dressed on quiet feet and slipped from the home, all without Erix even stirring from his position. My eyes lingered, only for a moment, on the slow rise and fall of his broad chest and the way his breath whistled out of his parted mouth.

He was my distraction, but now I needed a distraction from him, and seeing Berrow in daylight was the perfect thing to stop my mind from wandering to his touch and how my lips felt sensitive. Or, how my body still echoed with the memory of him.

The world beyond the home was white and endless. A light flurry of snow fell from the thick clouds above, not a single one allowing a slip of sunlight through. It was hard to tell the time of day without knowing where the sun was in the sky.

I stepped out into the street, footsteps blurred behind me in moments as fresh snow filled the divots I made with my boots. It was cold. Freezing. So much so that my teeth chattered in my jaws, threatening to shatter if I didn't stop. But I cared little for my own discomfort as the muffled daylight gave view to the true vision of Berrow.

Homes weighed heavy by timeless bouts of snow and ice. I couldn't imagine anyone having lived here. This was a place only of frozen, frigid air brave enough to tenant the empty and ruined homes that stood around me.

I walked up the street, footfalls muffled as though I walked on clouds of cotton. Even as I wrapped my arms around my chest, I couldn't keep the cold at bay.

The worst part of this place was the silence. Not a sound dared shatter the peace of the frozen village, which gave way to my mind's own roaring of thought.

On I moved, trying to make sense of what life in Berrow would've been like before the ruin. And in a way, it reminded me of Grove. Home, small yet cluttered, a place for working people who never got to benefit from the wealth of coin – only the wealth of life.

Skeletal trees – bark blackened with frostbite – haunted the sides of streets like guardians of death. Waiting and watching. And what unsettled me the most was the lack of wildlife. Birds didn't fly through the tense air. There were no signs of prints across the ground from deer or rabbits, creatures I would've expected to see thriving among the ruins of a village like Berrow.

It quickly became clear why.

At the end of the street, the houses and buildings simply stopped, giving way to a view that snatched my breath away. Besides the ruins of winter, there was one great difference between this place and Grove. Grove wasn't built on the precipice of a cliff. Berrow was.

Winds whipped around me, tugging at the black strands of hair and at the unfortunate bits of loose material I wore. One moment the street was ongoing, and the next, it stopped. There was the hint of an old stone wall before me, almost invisible above inches of thick, white snow; and beyond it was a view unfathomed and unimaginable. It was as though the fey god Altar punched down from the skies, carving a crater into the earth so deep and wide that I could see from here to the coastal line at the far edges of the Icethorn Court.

I raised a hand to my brow, trying to stop the fat flakes from ruining the vision before me as I looked over the land for as far as my eyes would allow. Far ahead of me, a crown of mountains proudly stood from the ground like the edges of jagged teeth, each topped with grey, white and black. From my standing, they looked small enough to pick up. But I recognised that they were each a grand size that it'd take days – if not weeks – to climb to the peak.

The land beneath me was bursting with fields, forests and hills, each covered in the white of winter but a blanket of different shades. Patches of deep ivory gave way to the dark of coal and the pure, glistening sheets of moonlight silver.

But the sight that stood out the most, where my eyes seemed drawn to, was a shard of black and ivory which stood out in the distance. Nestled among the mountain range, pointing skywards like a blade of night thrust from the bellies of the earth, was a castle.

An impressive building had been built into the walls of the mountain. The stone glistened like crystal, winking light over the land around it.

"Imeria."

I jumped out of my skin, turning to see Erix step in beside me, his face a grimace as he battled the harsh weather. He didn't apologise for his sudden appearance, even though it made my soul split from my skin. "What you are looking at is the capital of Icethorn. Your home, or what could be if you accepted it."

I glanced back from his scrunched face to the shard of obsidian stone. "Home? It feels far from it."

"The title is one that is earned. And since this is the first time you are laying eyes on it, I do not expect you to make a choice now. I only ask that you recognise it for the possibility it could be. Perhaps I should have used another word to describe it, but I am not one to sugarcoat the truth."

From a distance, it was hard to believe that the shard was anything but a shard. I couldn't make out any details. But I could imagine the grandeur. And I wanted nothing more than to stand so close before it that I could touch its walls with my bare hands.

"You should have woken me," Erix said, a tired edge to his voice. "It is not safe for you to roam alone."

"I am fine, Erix." A bubble of frustration popped in my chest.

"All I want is for you to be safe."

"And all I wanted was some fresh air. That's all."

I felt his eyes on me, but dared not turn around, frightened of what I'd find in them.

"There's something you need to understand, Robin." Erix's hand found the small curve at the bottom of my back and stayed there. "The gryvern aren't the only threat that I worry about. Look…" He lifted a finger and pointed in the distance. His arm angled upwards as though gesturing to the cloud-grey sky. "Do you see it?"

I squinted, narrowing my focus on whatever Erix wished for me to see. "I feel as though I'm searching for a needle through curtains of heavy lace. What exactly do you want me to see?"

"Just focus," he purred. "Open yourself to it. *Feel* it."

I almost gave up, sure Erix was pulling my leg. But then my eyes caught something – a movement in the distance. An unclear shape, violent and sharp. It shuddered through the sky above Imeria no different to a beast of wind, ice and ruin. It was close to impossible to make out the details, but like the mountains and the castle, it was also imposing in size. It was the colouring that made it hard to see among the rest of the grey and white of the sky. A mass of power, like a cloud of frantic energy slicing and jabbing, sped through the sky. It reminded me of a dragon, or even Gyah in her Eldrae form, but it was without wings, just a form of cold, winter wind and ice that circled the castle from the skies like a flock of birds.

But, even from my distance, I could *taste* its power. Laying my eyes upon the wild magic, it tugged at the cord that had settled calmly in my chest.

"So that is what could destroy Durmain?" I asked, almost fearful of speaking loudly as though it would hear me across the great divide and come to devour me.

"Yes. Your magic. The unclaimed power that is the threat to the Wychwood boundary and those within the human realm beyond. Robin –" The use of my name chilled my blood to ice far more than the horror we witnessed. "– it was important you saw this for yourself. Maybe it can help inform your decision."

As if what I'd seen hadn't already helped with that.

I'd listened to the talk of accepting the court and claiming it as my own, but I had not once imagined it being a physical obstacle to overcome. In fact, I'd not truly allowed myself to imagine what it had meant. Now, standing on the edge of a cliff that gave way to the rolling view of a court, *my* court, I had never felt so small.

This was the magic that came to my aid last night.

My birthright.

"No matter what decision you hope to see me make, I must tell you now… I don't think I can do it." I admitted my worry aloud, letting the words cloud before me in a puff of condensation within freezing air. "Look at it. I hardly know what I am doing with this… this power inside of me, and now I am expected to control that thing? I met a fraction of it last night, and almost didn't see it through. If you hadn't–"

I couldn't finish what I was trying to say. But Erix didn't need me to. In the silence that followed, the answer was loud.

If you hadn't have saved me with your touch.

"Do not doubt yourself." Erix's fingers tensed on my back. "It is unbecoming of a prince."

"I'm no prince," I scoffed, disagreeing. "I'm a simple man who can pour a pint of ale without wasting foam, who wishes for a family but will only ever have half of one. I'm no prince, no matter if that is the title you believe I should have."

"Actually, little bird, you're right. You are no prince, you are a king. And, most importantly, you are what you decide to be."

I sighed, tearing my attention from the cloud of frantic, jolting power to Erix, my stomach hardly settling from one beast to the other. We shared a moment of silence, my mind quickly drifting to the entanglement of our limbs in the dark room. Did he think of the same thing? His brow lifted, and his lips tightened as though something crossed his mind.

"Even if I'm to claim the court, how exactly am I to do so? That thing out there will destroy me. I'm one person, look what it's done to án entire kingdom. I'm no match for it. You cannot disagree with that."

"I have already made my thoughts clear on the matter," Erix said, his voice a rumble of deep, lush tones. "You are an Icethorn. You *are* the kingdom, whether you are willing to believe it or not."

"Your poetic words are doing nothing but distracting me from the answer I seek. Or do you not even know how I would accept the court, *if* I decided to?"

I studied Erix, waiting for him to drop my gaze or nibble on his lower lip to hide that he was going to follow up with a lie to calm me. But he never did. He held my gaze as though he watched on at a storm coming to sweep him away in a rolling wall of power. He didn't falter from my questioning, only faced it head-on.

"We were all brought up on the story of the first four children of Altar and how they claimed the courts which we live beneath to this day. It was said that they each bled for a season, blood giving way to power. It was taught that they claimed the powers, whereas I always believed it was the other way round. The aged and twisted story of the first members of the courts is the only indication of what is expected of you. But there are scholars and ancients across Wychwood tasked with researching if that is myth or guidance."

"I'm to bleed?" I repeated, skin prickling at the thought. "And let that… that *thing* enter me? That is what I must do? Seems like a risk to me."

Erix's face pinched with worry, but it was little in comparison to what I felt storming inside me. "If it is, in fact, a tale of truth, then it may be what is required. But it is far beyond my knowledge to confirm. It is merely a story, one that we should treat with caution until it is researched further."

"Then I hope they find another way," I whispered, looking back to the thundering of power as it dominated the sky above Imeria. "Even if I stop the promised storm, what is to stop the fey from still following through with war?"

"That is yet to be determined."

"I hope we find the answers we need then," I replied.

"As do I. But, little bird, remember that you have called upon the magic before. I do not doubt you can do it again. There's a seed of it within you; the tree to which that seed belongs is far out there. Like calls to like."

Watching the physical mound of power wither and thrash, I could imagine how it had damaged the Wychwood barrier to the point of destruction. It was like the smashing of an angered fist against the splintered wood of a door, banging over and over until it was ready to knock the door from its hinges.

I looked back to Berrow, then to the white sheet of the world beyond, imagining Grove and the rest of Durmain in the same state. A worry so great gripped its nasty, poisonous talons into my heart and squeezed, snatching my breath away.

"Do you really think I can do it?" I asked, my voice whisked away by the wild, roaring winds.

"I believe you can do anything you desire," Erix replied, soothing the beating of my heart like balm over a wound. "But for you to be successful, it is you who must believe. It matters little of what others think, wish or believe."

Erix echoed something I'd felt my entire life leading up to this point. I was never one to worry about what others saw of me. I'd grown used to seeing my reflection in their wide, untrusting and sometimes belittling stares. I'd hardened myself, like a rock, layering a shell of protection around my psyche to stop people's thoughts and views from hurting me.

But that'd all been stripped away, and I'd not been brave enough to realise until now.

"You must think I'm soft," I said. "Because I feel as though I couldn't live with myself, knowing what I'd unleash across the realm if I didn't do something about it."

"I think you are perfect." Erix's hand slipped from my back and wrapped itself around my side. One great tug, and I was pressed to him, his arm holding me like the folding of a wing. "Soft, maybe. But you are also brave. A brave, soft fool, who will change the course of history. I sense it."

I thanked him with a smile, but from the concerned tug of his lips, I could tell he knew I didn't think of myself the way he thought of me.

"If I have to bleed to prevent others from doing so, then my decision should be an easy one."

"And is it?" he asked.

"I don't know," I answered honestly. "But I'll figure it out."

"And I will be beside you when you do, little bird. Every step of the way."

Tension was thick in the air of Aurelia. Even the trees seemed still, as though they suffocated beneath the heavy atmosphere that'd settled over the city.

Gyah had collected us from Berrow as promised, her midnight-scaled body touching down clumsily in the snow-covered streets sometime in the early afternoon. At least, I believed it was Gyah, and not another Eldrae. Only when she landed beyond the grand castle in Aurelia did I truly know it was her. Exhausted, with eyes rimmed with shadows and skin ashen, she stumbled a step the moment she reclaimed her fey-form, weak in the legs. Erix tried to assist, but she waved him off, instead urging us to follow her immediately.

We walked through the quiet corridors of the castle, hardly a person or guard to be seen, only our footsteps echoing over the tall walls and high ceilings could be heard.

There was no room for questions, not that Gyah had refused answers, but we both knew not to speak, otherwise, it would've shattered the strange nature of the manor and the city beyond.

Mourning. Aurelia was locked in grief. That was what this feeling was like. Quiet, still and never-ending mourning. For Orion.

Guilt pinched in my gut for taking so long to notice it or even think of him. After my night with Erix, it seemed the hardness of his body and the gentle nature of his touch was all I could contemplate. It was the distraction I had longed for, but as we passed through a hallway that Orion would never have the luxury of wandering again, all I felt was selfish and wrong.

I wondered if Erix felt the same? He hardly spared me a glance the moment Gyah had collected us. But even now, walking side by side, I sensed his desire to flex a hand just for our fingers to brush.

I longed for it too, another distraction, even now.

We passed down a corridor of banners, each one barely moving, the emblem of Cedarfall's burning tree as still as water on a frozen lake.

Windows lined the opposite wall, stained with orange and red, causing waves of colour to wash over our boots. I knew this walkway from the night of the ballroom, making it clear where Gyah escorted us to.

I was thankful when Gyah broke the silence, standing before the great doors. "Good luck in there."

"Dare I ask why we require luck, Gyah?" Erix replied, lips pinched with tension.

Gyah blinked slowly, eyes heavy as though she fought to keep them open. "I am too tired for questions, Erix. Let the Cedarfall family explain. I have done what I have been required to do."

I offered her a smile, trying to show my gratitude. "Thank you, for everything, Gyah."

She studied me for a moment, eyes more alert than they'd been up until this point. Then she bowed her head as though I was both a stranger and someone of great importance, not a person she had travelled and fought beside. "It was and is my honour."

With that, she left us, one hand steadying herself along the wall as she walked away on heavy feet.

"Any guess as to what is going on?" I muttered, unable to shake the strange way Gyah looked at me.

"The vendors and shops are closed, meaning that the city has ceased normal activities in response to Orion's death. It is customary to stop normal life when a member of the head families of the courts perishes."

I swallowed the lump in my throat. "That's understandable."

But what about guards that had been my shadow since we've returned? Where are they? I'd not seen a single person here besides Gyah and Erix. The manor felt so empty.

Erix raised a palm and pressed it against the door. "Let's not keep them waiting. I have the sense that those left are behind here, waiting for us."

"Althea?" I asked, keeping his gaze even though I wanted nothing more than to look at my feet.

"Only one way to find out."

Althea did, in fact, wait for us beyond the door. She paced the empty ballroom floor with her knuckles pressed to her mouth in contemplation. She looked up at us as we stood on the balcony. She wore a fresh set of fighting leathers, with belts hugging weapons to almost every limb I could see. Even the twin-bladed axes waiting patiently at her hips had been cleaned, and I could only imagine that the curved ends of the blades were sharpened for the next time she needed to use them.

"About time," she shouted up at us. "I was moments from sending out a search party for you all."

"We are fine, Althea," Erix responded, urging me to follow him down the curved staircase. "I have never seen someone as tired as Gyah. She did her best at returning us."

"I told her we could have sent another for you, but she insisted. Do not make me feel guilty for her decision." Althea was on edge, I could tell, as though her emotions danced on the edge of a sharpened blade.

Anxiety swelled in my chest as I put myself between Althea and Erix. "Where is everyone else?"

"Taken for questioning. This is my aunt's domain, and my mother felt it necessary to ensure that every member of her household and staff are investigated. It is clear your life is at risk, and I will ensure that no member of this family, or yours, is threatened until the Passing."

"Kelsey, she *was* behind it?" I asked.

Althea shook her head at me. "Still unconfirmed. She is refusing knowledge and pleading ignorance, but my brother has lost his life. But Mother needs someone to blame. The Hunter is in for questioning, but it is clear that, beside the information he has already shared to us, he knows little more. However, for the sake of my mother's sanity and Aurelia, it is best her wrath is kept smothered... for now."

An image of fire burning through the city, and everything beyond, filled my head. Was that the power of the Cedarfall Court, much like the storm of ice that threatened the world if left unclaimed? I'd seen the destruction my family's magic could wreak; I could only imagine the burning wrath of Queen Lyra rolling over the lands and leaving nothing but ashes behind.

"How is she?" Erix asked, snapping me from the horrific image in my mind.

"Taut, like a string pulled too tight," Althea said through gritted teeth. For a moment, her stare was lost to a place behind us, but she soon snapped out of it, eyes focusing back in on me.

"My parents have awaited your return. They almost refused it, agreeing you would be safer in the lands of your court than returning here. But it set them, my mother in particular, at unease knowing you were alone there."

"He was never alone," Erix quickly added.

Althea looked to him, then back to me, as though she mentally measured the cord that glowed between us.

"I suppose he was not." Althea swept between us towards the staircase we had not long come down. "They wait for you in the next room. I would join you, but I have another that I must see first, although I will find you once we are equally well-rested."

"Briar," I called out to Althea, who faltered for a moment. She glanced back over a shoulder, her face framed with red curls that made her pale skin stand out with dramatic beauty. "Is she well?"

"Tarron Oakstorm was right. The antidote was what she needed." A faint smile, one that sang with relief, cracked across her face. "Briar is awake, and her condition has been improving rapidly since we came back."

I let my shoulders relax, fists flexing into splayed hands at my sides. "That is really good to hear, Althea."

"It is. Perhaps you can thank him for me. Saves me having to speak to him."

"Thank whom?" I asked, brows furrowed.

Erix stiffened, his fists balling at his sides, a faint rumbling building in the back of his throat.

Althea flicked her stare to the doors at the far end of the ballroom, the very same that led to the council meeting nights prior. "Our esteemed guest. Tarron Oakstorm, only son and heir to the Oakstorm Court. But make it quick. The sooner he leaves Aurelia, the better."

CHAPTER 23

The queen and king of the Cedarfall Court sat slumped on twin chairs, eyes red-rimmed and cheeks flushed with sorrow. Their pain rolled off them in waves so intense it nearly had me stumbling back. I was evermore thankful for Erix's presence and the hand that he'd not removed from my back the moment we entered the room.

"Orion's body is kept at the capital of Farrador, ready for the burial ceremony, which will be held in a matter of days," Queen Lyra explained, voice horse and quiet. "It would be custom to invite the members of each court, but as it stands, a family affair would be preferred. It is what he would have wanted. Orion was never one for fanfare."

I hated the silence that followed, so I filled it – giving myself something to say.

"I am deeply sorry for your loss." I felt the need to say it aloud but regretted it as Queen Lyra winced as though the sincerity in my voice pained her.

"As am I, Robin." Lyra bowed her head, eyes glittering with unspent tears. "It should be criminal for a parent to see the life cycle of their child end so abruptly. I only wish there was a law I could implement to prevent this from happening, but alas, here we are."

I bowed my head as Erix spoke over my heavy thoughts. "We will see that the Hunter is punished for his crimes."

"Settle down," King Thallan added, leaning forward in the

chair, his knuckles white as he gripped the armrests. "It is believed that Lady Kelsey is as much to blame. And it is her head I would prefer to see severed and spiked for this. She was the puppet master, the Hunter was merely a boy at the end of her strings. As much a victim as Orion."

"*If* her involvement is proven, my sister will answer for her crimes. But only when I am certain she was, in fact, involved. I have not come to a conclusion as of yet," Queen Lyra added, sparing her husband a look with grief-stricken eyes.

It was clear that both the queen and king held different views on what had occurred. King Thallan held darker thoughts towards his wife's sister, whereas Queen Lyra was not prepared to solidify her decision.

Lady Kelsey might have aided in Orion's death, but she was still family. And until proof was found that she was directly involved in the Hunters being on Icethorn land, or the gryvern attack, no brash action would be sought after.

"Do you require my assistance with the Hunter's interrogation?" Erix asked. "I offer myself if you do."

"You are to shadow Robin until the Passing. Only after he claims his court will you be required to leave him. Not for a moment before. I trust I don't need to explain why this is necessary?"

My skin itched as they spoke on my behalf as though I was not here. "I saw the power which I'm to claim. Forgive me for distrusting in my own ability, but do you know how or what I'm to do? I feel as though I'm going in unprepared, and I know that'll only lead to failure. I don't like the idea–"

"And I do not particularly like that my son lost his life, yet here I am, and there you are." A sudden flare of heat boiled in the air, making me turn my head to the side. There was no visible fire or flame, only the sizzling ripples of air melting from Queen Lyra's skin.

I bowed my head, apology for my stupid use of words fumbling over my lips.

"History of the fey is a long, complicated thing, and I can assure you my finest scholars are searching for confirmation as to what is required for you to claim your birthright. We have our suspicions, but I cannot deny it is an uncertain path, one that is not clear. Yet. Never in our history has the power been left without someone to control it. If Julianne had introduced you to court when you were born, your tie to the magic would've been already accepted."

"Understood," I replied, trying not to shy away from her controlled flare of anger. I wasn't ready to dive into my mother's actions, or lack thereof. "Erix has explained as much as he could, but I'm still cut short on what I can do."

"If I had known *he* was such a well-taught historian, then perhaps he would have been in the libraries, and you would have another as a shadow." There was a sharpness to King Thallan's comment, as though he meant it to sting. But Erix did not flinch, only stared ahead, seemingly unscathed and unbothered.

"Well," I bit back, unable to stop myself. "Considering he's the only one who is willingly giving me answers, I think it is best that he is my shadow." I felt defensive at Thallan's remarks about Erix. The strange feeling twisted and coiled within me, ready to strike in protection like a snake made of steel.

"Robin," Erix cooed, fingers tensing on my back. "Best not ruffle anymore feathers."

"No. Regardless of what has happened, no one is granted the right to speak to a person like that. Especially not someone like you, who has offered nothing but support." I spared him a glance, but only briefly before focusing my daggered stare back on the grieving queen and king. "I might not know much about the courts and the fey, but I understand that if I'm to claim my mother's court, then it puts *us* on equal footing, so I request that you treat me as such."

A king – just as Erix had told me.

"Are you so absorbed that you cannot see what we are doing for you, Robin Icethorn." Queen Lyra used my name as a weapon, carving it into me as if to prove it belonged there. "This entire manor has been cleared out to ensure your safety and success. My own family's lives are put on the line in order to keep you breathing. Do not think for a moment that we are not taking this matter seriously. You may be our equal, but a lesson for you to remember is you are still a guest in my court. Ensure it is known that my own bloodline is suffering for a mistake your mother has made. If you hold resentment, do not take it out on me."

"Mistake?" I asked, head tilting in question as though I had not quite heard her correctly. "Care to elaborate on what you mean by that?"

"Oh, I believe it is very clear." Tears glistened in her widening eyes, yet not a single one spilt down the curve of her pale skin. "Leaving you to be brought up by a man who would never truly understand you. Keeping you in the dark of who you are, and what you mean to our people." Her tears fell furiously over her cheeks. My eyes pricked too, as Lyra spoke every hurt I had harboured in the dark, and brought it to the light. "And yet, her gravest mistake of all, was not getting to cherish the little time she had with her own son. What I'd give for one more conversation with Orion, and yet Julianne had no qualms with leaving you–"

"I think that is enough." King Thallan's voice boomed over us all, a wave of command that I had not yet seen from the man.

I couldn't breathe. Lyra's words cut deep, because they were true.

If my legs worked, perhaps I would've fled the room entirely. As if reading my intention, Erix stepped before me, blocking the view of the queen, although her sobs persisted. He laid both hands on my shoulders, anchoring me to the ground. "They are only trying to help, little bird. But you are no mistake." His hands ran down from my shoulders to my upper arms and squeezed. "Do you hear me?"

"She is right," I gasped, struggling to catch my breath. "Nothing she said was wrong."

I brushed him aside, facing Queen Lyra, whose eyes darkened with regret. Before she could apologise, I began to speak.

"I spoke out of turn," I said, trying to soften my voice as I spoke through gritted teeth. Erix moved back to his post beside me, returning his hand to my back. "And for that, I apologise."

Queen Lyra simply tipped her head but did not say a word.

"Your father has been asking for you." King Thallan quickly changed the subject, grasping my attention. "We have kept him to his room, ensuring he is out of harm's way. Unlike your arrival, we have been able to keep his presence in Aurelia to only those we trust. You may want to visit him to let him know you are well."

Witnessing Lyra's grief over her son, hearing her words echo in my skull, made my desire to fall into my father's arms unignorable.

"Thank you," I said, bowing my head.

King Thallan's unwavering gaze dropped to the floor as though he'd been struck with a memory too hard to ignore. And it hit me, that look of grappling grief. Unlike me and my father, Thallan would never get the chance to look into his son's eyes again.

I almost turned to leave, but something stopped me. A need to speak my truth, in hopes it helped them.

"Orion fought valiantly by our side, even though his views on my... future differed from yours," I said, allowing every bit of sincerity into my voice.

Queen Lyra reached for her husband's hand and squeezed it, gripping onto him as though the tide of sorrow was moments from dragging him away. He slowly lifted his spare hand and placed it upon hers, a tethering of flesh and bone to one another.

"I do hope you both get the time you need and deserve to deal with this. My deepest condolences."

"Your kind words are appreciated, Robin," Queen Lyra thanked me, voice breaking enough to notice. "I suppose we have already required a reminder as to just how important kinder words are. So, with that, I too am sorry."

"No, Queen Lyra. For once, it's refreshing to hear the truth, no matter how painful it is."

"The truth may be painful," she replied, "but it is also what will set us free. We are old enough to know that the pain will soon fade. But I am also wise enough to understand that this wound, deep and terrible as it is, will never truly go, and nor would I want it so. Orion was my firstborn. The reason why we had so many children was because the feeling of swelling love when I first held him was like no other in the world."

Erix placed a hand across his chest and rested it above his heart. "May he rest."

"May he rest." King Thallan looked up, echoing the sentiment like a prayer or song.

"May he rest indeed," a new voice spoke, appearing from out of nowhere.

Beside the twin thrones, the air seemed to shiver. I looked, narrowing in on the empty space the deep voice had come from. One moment there was nothing. The next, the air seemed to split in two, carved by an unseen knife. Yellow light shone from the seam in the air. It was as if a doorway had opened, revealing the very sun within it. But this was no door. There were no doors on this side of the room.

Erix tensed but didn't reach for a weapon. Queen Lyra and King Thallan hardly reacted to the miracle I beheld, whereas I couldn't do anything but watch as the spindle of light gave way to a tall form, haloed in a bright glow that blurred all features and secrets.

Until the man stepped with both feet beyond, and the light simply vanished, leaving the room as though nothing had changed. All besides the person who now stood with us.

Long, curling dark-brown hair fell on either side of his face, resting over his shoulders; although thick, it did little to hide the sister points of ears that poked free on either side. He smiled, staring at me as though I was the only person in the room. I watched his deep, sun-kissed skin pull over high cheekbones as he held his grin, bright ocean-blue eyes devouring me where I stood.

I knew those with unending wealth would pay hoards of coin for jewels as blue as this man's eyes. And from the knowing smirk he showed me, he knew it himself.

"Tarron," Erix groaned the name from my side.

So this was the Oakstorm heir Althea was talking about. He wore a white shirt, sleeves rolled up to the elbows. Rings of dark metal flexed across almost all his fingers as he twisted them before him as though he longed to keep them busy. His leather breeches were form-fitting, highlighting just how long his legs were, but not taking away from the fact he could kick a door down with little effort if he so desired. The boots he wore showed no sign of scuffing across their polished surface.

"Well, I do hope I did not interrupt anything too important," he said, voice almost purring.

I almost answered, still entrapped in the strange trance that I felt as though he only spoke to me.

But then King Thallan called back, bringing me back to the room. "Never, your presence is always welcome here."

"That *is* good to know." Tarron ran his fingers through his hair, tucking some behind an ear. It gave way to a view of his long neck and broad shoulders. He was a specimen, and from the sly smile he had still not dropped, he knew it. "An invitation is an invitation. No matter the form of entrance, I suppose."

"Robin, this is–" Queen Lyra began, only to be silenced by heavy footfalls as Tarron strode forward towards me, finishing her sentence.

"Robin Vale," Tarron said, mere steps before me. He looked down a strong nose as he inspected me, hardly blinking as he did so. "It truly is a pleasure to see you in the flesh. And my, I must admit I am in awe of your story thus far."

Regardless of his words, I was hooked on one thing in particular.

"You just said my name," I muttered, intrigued.

Not the one I was told I was, but the one I'd only ever known.

"What else am I to call you?" He cocked his head to the side, playful eyes ablaze with light.

"Vale. That isn't something I've heard since being here." No one had called me that since arriving in Wychwood. Yet here Tarron stood, and he'd not called me by the court I was *destined* to claim.

"Well yes. That is all I know you to be. Perhaps you will tell me otherwise. But, oh my, how awfully rude." He stepped back, forced surprise plastered across his face. Then he bowed a head, only slightly, still with that grin cutting across his cheeks as though it always belonged there. "Robin Vale, it is a pleasure to meet you. A surprise as well, but a pleasure all the same."

I couldn't ignore the emphasis on my name this time. He dragged it out, rolling the letters over his tongue as though tasting it for the first time.

"And you," I replied, trying to steady my voice. I felt a hand on my back stiffen and remembered Erix was close beside me.

"Erix," Tarron spared him a glance, turning slowly to regard my shadow. "I would say I am surprised you have been chosen as his personal guard. Only the best, I suppose."

They knew each other. That much was clear. And not simply on a first name basis either. History hung between them, thick and thunderous, at least from Erix, who likely flexed every muscle in his body as he studied Tarron. Whereas Tarron just smiled, which only seemed to agitate Erix further.

"Tarron Oakstorm," I said, retrieving his attention back to me. "I have been told I am to thank you."

"Well, do go ahead."

"I think that is sufficient."

The prince of the Oakstorm Court stood before me proudly, releasing a breath that stirred the hairs upon my head.

"Tarron has been sharing his gift with those who require it," King Thallan said from his seat. "Without his knowledge, Althea's little friend may not have seen it through."

"That dear girl – Briar, is it? Ah yes. The Taster. It was a challenge to heal her, but then again, I do enjoy a challenge." My skin itched as Tarron repeated words I'd not held in relation to Erix. "Tugwort is a nasty poison, but even that has an antidote if you know where to look."

"And I suppose you heard about what happened when we went to get that antidote?" I asked, unable to stop myself.

The queen shifted awkwardly in her seat, leaning forward as if equally desperate to hear how Tarron would respond.

His entire body changed. His expression hardening into one of disgust. "I did. And, trust me. I will personally be checking in on that Hunter to make sure they pay for defiling your homeland, Robin."

Well, that wasn't what I expected him to say. But even if I didn't want to, I believed his reaction was genuine.

"Briar will not be tasting a single speck of my food again," I said, choosing to skip the thank you... for now.

"Putting others before yourself, Robin." Tarron turned on his heel towards the queen and king. "I am beginning to think it is a waste if he does not accept Icethorn and its power, no matter how disappointing that would be for me. He would make a fine king."

"It is not clear what decision is being made," Queen Lyra spoke up. "But for the sake of his aid in saving my daughter from Hunters, we will support him."

"You will?" Tarron paced the floor as though he owned it. "I suppose you have the perfect reasoning behind your sudden support *against* our plans. I cannot fault you for that. However,

I do find it strange that a year since the last Passing, you have suddenly changed your tune over a single man. Was it not yourselves who donated a rather large fund towards the campaign only a year ago? Is it not your capital that houses our armies?"

"Minds can change like the tide," King Thallan spoke up. This time it was he who seemed to want to pounce from his chair.

"They can do indeed." Tarron shot a glance back to me, lower lip nipped briefly between straight, white teeth.

"If you do not mind," I said, wanting nothing more than to leave this conversation. It had been a long day, with an even longer night prior, and I wanted to see my father before my legs gave out from exhaustion. "As much as I enjoy being spoken about as though I am not here, I think it may be my time to visit my father."

"Understood, he will like that," Queen Lyra said quickly, as though she were waiting for a reason to end this conversation. Even Erix relaxed by my side for a moment before Tarron spoke up once again.

"If that is the case, I must insist I escort you to him. Firstly, to apologise for making you feel so... unseen. And secondly, for I have much to ask you, as I am sure you have much to ask me. The walk would give us the perfect time to speak."

"No," Erix snapped, standing before me as a shield of height and muscle.

"Settle down, *pup*," Tarron said, laughing through his dismissive tone. "I understand you take your job rather seriously. Believe me, I do. However, my skill set suggests I am far more prepared to protect Robin than those dirtied blades at your hips."

Erix shook violently, looking to the queen and king for aid, but they didn't provide it.

"The choice is Robins to make," Queen Lyra finally said, tired eyes falling shut with each prolonged blink. "Erix, you could do with a rest yourself."

"What do you say, Robin Vale?" Tarron extended a hand. The tips of his fingers were not the same golden glow as the rest of his skin. Down towards his knuckles, his skin was pale, as though overwhelmed by frostbite or molten silver. It made the dark rings only stand out more. "Will you do me the honour of your time?"

"No…" Erix repeated through a jaw clenched shut. "He is in *my* care."

"And Robin is in my court," Queen Lyra snapped. "Erix, take this as an excuse to rest. You clearly need it."

"But–"

"Dismissed, Erix."

The decision was made for me, however, I had time to answer for myself. Deep down, I did want to explore the stranger before me whose blue eyes glowed with willing stories.

I reached for Erix, trying to slip my hand into his closed fist. "I'll be fine. I'm only going to see my father, and for that I would want space for anyway."

He turned on me with wide eyes of surprise, mouth parted as though he could not decide on what to say to me.

"Is that a yes to my invitation?" Tarron's smooth voice interrupted the moment. I waited for Erix to speak, wondering if he would say the right thing and encourage me to come with him, but he said nothing. He pulled his hand out of my reach and turned for the double doors.

Anger pulsed through me, a feeling I didn't expect to feel as I watched Erix walk away in his boiling silence.

"Yes," I replied, as Erix reached for the handle and stilled. "I accept."

Erix ripped the door open with such violence I almost expected it to part from its hinges.

"Well…" Tarron offered me the crook of his arm. "Where *shall* we begin?"

CHAPTER 24

Tarron strode beside me, straight back and chin held high. I tried to keep my expression void of emotion, but I was confident he caught me side-eyeing him as we moved through the manor.

It was his ever-widening grin that gave him away.

"I feel as though it is only polite to ask how your stay in Aurelia has been. Although I am more than aware of the events that have occurred, which seem truly ghastly. And I admit, Lady Kelsey may have the same goal in mind as I, but I would never go so far as to threaten a guest in my home."

His arrogant tone had my hackles rising. "Lady Kelsey has not yet been put to trial."

"Do you believe she is innocent?"

"Until proven guilty... isn't that how the saying goes?"

Tarron clicked his tongue over his perfectly straight teeth. The sound made my skin shiver. "I know little of the humans and their ways, nor do I particularly care to know. But I admit you intrigue me."

"I'm not human," I retorted, wishing our destination would hurry up. "Not completely."

"Well, wouldn't that depend on your decision?"

Perhaps accepting Tarron's invitation was a mistake. Queen Lyra had made it clear that Tarron knew the location of Father's dwelling and was well equipped to guide me. It aided in confirming that he was clearly trusted by the queen, but something about him unsettled me.

As soon as we'd left them, grieving in their thrones, I wished I had listened to Erix. I wondered where he would be. What he would be thinking. Even now, I could still feel the lingering taste of his distrust and anger towards Tarron. Compared to Erix and his rather lacklustre ability to talk about himself, I placed my bets that Tarron would be easier to get answers out of. He was clearly the type who enjoyed hearing his own voice.

"I think my blood, and ears, would already suggest that my end decision has nothing to do with who I am."

"But you are not full-blooded fey. Not an uncommon occurrence among our kind. But you are not just a mundane human either. You are an Icethorn, if you wish to be. I still cannot believe an Icethorn would have found themselves entangled with a human, creating off-spring."

"You speak of me as though I'm cattle." Even I winced at the snap of my voice. "Don't. It's not very becoming."

"Becoming." Tarron repeated, chuckling as though this was a game. "I suppose it is not. I am simply trying to explain how this works and what makes you such an interest in my eyes. When word about you reached me, I knew I had to see for myself. I practically waited for the invitation at my borders. Then when I arrived and found you had gone, I felt some disappointment."

"Nice to know that I cause you discomfort, Tarron," I said coldly. "Even if I'm a little sorry about that."

Tarron slowed his pace as we rounded a corridor, approaching two closed doors before us. Without hesitation, he reached for the one on the right, as though he knew these pathways and rooms beyond like the lines on his palm. This was not his court, but he clearly believed it could be. He knew it well enough.

"Take my advice, Robin. Those of our standing should never apologise."

"So people keep telling me." I followed him through the door, the smooth ground giving way to a narrow, winding staircase. "I believed you didn't want to see me as an equal though. Like you said, you and Lady Kelsey have one thing in common. Neither of you wants to see me claim Icethorn as my court. It would ruin your precious plans of domination of the human realm."

"Domination?" Tarron pondered the word as he climbed the stairs first. The space was so narrow we could not walk side by side, which meant I could allow the torrent of faces to be made behind his back. "I do not see it as such."

"You do not deny it then?"

Tarron trailed his pale fingers along the curved, brick walls, rings glinting in the dull light that seeped through the many, narrow glassless windows. "You are right, I will not lie. I do not want you to claim Icethorn as your court."

His words should have made me feel unsafe, but the worry and nerves didn't greet me. If Tarron wanted to harm me, he would've done so. He could turn on me now and push me down the stairs where I'd have little chance to soften the fall. Whatever it was he wanted from me, it was not to see me harmed. Erix had left me with him, even if he did not want to; that told me enough.

"Then what do you want, Tarron?"

"To avenge my family."

It hit me then, as though the wall beside me crumbled and toppled above me, burying me in a memory, a story about Tarron's mother and brother being taken by the Hunters years ago.

I softened my voice, honest sorrow for his loss coursing through me. "I know the feeling of losing a family."

"I do not mean to offend you, Robin, but you cannot lose something you never had. Grieving the idea of a person you wished to know is far less painful than it would be if you knew her in blood and flesh. I was young when they took my mother and my brother. But old enough to still remember the pain as though the dagger stabbed in my heart shattered, pieces of steel still lost within me. That feeling never goes."

"And seeing the humans suffer will help locate those pieces in you and remove them one by one?" The question was blunt but honest. Flashes of Berrow covered in snow and torn by winds had me thinking of home once again.

"Maybe it will ease the pain, I won't know until it happens." Tarron paused, one foot resting on the step before him, hand holding his weight as he leaned against the wall as though he was catching his breath. "Maybe it will do nothing. How does it feel knowing the people beyond our lands also killed your family?"

My own breath caught and lodged in my throat as Tarron turned to face me. He was steps ahead, towering over me in the shadow of the stairway. His long, dark hair hung in curls over his shoulders, cloaking his face but not doing anything to hide the glow of his lightning blue stare.

"If I knew who was behind it, I'd happily hold the knife that would end them. But I wouldn't want to see thousands suffer in my search for that one person." It was the first time I had said it aloud, as though I'd not allowed myself to think of what I would do if I faced the person who was responsible for my mother's death.

"Then you are a better person than me."

I held his stare, my heart in my chest. Tarron leaned towards me, his loose tunic shifting to reveal the curve of a hairless chest. He was tall and narrow, like a weed, no doubt as stubborn as one. However, there was no denying he was beautiful. But then, the deadliest things often were.

"That's yet to be determined," I replied. It was the first time I had not seen him with a smile as that was all he had done since meeting me. His lips were straight, eyes empty of anything revealing as he studied me.

"What if I told you that your mother was not the only thing you lost the day the humans sent their gryvern to attack?"

"What do you mean?" My mind could not comprehend what he had to say next.

"Like me, you lost a brother, but you also lost three sisters in the murder. A family you would have no doubt met one day down the line if that future was not snatched from you."

I looked to the floor, mind racing. "I did not ask for the reminder…"

"Of course, you did not. I trust you have not been told much of your home and heritage. Ignorance is bliss in the eyes of many, but I wish to know that no detail has been kept from you." Tarron stepped down, closing the space between us. I hardly cared or noticed as he placed a ringed hand on my shoulder. "There is much I can tell you that others may want to keep secret, locked away just like they are doing with you now, and the man who waits behind the door at the top of his tower. It is not long before the Passing when you are required to make your decision. No better time to become king then when seasons change, and autumn passes to winter. But the outcome, if you choose not to claim Icethorn, does not need to end in your demise, all of which I can explain if you give me the chance to."

I looked up through my lashes, body numbing as what he'd hinted at sunk in. Siblings. Something I'd longed for but also long had given up hope of. Did Father know? If he had loved Mother and she him, he must have. I couldn't imagine keeping anything from those I loved.

Unlike my father, who kept a lot from me.

The curling of power lifted its presence like a snake, uncoiling as it woke.

"You look so much like them," Tarron said, voice no more than a whisper. "Even if I had doubts before seeing you… they all disappeared the moment I saw you. It is like looking at a memory brought back to life."

I lifted a hand, touching my fingers to my cheek gently, then the vision of dark hair billowing in winds, and the lullaby voice returned. "You know, no one ever wants to talk to me about them."

"Or have you simply not asked the right questions?" Tarron asked calmly. "Secrets are only secrets because of selfish people and their selfish gain. I would ask yourself why you think those around you believed this information was not important to share. They all want you to claim the Icethorn Court but are not telling you what it is, exactly, that you are commanded to take."

"I wish to know everything," I said. Tarron's smile returned, this time void of arrogance or sarcasm.

"I am an open book, Robin. You simply need to turn my pages and read."

My father's room lacked the comforts of my own. This was a prison of brick and barred windows, high up in the tower with no other exit than the one door we had opened to get inside. A single guard was stationed, armed to the teeth with blades, though whether to protect what was inside or to stop him from leaving, I wasn't unsure.

"I thought you'd forgotten about me." Father's voice was rough, as though he'd not used it for a long while. But still, he stood from the bed, waiting with open arms. Reluctantly I let myself fall into them, wondering of all the truths that Tarron had revealed to me. Father pressed a breathy kiss to my hair and held me firmly.

"Never," I replied, my arms hanging limp beside me. "I left Aurelia for a couple of days. I would have come sooner, but…"

My voice trailed off.

"You were busy learning the side I've kept from you. I understand, Robin. You don't need to explain yourself to me. Just do your old man a favour and tell him everything you've discovered."

I slipped from his hold, turning my back on him to inspect the room. Trays of empty plates and scraps of food littered the floor, equally as forgotten as my father in this room. Tankards of water, some empty and most full, waited for someone to drink. They must have been here a while, for dust layered their still surfaces.

"Nice prison cell you have here," I said.

"Could be worse, son. The walls are thick, they do well at keeping the cold out. It might not look like much, but I've slept better in the days passed than I have in years."

"It's still a prison though."

Father stepped in behind me. "I can leave if I choose to. Return to Grove and await what is to come. Instead, I stay here. With you. *For* you. If this is a prison, then lock the door and throw away the key."

I could've laughed, but I didn't have the energy to spare.

I loosed a breath and let down the floodgates that kept in my thoughts. "Did you know I had siblings?" I wrapped my arms around my waist, hunching forward as the weight of my thoughts became too much to bear alone. "A brother and sisters?"

"I did."

The air chilled between us.

"And you decided that I wasn't welcome to that information as well?"

Father reached a hand for me, but I pulled away. It hurt him. His rugged, aged face showed signs that my rejection pained him. "I didn't want to give you reasons to go searching for them. I lost your mother. I didn't want to lose you too."

"It's clear to me now that the fey and humans share one thing in common. You all lie." I took a deep breath in, noticing the swell of my anxious heart. "You should have told me. I deserved to know."

"There is much I should've done. In hindsight, I wish I'd dealt with everything differently. But I can't go back and change the past now. Just know that everything I did was to protect you. Or at least that was my intention. I see now that what I should've understood was you didn't need protecting. You grew out of that a long time ago."

Father reached for me again, and this time I stopped myself from pulling away.

"All of this has been put upon me all at once," I said, voice trembling. "It makes thinking about anything of importance rather difficult."

"You can ask me anything. I'll never lie to you again."

I wanted to explain to him that the damage was done, but a shifting silhouette caught my eye. A shadow, for a brief moment, blocked the light of the high window at the wall far behind Father. I blinked, expecting it to be tiredness that caused the illusion. Maybe Tarron had come in to get me, or Erix had returned to check I was still in one piece.

But the person I saw, landing on soft feet upon the floor of the room, was not either of them.

Cloaked in black, they crouched down, ready to spring forward at the quickest of moments.

I tried to move Father behind me, but the figure was faster. A flash of metal glistened, brought free from the dark material that covered the intruder's body. Then they sprang forward, pouncing across the air like a cat chasing its prey, all before I could utter a single word.

CHAPTER 25

Father's back was to the assailant, blissfully unaware of the weapon outstretched inches from him. I pushed at his frame with as much force as I could muster, trying to get him out of the way. There was no time to regret the clatter of his knees as they smacked into the floor. I preferred his pain over his death.

Then it was only me and the attacker, who I quickly realised was not here for my father but for me. But this was different to all the attempts before. This time I was prepared to face them.

Their dark eyes, shrouded in shadow, stayed on me, caring little for the older man gasping on the floor to our side. A knife, dark and ominous, jabbed towards me with lightning precision, its tip catching the dull light, revealing the layering of liquid across it. More poison, no doubt.

I threw myself backwards, blindly, back slamming into the corner of unmoving furniture. Pain lanced my side as the wind in my lungs was knocked out of me.

"Robin!" Father shouted, pushing himself to stand. I recognised the faint noise of a struggle on the other side of the door. There was no time to focus on that when a fist gripped a hold of my tunic and lifted me from the ground.

The assailant was on me, arm pulled back and ready to stab. Then we both clattered to the floor as my father's hulking body tackled the attacker off me. We were a mess of limbs and panic as the three of us wrestled for control. Father had a hold of the attacker, arm wrapped around their throat as he pulled them off.

"Get out of here," Father shouted. "Now."

There was no *fucking* chance I was leaving.

I crawled out of harm's way, watching as the attacker raised a curved hand and sliced the dagger across Father's arm. Blood blossomed, dark ruby. Father called out in agonised anger, arms loosening in response. It was exactly what the attacker needed to get free from the hold.

Father tried to reach out again, but his hands were slick with his own gore. Out of his reach, the assailant was upright once again, racing on soundless feet for me. Cold, frigid tendrils of power escaped from my chest and filled my consciousness. A cloud of silver breath fogged beyond the attacker's face covering. The dark swathe of material that rested perfectly across the bridge of their nose did little to keep my power out. I threw my hands out, willing the magic within to assist me.

The attacker halted before a jagged slicing of ice burst a step before them. Another moment later, and they would've been impaled. My attempt didn't end them as intended, giving me little time to ready myself for my next move.

I was quick, but the attacker was quicker – skilled and clearly trained.

Father was up again, swinging a wooden chair with a mighty roar. That was his grave mistake. It warned the attacker of his attempt to save me. The attacker turned on light feet, dodging the attack. The unbalanced momentum sent father pinwheeling straight into the attacker's embrace. Time stilled. I locked eyes with my father, hearing the light gasp he released as if I stood an inch from his mouth, not a room apart.

The chair clattered to the ground; wood splitting terrifyingly loud.

I could no longer see the attacker's blade because it was buried deep in my father's chest. I screamed in denial as I watched the realisation dawn in my father's eyes. Then the attacker peeled back, drawing the blade with him, a spurt of blood pumping out of the wound it left behind.

Father fell to the ground, clutching at himself. Gasping for breath.

The attacker turned on me, ready to complete their task. But the moment was brief, interrupted by an explosion of pure, white light which blinded me. I saw nothing but the halo of sunlight, even in the darks of my eyes as I scrunched them shut. The light seemed to drown all noise, all reality of what happened in the room beyond my closed eyes. I wanted to see – to help – to rip the attacker from Father's body with my own hands and unleash a swarm of pain that built within me.

But I could do nothing but shy from the brightness.

It could have gone on for an eternity, but as the welcome gloom returned, I threw my eyes open to inspect the scene before me.

Tarron Oakstorm held the attacker by the neck, their feet kicking wildly in the air. His hands seemed to glow from the inside, a star trapped within flesh. But it was the long blade of golden light that buzzed in his spare hand that entrapped my attention. A shard of light. A blade of sun.

The cold air – *my* cold air – fizzed around it as though it recoiled in agony.

Tarron was saying something, but it was hard to hear over the screaming of the man at his feet. Father. Pain ruled his body, limbs spasming as he thrashed in a puddle of his own blood.

Wasting not another moment, I crashed through the spears of conjured ice, throwing myself towards him.

"I've got you," I said, hands shaking, hesitant to touch him in case it caused him more pain. "I'm here."

Father's eyes were bloodshot and wide, lips paling as they trembled as though he was encased in a blanket of winter. Colour drained from his expression, only making the deep red of his blood stand out more.

"Silly... bastard nipped me," he managed to say, all while he was breathless and imprisoned by pain.

He tried to sit up, but I kept him in place. "Stop moving, Dad. You're going to bleed out. I need to staunch the bleeding."

Should I have cared about what was occurring between the attacker and Tarron? Not once did I believe he would find his way free again to wreak more havoc. With Tarron here, there was a certainty that settled over me; the attacker would not get close enough to us again.

"It is just a scratch, son. I will be fine–" Father's words of dismissal soon stopped as I pressed both hands down upon the wound. I felt the tickling of warm blood but didn't care, not as I tried everything to stop the flow.

"What should I do!?" The question was not for Father, or anyone really. It was more to myself as I went through my memory, trying to find some fragment that would aid in helping Father.

A scream broke the moment. I turned in time to see the blade of golden light thrust through the base of the attacker's skull. Blood and skin sizzled as the shard of light cut through with ease. The scream soon stopped, swapped for the gargling of blood as death welcomed the attacker.

Tarron discarded the body with a careless gesture of his arm. For someone of his size and build, he had kept the attacker from the floor with ease, helped by his clear yet hidden strength.

The shard of light recoiled, melting into the skin of his closed fist. One moment his face was lit by the conjured golden glow, the next only the shadows of the room graced the angles of his enraged expression.

"Take his shirt off," Tarron commanded, snapping his furious gaze towards me.

"I can't – he'll bleed out."

Tarron's intense stare burned holes through me. "I can heal him, but for that, I need to *see* the wound. Now take his shirt off."

There was no room to argue. To refuse. Reluctantly, I lifted my hands from the wound, watching as the force of blood pumped freely without my pressure. The weight of Erix's dagger made itself known at my waist. I pulled it free quickly, slicing the material of Father's bloodied shirt from the bottom to the collar until his skin was exposed, or what little I could see beyond the coating of dark blood.

Tarron leaned over Father, hands splayed inches above the leaking slice. I rocked backwards, wrapping my arms around my legs as I watched, helpless to do anything but hope that Tarron's confidence was not wasted.

A splintering of light glowed from the pale tips of his fingers. Much like the blade he had held, it was golden and bright, but not sharp and cold, it was warm, like melted butter, or a glow of firelight.

Concentration silenced Tarron. He leaned his head backwards, eyes closed as he urged his strange power to slay across my father's body. It encased him in the glow shared between both men.

Tarron was healing him.

The blood didn't retreat, not that I expected it to. I had no clue of what to expect as the scene played out before me. Only the calming of Father's breathing suggested that he was brought some form of comfort. Even the lines across his tense face had smoothed.

Time dragged until it was unbearable. Watching and not helping made discomfort itch at my very soul. But soon enough, Tarron pulled back, breathless, his glow retreating to darkness.

"He will be fine," Tarron announced, relief flooded me. "The wound has healed. Without further inspection, I can't sense the internal damage, but I trust that I have stilled the bleeding both inside and out."

I couldn't ignore how exhausted Tarron sounded as he spoke, how his words slurred and seemed heavy.

"Thank you," I said, blinking. Unable to truly believe what I had just witnessed. I had a hand on Father, and the other reached out for Tarron as though to prop him up.

Father seemed to be sleeping peacefully, his breathing shallow and slow but regular.

Tarron winced as he opened his eyes, his skin paled to a dull grey. "The guard at the door was in on the attack. As soon as I heard the struggle, he lunged for me. He fought hard but failed. I am sorry I did not get in sooner."

My eyes drifted to the door, noticing two booted feet lying on the ground beyond. Then my gaze drifted to the body of the attacker. Even from a distance, I could smell the tang of burned flesh.

"We should get someone." My voice shook, hands reaching for Father's bloodied torso. "What if someone else attempts it? Lady Kelsey has been locked away. How did this happen?"

Maybe it was never her at all.

"I can assure you nothing will happen again. My judgement lapsed for a moment, but that moment has passed. I dare someone else to enter this room unwelcomed."

"I don't," I replied. "It is only a matter of time until they succeed."

I couldn't help but feel... defeated.

Every time an attempt on my life was made, another was taken as payment. This time, thanks to Tarron, he might've just spared my father from death.

"Then we must find out who *they* are." Tarron rocked forward, leaning over his knees as he caught his breath. "You should not live in fear of being attacked at every turn."

"Queen Lyra will–"

"Is taking too long of a time in locating those behind the attempts on your life. In my court, this would have been resolved before the second attempt was even made. I am not satisfied your hosts are acting in your best interest."

My mouth dried. There was a part of me that wanted to disagree, to stand up for the Cedarfall family and all they had done for me. But then I sat back, rocking on my heels as I pondered that very thing.

What *had* they done for me?

"I should clear the blood from him." I was thankful for Tarron changing the subject, as though my prolonged response begged for a reprieve. "It is close to impossible to fully heal a wound that I cannot see. I would feel far better knowing not a scratch has been missed."

I reached for the bedsheet that was half fitted, and half dragged across the ground. Wasting no time, I bunched the material up in my hands and gently ran it over Father's slow-rising chest. If Tarron had missed any wound with his healing abilities, I didn't want to cause him discomfort.

It took a few sweeps to catch the deep ruby gore until skin could be seen.

It was strange seeing Father so vulnerable. He winced with almost every inhale, brows pinched and lips pale, and there was nothing I could do to help give him ease. Only Tarron beheld such power.

"He will be okay, won't he?" I asked, eyes almost filling with tears. I blinked them away, not wanting to show this side of me to Tarron, a vulnerability that would make me look weak.

"I would like to hope so," Tarron replied. "It has been many years since my powers have failed me. Although he is the first human I have had to aid."

There was a strange, tugging discomfort as he spoke it aloud, as though it pained him to admit what he had done.

"You hate them," I added. "And yet you healed him without thought."

"I did what I felt was right in the moment."

I paused, pulling the now bloodied sheet from Father as I studied Tarron. "Am I supposed to ignore the clear underlying message in your words?"

"Take from it what you will, Robin. My presence is not to be a teacher for you, someone to make you see what I wish you to see. I simply desire for you to learn how to see the world and make your decision based on your own knowledge of it. I do not wish to see the humans – people like your father – killed. But I believe a time has come for *our* kind to stop playing by the rules. The years the humans have come into our lands, taken our people for their own twisted and unimaginable needs, not once have we done the same." He sighed, looking back to my father beneath us. "Perhaps now is not the time to discuss matters."

I followed his stare. "Perhaps not."

My eyes caught on a dark marking on Father's side. Smears of blood still covered it, but the symbol inked on his skin was obvious. I reached for it, feeling his warmth beneath my thumb as I cleared away the blood.

"What is the matter?" Tarron asked, concern rumbling in his voice.

I couldn't answer. There were no words to say what tore my heart into ribbons of flesh. With great force, I backed away. Tarron pushed himself up, watching my reaction with furrowed brows.

"Robin, if I have missed a wound, I will–"

"Hunter." It was all I could say. My hand slapped to my mouth a moment too late to stop me from admitting it. Deep down, I knew what this would mean, but the horror before me couldn't be ignored.

Across the side of Father's ribs, inches away from being hidden and covered by his resting arm, was a marking. A permeant staining of ink that I'd seen branded on the neck of the Hunter who killed Orion.

Not on Father. But it was not the fact that he had the marking but what it was that cleaved my world in two.

The outline of a palm, fingers pointing north with a thumb pressed tightly into its side. The same hand outline that covered the Hunters' cloaks and wagons. A symbol I'd seen up close when the executioner lifted his rusted, blood-covered axe above my head. And that mark was now etched into the darks of my eyes, neatly drawn across my own father's skin.

My eyes snapped back to Tarron. I was ready to stop him, magic poised and coiled like a spring, waiting patiently for my command. Even though the truth of what this meant horrified me, I also understood what this meant to Tarron. To every fey within Wychwood.

"I didn't know." I kept my voice as flat and unwavering as I could muster, all whilst watching Tarron, expecting him to conjure yet another blade of light to end the man on the floor between us.

"He is one of them." Tarron's lip lifted, flashing teeth as he battled to keep a snarl hidden. "A Hunter."

"You're wrong," I said, cowering over his body, ready to do anything to protect it. "If my father has been branded, it could've been against his will."

I grappled for excuses, but the only one who could prove otherwise was dying in my arms.

"Tarron, I will not let you hurt him." I was no match for Tarron's control over his magic, but deep down, I knew the power within me was far greater than his. As it had been explained, magic was diluted by the members of the ruling court. He may be the prince, but he had other family.

Whereas I was one of a kind.

"If *they* find out, they will kill him. Not put him on trial. Kill him. Right where he lies."

"I know." I bit down on my lip, trying to stop it from shaking.

Tarron looked back down at Father, and I wanted to scream at him to stop, to look at me and never even think of my father again. But I asked the question that coursed through me, the one that made making a plan impossible, a plan to get Father out of here, far before anyone else found out. "What will you do to him?"

My breathing rattled in my head, my heart thumping painfully in my chest. I felt my ribs, like a weakening cage, scream to shatter and release the anxiety within.

Tarron focused in on me, bright eyes glinting with a light that I did not expect to see. "Nothing that you are imagining. Robin, I am not going to hurt him."

"Why?" I snapped. From relief or shock, I was not certain.

"Because... I do not know."

Trust was a hard concept to grasp, especially since I looked upon a boy whose family had been torn apart by Hunters.

"Tell me what it is that *you* are going to do with this secret, Robin?" Tarron asked in return.

I lowered my hands, feeling the tickling of cold recoiling. What was I going to do? I felt the need to run. Get as far away from Wychwood as possible. But they would find me. This side of the Wychwood border, or the other when the barrier was destroyed by the unclaimed power of the Icethorn Court. The only feeling I had was the burning, overwhelming urge to get my father out of here. Even if he was a monster. Even if he likely deserved all that was waiting for him.

I couldn't let it happen.

"I want to get him as far away from here as possible. It is not safe..."

"Safe for who?" Tarron added. "Him? Or the fey around him which his very presence threatens?"

His expression was calm and warm, even though his question stung.

"Both," I answered.

I waited for him to refuse, to tell me what I already knew about Father having to be handed over for his crimes. Even though I'd never seen, nor could believe, he was linked to the Hunters. The inking on his ribs suggested otherwise. Until I could ask him myself, I would choose not to question it.

And I had to trust Tarron would do the same.

"Then we do just that." I could've dropped to my knees as Tarron spoke, his voice commanding in tone but gentle in nature. "We will help get him away from the Cedarfall Court, but I cannot promise his secret would be safer where I can take him."

"Why? Why would you help me?"

Tarron shook his head, dark locks of hair swaying over his shoulder. All I could do was listen, completely still, as he revealed his plan. "Because I feel as though it is the right decision. For now, time is on our side. No one will know of the attack until we tell them, so we act whilst we can. I shall tell them your father was harmed, but my healing can only do so much. He will need to be sent to my family's court where he can complete the necessary treatment."

"When?" I gasped.

Tarron mused my short question for a moment. "As soon as you convince them that is what you want."

"How do I know I can trust you?" I asked above the crashing of my heart in my chest.

"You are the son of a man who hunts fey. It is I who should be asking that question of you." My lips parted, ready to scream the tower down that I had no idea of Father's ties to the Hunters. It felt like the truth was a lie in disguise for all this time.

Then Tarron spoke, closing the space between us where he reached for my hands. "Trust is earned, so allow me to do just that."

I stared at him, allowing my hands to squeeze onto his as his did to mine. A twisting of a frozen storm built within me. I harnessed the emotion and forced it into my words, making my tone as serious as I could muster. "Then earn it."

CHAPTER 26

It took little persuading for Queen Lyra and King Thallan to agree for Father to be put under the Oakstorms' protection. I knew it from the moment I saw their mortified expressions as we interrupted their dinner, covered in his blood. There was no room for disagreement, nor did Tarron allow for any. Clearly Aurelia was no longer safe. They had no grounds to argue against that fact. So, to my relief, it was agreed Tarron would arrange proper protection for my father – away from here.

Tarron had split the air in two with no more than a swift slice of a hand, much like he had the first time I'd seen him, creating a portal we could step between without walking a great distance. It was easier to pull Father's body through it and allow the swarm of the queen's personal guards to enter and obtain the bodies of the attackers whom Tarron had discarded in a pile beyond the room's door.

Everything happened so quickly. Father was still unconscious as Tarron took him away, promising that he would give me time with Father before they left for the Oakstorm Court. In a blink, he'd stepped through another spindle of light, Father's unconscious body draped over his shoulder as though he weighed no more than an empty satchel.

Queen Lyra tried to engage in conversation, but I was unable to say much. She likely told me what we waited for, yet I couldn't focus on anything but the storm in my mind.

My father might have been a Hunter. I wasn't sure what it meant to me. Beyond my suspicions, the marking across his skin suggested he was an enemy to everyone in Wychwood. And after what had happened to Orion, I didn't doubt the Cedarfall's were still looking for someone to blame.

Those questions, and more, haunted me with each laboured breath.

"I should never have left you." Erix stormed into the room, which had turned out to be the king's own personal quarters. It was a bedchamber, but one he never used as he shared a bed with his wife. It made sense because it was richly decorated, with a lavish covering of food across the table in the living section of their rooms.

I'd not long climbed out of the bathtub, leaving the water almost black from father's blood and grime.

Erix's hands found my arms, gripping hold of them as though a sudden, threatening gust would blow me away in a moment. "Are you hurt?" His silver eyes searched every inch of me. "Tell me what happened."

I hung my head, so relieved to finally see him. "It was horrible," I admitted.

"I knew I should have continued to refuse leaving you. It is my duty – *you* are my fucking duty, and I gave in to a command I did not feel comfortable with."

"Please…" My voice was a whisper, it was all I could manage. "Not here."

Erix snapped his attention upwards, surveying the room and those who filled it as though it was the first time he realised where he was. Guards and serving staff looked at Erix as though he was the most frightened man in the entire world. He noticed, softening his voice. "Forgive me for my intrusion, but I have it from here."

"Forgiven." Queen Lyra's voice was blunt but coated in a false softness to dull the sharpness hidden within it. She parted from the shadows, unannounced and yet blooming with authority.

"Permission to take Robin to his room, my queen?"

"I cannot grant you that," Queen Lyra said, pacing the room. "This room will do. It isn't being used by my husband, or anyone else, for that matter. I have had every shadow and corner searched for threats. I fear this palace is no longer safe to stay at all. For any of us. If my sister's poisonous influence has spread further than my investigation can reach, then I cannot ensure Robin's safety... no matter the company I believed I could trust."

My body felt numb, my mind the only part of me alive like a bolt of lightning had crashed across my skull.

"He needs to rest." Erix's tone matched that of the authority of the queen; he was both demanding and pleading.

"And he shall. Once we reach Farrador, we will *all* be welcome to rest knowing we are far from the threats faced here."

Farrador, the capital of the Cedarfall Court, where Orion's body was travelling to, where Althea had grown up.

Erix flinched, stopping himself from wrapping an arm around me. I almost urged him to do it, to not hold back and take me in his arms.

"What is to say yet another assailant does not wait for me in Farrador?" I questioned. Every head in the room turned to me. Perhaps it was the surprise that I had finally uttered a word or the frozen touch my statement left upon the room.

"I can only give you my word," Queen Lyra declared. "And know that every possible power I have will be exhausted, ensuring another hair on your head is not threatened."

What about the people around me? I dared not speak it aloud for fear it would become too real.

I wanted to remind her that the word of her family had yet to mean anything, but then I remembered my father with the mark of a Hunter across his ribs, and I felt I was in no position to say anything with the secret I kept from everyone in this room.

"When do we leave?" I asked, hands clenched into fists so tight that my nails marked crescent moons across my palm.

"As soon as our means of travel allows. Until then you can stay in this room. We will send for you when we are ready to leave."

I drank from the bone-carved cup slowly, not because I was thirsty, but because I needed to keep my hands busy. I didn't long for the water that passed my lips. It was a stronger substance I desired, something that would warm my chest and make my mind hazy.

As I took the short, uninterested sips, I couldn't take my eyes off the elegant, green, glass bottle full of a honey-coloured wine waiting patiently on the table before me.

"I will drink from it first if it makes you feel more comfortable," Erix offered, noticing my hesitation.

Erix and I had been left in the King Thallan's personal quarters whilst the plans for our quick departure were underway. It was clear the room had never been used, but that didn't make me any less comfortable.

Erix had done everything to ensure my comfort, offered to fetch warm water for another bath, even to rummage through the clothing provided to check for something – anything – that was hidden or could harm me. But most of all, he ensured he took the first sip or nibble of food before he gave them to me.

Although his attentiveness picked at the corners of my annoyance, I also didn't complain. It was calming knowing I could trust Erix without him giving me a reason to. Unlike Tarron, who hours before I could never have shared a secret with, nor longed to converse with a person of his personality type. That had changed now, as he had my father, and I could only pray that he kept his word, even though he had many reasons not to.

"You don't have to do all this," I replied, truly wincing at the thought of Erix trying anything; I didn't want him to be bedridden like Briar had been.

"I want to. It is not a case of if I have to or not. It is the least I can do."

I looked up to him, focusing on keeping my hands steady as I gripped the cup. His wide, silver-clouded eyes were wide with concern. He hardly blinked as he studied me with his unwavering intensity. His skin was freshly washed, but his underlying scent hadn't wavered. He'd dressed in his usual dark leather trousers and form-fitting top. This time his sleeves didn't hide the outlined muscles of his arms. The material had little room for movement, as though the shirt was made for someone with a lesser build.

I distracted myself with the vision of him, tracing his features as a silent game to keep my own dark thoughts at bay. But it was failing, lasting only for a moment of reprieve. I needed something more as a distraction.

"Back home," I began, "when days were equally as draining, all I would want was the burn of a homebrewed ale to wash away the stresses. Since I cannot imagine this pretty little city has anything so hearty, why don't I crack open that bottle of wine and not let it go to waste?"

Erix lifted an eyebrow in surprise, turning in his seat to follow my gaze. "I am not sure that would be a good idea... it is best you have a clear head."

"Erix, I am sitting on the edge of a bed made for royalty, dressed in clothes meant for a king. I don't imagine drinking the wine is going to make much of a difference to the wild storm in my mind right now."

"Well, you do look rather handsome in that oversized tunic." Erix turned back to me, narrowing eyes looking across my body. My legs were bare, the shirt falling below my undershorts.

"So, is that a yes to the wine?" I held up my cup, sloshing the water over the sides until it splashed upon the bedding beneath me. "Or are you going to make me say please?"

For a moment, his stare became serious. Anyone else might've felt threatened. But to me, it only made my longing for a distraction burn hotter.

In moments the downed cup of water was refilled to the top with the golden-hued liquid. Erix didn't pour himself a glass, instead he took the bottle in his large, closed fist and sat back down before me.

"You have done a masterful job at dancing around the topic of what happened with Tarron," Erix said, lifting the rim of the bottle to his full, parted lips.

Because you made it clear that any mention of Tarron irked you.

"I visited Father, someone attacked, and he was hurt. Tarron healed him and promised to protect him under his own care. There is nothing more to the story." I took a long swig of wine, letting my tongue melt beneath the beautiful, unworldly taste that followed. I kept the liquid in my mouth, behind closed lips, allowing the flavour to rock around every possible inch of my tongue, before swallowing.

"I do not want to be the one to darken the mood even more so, but Tarron is not to be trusted. We should petition for your father to stay with us. Queen Lyra would not decline if you asked for him to travel to Farrador. Gods, I would feel better even if he was left in Aurelia." Urgency made Erix speak quickly, hardly breaking for breath until he got every last word out.

"Dare I ask what Tarron has done to you that you hold such dislike for him?"

The question hung between us. I could see Erix contemplating my question as he lost himself to his thoughts, gaze drifting to some forgotten spot on the headboard behind me.

"It won't change matters."

"Maybe not." I reached a hand for him, placing it softly upon his knee. "But you can tell me. At some point, you are going to have to open up if you keep expecting me to do the same."

"Fair enough, little bird." Erix loosed a sigh, took a rather large swig of wine, and relaxed back in the chair. "My family were from the Oakstorm Court. Tarron and I are of similar ages and had been forced together, in social events, from a very early age. You see, my mother was a lady-in-waiting, helping and aiding Tarron's own mother for years. Far more years before Tarron and I came into the world. I have known him for a long time and can see through his cracks. Believe me, there are many. He..." Erix shook his head and took yet another swig of wine, tipping the bottle back and inhaling the liquid. I watched, enthralled by the rhythmic bob of the lump in his throat. He came back for air, clearing the remnants of glistening wine from his lips and chin with the back of his hand. "Tarron once took someone I cared dearly about. To prove a point. Or just for a game, I still am not certain who won. It was one of the reasons I left, to get away from the unfair games between us that I had found myself entered into without a choice. There is far more to the story, but nothing that cannot wait for another day."

A twisting of emotion thrummed within me; it was not a nice feeling but a familiar, bitter one that soured the wine as I drank it. "Who was it?"

I didn't need to elaborate on my question for Erix to know what I asked. Part of me didn't want to know the answer either, but I found myself craving the knowledge.

"A girl. Someone I once knew from my past that I try extremely hard to forget. It was many years ago, and her memory is no more than a closed chapter. But to Tarron, she was a trophy. A prize to be won. And it broke her beyond the point of..." Erix trailed off, words dying on the tip of his tongue.

"Of what?" I sat forward, longing to know more.

"It is not for me to say." There was something thunderous behind his stare; it came on as fast as a storm, darkening the mood in seconds. "Not now, please. That part of my life means nothing now. Forgotten. And I would very much like to keep it that way. Although it may seem therapeutic to peer through the crack in the door, I would like very much to keep it closed."

The version of Tarron that Erix saw was far different to the man who promised my father's safety, someone I had shared the greatest secret of all with. "Perhaps he has changed."

Erix looked at me, lip curling slightly. "For the better or worse, it is too soon to tell."

I regretted speaking of Tarron. It only conjured an image of Father's bleeding body and the mark that had engraved itself into my very brain; it waited for me in the dark behind my eyes with every blink.

I needed a distraction.

My eyes glanced back to Erix, who stole gulps of wine from the bottle again. What he spoke of had troubled him to the point his hands shook with anger. A bottled emotion that he struggled to keep caged. I almost felt the tension he wrestled with.

"How long do you think we have?" I asked, voice no more than a whisper.

Erix slowly lowered the bottle, eyes wide as he regarded me. "Why do you ask?"

Was that hope I caught in the lift of his voice? I hoped not. Now, more than ever, I was not in a position to commit to someone's feelings when my own was uncontrollable, but his ability to take my mind away was a blessing, and I didn't want it to go to waste.

And I could see that he too required a distraction. One I was willing to become.

"It's just…" My words tapered off.

Erix scowled, leaning in as he no doubt tried to work me out. Good luck with that, my mind was a maze. "You are making me nervous with your questioning, little bird. And your silence."

"Was it just a one-time thing?" I asked, ignoring his use of my nickname. "Or, I mean, should it be a one-time thing?"

Silver eyed widened, lips parting. "Is that what you want?" He threw his question at me, dodging my own as though it was a sharpened blade. "Because if it is, I will respect your answer."

What did I want?

Him.

I stood from the bed, nudging his knees apart enough for me to stand between them. He looked up at me, fist gripped around the elegant neck of the bottle. I was surprised it did not crack beneath the strengthening of his grip. "I know it should be. Deep down, I'm screaming at myself to dismiss it and move on. But–"

"But?" Erix echoed.

"Maybe I don't want it to stop. Not completely."

"I'm good at many things, little bird, but reading between the lines is one skill I haven't mastered. Tell me what you want from me, and you can have it. Be clear with your words."

The tension between us thickened, growing serious in a matter of seconds. Erix didn't smile as he looked up at me. I felt like a delicious meal that he was being kept from, although he was starved.

I reached for his face, pressing a hand to his cheek. His skin was warm and welcoming. His hard, straight and tall posture relaxed into my touch as I told him what I thought. "I want to stop thinking. I want peace in my own head for just a moment."

"And you need my help for that?"

I nodded, fighting the urge to grin at the thought of using him for my own peace of mind. "It may make the process of what's happening, and what has happened, easier to organise from chaos to clarity."

"And how," he murmured, his deep voice sending a lightning bolt through my spine, "can I help with that?"

"Distract me."

Those two words were all that was holding Erix back. He sprang from the chair, wrapping an arm around my back and twisting my body towards the bed once again. Air whizzed past my ears, my stomach jolting under the impact.

I giggled as my back hit the soft cushioning of the bed. Erix prowled above me, wide arm sweeping the many decorations from around us until pillows and blankets softly plopped onto the floor, forgotten.

His lips were on mine, tasting like fruit and spice. My tongue moved, lapping up the remnants of wine which exploded within my own mouth, tastebuds as alive as the skin his rough touch brushed over.

I wrapped my arms around his neck, pulling him down upon me. All I could think of was keeping him close, preventing him from stopping.

My lips tingled when we finally broke away from one another. I took the moments he trailed his mouth down my cheek, along the curve of my jaw and onto my neck to catch my breath. He slipped from my hold, his hands lifting the bottom of King Thallan's oversized shirt and exposing my stomach. No matter how many deep inhales I took in, I couldn't seem to catch my breath. Not as his kiss moved from my neck to my chest, to the tensed muscles of my lower stomach, all the way to the band of material that signalled the start of my undershorts.

Then Erix stopped. It was so sudden I craned my neck up and looked down at him.

He was staring up at me, his grin turning the corners of his glistening, full lips up at each corner. Mischief made his silver eyes glow from within. "May I?"

It seemed words were not an option. Instead, I flopped my head back down onto the bed, closing my eyes until all I saw was star-speckled darkness. It wasn't what I could see that thrilled me, but what I felt. And his hands had not stopped moving, fingers inching closer to the cock that throbbed within my undershorts, all I did was *feel*.

It was enough of an indication that I wanted what Erix had to offer. The feeling was strange but welcome. It sent burning nerves through my core, but his touch seemed to smother those embers.

I was usually the one on my knees until my jaw ached. Never had it been me on the receiving end; by choice, maybe, or the fact that the others I'd been intimate with were more worried about their own ending than mine.

Erix didn't seem to think of himself, not once. Even when he rode inside of me, it had felt as though each movement was a gift or treat meant for me.

This was no different.

Erix gently tugged at my undershorts with one hand, the other scooped beneath my back until he lifted me from the bed. Enough to pull them from me and discard them on the pile of pillows. A breeze dusted across my cock, making a shiver cross my skin, but then it was gone, warmed by the touch of Erix, who wrapped his fingers around it.

"You asked for a distraction, and it is my duty as your personal guard to provide you with one."

"Erix," I exhaled his name, arching my back until the flat of his hand pressed down on my stomach and I was lying once again. I looked down at him, expecting to see him staring back, but his focus was on the hard cock that waited in his hand.

"You want this, don't you?" he asked.

I gasped as his hand began to move. Up and down, slowly twisting at the wrist with each stroke. "Yes."

"Let me hear you say my name." His hand quickened in pace.

"Erix."

"Again," he demanded, hand quickening in pace yet again.

"Eri – Erix!"

I tumbled into the thrill of pleasure, unable to think of anything but his touch.

"Good," he breathed slowly. "I do love it when you say my name."

The feeling that followed was unlike anything I'd ever felt before. Erix placed me within his mouth, swapping his hand movements for the upwards and downwards dance of his head. I'd done it many times before but never realised what it felt like on the receiving end.

Now I did; I scolded myself for never having it done to me before.

I gripped at the sheets. Pleasure had me making sounds with each exhale. It urged Erix on, his pace changing and altering without warning. I felt as though I rode atop a wild stallion, not knowing if it was trotting, cantering or galloping. The unknown was thrilling as I gave into it. If this was like riding a horse, I was ready to be thrown from the saddle.

A pressure was building within me. The more it grew, the more sensitive I became. Erix's lips tightened, his tongue moving in quicker and more frantic circles around my cock. I wanted it to end, but in the same way, I didn't. This feeling was one that I wished would last forever, but I knew the sensation that was waiting to happen was pure divinity, and the promise of that release, with Erix at the helm, almost sent me over the edge.

I looked down at Erix's bobbing head. His mouth was busy, and so was the hand that aided him. But his other hand, the one spare, couldn't be seen as he gripped onto his own cock. His arm moved, pleasuring himself just as he did me.

And it was that sight that threw me over the chasm, knowing he shared in the feeling made it impossible to control it. My breathing laboured, my moaning increasing in volume and pace. The feeling crept from the pits of my stomach, warming my groin as his wet mouth worked on me. I tried to pull back at it, but it was impossible to control. Erix made noises, deep huffing as his own arm jerked wildly at his cock.

Then we finished. Together – *again*.

I closed my eyes but felt it as though that sensation was all that mattered. Our breathing entwined into one thread, our bodies tensing in the same overwhelming waves.

For one long celestial moment, we were united as one, and that was a feeling I would never forget.

My head spun as I lay back on the bed. I felt every touch as Erix peeled his hand from my length. I was too enthralled in the reoccurring spasms of joy that took over my body to care about what occurred in the room around me.

"Thank you," I murmured, revelling in the peace and quiet of my mind.

"I do not expect you to thank me for anything, little bird." Erix was at my feet, pulling the undershorts over them and up both my legs. He dressed me with sure fingers, just as he had undressed me. "For another, careless night, the thanks may have been nice to hear. But you do not thank me for something that is quite literally my pleasure."

I sat up, reaching shaking hands to help him as I pulled the undershorts back into position. "Do you need me to finish too?"

Erix shook his head. He knew what I asked before I even had finished what I had to say. "I am *more* than satisfied, trust me."

I looked at the bulge within his trousers. He was still large, but I knew that he had shared in that climax. The splash of liquid staining his undershorts confirmed as much. Just seeing the imprint had me ready to go again, a feeling that usually returned after a good sleep and a meal, with previous lovers.

It was Erix's turn to walk between my legs, nudging them open with his knees. He placed both his fists on the bed beside me, leaning down until his face was inches from my own. "I hope that helped clear your mind."

I blinked slowly, not wanting to take my eyes off him. "It did."

Erix puckered his lips and placed a small, kind kiss to the tip of my nose. "If I cannot do anything but take your mind off the world, then I sacrifice myself to the cause. Willingly, of course."

"I–"

"Are you both done…?" a voice yawned at the edge of the room.

I snapped my head to the door, just as Erix did, our noses a splinter from cracking into each other. Althea leaned against the doorframe, inspecting her nails in the dim light as though she hid gold within them.

Erix bolted from me. I couldn't move, I was frozen to the spot. Damn. Her father's spare bed.

"Oh, Erix, no need to act so bashful now." Althea hardly spared us a glance, her entire demeanour screamed with her lack of care.

"It is not what it looks like," I uttered, snatching Althea's attention from Erix before she truly had a chance to look at him.

"Is it not?" Althea pouted, hand landing upon her hip as though it were a walking stick. "Well, that is very disappointing. Do not get me wrong, you would not be the first story of a royal falling for their personal guard. Even my own father has had those rumours linked to his name. But to do it in this bed, how very…" I readied myself for the mortifying dread that was coming to bury me alive. "…repetitive."

I glanced at Erix, who shared the same look of embarrassment, but confusion about what Althea said.

Althea sighed heavily. "Oh, boys, come on. Do you think you are the first to spoil those sheets? My father doesn't sleep here, so someone better get the enjoyment out of them. Please, welcome to the club. As the leading member, I should likely hand out badges or create a banner to unite us, but perhaps that would be in bad taste."

"I don't get it…" I said, noticing Erix as he stared at his boots with a knowing smirk.

"Apologies, Althea, we did not expect your presence," Erix said, looking up at her through his lashes.

"I am only sorry to be the one to interrupt. Erix, how about you clean up the mess, and I will get Robin something more suitable to wear."

I sprang from the bed, skipping on light feet for Althea, who waved me to join her. Her father's shirt fell back down to my knees, hiding what little modesty I had left.

Althea hooked an arm around my own and patted her hand on mine. "Forgive me if I am wrong, but I am starting to understand how you both kept warm during your night in Berrow." My cheeks flushed red. "And do not worry, I hardly saw a thing. Your secret is rather safe with me. And believe me, I am excellent at keeping secrets."

CHAPTER 27

My father was already awake by the time I entered the infirmary. I could hear him before the door was opened, suffering from heavy, debilitating coughs. Each of his breaths sounded like stone grating against stone. He wretched and hacked, trying to catch a breath between the fits. Each time it made my body wince.

Tugwort. The note from Tarron had revealed the poison that'd been laced on the dagger. Thank Altar, the Creator – anyone – that Althea had plenty of the antidote spare.

My father was going to live, but that didn't take away from the knowledge that anyone close to me was under threat.

Tarron's note was rushed and apologetic, explaining he required rest before completing the necessary healing of my father's wounds. It also explained how it could take days to rid his body of the poison, since the antidote wasn't as 'fresh' as it had been when Althea picked it. This part of his message was tactical, in case anyone else read it. The mention of Tarron needing rest, how it would take time to heal my father, only benefited the need for them both to leave for the Oakstorm Court.

The perfect cover-up.

I panicked, as Althea let me enter the room alone, that a healer would stumble across the mark on my father's ribs, revealing him for what he was. A Hunter, but worrying about that outcome would do nothing to prevent it.

Getting him out of Aurelia would.

Tarron would rest and – as promised – take Father from here to keep him safe, even if his past didn't suggest he deserved it.

"You're back... back for me," Father rasped, our eyes locking across the room.

"I'll leave you to it," Althea said, offering me a sympathetic smile. "Shout if you need me."

With that, she left me, my father and his secrets alone.

He looked like shit warmed up. At least my presence seemed to calm his coughing into small, manageable rasps. He lifted a hand, his arm shaking as though it weighed a tonne, and beckoned me to his bedside.

My feet were slow, like wading through mud, their own refusal to heed his silent command. But still, I joined him, wanting nothing more than to lay my head on his chest and hold onto him. Father winced, and not from the pain his body was in, but more from the expression that creased my face, one he was all too familiar with.

Disappointment.

"Did you expect me to leave you alone?" I asked, taking my seat, chair squeaking violently against the tiled floor.

"I did, actually. I've... been told of your plans to ship me off to the summer court."

Father opened his mouth to speak, but I quickly pressed a finger to my lips and gestured towards the now closed door. Althea had stayed outside the infirmary, but I was confident the walls would do little to muffle our conversation. Only when I was right by his side did I dare a whisper.

"We must be careful," I warned. "If they hear us, it will not end well for you or for me."

"Son," he said, face pinched with dread. Did he know what I knew? His red-rimmed eyes searched my face for a reason for my distance. "Tell me what is bothering you. I can see it in your eyes."

I placed my hands by my side, pinching nails into my palms to stop them from shaking. "You."

Father tried to push himself up to sitting, but another wave of coughing overtook him. I waited for it to pass, not offering a hand to hold for comfort. I wanted to, desperately, but felt wrong to award him such things after uncovering yet another secret he'd kept from me.

This one I understood the need to keep secret. If he was a fey-hunter, and I was part-fey, it only created more questions.

Finally, after he caught his breath enough, he continued. "I remember the blade piercing my skin. When I woke in this bed, I searched my chest for the mark but found nothing. Not a scratch or scar. There… there were no scars. Everything, all marks of the past, had healed. Even scars I'd created to *hide* the past."

"I saw it," I muttered, eyes stinging. I refused to spill a tear until I understood what emotion brought them forth, anger or sadness. "The inking on your ribs."

Father's eyes widened and paled lips pulled taut. "I thought as much."

"Tell me it was forced on you," I pleaded. "Some nasty brand from terrible people. Please," I choked on the sudden urge to cry. "Tell me I'm wrong."

He lowered his tired eyes, and my heart sunk.

"I prayed you'd never see it. But when I woke here – alive – I tricked myself into believing that no one saw it. Because if they did, if they discovered the mark of my sordid past inked on my skin, they'd have me killed."

I shook my head, feeling the copper tang swell in my mouth as I bit down hard on my lip to stop myself from shouting. "What is that even supposed to mean!? You are a… you were… I don't fucking understand. Help me understand!"

There was no one in the room to listen to us. But that didn't stop me from trying to control myself.

Father reached a hand to grab mine, but I pulled away. I could hardly hold his gaze for fear of breaking down, let alone allow the comfort of his touch.

"We all have a past we hide from. Give it time, and you will too. It's a lesson my own parents neglected to teach me."

"So you're blaming them for becoming someone who hunts innocent people?"

Father winced but didn't tell me I was wrong.

"I thought I'd mutilated the inking enough to hide it beneath a bed of scars. It disgusted me, knowing it would curse my skin for an eternity. But that issue was resolved when my fellow comrades discovered what I did. They... they carved the ink out of me themselves as punishment. I wasn't supposed to live through it. I knew, in time, my wrong-doings would come back and deliver me my just punishment. And now it's back, and all the other scars I'd gotten during the years are gone. But now you know."

I didn't want to blink for fear my mind would paint a picture of my father, held down by Hunters, as they took a knife and mutilated his skin. I once craved the stories of his past, now I wanted to run from them.

"Would you have ever told me?" I looked at him finally, truly searching for his soul in his tired gaze. It sickened me to think Father had used a blade to scar his own skin, an echo of the pain that must have caused gripped at my stomach. "Or did you become complicit by adding that secret onto your ever-growing list of them?"

"Truly, I wish that was one secret I'd take to my grave," he admitted softly. My heart cracked, not into two, but into a scattering of a million pieces. "But that luxury of lies is no more. Sit with me, and I'll tell you everything."

"Everything?" I scoffed, almost laughing aloud in a sharp bark. "This is a reoccurring theme of our conversations, Father. I find something out, you have nowhere to hide and promise me answers. What will it be next? What else hides in the dark trunk of lies that you have so perfectly kept locked?"

"Sit, son." His voice darkened like it would when I was younger and he reprimanded me for misbehaving. In that moment, I was like a child again, beckoned to his call. "I understand you are angry... but let me try and make sense of this for you. You don't owe me the chance to speak, but I owe you the opportunity to listen."

Father was struggling to speak, his sentences broken by breathless, raspy growls that came from his chest. He did well to keep the coughing at bay. He clearly felt some urgency to tell me his truth, even if I would have a hard time believing what he had to say.

"Fine," I said, anxiety fluttering like a flock of birds in my chest. "Talk."

Father shifted his legs in the bed, making room for me to perch at the end. I took it without hesitation this time.

"I was a troubled child," he began, eyes drifting as though he focused on everything and nothing all at once. "It's not an excuse, far from it, but it led to me being tangled with the wrong people, in the wrong groups at the *right* time. Grove has always struggled for coin and comfort, even more so when I was a young man. It resulted in resentment igniting in the hearts of many. And I admit that kindling was a raging inferno within me far before I was offered a way to exploit it. To join the Hunters, under the employment of the Hand, was an honour. A way of fixing the scales of balance that greatly tipped in favour of the fey beyond the Wychwood border. We were sold stories of the lack of struggle and undeserved power when we were living only a breath away. Whilst we fought to even put food on the table. At the time, it was an easy choice to join the legion of... *Hunters*." He fumbled over the word as though it truly disgusted him. "In hindsight, a lot of us joined in blindness, encouraged by the promise of payment in return for the capture and deliverance of fey to the capital. It was easy work for us in Grove, being so close to the border, we were the first to intercept those who wandered far from the safety of their lands. We got paid handsomely for it, which encouraged those in our group to work harder, and longer. When you give someone something they've never had, it makes it harder to imagine life without it again. Coin did that. It warped the lines of right and wrong."

I listened without interrupting, trying to understand his reasoning but being unable to connect to his struggle. We hadn't exactly had a lot of money like those in Lockinge or the surrounding towns and villages. But it wouldn't have led me to hunt the innocent. I'd been up close and personal with a Hunter, with a bloodied axe ready to meet the soft skin of my neck. Was the executioner motivated by coin to kill? Or had time warped the motivations of the Hunters now into something else? Something darker.

"Am I supposed to feel sorry for you?" I said, voice numb and cold. "Because I admit I'm finding that emotion rather hard to grasp at the moment."

"I'm not going to tell you how to feel about me. That is your decision. But perhaps you will change your mind when I *finish* my story."

I waved a hand, both of us noticing how it shook. "I'm all ears."

"It all changed when I met your mother. Julianne Icethorn. The most incredible woman I've ever had the pleasure of meeting in this life. No one would compare to her, not before and certainly not after." The words conjured the icy coil and brought it to life within me. I was not prepared for this part of the story, nor did I believe it would lead here. "She was a captive from a neighbouring party of Hunters who'd come from another town and made claim to our lands and the bounty on it. We turned on one another. My party overtook theirs and claimed their bounty, because we believed it was rightfully ours. Julianne was with them. Our story is far longer, but between travelling from the border of Wychwood to Lockinge, I'd a change of heart, and it was your mother who contributed to that. We escaped together, fled and lived off the land until you were born. She couldn't return home, not whilst she carried you, and I couldn't return to Grove as a deserter either."

"But you did," I interrupted, a sheen of wetness covering my eyes; one blink, and it would release the tears down my cheeks. "You not only returned, but with me, proof of your affair with her."

"My relationship with your mother was far more than an affair. It was love. True, honest and frightening. When she left us, I'd no choice but to return to Grove. I changed everything I could about myself, my name, even my appearance with the help of your mother's friend. He created a glamour, shifting my features, that would last for as long as I did." His hands lifted to his face, thick, calloused fingers pulling at his cheeks as though it was a mask ready to come off. "Keeping my past a secret was easy, but hiding the truth of what *you* were was more difficult. Your kind were rare but not completely unheard of. It took a few years for those in Grove to grow used to you. A mundane, powerless boy. Most importantly, harmless. The more time passed, the less of a threat you were. Over the years, the talk of Hunters reduced, disbanding to whispers, and I grew comfortable knowing they'd left you alone. It'll be the gravest mistake I ever made.

"Because they did find me," I added, "And here we are."

"Yes." Father reached for my hand. I let him take it. "Here we are indeed."

I felt as though his story was short and rushed, but Father had explained the main plot with clear ease, as though he was reading from one of my favourite books as a child. He was the narrator of his own story now – the good, the bad and the downright rotten.

"I don't know who I'm looking at." My voice shook as I took in my father's face. What had it been before the *glamour*? Had his hair been a different shade? His nose longer or lips thicker?

"It's the same man, the same face, you've always seen. It may not be real to me, but for you, it is. You have known no different than this face. Don't allow the thought of what *was* cloud what has been."

I searched father's face for the edges of his perfect mask. But he was right. It was the same I'd always seen, a face I'd know even if the world went dark for an eternity.

"Thank you," I forced out, swallowing the lump that had embedded itself in my throat. "For telling me your truth."

"It was about time." He closed his eyes as though the weight of our conversation was heavy on him. "Do *they* know?"

"Only one," I admitted. "A friend."

When Father conjured the strength to open his eyes, I could see fear in them. "Well, I'm still alive, struggling with pain and a chest that feels as though it is drowning, but alive."

"He's promised to keep you safe." And so far he had stuck to that promise. That had to mean something.

"And you trust this... person?"

"I don't have any other choice." I dropped his gaze. "His name is Tarron. He's the one who saved your life."

Father's eyes narrowed on me, flickering across my face as though trying to read the nuances of my expression. "Oh, my son. You can always tell deep down if someone is unworthy of your trust."

"Then yes," I said, hard and fast. "I believe I do trust him. It's not safe for you here. Tarron has assured me he'll keep you far from the action, until everything has calmed to some normalcy. I can't have you in harm's way again, nor can I risk anyone else finding out about you. I don't imagine every person in this court will take kindly to your personal redemption story."

"Understood. Tell me though, when will I see you again?" It was all he could manage to say. Father looked exhausted, to the point that he fought to keep his eyes open. I held onto him, hoping he could stay awake just a moment longer. The last part of Tarron's note was that Father would be leaving by nightfall. This was the last I would see of him. But to answer his question, I didn't know when we would be together again.

"Sleep, Dad," I replied, squeezing his hand. I could not answer him without lying. And if time was unkind, I did not want a lie to haunt our last words together. "I will do what is right and return for you when I can."

Father smiled faintly, fingers relaxing their hold on my hand. He didn't notice my lack of answer, which I was relieved about. When he replied, it was slurred words broken by a yawn. "I am proud of you... and *she* would've been too."

CHAPTER 28

Dawn washed across our travelling party with the breeze of frigid air. The flame-jewelled lanterns dimmed, no longer needed to light the way from Aurelia to our new destination. The very sky felt tense, white clouds threatening to unleash hail or rain at any given moment. Maybe snow.

Winter was truly upon us. Whereas the many fey who travelled with us pulled fur-lined coats around their necks and hugged arms around their bodies, I hardly felt the cold anymore. And what chill I *did* feel felt oddly calming.

It'd been night when we vacated Aurelia, perfectly timed under cover of darkness. The familiar trot of the stag had me falling asleep long before we left the cover of the ancient trees. I woke with Erix pressed close behind me, mouth dry and neck cramping with an awkward ache.

"Now that you are awake, can I suggest talking as a form of passing the time? Might help make the journey feel quicker," Erix said, tightening his hold on me as I sat before him on the stag. "Or we can continue sitting in silence. At least I would have your snoring to keep me entertained."

"I'm tired," I replied, scanning the crowds to make sense of my slight disorientation. "And if you make one more comment about snoring, I swear you'll not have the luxury of seeing me sleep again."

Erix leaned in, whisper tickling my ear. "There are many other things I can imagine that sound more highly entertaining than sleeping, little bird. I have the stamina to see an entire day through if given the choice."

I shrugged him off, fighting a smile as I craned my sore neck and looked back at the crowd of mounted fey behind us. "Swallow your tongue. Someone might hear us."

My heart sank to the pit of my stomach when I caught sight of Tarron riding at the back of our campaign. Erix might've replied, but I lost all ability to listen as my eyes settled on the Oakstorm prince. Tarron's face was one I didn't expect to see in our convoy. He wasn't meant to be here. He should be with Father on their way to Oakstorm.

I held my eyes on him, waiting for Tarron to notice me, but he was too captivated by his surroundings.

Or he was purposefully trying not to meet my eyes.

"Robin, what is wrong?" Erix's hand found my shoulder and squeezed gently. "You have been oddly distant since our… interruption yesterday. Have I done, or said something to offend you?"

"Nothing," I said, snapping my attention back to the procession before me. "It's not you, it's–"

"Let me guess what is coming next," Erix interrupted, looking ahead, mouth drawn tight. "'It is me.'"

"Well, yes." I scrambled my way out of the awkward conversation. "It is me. Because the ache in my arse is terrible, and my mouth tastes like the bottom of a birdcage."

I wasn't ready to tell Erix why Tarron's presence concerned me. And from what I could see, Father wasn't with him. There would be a time to question Tarron, but in the presence of so many fey, now was not it.

Erix leaned into my ear and whispered again. "Do not fret, little bird. I am confident I can assist with your first concern. The latter… that's what you get for snoring with your mouth wide open."

I nestled into him until all I felt was the warmth of his body through our travelling attire. It was as much of a distraction from Tarron's presence as I could afford.

"I'm beginning to think you have a fetish for men snoring, you bring it up so much."

"Not men who snore, little bird. Men who enjoy having their mouths open–"

I jolted him in the ribs, conjuring a breathy laugh from Erix.

Althea rode ahead of us, her face turned to the side, ears twitching as though she listened in. The smirk across her face suggested she'd heard, but it could've been from the young woman nestled on the stag before her. Briar. My Taster. I'd not noticed her before but felt a pang of happiness that she was healthy and well – for Althea's sake as well as her own.

"Is there not something thrilling about sharing such thoughts among a crowd?" Erix asked. "It gives the sense of being rather..."

"Don't say it, Erix." My cheeks flushed as I bit down on my lip to stop the giggle that threatened to expose me to those who rode close to our sides. Gyah was one of them, constantly scanning the surroundings of the forest and beyond for threats. Her hand never strayed far from the handle of the sword that bounced at her hip. She offered me a quick grin, one that hardly lit her golden eyes.

"We still have a while to go until we reach Farrador. But I'm afraid to admit, all this bouncing in the saddle is making me lose my head a bit." Erix's large hands gripped on the reins, leather gloves crunching as he did so. Then he rested both hands on either of my thighs, his touch sending a bolt of excitement through me as a shiver shot up my spine.

"What has gotten into you?" I said through the corner of my mouth, looking around to see if anyone else listened in.

"Perhaps it is my desire for you or the fact that this journey has you bouncing before my crotch which has made me rather... starved."

I suddenly became aware of the movement of our stag, and tried everything to stiffen my body by clenching my stomach muscles and clamping down with my thighs. "One more word, and I'm pushing you from this mount and leaving you in the dust."

"Is that a threat?" Erix purred, tongue brushing the nape of my neck.

"A promise," I replied, unable to stop my skin from erupting in gooseflesh. "Now shut it."

Erix chuckled deeply, leaning back from me and lifting his hands from my legs. I suddenly felt the urge to scold him and return his touch upon my legs but decided against it because he was not the only one who felt starved. I was famished.

"Tell me about Farrador." I thought it was best to change the conversation. And quickly.

"What is it you desire to know?"

I sighed, trying to conjure an image of the mysterious city. Was it built into the side of a mountain like Imeria? Etched into the stone as though it belonged there without question? Or was it burrowed beneath monstrous, gold-leafed trees like Aurelia?

"Well," I began. "Do you really believe it's safer for me there?"

"Queen Lyra believes it, and so do I. The gryvern have never ventured that far, and the city is... well guarded." There was something in the way he said those last two words that made me tense. "It is the home to the Cedarfall family, and the power within the family's veins also fills the city. Gryvern are stupid monsters, but smart enough to know where their attempts are wasted."

"And what about the people of Farrador? What's to say they'll not try, as others have, to kill me? To them, I'm the biggest threat to their hopes of war."

Erix pondered my question in a moment of silence. I looked back at him, catching the glint of his serious, silver-gleaming eyes. "Because those who are against the idea of war are the soldiers themselves. And the city is full of them, and their loved ones. Those who risk their lives and put futures on the line are the very same who would pray for an excuse to not leave their families with the uncertainty of never returning."

"Makes a lot of sense," I muttered, feeling a sense of ease rush over me.

"I am full of sense." The return of Erix's thick, sarcastic tone broke the seriousness of the conversation. "And other things, of course."

"Did you forget about my promise to push you off?"

"I am merely seeing if you are good with your word."

I nudged him with an elbow, driving the air out of him as he wheezed a surprised laugh. "I will take that as a yes."

"Remind me how long I have until the Passing?" I asked, the question sprang to my mind quickly, like a cat stalking a mouse. The Passing was still a topic that interestingly skipped most conversations, although it was the most important. Since I'd left my father, I felt as though my heart was made up. Even though my mind still pondered the option of leaving the Icethorn Court unclaimed.

I knew what I had to do.

Father's words repeated in the back of my mind. *"I am proud of you… and she would've been too."*

"Not long." Gone was the sarcasm from his tone. In fact, it was my turn to sense his body stiffening.

"Care to elaborate?"

"The festivities begin within the week." I looked ahead at the straight backs of Queen Lyra and her husband as they led the campaign, flanked by their own guards.

"Within the week, and I still don't understand what is being asked of me."

"I would not worry. Queen Lyra has informed me of the preparations over the coming days. Your days, although limited, are going to be full of lessons and council. The other ruling families of Wychwood will be arriving for the Passing, which will keep the Cedarfall family preoccupied. I have been informed the very best scholars and historians will be reporting to you daily to shed light on what is *required* of you."

"Is that what you believe?" I asked, not caring if anyone listened in. "That I'm required to claim the Icethorn Court? And who requires that of me?"

"Every living soul both sides of the Wychwood border. They require it."

"And what do you require?"

I couldn't see Erix's expression as he replied, but I could imagine how his eyes narrowed as though he was in pain. "For you to survive, and thrive, far beyond the Passing."

The city of Farrador was far different from anything I could've ever imagined.

The dense forest thinned at the end of our journey just as the day darkened with the arrival of night. Or at least, that was what I first believed was the reasoning for the shift in daylight. What actually shadowed our final stretch was not, in fact, dusk, but the towering wall of polished stone that shot up into the sky before us. A wall, endless and proud, travelling as far as the eye could see into the sky whilst also wrapped around the city. For as far as my eyes could see, there was a slight curve to the wall, but no end in sight.

Our campaign fanned out, each stag coming to a stop in a line as we each faced the impossible wall, all but Queen Lyra and Althea, who rode ahead, side by side. I couldn't see if Briar still sat before her, nestled in Althea's arms. But I got the impression that Althea, much like Erix with me, would never leave Briar too far from sight again.

I noticed Tarron at our side, his gaze finally meeting mine for a brief moment. There was something tense about his presence, and it was likely conjured by the fact that I'd been led to believe he was on his way to Oakstorm now. If Erix noticed me looking at Tarron, he didn't mention it.

It wasn't that I didn't like his presence. There was something reassuring in knowing that the keeper of my deadliest secret was not too far away. But all I could think about was *why*.

A flash of deep ruby light burst from the front of the crowd. I snapped my head to see what'd caused it. Althea and her mother each raised a hand skywards, and a ball of twisting fire exploding from their palms. Up it flew, as though it was a fallen star reclaimed by the night. The flame was so large that I felt the heat from it where I sat, even at a distance. Upwards it flew, throwing deep light across the grey stone wall. Then it stopped dead in its flight, hovering in mid-air before imploding into nothingness in a shower of sparks.

"What was that about?" I asked.

"A signal," Erix replied, voice a whisper to avoid shattering the illusion of silence around us.

"For who?"

"To open the city. The Cedarfall family have returned."

A loud, earth-shaking crack sounded, and the wall began to split in two. The door to Farrador slowly opened, the grinding of metal ringing out across the night.

I expected to see a sea of buildings beyond, streets as full of life as Aurelia had been. But Farrador was void of city life, at least how I'd imagined it to be. When Father talked of the human capital of Lockinge, he'd made it seem as though the smell of cramped bodies was enough to spoil fresh food, or the noise of city life would ring in one's ears weeks after leaving. But what waited beyond the wall was not that.

It was... silence.

The hidden gate opened slowly, and Erix guided the stag into line as we all began following through. I tried to crane my neck to see more, only to be pulled back with Erix's steady hand. His low promise sent a shiver across the back of my head. "All good things come to those who wait for them."

Ash and smoke hung in the air, poisoning my lungs with each inhale. I clapped a hand over my mouth to stifle it.

Campfires raged all around me. Large fields stretched as far as I could see, not the types I'd seen before, square patches of different shades of farming and land, but an ocean of tents pitched across the flat and empty land, all leading up to a tower that stretched up into the sky ahead. Trees had been cut down to make way for the army soldiers who filled the cramped spaces between.

An army. Thousands of them. Maybe more. There was no possible way of counting or even dreaming up a number.

All this discussion of war and the threat to Durmain became real at that very moment.

I couldn't focus on anything but the camp. How it stretched as far as I could see, even to the edges of the circular wall that surrounded Farrador's land. It was overwhelming – horrifying and very real.

There wasn't a single sound from the campaign as we trailed the path that cut directly through the camp, leading up to the inner wall that surrounded the many towers of the Cedarfall castle. Soldiers stopped what they'd been doing as we passed, each looking at us with blank and unreadable expressions. Some tipped their heads to Queen Lyra in respect. Others didn't. Many even bowed as Tarron passed them.

These men and women weren't only from the Cedarfall Court, that much was clear, confirmed by a quiet murmur that Erix shared with me. They were the recruits from Elmdew, Oakstorm and Cedarfall. And from the few who couldn't hold my stare, I could only guess they may've been survivors from the Icethorn Court, before the land became a death trap to any who had inhabited it.

This part of the journey, cutting between the crowds towards the castle, felt like the longest. Before we reached the end, I kept my gaze to my lap, unable to look upon the soldiers a moment longer. If the unclaimed power of the Icethorn Court was a threat to the humans beyond Wychwood, this scene prompted a far greater concern for them.

It was impossible to choose which reality was most frightening.

Long after we passed through the second circular wall that gave way to the castle within, could I hear the rumbling noise of countless people. Erix was right about Farrador being a city full of soldiers. But what he failed to reveal was it was, in fact, a city *made* for soldiers. Fields trampled, trees chopped down, and even buildings levelled to give way for a sea of people ready to conquer a realm, using the Icethorn magic as their key for entry.

And if I had to bleed dry to prevent the war, then I was ready to be the one to wield the blade to ensure it never happened.

CHAPTER 29

I leaned against the rough stone wall, peering beyond the narrow window to the monstrous army that lay across the land far beneath me. It'd been over a day since our arrival in Farrador, and I still couldn't stop looking at the view. Even when I dreamed, I saw the image. It was as though I hoped it would become an illusion, a hope I clung to every time I gazed out the window and the reality of the situation sunk in.

The room I occupied was far up the western tower of Farrador castle. Brisk winds ripped around the tower, whistling and screaming. The narrow glass shuddered in the thin brass frame, the only noise besides the deep thump of life among the endless camp. The view was yet another reminder of what was to come if I turned my back on my birthright.

War.

"These books are not going to read themselves, Robin," Althea called, discarding a large tome on the chair beside her. She had to be careful not to drop it upon Briar's head where it rested in her lap.

"Wouldn't that be nice," Erix scoffed, barely looking up from the leather-bound journal he skimmed through, his brow set in a constant frown, his eyes narrowed in a squint of concentration. "The sooner the scholars arrive to help, the better."

The scholars' arrival had been postponed time after time. They should've arrived this morning, but lunch was upon us and still there was no sign of help.

"When will they come?" I asked Althea, noticing her shift on her reading chair.

"Soon, I hope," Althea drawled.

"That doesn't sound promising," I said, refusing to look away from her.

Althea chewed on her lower lip, sparing Briar a glance for confidence. "So far no scholar has answered our call for help."

"You've got to be joking," I snapped, my blood turning to ice.

Althea shot me a look; one I didn't need her to vocalise for me to understand. "Mother is trying everything in her power. They reply to our summons, but something is stopping them from actually following through with it."

Erix's stare bore into me. I dared not look, knowing it would likely bring me to my knees.

"They don't want me to find the answers," I said. "That's why, isn't it?"

"Most likely, but that doesn't mean we give up. Not yet," Erix answered.

"This is no good," I moaned, refusing to rejoin the circle of chairs and piles of books that had overtaken the majority of the chamber's living quarters. "Surely those who obtained these books could've narrowed them down. At this rate, The Passing will have come and gone long before we find any answers."

"If there are any answers to find, that is," Erix mumbled.

"Is he always this positive?" Briar's light voice filled the room. Some might've found her tone grating, but Althea seemed to love it, smiling at her as though Briar was a mythical siren, drawing her into a trance with her dulcet tones.

Althea placed her now empty hands upon Briar's short hair and began to comb it with her fingers. "Erix is just struggling to make sense of the words and is losing in our little race. He is bitter that his read pile is smaller than ours."

"Perhaps we refrain from talking about someone as though they are not in the room, huh?" Erix sat up in his lounge chair, dragging his boots from the stool before him and thudding them onto the ground. "And it is taking me longer to sift through my pile because you, so dutifully, gave me the thicker books."

"Is that an excuse, I hear?" Althea chirped, spurring a laugh from Briar, who clapped a hand to her mouth to stifle it. "And I thought you were well adept with thick things, Erix."

Erix closed the book and chucked it across the room at Althea. One quick swing of a hand, and she had knocked it to the floor.

"Would you both stop?" The back and forth between them was fun to endure at first, but we'd all had been in the same spot since before dawn, flitting through the scrolls, books and parchments for some clue as to what was required of me to claim Icethorn. It had been a long day, and my patience wore as thin as ice in spring. The only breaks we'd been allowed were when Althea had me practising calling upon the power within me; short exercises or excuses depending on how you looked at them. It gave us a reprieve from having sore fingertips as a result of turning countless pages. Between the conjuring of magic and the reading of never-ending books, my head felt as though it would implode. "This isn't helping."

"Robin's right. It has been a long day," Althea began. "I say we take a long break, and pick it up tomorrow. I can go and check on the court and see how they are getting on with the scholars. It is no good if we are trying to find answers but our minds are too tired to actually notice them among the pages. We could be skipping over information even now."

I crossed the room, snatching a book from my own pile and falling back into my chair. "We keep going until we find something." No one moved to join me until I looked up with a gaze of pleading. "Please."

Erix reached a hand for my shoulder and held it. "You deserve a rest, as do we. There is no harm in stopping for the day. We will always have tomorrow."

My mind slipped to Tarron, who I'd still not managed to speak with since arriving. This break from researching would be exactly the excuse I needed to see him. Maybe he had answers – he seemed to have them for everything else.

"And what happens if we are still in the same predicament tomorrow evening?" I asked, hands shaking. My heart hammered in my chest, making me press a hand above it as though that would stop it jumping out of its place. It'd been clear that the scholars and historians required to aid our search didn't want us to succeed. I understood why. They wanted to see the soldiers beyond the tower cross the ruined border of Wychwood and lay claim to the land and knowledge beyond. If I didn't accept the Icethorn Court, the magic there would simply make the claim to Durmain easier for the fey.

Not everyone in Farrador nor the Cedarfall Court wished to see me succeed, which only encouraged me further.

"Secrets cannot stay hidden forever," Althea said, snatching my attention. "If there is something to find, we will find it."

"And what if we can't?" I pressed on, anxiety a storm of wings in my chest.

"Put *can't* in your pocket and pull out try, because that is all we can do," Briar said, smiling as though she didn't realise tension bathed the room.

I didn't know Briar well, but I felt as though I couldn't be sharp with her. Firstly, because she rested in the lap of Althea, who was always deadly like a new blade, and secondly, she was far too kind. Even during this search party through the books, it was all one big game to her. Optimism poured off her in waves, and it was exactly what the room and I needed to hear.

"Briar, you're full of wisdom." *Just not the answers I need.*

I thanked her in my own way before burying my face in my hands. "You all go. I'll carry on until my eyes bleed. And don't bother telling me not to. You won't get far."

"*That* is exactly what I was expecting you to say," Althea said, as though she had finally realised something she'd pondered on for years. "Something has changed in you, Robin. Since we arrived to Farrador, you've been like a cat with a thorn in its paw."

"What did you expect of me?" I tried my best not to snap, even though I wanted to. "I didn't know what to imagine when we arrived, but a sea of soldiers from all the courts was not it. No one warned me."

"Robin, stop suggesting you are entitled to information you are not privy to." Althea's words slapped me from across the room. "No one told you because you didn't ask, nor have we particularly had the time to update you on such matters."

My cheeks warmed, and I felt the need to apologise, but I swallowed that need and buried it deep in my gut.

"Althea–" I raised a hand to silence Erix from carrying on.

"I won't let them march on Durmain," I said. "Whether the answers are in these books or not. I will accept the Icethorn Court, and then I will stop this war."

Briar sat up in time for Althea to lean forward, elbows on her knees. "Good. He knows what he wants. And how are you going to ensure it does not happen, Robin?"

Stupid question, since we'd just spent hours trying to find out that answer.

"I just told you," I said, finding her to be slightly grating. Even Erix winced, noticing my reaction.

"Yes, I get that. But then what?" Briar asked, smiling as she spurred me on. "The border may be safe, but the army will still be ready. Hunters will still take fey as they had before your family were killed. What next?"

"I… I…"

Had no words. No answer. Nothing but the vision of thousands of decorated soldiers, weapons in hands, rolling over Durmain like a tidal wave of steel and bone.

"You are merely strengthening the weakened fence that keeps us here and *them* there. The desire for revenge burns brightly in the people's hearts. That will need smothering if we are ever to have the opportunity to truly say that war is not an option."

For a Taster, she clearly knew more about politics than I did. Perhaps being in the right rooms, around the right people, had filled her with the knowledge.

I fought to keep Briar's gaze, seeing how the skin around her eyes softened as her expression melted into one close to sympathy, aided by a gentle hand that Althea placed upon her thigh.

"I don't know yet," I said.

"Then that is another problem that will have to wait in line. None of that matters if you do not succeed in claiming Icethorn, I suppose."

"Thanks, Briar," I mocked sarcastically.

Her eyes narrowed as her smile grew brighter. "You are welcome, Robin."

All we had found were poems and recountings of the first beings who were given the promise of power in return for ruling what we now knew as the courts, muddled and lyrical stories of Altar, the first fey, bleeding his children dry and filling them each with the soul of a season. And we all had agreed that could not be the answer, at least, I hoped it was not.

"Do me a favour, friend." Althea locked eyes with me. "Take a break. Or I'll order Erix to make you."

"But there are still more tomes to search through," Briar spoke up, breaking the tension. It was the first time I saw her with a frown. "I could stay and help. Why not think of it as a game? That might make it less daunting. And if we have no luck, we just have to move our search to a different source."

I fought the urge to snap and tell her that 'help' wasn't what I wanted right now.

Erix cleared his throat. "We are all open to suggestions."

"Over the coming days, many important figures will arrive in Farrador for the Passing. It is simply a case of listening and talking. Someone may know something that these books do not. I can help."

Guilt sprung in my core. Up until now I'd waved Briar off, disregarding her requests. But this might actually help.

"No," Althea snapped, eyes widening in panic. "I know what you are suggesting, and the answer is no."

"Oh, Althea." Briar cupped Althea's cheek. "You can't keep me swaddled up for all of time. Serving staff are the best for spreading news. If anyone holds information that they should not, it will be them. Give your word, and I can return to my station and dig for a lead. Someone would have heard old tales passed down from families. Others may just know gossip. I can help separate the useful from the not so."

"It is not a bad idea," Erix added, leaning his head back and crossing his arms over his chest as though he was ready to sleep.

"It is a *terrible* idea, Erix. Do not encourage her." Althea looked as though she could have jumped from her seat and tackled Erix to the ground. "Briar, it is not safe."

"As long as I'm not tasting Robin's food, I'm sure I will be fine," Briar said, not realising the pain her words caused me. Because she was right. I was the only person people wanted dead – it was me who threatened the lives of those who got too close.

"Briar, do not make me beg you to give up on this idea."

"I do not need to return to my station as taster, there are plenty of other jobs I can do." My throat dried at her comment, making it impossible to swallow without making a gulping noise. "Althea, you may be *my* princess, but I'm grown-up and can make this decision."

Briar may have been quiet and kind, but I could see she knew how to work someone into a corner to get what she wanted.

"Fine," Althea barked, although her face was pinched in tension as though that single word took effort to spit out. "But only until The Passing. Your pardon from your station still stands."

Pardon? I shared a glance with Erix, who noticed the strange choice of wording.

Briar leaned forward, smacking a kiss upon Althea's lips. I felt my mouth tug upwards without realising.

"Whilst Briar is doing that, I will use the time to speak with the courts themselves," Althea said. "I will have to be cautious as Elmdew and Oakstorm don't want you to stop the war, but I have ways of getting answers to questions without truly asking anything."

"I feel as though I should have some clever idea to help." Erix's deep voice rolled over the room. "But I suppose I will stick to the books for now."

"Make sure Robin's eyes don't fall out," Althea added. "He's going to need them."

The tugging of my lips turned into a full smile as I surveyed the group before me. Erix, Althea and Briar had become a team that I did not know I needed.

"Thank you, all of you," I said finally. "It helps to know I have others backing me; it makes the idea of the unknown that bit less daunting."

"But still pretty daunting?" Althea winced before laughing.

"Nasty girl." Briar nudged into her side, joining in with the laugh.

Erix reached for me and took my hand. I didn't care if Althea watched, she had seen us in a far more incriminating position than this. So I let him entwine our fingers together. His hand was warm, large fingers folding over mine and holding tight.

"Surely you did not think we would let you face the unknown alone?" Erix said softly, brows peaked above his grin.

I smiled up at him, wanting nothing more than to lay my head on his lap, as Briar had with Althea, and lose myself in his touch. His taste. "With you, how could I possibly feel alone?"

"He is like a weed, isn't he?" Althea whispered, conjuring a sharp giggle from Briar. "Sticky and entrapping."

I gave them a wink, which pinched Erix's chiselled cheeks pink. "I'm certainly pretty ensnared by him."

"Good," Erix whispered, his strong nose scrunching as he made a face at me. "That's exactly how I want you to feel."

Althea and Briar grew bored of our company and left in a cloud of pinching hands and light kisses, discarding their books on the remaining pile for Erix and me to search through without much of a thought.

Erix grew tired, eyes hardly able to stay open whilst he scanned the book across his lap. Whereas I didn't have that luxury, with the horror of possibility that clung to my mind, I could hardly imagine sleeping until I found the answer… whatever form that came in.

We did well for a short while, until a knock sounded at the door of the room. Reluctantly, I left the warmth of the nook I had made in Erix's embrace to answer it.

"Gyah," I murmured, surprised to see the warrior waiting beyond the threshold. I looked behind her, half expecting food to be brought as it had been the night prior, but the corridor was only full of new guards that lined the length of it. "Do you want to come in?"

She shook her head, dark curls tucked neatly behind the points of her ears. "I have been asked to provide you with this letter of summons."

Gyah revealed a small, folded parchment from her breast pocket, offering it to me between two fingers.

I took it from her, unfolded it and read the short note twice, then once again, because I could not quite believe the invitation that waited upon it.

We have much to discuss. Join me for dinner.
Tarron.

I looked back at her, wondering if she knew the contents. A flash of my father's image filled my head, followed by the stoic face of Tarron as he rode with our campaign when he should've been returning home. I put his presence down to the fact that his court was required in Farrador for the Passing, but that still didn't explain why I felt misled.

"I will wait for you, if you accept the invitation," Gyah said, face void of any expression. Her eyes flickered towards the room as though she expected Erix to be inside. "Tarron will not like to be kept waiting."

"Do I not have the luxury to decline?" I asked, unsure how I would tell Erix of the reason for my departure.

Gyah looked through me as she replied. "*Tarron Oakstorm* told me to tell you that it would be a waste of delicious food and equally delicious conversation, Robin." She repeated her words again, this time slower as though I hadn't truly understood them before, emphasised by the scolding use of my name. "So I will wait for you here."

Something was wrong; I could see it clearly across the taut, tense lines that haunted Gyah's expression.

I closed the door on her slowly, closing my fist around the note, already giving her my answer. My mind raced with what to tell Erix. Lie after lie filled my thoughts as options, but as he looked up at me over the top of the book, I could only tell him the truth.

"Tarron has invited me to dine with him tonight."

Erix laughed, returning his attention to the book dismissively. "Then he is going to have one very lonely meal with far too much to eat."

"I didn't decline."

"Pardon?"

I closed the space between us, plucking the book from his hands and placing it cover-spread on the table beside his chair. "He might have answers we've been looking for. I could speak with him and–"

"Tarron would be the first to gladly see you fail. You and I both know he won't aid you by revealing any information that will jeopardise his plans of domination and revenge." Erix scooped me into his arms, pulling me down onto his lap. "Refuse his invitation, and we can eat together. I promise for more interesting conversation and even better dessert."

"I'm going, Erix." I kept my voice stern, not wrapping my arms back around his shoulders even though I longed to. There were other answers Tarron could give me, ones I hadn't dared share with anyone else. "I understand you have a history, but I promise it's not like that between us. I'm not a prize to be fought after. But I must go – for my father."

Erix knew he couldn't argue with that, but he tried anyway. "What if I told you I don't want you to go to him?"

"I would apologise–" My lips tugged downwards, the frown creasing my forehead, revealed by Erix sweeping the strands of dark hair from my eyes "– then remind you that you don't control me."

Erix's frown set my stomach at unease "Little bird." He was panicking. I could see it in the fidgeting of his hands and the inability to keep his eyes from darting around my face and body. "I do not wish to control you. But I cannot lie and pretend this does not make me feel uncomfortable… the thought of you both sharing a meal. Alone."

"Why?" I asked him. *Give me a good enough reason, and I will decline.* Push my questioning for another day and stay with him here. I wanted that. Not to go to Tarron, but to stay locked within this room with Erix.

"I do not trust him, that is why." There was an urgency in his deepening voice.

"Do you trust me?" I asked.

He leaned into me, pressing his nose to my own. My eyes crossed as I held his gaze. "Am I a soft fool to say I do?"

I smiled. "A soft fool, yes. But not for that reason."

"Then I will come with you. I am your personal guard after all, and what he has to say in front of you, he can say with me in the room."

The invitation had not suggested a limit on who joined the dinner, but the conversation I needed to have with Tarron was not for Erix's ears. Not yet. *Not until I learned to trust him in return.*

"Erix, I'm going to ask you to wait here for me," I said, pulling myself from his grasp and standing from his lap. "Keep the bed warm for my return."

"But–" He pushed himself to stand, but I stopped him with a hand on his chest.

"Please… let me do this." The cord in my chest tightened as I looked back at Erix. "Gyah brought me the note. If you don't trust Tarron, then believe that Gyah will be my escort. I'm safe with her."

Erix trembled with the desire to reach for me, to hold me in place. But slowly and with arms shaking, he lowered himself back to the chair. "If Tarron makes a move, I give her permission to shift and rip his head from his shoulders."

"Now, now, Erix," I replied, wanting nothing more than to kiss away those lines across his tensed jaw. "Back in Durmain, that treasonous talk would get you killed if referring to a royal."

Erix's head tilted forward, looking up at me through his dark lashes. There was something sinister about his stare; it was the first time he looked at me like this, and hopefully the last. Then he replied, tone pointed and dangerous. "I would love to see him try."

CHAPTER 30

Tarron's chambers were modest in size, filled with the necessary requirements and nothing more. Not what I expected to find fitting for a royal prince. In its heart was a small table with two plush seats tucked beneath it beside a lounge chair which filled most of the space. His bedroom was in the north of the room, open doors giving way to a rather large four-poster bed, the sheets straight and untouched.

He smiled as I entered, looking up from the table which hosted silverware and food-covered plates. It was clear from his wide, azure eyes and subtle grin that he expected me.

Again, not that I had the choice to decline. We both knew that. It was clear from how prepared he was for my arrival.

"You came," he said, hands linked together before him as though he did not know what else to do with them.

"I was not under the impression I had a choice in the matter." My comment was said in jest, but even Tarron should not deny the sharpness that was hidden beneath my light tone.

"With me, you always have a choice." He looked to Gyah, bright eyes glowing as he dismissed her. "Thank you for your assistance in collecting Robin. I have got him from here."

She bowed and left swiftly, the door clicking shut to signal her departure. I was certain she mumbled something beneath her breath, but I didn't have a moment to grasp it.

"I feel as though I should ask you how you have been...

Forgive me if you have been waiting for my company, but court has been abuzz, and the time has not been right."

He had an air of cockiness about him as if he couldn't imagine a scenario where I didn't, in fact, desire his presence. But deep down, I knew that he was right. I had longed to see him and question why he was here and not in his own court with my father.

"What makes tonight any different then?" I asked, taking tentative steps into the room.

Tarron simply shrugged, pouting his lips as though he chewed the inside of his cheek in contemplation. "I suppose I simply couldn't wait another moment."

I studied him at a distance, hoping my focus would stop the creeping of red from flushing my cheeks. Tarron's jacket was a deep maroon, with gold threading twisting across his chest and sleeves like thorned vines. Buttoned only at his waist, it gave view to the low-cut tunic that scooped to reveal his strong bone structure across his collarbone. He wasn't crafted from muscle like Erix, but his tall, narrow frame still gave the impression of power, just in a different way. Tarron had gathered his long, curling hair into a bun that rested atop his head, unmoving like a crown. A single, disobedient strand draped to the side of his sharp and handsome face, defining the line of his jaw where it rested.

"If the invite had outlined a dress code for this evening, I would've put in more effort." My comment only tugged at his lips, creasing lines beside his azure gaze.

"You look…" His eyes ran the length of me, from head to foot. A shiver responded across every inch of skin, exposed and hidden. "Perfectly fine."

"Is that it?" I asked, forcing the joke out unnaturally. "I suppose I've been referred to as worse."

"Haven't we all?" Tarron swept into action, standing from the small table and moving until he stood guard behind one of the chairs with both hands gripping its back for support. "I do hope you are hungry. I would have sent word to ask what foods you like but thought that someone of your history would not be fussy with what is on the plate."

I joined him at the table, pulling a face as his words settled over me. "Because I am a poor boy, from a poor human village with no taste or trained palate?"

"Perhaps. Am I wrong?"

"Well, not exactly. I've never cared about what food I ate, only that I had some to stuff in my cheeks. Although I must say, I cannot imagine how anyone could turn their noses up at this." The table was covered in plates of all sizes. Some had thin-sliced meats folded over one another, layered with a drizzling of what smelled like mint. Another plate spilt over with grapes on the vine, another with potatoes whose skin looked crispy to the touch.

"Please." Tarron was beside me in two steps, pulling out the chair closest to me and ushering me into the seat. "Carry on standing in awe, and the food will be cold before you eat it."

I slipped into the chair, back stiff as I allowed Tarron to tuck me in. There were so many questions I had to ask him, but as he hovered so closely behind me, I found it hard to grasp onto a single one.

"Not that I don't appreciate the effort, but the last time I sat down for such an elaborate feast, someone tried to poison me," I reminded him, the memory doing a swell task at spoiling the food before me.

Tarron moved around the table, pulling his own chair free and sitting upon it as though it was a throne. Even with the table between us, we were close. His long legs stretched out beneath it, and I felt the brush of a knee against my own.

"If it makes you feel more at ease, no one but Gyah and I know of your visit here tonight. And the food was already brought to my room before Gyah was asked to send word of my invitation. If the food was poisoned, it would be to kill me, not you."

"Or you could be the one trying to take my life," I reminded him of the possibility.

Tarron smiled, flashing teeth. "If I wanted to kill you, Robin. Trust me when I say you'd be dead by now."

"Wow, that makes me feel fantastic. Thanks."

His wink sent a shock to my core

"Do you not have your own Taster?" I asked.

Tarron scoffed, tugging out a napkin and unfolding it across his lap. "Of course, and he is still standing, unharmed. Believe me, it is safe to eat. You look like you need something… sufficient."

There was an insult somewhere in his words, but my stomach distracted me with a rumble that made him laugh.

Polished silverware rested upon the table in front of me, catching the golden glint of light from the many candles that filled the corners of the room. Each wink was an invitation for me to reach for them and begin piling food on the empty plate that waited patiently before me.

I picked up the fork, stabbing it down into a hunk of sliced white meat, which I hoped was chicken. "It would solve the problem my presence means to you."

"Care to remind me which *problem* you refer to?" Tarron said over the rim of a glass. The warm glow of candlelight revealed the mark his lip had already left on the drink. He had clearly started that before I had arrived.

My cheeks flushed, so I popped the piece of chicken into my mouth and chewed on it to keep myself from saying something I would regret. Swallowing, I spoke. "Me putting an end to your plans of war and domination."

A flash of what could only be disappointment passed behind his eyes, darkening them for a moment. It was brief but I noticed.

"So you have made your choice?" Tarron asked whilst plucking a pale green grape from the vine before him.

"Are you dissatisfied? Want to tell the cooks that I'm eating with you tonight, just so they can quickly pop a dribble of poison in it?"

"Well." Tarron shook his head, popping the grape into his mouth and chewing politely with his lips closed. Only when the lump in his throat bobbed from swallowing did he continue. "There is still time to convince you otherwise, nor would I like this meal to be ruined by more death. It would truly spoil the evening."

"Is that why you invited me for dinner? To try and convince me that sending the army beyond these walls to level Durmain is the right thing to do? Or does it have anything to do with Erix and the response he'd have had knowing you called upon me?"

"Am I missing something?" Tarron ignored my initial question, which set me at unease. "Erix is your personal guard, not someone who should feel any type of way for you accepting a harmless invitation to dinner."

"Except he told me about you and him. Your past," I said quickly, enjoying the look of surprise that pinched his handsome face. "Interesting stories he had to share."

"He did?" Tarron's dark brow peaked, his stare unwavering from mine as he popped yet another grape into his mouth. "And what stories did *he* tell of me? Please... I would love to hear this."

I narrowed my stare on him, stabbing the fork in yet another piece of meat. Tarron did not flinch as the table shuddered beneath the impact. "Erix doesn't trust you. What I know of your history is disjointed and unclear, but the way he feels about you screams volumes."

"If he distrusts me so greatly, then what made him allow you to join me this evening?"

"I make my own decisions. He might not like you, but he does respect me–" Tarron's knee brushed against mine again, this time the connection silencing me.

"Have you told him about the secret we share since you are both such open books for one another?"

Father.

"No."

Tarron placed a finger over his lips, eyes wide. Then he pointed to the door behind me, then to his ears. I knew instantly what he warned. Gyah, and the many of Tarron's own guards who we'd passed on the way here, lining the hallways beyond. They'd likely be listening in, and that set me at unease. It also ruined my chance of asking the important questions, at least in the way I originally planned to. I supposed I'd just have to alter them.

"Of course, he doesn't know," I hissed.

"Then surely that suggests you do not trust him as you say you do?"

My grip on the fork tightened until my knuckles went white. "I'm getting the sense that you are using this against me. Is this all a joke to you? To get me in here just to make me feel like an idiot?"

Tarron's expression tensed, the blue of his eyes darkening to rough oceans. He reached across the table, jacket sleeve brushing over the food. His hand found mine and held it. His touch wasn't warm, not like Erix's. But it was still grounding and certain. The metal of his rings left a cold kiss across my own skin.

"Robin, I assure you I take what I know extremely seriously. I apologise if I have come across as disrespectful. Please know that is not my intention. I just... I have not had the chance to be in a setting like this for a long while. My years have been so taken up with planning and war council that it seems I have forgotten ways of conversation when in such... close proximity."

I looked at his hand and the pale tips of his fingers as he held me. It was this hand that had led the current of war and encouraged it. Tarron and his revenge were what likely sparked the creation of the overwhelming camp that waited beyond the layering of brick separating the castle from the outside world.

"You should practice more then," I said quietly, unsure if I should pull my hand away or let him carry on holding it.

"Oh, I do hope I get the chance to."

A flush of warmth crept into my cheeks the second Tarron let go of my hand. He sat back in his seat, lips parted as though he thought of what to say next, but I spoke first.

"I was under the impression you would be returning to Oakstorm with my father. Does he not need your magic to help him heal?"

"He is in safe hands. There are others in my home who can help him. The antidote has done the necessary, all he needs now is time. And anyway, with the Passing sneaking up on us, I didn't feel comfortable leaving you."

"But the inking—"

"*Has* been removed. I personally saw to the deterioration of the ink. His body took to it well, absorbing it into the blood stream. There is nothing amiss for anyone to discover."

My cheeks burned with his intense stare. "Thank you."

"Of course." Not *'you're welcome'* which suggested he didn't do it for me, but actually for himself.

"Aren't you going to ask me what he said about the mark," I said.

"His excuse? No. I trust you will tell me if I needed to know. And anyway, spoiling dinner over a discussion of Hunters and their hate for our kind would really not be ideal. Instead, tell me what you think of the legion of soldiers outside that window. Are you impressed?"

"Should I be?"

Tarron shrugged. "Part of being a king is caring about the movements of your people."

King. Your people. I hadn't claimed the fey, or my heritage yet. And I got the impression Tarron knew exactly what he was saying, and how his words had an effect.

But he had my father. I couldn't say the wrong thing.

"I don't feel a sense of ownership over anyone, Tarron. Not those soldiers, only the innocent lives they could threaten."

"So you do feel a sense of ownership? Just over the humans."

Blood rushed up my neck, spreading cold fingers across my back. "I'm not going to answer that."

"It's ok. Anyway, there will be plenty of festivities to follow. Not all the perks of being a king are negative. How has your research been coming along? I've heard that Queen Lyra's scholars are being a little tricky in coming to help you."

"Court gossip?" I asked.

Tarron nodded. "Seems like you are really up against some barriers, Robin."

He was talking about the war, the soldiers shifting their camp closer to the Wychwood and Durmain border, readying to strike once the unclaimed power of the Icethorn Court did most of the initial damage, information I had dragged from Althea the night we had arrived in Farrador.

"I know you want to go to war, Tarron. But for that, wouldn't the term war suggest you have someone to fight against?" I asked. "Surely you know that the humans are not prepared for what is to come. If you succeed, then you'll have no resistance from them."

"Does not seem fair, does it? But why are you talking about such matters if you are decided on the choice of accepting your court, what it means for the realms if you do."

"Wouldn't I simply be halting your plans rather than stopping them all together?" I retorted. "Even if the border stays strong and a ravenous winter is not sent over Durmain, would your army not simply wait for another moment to strike? I trust that revenge will linger far longer than the border."

"You are very smart for someone with human blood running through your veins."

"That sounds much like a compliment but *feels* more like a punch to the jaw."

"I admit if you claim the court it would ruin the map of plans we have spent years conjuring. But you are right that it would not stop a war, only postpone it. It is why you should give up on the idea of stopping me. Revenge is ancient and inevitable, and my urge for it only grows with each passing day."

I knew what it was like to lose a loved one, and knowing the humans were to blame for the fact I'd never see my mother pained my heart as though a dagger was twisted within it. But it didn't make me want to lay waste to an entire civilisation.

"Revenge cannot be your only motivator," I said, my hunger almost non-existent now. "Is it land you want? Isn't that what old leaders fought over? Land, love and pride. You would really lay siege to thousands of innocent lives just in the pursuit of revenge for what happened to your family? What of those who survive your attack. What is to stop them from seeking the very same revenge against you?"

"It is not only land, love or pride that motivates war. Even coin doesn't come into play. For me, it is duty," Tarron growled as he replied, the last three words let out with effort as he gripped the table before him. "I do it for family, but those who want the same as me have their own reasonings. Perhaps some are motivated by land. Each year our numbers grow, and space unconfined by a border would be luxurious. Maybe some want war for love, slaying the monsters who clawed families in two as they did with mine. We all have our reasons, each as valid as the other. I am surprised you choose to stand in the way to protect the people who tore so much away from you. Not everyone is that *good*, Robin."

"I'm not good," I told him; it took a lot not to stand abruptly from the chair as I said it. "My choices are made for selfish reasons. Whether it be the need for a distraction." My mind flirted with the image of Erix and his strong touch. "Or the desire to finally feel like I have something. Growing up in Grove, I never really belonged. But here I do. And this is a feeling I don't want to let go of."

"Which leads us back to our new issue. Accepting the power

of your lineage will not *prevent* a war, but postpone it, Robin. With or without the aid of the enteral winter your family's power will lay across Durmain, the war will happen one day. Surely you have understood that? Those who wish to seek vengeance for the pain the humans and their Hunters have caused will find another way."

"Do you have a habit of speaking about yourself in the third person, Tarron?"

He bit his lower lip, carefully holding back whatever he was going to say next.

There was a tension between us, so taut, the very air felt as though it was going to shatter. Neither one of us spoke for a moment. All I could do was look at him as he looked at me. Part of me felt the strong need to stand and leave, demanding Gyah take me back to my room where I'd lose myself to the distraction that waited for me. Erix, not the piles of unhelpful books. But there was another part of me, small but undeniable, and that told me not to leave Tarron.

At least not yet.

"Do you know how your mother was murdered?" Tarron asked me. Even the flames across the candles seemed to stop dancing as the question settled over the room.

"A gryvern attack." My voice cracked as I replied.

"And who sent them?"

"If you are trying to prove a—"

"Who sent them, Robin? Answer the question."

"A human. Someone from Durmain. It doesn't matter because it will never change what happened."

"Yes, the humans did, but specifically the Hand. The mysterious leader who instructs the Hunters to continue abducting and killing *our* kind."

It was hard to conjure an image of a person who hid behind a legion of murderers who proudly wore the marking to join them all as one, the same mark inked across Father's ribs.

"What are you trying to prove? That the command of one man should make me feel the need to justify the killing of many?"

"Why?" Tarron added coldly. "Why did they attack the Icethorn Court specifically? No other attacks occurred across Wychwood. The gryvern attacked your family and your family only. Why?"

I shook my head, unable to conjure an answer.

"Rumours started before your mother took her final breath, stories of a child, made from an affair, between Julianne and her human lover. At first, it was courtly gossip, something the nobles and dignitaries would whisper behind backs as entertainment. It was believed that it was that link that caused such a targeted attack. Why else would she have been the focus of the monsters? She was the one who got away. And the Hand's victims… they never escape him."

Father would never have done that. I knew it as clear as a summer day. I had never been so certain of anything in my life before.

"I was invited here to eat, not to answer double-sided questions." I moved to stand, but Tarron beat me, pleading me to wait with an outstretched hand.

"There is something I need to tell you, but it needs to be somewhere more private…" My eyes darted to the open doors that led to his bedroom. He must've caught my glance, because he looked down to his clasped hands, trying to fight the grin.

I felt the need to shout at him, to remind him this was no laughing matter. Instead, I just stood, pathetic and shaking, as his accusations riled through me.

"And I want to return to my room. If I'd known this dinner would've gone down such a dark and disagreeable route, I would've refused it in the first place."

"But you did not, and you are still here. There is one last story I need to tell you, and then I promise not to bring it up again."

"I'm not going to your bedroom." I didn't know why I said it so abruptly. He had not once suggested that was where he wanted me, but it was the only place of privacy I could see.

"A shame, but understandable. But there is somewhere else I would like to take you equally as much."

There it was again, the creeping of guilt, as Tarron's throwaway words proved Erix's theory that this was all some game to him. And I was the prize.

"Why can I never say no to you?" I asked.

"Because you are a smart man."

Tarron closed most of his hand into a fist, leaving only two extended fingers free. He stepped beside the table and sliced his fingers down through the air. At first, nothing happened, the action random and alarming, but then the air shivered and separated. Two beams of light peeled away from one another to show one of his spindle-like portals. Where it led, I was unsure. The scene beyond was dark, but the wind that escaped through it was real as it tugged at the dark strands of my own hair, even from a distance.

"We can talk freely, where ears do not follow us," Tarron whispered, standing before the spindle of light, half his body engulfed by it.

I hesitated before stepping towards him. My body, although my mind screamed for me not to follow, refused to obey. One step after the other, I moved towards him.

"Is this the part you take me somewhere unguarded and stab me in the back?"

Tarron extended a hand for me to take. "Robin, I am not one to stab my enemies in the back. If I were to do it, I would want to look at you, face to face, with nothing but a blade width between us."

A shiver ran up from my legs, across my spine and down my arms until my fingers numbed as a response to his words. But still I took his hand. "You are the type of man I was warned to run from."

"Then why are you not running from me?" he asked, guiding me towards the portal of light.

"Because my father always taught me to face danger and never turn my back on it."

With that, we both stepped into the portal, leaving his room behind us as we were greeted by cold night air and deathly silence.

CHAPTER 31

The dark, dank air slapped me in the face the moment our feet stepped through the portal of splintered light. When Tarron's power receded, it gave way to nothingness. There was no light here. Without the reassuring hand holding my own, I'd have believed that I'd been tricked into meeting death itself.

The darkness was heavy, each breath a struggle as though moisture filled the air in abundance. I dared not let go of Tarron's guiding hand.

"Where are we?" I asked, and the echo of my voice carried on as it travelled through the space. No matter how hard I focused or strained my eyes to make out just a small detail of the destination, I saw nothing. Fear should have reached me, but it seemed to be kept at bay by Tarron's touch.

"Somewhere we can talk freely." Light exploded to life at my side. It illuminated a glow over Tarron and me, a small spinning orb which hovered above Tarron's free hand. It was as though he held the golden sun in his palm. The light spread as the orb grew in size until I could make sense of old towering walls and a curved ceiling above.

"Farrador has always been known for having one of the greatest tombs across Wychwood." Tarron smiled, skin glowing with golden light as though he too gave off its power. It lit him up from the inside as though he harboured a star beneath his skin. "It would not usually be my choice of visits after a dinner, but needs must, and all that."

"You've brought me to talk among the dead?" A shiver passed over the skin of my exposed neck as though a ghostly finger tickled across it.

"Well." His smile reached his glowing eyes, giving him a sense of mischief. "When you say it like that, it sounds as though I have bad taste. But we can speak freely without the worry of the dead relaying the secrets we have to share. Are you frightened, Robin?"

"Creeped out yes, frightened hardly."

I let go of his hand now that I could see around me. There was a reluctance from him to pull his fingers away, but he did so without refusing. I put space between us, noticing how the barren tunnel before me made even my footsteps echo. "I have so many things I want to ask, but all I can think about is knowing how you do this."

"Do what?" Tarron followed me at a distance.

"You use your power so freely, in ways that I cannot fathom." I'd seen Althea conjure flame with ease, but it seemed Tarron's power of light gave him more uses than I would've thought possible.

"You understand the law of magic in Wychwood, do you not?"

My eyes traced over the stone figures that stood guard on either side of the tomb. They each were unique, faces differing in detail, but all sharing the same look of rest with eyes closed and hands crossed over their chests, men and women, young and old, and each shared a resemblance to the living Cedarfall family; I could recognise the familiarity in each etched stone.

"Power is in blood. The larger the court's family, the weaker it is. The smaller, the more from the pool of magic they can call upon."

"So, they have not kept everything from you..." I wanted to ask what he meant, but Tarron carried on as though he meant to interrupt the time for questioning. "There are only a few of the Oakstorm Court living, myself and my father, and an uncle whose way I prefer to stay out of. Whereas the Cedarfall family share the magic bestowed upon their line across the hordes of their children and family, I do not. It gives me access to the strains of magic that would have been shared out if my family had not been taken from me. When an Oakstorm dies, their power returns to the pool. That is what determines the potency magic, how many have access to it. We've all paid unfair prices in this life, no cost weighs heavier than another."

"I'm sorry," I felt the need to say, as his light wavered at telling the story. My question had, unnecessarily, caused Tarron to explain the loss he had endured.

"Never be sorry for something you are not responsible for. You have lost far more than I could imagine. At least my father still lives. Whereas you don't have a family. You share your magic with no one else. It is solely yours."

"Still does not mean I have any sense of controlling it. The power inside feels wild and untamed." I raised a hand before me, focusing on the coil of magic in my chest. I had to coax it to listen, silently begging for it to do as I wished. The air around my hand crackled as I forced the coldness within me to reveal itself. "Even now, I'm not sure whether it will listen or decide I'm unworthy of command and devour this room entirely."

Tarron's lips pursed into a line of concentration. He closed the space before me, pressing his free hand upon my wrist to hold my hand up in place. "I see that the power you were destined to have was kept from you by iron all these years. I heard about the bracelet your mother bestowed upon you and how it kept your destiny at bay. You may believe that it is the reason as to why you struggle to command your abilities, to fully explore them, but you are wrong."

"Enlighten me then, Tarron."

He released a sigh, eyes narrowing in on mine. His touch was warm and assured, and so was his attention as it was completely on me as though I owned him.

"The moment you realise that the magic within is not a separate entity to who you are, will be the same moment you finally command it without hesitation and fear. The magic is you, just as you are the magic."

"You make it sound easy." I looked up at him through my lashes. His fingers drummed across my wrist as he still held it, a shackle of flesh, tethering us to one another. If he didn't need to hold the light across the tomb, I was certain both of his hands would've been on me.

"Being yourself should be easy, Robin," Tarron said, voice quiet. There was no need to talk loudly as we stood so close. "Now, show me what you can do."

"I shouldn't."

"Why not?" His eyes never left me.

"Well, what if I hurt you?" *Or myself.* The last time I'd used my magic to stop the gryvern, I nearly lost myself to it.

Tarron looked at me dead in the eyes as though he wished to study the soul I hid within. "Then I would wear the scars like a badge of honour. You think I should fear you, but I do not. I have faced far greater threats. Now do it, Robin. Show me who *you* are."

Part of me longed to pull away from him and refuse, but there was something about his bright-sky gaze that I knew deep down I couldn't say no to. Even if refusing was the right thing to do, everything about the princeling before me was the opposite of right. I wasn't certain if that was a good or bad thing.

With Tarron holding onto me, I closed my eyes, giving in to my inner darkness. I reached down for the coil of power, keeping my reluctance at bay as I took hold of it. I imagined it as a hand, reaching for something that belonged to me and no one else. I took it without hesitation and lifted it from the cage it had so willingly made within me.

I scrunched my face as the gentle kiss of cold fell upon me. With my eyes still closed, it felt as though butterflies of ice flirted with me, landing upon my head, my cheeks, and any exposed parts of skin that I revealed. When I opened my eyes, I saw what caused it.

Snow fell upon us, released from the pregnant cloud of mist that grew above our heads. I laughed, surprised by my reaction. But I was doing this. Me. The magic was beautiful and calm, not frightening and dangerous. I knew it could be at my whim, and that made me feel a sense of control I hadn't experienced up until this point.

"See," Tarron whispered, flecks of snow falling upon his brown curls, where they melted. "That was not so bad, was it?"

"I can't believe I'm doing it." I couldn't comprehend how I held onto the power, but it was as though it reflected the inner calm I felt, thanks to Tarron and his words.

He let go of my wrist and reached a hand for my cheek. My breath hitched as he reached for me, but his thumb only brushed away a flake of snow that rested upon my cheekbone. "Perhaps I am a fool to give you the advice to embrace who you are meant to be. It will likely scupper the plans I have spent years aiding and perfecting."

There was a sense of hesitation to his touch as he pulled away. The snow thickened as my emotions changed from calm to a type of disappointment that surprised me. "Then why do you want to help me? You keep doing it, and I don't understand why"

Tarron's light dulled for a moment, and the orb he controlled without effort shrunk in size until the tomb became dark and only we were bathed in light. He finally dropped my gaze, looking to the floor as he contemplated a thought that clearly bothered him. "I do not believe I have the ability to answer that question."

I reclaimed the magic that I'd released until the snowflakes ceased their small kisses across my exposed skin. Tarron didn't look back at me, even though my mind screamed for his attention. The silence between us was long and painful.

"I think we should head back," I said finally. "Before Gyah discovers we're missing and alerts Erix."

"Yes, perhaps. We wouldn't want to make him feel... contested," Tarron replied. "But do you not wish to know what I wanted to tell you before you run off? The very reason I asked for your company tonight?"

With everything that had happened – had been said – it had escaped my mind. "I do."

Tarron sliced his hand, the air before him parting in two. He conjured a spindle of light that exposed the view of his chambers once again. I expected him to offer a hand for me to follow, but he did not. He kept his back towards me as he spoke. "To claim the court, you must offer a trade to the power, just as the founding fey had. Magic is in blood, and it is that blood you will exchange, in full, as the first did."

It was the same story Erix had shared – the answer staring at me in the face this entire time.

"Why would you tell me this?" In little words, he had confirmed what the stories and poems suggested.

"As I said." He glanced back at me. "I am a fool."

He took a step forward, one foot through the portal of light. I snapped out, willing for him to wait. "I have to bleed and make room for the power that is left unclaimed."

Tarron was hesitant to respond. In a way, I believed he would not, that he'd step fully through the portal without answering my question. "Magic isn't simply in your blood. Magic *is* your blood."

I pondered his words as he finally stepped through the portal. I understood the difference between us finally, even what set Althea apart from me. And with his answer, I knew what I had to do.

As I followed Tarron through the portal, my mind could only contemplate one loud thought. The answer to what was required of me to claim my fate.

And I knew it involved visiting the Icethorn Court without another moment to waste.

CHAPTER 32

"Robin!" an exasperated voice called as I stepped through the spindle of light into Tarron's chamber. I barely had a moment to register what was happening before strong hands took hold of my upper arms. Erix was before me, a broad frame blocking Tarron from view. If the quiver of his deep voice didn't indicate his panic, the pale expression I looked up at did.

"Has something happened?" I asked, wincing as his grip tightened into a pinch at my skin. It must have been something terrible from his reaction. My mind instantly went to Father.

"*He* took you," Erix growled, body trembling, the darks of his eyes devouring the silver. "What did he do... Where did you go?" With each question, Erix's voice grew raspier and more urgent.

"Always the one for overreacting," Tarron spoke up, voice laced with poisonous sarcasm. "I should have known you would come looking. Could not bear to sit and wait, like the patient puppy you are hired to be."

It was my turn to reach for Erix as he snapped from me and turned to face the Oakstorm prince. "This is all a game to you, isn't it?"

"A game? Do I look like a child, *berserker*? You could not even comprehend what this is." Tarron spat the last two words, straightening his posture to add as many inches of height as he could in comparison to the man before him; Tarron would have had to stand on a box to meet his eyes.

I pulled at Erix's arm, working myself between the men. My fists slammed into his chest, demanding his attention, but it only pained me as though I had connected with a wall. Erix hardly looked my way, as though my attempt was futile.

"Stand down," I warned. "Tarron is only trying to help us."

"That is right," Tarron agreed, light and unbothered, as though a goliath was not moments away from throwing fists. "I suggest you calm yourself down, preferably outside this room, before you make more of a fool of yourself. Not only are you without an invitation to this dinner, but you are embarrassing yourself in front of Robin."

His comment caught me off guard, so much so that Erix pushed me to the side and stepped toe to toe with Tarron. There was no getting between them now.

"Speak carefully, Tarron."

"Losing control, are you?" Tarron huffed, lifting his hand to inspect a nail. "I can see the fractures clearer than I had all those years ago."

Spittle flew beyond Erix's paled lips. "Provoke me again and watch me shatter."

"Oh, I would love that. You may not claim it, but you are an Oakstorm-born fey, which makes me your ruling court by birth. And I have a sense that you are asking for a reminder as to what can happen when one threatens someone of, how do I put this? Higher rank."

Erix cocked a fist back, but before it connected, I forced myself between them again.

"That is enough. Both of you!" I shouted. "Erix, I want to go back to my room. Right now."

He ignored my request, his back heaving as he took in shuddering breaths. "This will be the last time you see him alone."

"Tightening the leash are we, Erix?" Tarron almost laughed as he spoke. "How daring of you to believe you can tell an Icethorn what to do."

The string of sounds that Erix replied with could not be translated into words. It was a feral growl that grew in volume throughout his extended exhale. My heart stopped as he reached for the hilt of a blade resting at his hip. Tarron hardly noticed, but I did, and I understood enough of what would follow if Erix acted upon the dark wishes that plagued his mind.

"Enough!" The command exploded from me, sending a rush of ice-cold mist across the room towards them. It made the air crackle as the warmth of the room dropped within an instant, the conjured, frozen winds extinguishing every dancing candle flame and burning fireplace.

The magic came more naturally, without thought or reasoning. My words hadn't been enough to stop the two men, so my instincts willed the next powerful thing.

"Tarron," I said, breathless, body full of magic and the potential it offered. "Thank you for your dinner and the time you have given me."

"The pleasure," he purred, eyes pinned to Erix, "was all mine."

"Erix," I said sharply. I felt his reluctance to look at me in the stiff turn of his neck. Only when his hand moved away from the hilt of the blade did I retrieve the cold magic from the room. "I'm tired and have had enough of this charade. It's time for bed. Now."

Everything about Erix was tense, all but his brows, which melted into an expression of sorrow and embarrassment as he looked at me. His simple reply was all I required from him.

"Is that a command, Robin?" Erix said.

"It is."

Erix snapped to attention, moving from Tarron, who bowed his head in farewell. I caught his smile, not once had it wavered from his face. I mouthed him a quick apology just as Erix came to a stop beside me.

"After you," he said, voice thunderous.

I swept ahead, needing to get out of this room, and put distance between us. Erix followed.

We left beneath a cloud of tension. It was clear Gyah, and every other guard beyond the door, had heard the commotion, but I faked a smile as though nothing was wrong, even though Erix exuded anger as though it seeped from every one of his pores.

Neither one of us spoke until we finally reached my room. I slammed the door, needing to take my fury and embarrassment out on something.

"What the fuck is wrong with you, Erix?"

He paced the room, one hand on his head, the other dramatically pointing to the door. "He is what is wrong with me. I should have never trusted that he would not have pulled tricks to get you alone. Anything could have happened."

"But it didn't! I'm fine." We were both shouting. Where Erix couldn't stand still, I felt that if I even took a step forward, I would reach for the nearest thing and smash it against a wall. "Why were you even there? You should have stayed here."

"Because I found something that may help with the claiming. I went there only to share the news and found the room empty. Gyah had assured me you had been inside with *him*, so I knew he would have blinded you with his magical tricks and lured you somewhere else. Do you know how dangerous it could have been?"

"You are completely missing the big picture. I'm fine. Untouched, unharmed and actually rather pissed off. Why can't you see that and realise your worrying and anger is all a result of your insecurities?"

He paused, looking at me with a face pinched in disgust. "What did you just say?"

"Well, what else could it be?" I laughed. "Tarron has done nothing but present himself to me with respect and kindness. He's given you, and me, no reason to label him as untrustworthy. Yet you fly off the handle at the smallest given thing."

"I am not insecure." His growl sent a cold shiver up my spine. Erix ceased his pacing and walked towards me; his sudden presence thrilled me, even if I hardly dared admit it.

"Then what is it?" I lowered my voice, unable to hold confidence in my shouting with him so close. "Ego?"

"I'm a–" Erix stopped himself, slapping a hand into his cheek until his skin was pink. "It is Tarron. You do not know him as I do. Not even a bit. I have told you what he did to someone I cared about, and I will not let that happen again."

"Maybe he's changed."

"People change. Monsters stay the same."

I stared into his eyes, feeling the weight of his tension; unlike his anger for Tarron, this was different.

There was no arguing my point against Erix's remark without giving away the secret about Father, so I gave him the second reason, the one that was still fresh in my mind. "For someone who wishes for war more than any other, he may have just suggested what I have to do to claim the Icethorn Court."

"It will be a trick," Erix seethed through gritted teeth. "Whatever he says is a lie only to better his own standing."

"I have to bleed for the court," I said quickly, silencing Erix from saying another word. "Just as you said. Magic is in my blood, but it should *be* my blood. It is just what you had first thought, or what the stories, poems and recollections suggest. And I know it is what is required of me."

I expected Erix to respond abruptly, to tell me I was wrong or what Tarron had said was a lie, as was everything else he believed came out of his mouth. But he didn't. "I really wished it was not true."

"Oh, so now you believe him?"

Erix moved from me and picked a book that lay, pages splayed, on the table within the room. Returning before me, he handed me the open book with a slight shake of his hands. "This depiction is the only similarity to all the books we have searched. Although the words around them, and the style of the drawing changes, they all show the same image."

I looked down at it, noticing the similarity to a drawing that was in the pages of another book I had searched. It was simple, showing the outline of four figures, the first fey. Beneath them, where their bare feet hung upon the page, were lines of flowing water, at least, that was what it could have been, except I now saw it as what Tarron had confirmed. Blood. The figures each had their hands extended upwards as though reaching for something beyond the page, and it was around each of those hands that the artist had drawn symbols. In this book, they held each of the court's symbols. The Cedarfall's burning tree, which I recognised first. Then there was the outline of a stag with a crown of sun between its antlers, a symbol I had seen pinned to Tarron's chest. There were two other symbols, one of which looked like a splash of dark water wrapped around an obsidian goblet, and the remaining one had my fingers reaching for it, a sword piercing skywards through the outline of mountains.

I knew in my heart, which voiced confirmation, that the symbol belonged to the Icethorn Court.

"It was as though the answer was staring us in the face, but we were too ignorant to notice," Erix said as I ran my finger over the drawing.

Finally tearing my focus from the book, I looked back to Erix. "Give me a reason not to do this."

"There is a risk–" Erix couldn't finish his sentence. He didn't need to either, because my mind screamed with the possibility.

There is a risk that I would die. That it would not work, and we were being falsely led by unclear drawings and the words of a prince who, deep down, wished me to fail. Although I couldn't let go of the hope that Tarron did, in fact, wish to help. Monster or not, I believed he could change. I had after all.

"If I don't at least try, I'll live to watch an army ruin the realm which I call home."

"Then we will try together, for it is my duty to keep you safe." Erix took the book from me, closed it, and discarded it to the floor without thought. His stormy silver gaze flickered across my face, his hands reaching up to hold my cheeks as though he wished to keep me before him forever.

"I have never asked you why."

"Why what?" His thumb brushed my cheek in a soothing rhythm.

"Why do you help me as you do? Why are you here? Is it because it is your duty as my guard, and you follow commands that have been issued to you? Or...?"

"Or is it because I care deeply for the brave man before me. It is not an excuse for my behaviour, but it is undeniable, and if I do not say it now, then I may live to regret keeping it from you. I once lost someone I cared deeply for, and when I am ready to share that story with you, I will. But seeing you with Tarron, clambering through that power of his, brought back a memory of the last time he passed through with someone I cared deeply for. They went in, claiming to share that emotion back in heart and soul, only to return again as though I was the vilest, twisted and most hateful person in the realm. Seeing his magic again triggered a response I have fought for years to control." Erix paused, steadying his breathing, and slowing his frantic words. "And it is all because I care for you, little bird."

No one had ever said this to me, not with such honesty as burned from the man before me or the way his gaze pleaded with me to believe him. At first, I was unsure if I could respond. But I breathed, gave in to the face that I couldn't bear to never look upon again and let go of my inner thoughts. I allowed myself to reply with the honesty he deserved.

"I care about you too. I don't understand it just yet, but if you are willing to be patient with me, then I hope I can explore what that means."

"As long as tomorrow is a possibility with you, I would do anything to ensure it."

A tomorrow. A simple sentiment that meant so much to me.

Erix smiled, which settled a wave of relief over me. I wasn't ready to express undying love or mislead him into lying about feelings I was simply not prepared to face yet. But I did care about him, and that was enough for me, and for him, by the look on his face.

"I can offer that," I replied.

"Then I wait for you, for as long as you require."

I thanked him the only way I felt was right in the moment. Stepping up onto my tiptoes, I pulled his face down, the prickle of a beard scratching my palms, and guided his lips to mine. The kiss was tender and soft, with the control of warm wanting kept at bay. Erix trailed his hands from my cheeks, down across my shoulders and to the small curve of my back, where he pulled me into him. Our lips moved as one, allowing our tongues to brush against one another for the perfect balance. Part of me wanted to bite down on his lower lip and spur him to wrap my legs around his waist and clatter into the wall behind us. But for the first time, I didn't need a distraction, nor did I wish Erix to be one. The next time he would have me, it would be for another reason entirely.

It was Erix who pulled away first, before the heat between us intensified into something unignorable. "It would seem we have a plan, finally."

My lips tingled, likely painted pink from the kiss. His were the same, tinged red and lips slightly swollen. "I need to get the message to Althea and Briar. Tomorrow, we head for Icethorn, and then I'll attempt to claim the court."

Erix winced, knowing it involved me bleeding out and the pain that would come with it. "You will succeed. I know it."

I swallowed hard, burying the bile that crept up my throat. "If we go and it works, I come back in time for the Passing and to stop a war. And if it fails–"

Erix stepped in, closing the minimal space, and laying a finger on my lip to silence me.

"We shall face that difficulty if it comes to it. Together."

CHAPTER 33

Morning came suddenly, as though I had slept for only a moment, but as my mind came to, I was certain I hadn't had such a deep and welcoming sleep for as long as I could remember. Unbroken, aided by the warmth of Erix's naked body, where he'd slept in the bed beside me all night. Perhaps it was his closeness that made me feel at ease and safe. It hadn't taken much persuading for him to agree to share my bed, not that we touched more than an inch of skin the entire sleep.

The plan was confirmed by a note that was delivered with breakfast. Althea and Briar had agreed to our request to leave for the Icethorn Court as soon as Althea convinced her mother to allow the gates at the edge of Farrador to open and to arrange our means of travel. Before the sun reached its peak, they promised to send for us. Until then, we were left to a morning of peace. We shared food and spoke of minor, unimportant things to distract me from what was to come.

I should've known this peace would not last.

We were dressed and ready to leave for Icethorn, when the gryvern's blood-curdling screams filled the sky beyond Farrador Castle. I reached the window first, peering out at the cloud of winged beasts as they raced through the dawn-tinged sky towards the castle. The army who camped in the barren fields beyond were alive with shouts, hardly audible above the ferocious noise the demonic creatures created. I could see arrows fired, swords drawn, but the gryvern ducked and dodged every attempt to bring them down.

Everything happened so quickly, but I was certain not a single beast was hit.

"You've got to be fucking kidding me–"

"Get away from the window!" Erix interrupted, tugging me with force from the window and into the belly of the room. "They can't know you are here. If they sense you, we will not stand a chance."

Of course the gryvern were here for me. On the dawn that would change the course of the realm's future.

It was almost too obvious. Someone knew of my plans and was attempting to stop me.

The thought encouraged the winter inside my bones to escape, laying the stone wall in a layer of famished ice.

"We can't let them stop us, Erix. We need to leave now," I said. I was ready for one of the monsters to break through the window and face the wrath I held back. The dagger Erix had given me was already drawn free, gripped tightly in one hand. My magic only a thought – a beat – away.

"If we leave, they will follow," Erix replied, brows furrowed in concentration. He, too, waited, his hand on the hilt of his sword as the other held me close to his chest. "I'm sorry, Robin, but it is not safe. If they come, then we fight. You stopped them before. You can do it again."

I had no doubt.

"Let them come," I warned, arms and legs beginning to shake as adrenaline raced through me. Pure, blinding anger filled my veins in a flash. How dare these creatures ruin yet another moment? We could not let them postpone our plan, but if they did, I was ready to give them a fight. "I get the impression this is to stop us from leaving?"

"I can't help but think the same, little bird. But we should see this through and then worry about who sent them. The important thing is we still have time."

But time was fickle and quickly running out.

The wait for the gryverns' destruction went on for long, painful moments. Surely, they had passed over the army's camps and reached the castle? I wanted to return to my post by the window and see, but Erix's strong arm held me in place.

All I could do was listen to the noise of leathered wings as they beat against slick dark bodies. How they screeched and clicked and made sounds that no person or living creature should dare make. The discomfort of not knowing, of being blind to their positioning, itched at my skin. I evened my breathing, trying to stop my mind from racing so I could focus. Each exhale came out slower, colder, breath fogging in a silver cloud just before my lips. Ice crept along the floor beneath my feet, spreading like flooding water across the room. Erix tensed as he noticed the release of my magic but did not loosen his hold on me.

Glass smashed somewhere beyond the castle. Then again, and again. The gryvern had reached us. I waited with bated breath for a creature to smash through our window. But as more of the heavy crashing sounded all around us, followed by the screams and shouts of horror within the castle beyond our door, none of the monsters found me.

"We should help them," I muttered, wanting to rush to our door and throw it open. It was hard to make sense of the terror that occurred as the gryvern had clearly crashed through the different levels of the castle, yet the screams tugged at my gut, and I knew that we had to do something.

How many more people would be hurt – or die – because of me?

"I am sorry, but I will not let you leave this room," Erix replied, deep voice more a growl as his gaze was now pinned to the chamber's main entrance. "We are safer here. There is an army to win this battle. This is not only your fight."

"But what of everyone else?" I let go of the wrath I held within, shouting at Erix for him to understand my urgency.

"I can't just wait for them to hurt people just to get to me. Please, Erix, we need to help."

My mind filled with images of their curved claws and fanged mouths as they tore through the guards, servants and nobles who dwelled within the expansive castle.

Erix's straight mouth twitched. He wanted to help them. He longed to; I could see it from the shivering of his body. But when he looked back at me, it was as though I was the realisation as to why he refused.

I was his duty, and he took that seriously.

It quickly became too much to bear, listening to the sounds of fighting and death. Erix held me to him with both arms, keeping me tight to his chest as the horror of what happened beyond the door went on and on.

I was beginning to believe it'd never end. Until something heavy slammed into the other side of the door. It snapped me out of the trance my horror had lured me into. Dagger gripped firm and ready, magic poised, I waited for the inevitable to break down the door.

Erix drew his sword and stepped before me, both hands on the hilt.

"Help!"

Our eyes met across the room. It was no monster outside the door. It was Briar.

Erix pulled the door open, slamming it into the wall beyond. Briar stumbled through. Her face was covered in blood from a wound that had already dried. Her short hair did well to cover the cut, but I could see the slice peeking out of her hairline.

Briar made it three steps before falling to her knees. Her own dagger tumbled out of her hands, covered in dark, slick blood that belonged to no fey. Gryvern blood.

"Althea…" Briar gasped, voice broken through hulking breaths. "I can't find Althea."

"Robin, we need to stop her bleeding," Erix commanded as he unsheathed his sword, readying for anything.

I dropped to my knees beside her, clasping almost too-cold skin. "Briar, look at me. Tell me what happened."

"The glass it…" That must have been what caused the nasty gash on her head. "Then *they* came in. The gryvern were everywhere. We… we tried to get away to find you. But Althea knew they wanted you, so she… she…"

"What, Briar? Keep going." My voice shook, needing to know the answer to Althea's whereabouts as yet more screaming and sounds of struggle reached us from beyond the now open door. Smoke crept up the walls of the hallway beyond. Briar lifted a weak, shaking arm and pointed into the dark of the corridor. That was when I noticed the three raw slices that cut into her arm. These, unlike the wound on her head, bled freely, causing a puddle of blood to spill upon the flagstone floor. "Althea fell… she is really hurt, Robin. I tried to find her, but there were too many…"

Briar cried wildly, tears spilling from her red-rimmed eyes, and threw her arms around me.

I looked to Erix, whose hand gripped the door. His knuckles were white as he held on, eyes lost as his thoughts raced with what to do.

"Go," I commanded him. He looked at me as though I read his mind. "Find Althea and make sure she is okay."

Erix shook his head, but I could see his internal struggle. "Your safety is what matters. I will not leave you."

"Erix, you must find her. If she is hurt, she *will* need you. Please go. I command you to do so."

I had to shout over the commotion and the crying girl who I held in my arms. Briar buried her head into my lap, tears and blood soaking the material of my trousers.

Erix's eyes widened as he looked at me. His pursed lips separated long enough for him to speak, but I could taste his regret before he even finished.

"Please," I forced out the final word.

Something dark passed behind his eyes, like the waking of a

monster. "I will not be long. If I can't find her, I will come back for you. Do not leave this room."

"Okay," I whispered, eyes stinging as I looked up at him.

"Promise me, little bird."

I nodded. "I promise, Erix."

We shared a moment of silence, not risking taking our eyes off one another. Then Erix released a deep growl, raised his sword and ran into the hallway, towards the terror that waited down it.

Briar's crying slowed into quiet, hiccupping sobs. She'd gripped hold of my hand as I studied the door for Erix's return.

"I need to check your wounds," I said quietly.

I worried that if I spoke too loudly, I'd risk alerting my location to the gryvern. Without Erix, my confidence in facing them had dwindled to a dying flame, hardly strong enough to catch in a dry forest.

"No…" Briar said, head still on my lap. "They will heal, I just need a moment."

Her demeanour had shifted from pure terror to something like poised clarity.

It was strange, but I understood she was likely dealing with a lot of trauma. I could only imagine what she must have seen.

"Can you tell me everything that happened?" I asked her, wanting to fill these moments of Erix's departure.

"Althea and I were on our way to get you as planned. Queen Lyra had agreed for us to leave for Icethorn as a matter of urgency. But then the attack happened and…" Briar choked on her words.

"Shh," I hushed, running my hand carefully along with her short, dark hair. "Althea will be fine. She's fearsome. I fear more for the gryvern than her. And Erix *will* find her. They will come back for us soon."

"Not too soon I hope," Briar said, her hold on my hand gripping noticeably tighter.

"What?" I tried to pull away, but her nails dug into my skin, drawing a splintering gasp from me.

It was the pause in her response that had my heart sinking to the pits of my stomach. Briar lifted her head, looking up at me through her lashes with a smile so terrifying I would've rather faced a gryvern. "I said, I do not want them returning soon. Not yet, at least. Would not want them to ruin all my plans."

I yanked my hand away from her, scrambling backwards as Briar stood before me. I met her stance, holding the dagger before me as she, too, held the bloodied one out before her. Words failed me as I could not make sense of the scene before me. It had all changed so quickly.

"Don't look so confused," Briar said through a pout, flicking the blade towards me.

"You have just been crying in my lap, and now you are pointing a blade at me. Forgive me, but I think I've every right to be fucking confused." I forced much hostility into my tone, but even I noticed my voice tremble.

"Didn't expect it to be me, did you?" Briar revelled in her questioning, looking as pleased as a dog with a new bone. She stepped back to the door and kicked it closed. "I admit I have been dying to see your reaction when my little secret was finally exposed. So, how did I do? Impressed?"

"Do what?" My hands shook. I could take her, with or without my magic. She was far smaller than me and housed no natural magic, but there was something goliath about her confidence that made me feel pathetic and small.

"As much as I could stand here and boast about my stellar performance, I'm not completely finished with my task." Briar's gaze narrowed as she stepped forward. "You've been one slippery little fish. But I've got you now."

"It was you. You've been trying to kill me." The words fell out of me, rushed by my panic.

"What a silly thing to say. Oh no, I am not going to kill you. At least not anymore. But hurt you, yes. The updated contract said nothing about causing you as much pain as I desire."

I raised a hand, calling upon the coiling of magic within me. In my panic, I couldn't think of what I required it to do. I simply let instinct decide. But I hit a wall. Reaching down within, I could not feel it. The magic –

It was missing.

"Not making the same mistake my predecessors have," Briar said, clicking her tongue across her teeth. She flicked the dagger to my wrist. I risked a glance down to see a thin band of familiar metal wrapped around it. "The iron will keep your magic at bay. Evens the playing field, one would say. Consider the bracelet a gift to soften the blow of what I have to do. And do you know what… when this is all over, I might even let you keep it."

The bracelet wasn't much different to the one my mother had left me to wear, cold and draining. Except before, I'd been indifferent to its effects. Now having experienced the freedom of my magic the iron had kept at bay, I felt… empty.

"Pretty, isn't it? Picked it myself."

Instinct had me reaching for the bracelet. As I tugged at the thin string-like metal, it got tighter.

"Oh yes. About that. The band was given to me by my employer, then spelled by another Asp I know," Briar said. "Only the hand of the person that beautiful piece of jewellery belonged to can take it off. The more you struggle, the tighter it will become. Too much and it will slice right through that dainty little wrist of yours. You can say goodbye to that hand, not that it will have much use where you're going."

A snarl broke free from me as I gave up on hopes of reaching my power. "I've spent more time without my magic than with it. Whatever you want, I don't need it to stop you."

"Oh, alright big boy. Someone's finally found some balls. If you were so clever, you would've noticed me slip that little band on in the first place."

It was clear from her wide eyes and roaming tongue, Briar enjoyed every second of this.

"Why are you doing this, Briar?"

"Don't take it personally. It's all part of the job," She laughed, throwing her head back but not once taking her eyes off me.

"The gryvern attacks. It was you."

"Altar, no. They aren't my doing. You've got to be joking, one nearly took my arm off. All part of the job. Comes with the territory. May even get me a little bonus for taking the role so seriously."

"Get to the point." I was backing away from her, edging slowly towards the bedroom. If I could get inside and barricade the door, then I could wait for Erix to return. That, or I would have to fight my way past her, and I was beginning to believe that was her preferred option.

"I want nothing from you. I'm simply doing the job that I've been employed to complete. It is the benefactor who wants you, and for me to get the coin I'm promised, you're coming with me."

I wanted to ask whom she spoke of, but I didn't have a chance as she sprung forward.

Briar moved with a grace that I didn't expect. I threw out the hand holding Erix's dagger, hoping the edge of the blade would meet skin. It didn't. At the last moment, Briar changed her footing, twisting her body and sidestepping out of the way, enough to miss the blade but close enough to wrap two arms around me and pull with all her body weight until I was splayed out on the ground. My shoulders screamed as she pulled back on both my arms, pinning them behind my back with the side of my face pressed into the floor.

"What were you saying about beating me without your magic?" she joked, leaning down close to my ear. "Care to remind me?"

"Fuck – you," I bellowed, cheekbone pressed against the floor, stone aching against my skin.

"That's no way a princeling should speak. I'm frankly appalled. Now, why don't you settle down and have a little rest? It will make what is to come easier."

I struggled, wriggling beneath her like a worm entrapped by the claws of a bird. Briar, only short, held firm and did not let go. Stradling my lower back, she was able to keep me secured on the ground. Erix's dagger rested on the floor, taunting me just out of reach.

"Who... are you?"

"Briar, Child of the Asp. And thanks to you, I'm about to be officially inducted into the Guild."

Nothing she said made sense. Not that there was much room for thinking with a face pushed to the floor and a dagger pressed to the soft skin at the back of my neck. The tip of her blade sunk into my flesh, and a cool rush of numbing exploded beneath its touch.

Briar let go of my arms. I tried to move them, but they didn't shift an inch. My entire body was numb, unable move at all. Even my breathing laboured as my lungs struggled to drag in air.

My body was shutting down.

I felt the lack of Briar's pressure on my back and watched, through strained eyes, as her boots came into view. I couldn't look up at her where she stood before me, but I got the impression of her winning smile from her tone.

"The poison will fade in time, don't panic."

I wanted to reply, but my tongue had swollen in my mouth. Dribble wet my cheek and spread across the dusty floor.

"At first, I wasn't bothered if you succeeded in your task to claim Icethorn or not. All I cared about was proving myself to the Guild and claiming the ever-growing bag of coin each time another one of the Children failed in the task."

Briar walked towards the chairs we had sat in the day before, searching the books for answers together. Carelessly she knocked a pile to the floor and picked one of the smaller chairs up until it was held over her head, not a bead of sweat visible as she kept it aloft.

"It started with the Tugwort. It was my idea to poison myself, to eliminate myself as a potential threat. Poor little Taster, no one would've thought that the person behind poisoning me was, in fact, myself."

She padded over to the large window, letting the dawn light halo around her short frame.

There was a name on the tip of my useless tongue. I longed to cry it out aloud, matching the keening scream in my mind.

"Erix. Erix. Erix."

"The only part of me that feels some sense of regret is knowing what Althea will think if she found out. But that does not matter now. No one will be able to tell her once you are gone."

I couldn't even close my eyes as Briar threw the chair towards the window. Glass exploded upon impact, raining down upon the world outside, and the metal framing bent and jagged.

"You do not know how lucky you are, Robin."

My eyes followed Briar as she walked away from the broken window in the direction of the door and out of view. No matter how I struggled to follow, my body was set in full paralysis now.

"When *Erix* comes back for you, he'll see that the gryvern got here first. They attacked me and took you without hesitation." Briar clapped her hands, rubbing them together. "No one will question poor, friendly little Briar. They never have before, and that won't change going forward."

My ears pricked at the sound of flapping wings. I no longer cared for Briar as the gryvern lifted itself into view beyond the shattered window, mouth wide, exposing the rows of fangs as it surveyed me.

I wanted to close my eyes, but even that was impossible. I was forced to watch the gryvern climb inside the room, talons gripped onto the window ledge, not caring about the spears of glass that embedded into its already mangled skin.

"See you soon, Robin."

The gryvern pounced towards me, screeching rotten air over me. I was swept from the floor, just as my consciousness decided now was the moment to protect me.

And everything went dark.

CHAPTER 34

I existed in a void of pure darkness. Even opening my eyes was torture. I couldn't see anything, no matter how hard I tried.

There was no concept of how much time had passed. Days, hours – since I'd been ripped from the floor of my room by the gryvern's uncaring claws, flown beyond the window of Farrador Castle, and taken to this tortuous place.

My initial instinct was to panic as I slowly regained the ability to move. But I had to stay focused. It wouldn't do me any good to give in to the horrific thoughts that plagued my mind.

So, I focused on the details – the little I could discover, using my touch to get the answers I needed.

I was in a room of some kind. A box of four walls, a hard floor and a seemingly endless ceiling. My fingers instantly went for the iron bracelet that Briar had slipped around my wrist. I'd forgotten Briar's warning, attempting to remove it, only to find the metal growing tighter. My skin ached beneath its pinch, digging into my flesh until I felt the dribble of warm blood tickle my arm.

There was no light in this place. No glow beneath a door frame or flirting of daylight through shuttered windows. It was just a box of darkness. I had no real understanding of where it began and ended.

And it was cold, so deathly cold that my teeth chattered and skin peppered with bumps as shivers rushed over me. Even

Berrow, where I'd felt the cold air as a familiar friend, wasn't as bad as this, the feeling close to unbearable. And I blamed the iron around my wrist for that. By cutting off my magic, it made me feel normal again. Human. That side of me that I had been most used to, which now felt like a stranger.

And no one came for me. Although it was impossible to grasp how much time had passed, I guessed it had been a while, from my starvation and overwhelming tiredness.

All I could do was wait. Get myself ready to face whatever was coming for me. I kept still, unmoving, and listened for some sign of life beyond this prison of shadow. But that soon made the echoing of my own breathing become unbearable to listen to; the smallest of sounds among the silence sounded terrible and loud.

I tortured myself, wanting nothing more than to stop breathing altogether, just to stop the sound.

But the worst of it was the darkness.

A promise Erix had made during my first day in Aurelia played over and over in my mind. *The next time you find yourself in a dark room, little bird, just call for me.*

I did just that. I shouted at first, screaming Erix's name until my throat felt as though it bled from within. My voice soon grew hoarse and sore, until I could barely whisper his name without being in pain. I pulled my knees up to my chest, burying my head into them to block out reality, still muttering his name over and over as tears dared to slip down my skin and soaked the ripped, dirty clothing that hung off me in tatters.

I woke to a new noise – a breathing that was not in sync with my own. My shoulders ached as I pushed myself from the floor, my heart thundering at the closeness of the threat. But still, I couldn't see anything, not even my hand, which I raised as a shield between me and the person that stalked in the darkness, the piercing heat of their gaze resting upon me through the shadows.

"I should thank you," Briar's voice hissed, so close that I feared to reach out another inch and touch her. But there was something about the traitor that seemed she belonged, cloaked in shadow, unseen like a predator stalking its prey. "It's been years of work to be accepted into the Guild. Yet all it took was a pathetic boy to stumble into a world he was not asked to return to. I have had many a target during my training, but never one as... simple as you."

"If you are searching for praise, you are looking in the wrong place." My voice cracked as I replied. I longed for something to drink, to ease the throbbing in my head and the fresh cuts that seemed to fill my throat with each swallow.

"Praise? I don't care what you think, but I admit I did come here to gloat." There was a shifting of feet across the floor, making me flinch. Briar laughed slowly as if she could see through the dark. "It's not common for an assassin to speak freely to a target once the task has been completed. Usually, you are stiff and cold by the time I get paid. This is a rare occasion."

"And did Lady Kelsey pay handsomely?" I needed answers, not that it mattered anymore.

"She has, for other jobs. But her hand has not been in her pocket for this one, nor the other attempts on your life. No matter how... pathetic they had been." Even cowering on the floor in an unknown place with a girl hellbent on murder before me, I felt relief that Lady Kelsey was not guilty. "Kelsey was merely a means to divert the attention from my current employer, someone who wanted your demise treated with efficiency and silence. Kelsey, like her family, is not known for those talents."

"And if I ask who wanted me dead all along, you will tell me?"

I could almost imagine the pout that Briar would have forced as she contemplated my question; from the huffing sound, she made, I could see it as clear as day within my mind's eye. "All will be revealed in time. It has been a rather busy couple of days since you were abducted in plain sight by the gryvern. You can imagine it would not be the smartest of ideas to come and visit you."

"Yet here you are..."

"Yes," she purred. "Here I am."

"And can I ask where *here* is? Or does it not matter if you are only going to kill me anyway. If that is my fate, you might as well tell me everything."

Briar sighed. "Did you not listen to me before, Robin? My employer changed their mind rather last minute. The plans for your future involve staying alive, do not ask me why. If it was my suggestion, I would have seen your throat cut days ago. You are valuable, I suppose, but only when the time is right."

"Oh, I do feel special." I forced as much confidence into my voice as I could muster, even though I felt nothing but the seedling of fear and weakness deep inside of me. Briar was unpredictable, she had proven that.

"You are currently in the domain of the Children of the Asp. A place I can now call home thanks to you. Do you know how many of my fellow Asps have tried to be inducted by completing the hit put upon you? All chose to rush and failed miserably. So many stopped long before they even reached you, attempts Althea had kept quiet to prevent you from worrying."

I couldn't believe what I was hearing, and the secrets Althea had kept from me. Had Erix known of these failed assassination attempts?

"If you had found out about the race and the multitude of Asps that longed to see you dead, you would never have looked to me as a suspect. Not silly, little Briar, who suffered the most to keep you safe. Sometimes it's not who gets to the finish line first who succeeds, but the one who is patient and waits. Slow and steady. And here I am, welcomed into a Guild I have longed to join for as long as I could remember."

"A guild of assassins," I repeated, taking in as much information as I could. "What would Althea think if she knew this side of you?"

"Althea is so blinded with her infatuation for me that she would never see me as a threat. That's what being an Asp is. We shed your skin to fill the roles in a false life. Althea, although a fun part of this role, is merely a bonus to the job. Anyway, who is going to tell her? You?" Briar's giggle ricocheted around the room. "With what is coming for you, I don't think you will ever have the chance to speak to her. And if you did, I would kill you before you got the chance, with a bounty on your head or not."

The threat was honest and true. I opened my mouth to respond, silenced by the outline of a face that presented itself a breadth from my own. Briar's snarl wavered in the dark, my eyes adjusting enough to see it. Her nose brushed my own, her breath sour as it washed over me.

"It has been lovely to see you again, Robin." Briar forced the sweet, meek voice that I had grown used to, her voice full of its childish tones as her features melted into a sincere and truly frightening smile. "It is awfully sad without you in Farrador. With the Passing terribly close, it seems that even Erix is giving up hope of finding you. And believe me… he has been searching. The berserker has almost torn down the castle in his attempt to find you. They all have. But don't worry. All good things soon become distant memories. It won't be long until that is all you are to them. To him. A distant and long-forgotten memory."

Briar slipped back into the darkness, leaving her words to stab into me. I was certain that the sudden silence of the room could pick up the cracking of my heart as it thawed like ice in summer.

I sat like that, knowing she'd left me. I felt alone again, with the dwindling wish of escape evaporating into the nothingness around me.

CHAPTER 35

I cared little for food but every sense of my body screamed for water. Those feelings never passed, torturing me throughout the seemingly endless hours in the dark room. I slept a lot, unable to keep myself awake for long enough to think of much. Nightmares greeted me now, so terribly real that it was hard to distinguish them from reality.

I dreamt of a winter storm exploding over Durmain, of cities and towns, villages and homes devoured by snow and frozen winds, each left in the same forgotten and empty state as Berrow. It was the sounds of thousands of feet thundering over the destroyed lands as a horde of fey warriors devoured the human realm and claimed it for their own.

Was it a vision of what happened? Had the Passing occurred, and the wild storm of my family's heritage broken free from its cage and consumed the world beyond Wychwood? Even now, my mind willed me to give up on my desire to stop it.

It wasn't long before I even started to wish that Briar would come back. I craved some form of company to break this horror I found myself within. I longed to hear her gloat if it meant that I had someone to see me through the dark. But she never came back. Even after I'd spent time calling her name until my voice could hardly make a sound more than a forced, croaky whisper.

Time slipped by with ease, as did my mental strength.

When the room was suddenly bathed in light, I was confident

it was yet another dream. I raised a hand, blocking the glare from burning my eyes from my skull. Then my name, spoken in a gentle and familiar voice, was the worst torture of all.

"Robin, oh Robin. I've come for you."

The outline of the tall, narrow princeling stepped through a portal when I had already given up hope that someone would find me.

Tarron Oakstorm had found me. And that thought didn't fill me with relief.

"No…" I muttered, slapping my hands into my head to rid myself of the unkind vision. "This is not fair. No. No. No."

Soft hands gripped my wrists, stopping me from hitting myself. "Do not hurt yourself, Robin. I am here. Touch me, see for yourself that I am real."

He certainly felt real, hard yet soft skin glowing with light from within, veins filled with golden light as though the sun was his heart, and it filled him with life.

"Tarron…" I reached for his face, dirty fingers leaving a trail as I could hardly hold him. His long, curling hair had been gathered in a tidy bun that rested within the circlet of a crown upon his head. The brass tones caught the light he conjured, highlighting the sharp points of metal thorns that wrapped around his forehead. "How… it was Briar. You need to warn them of her."

"Shh." He pulled me from the floor, holding me up without showing signs of a struggle. "I am sorry it has taken me this long to visit. I would have come for you sooner, but I could not get away. Are you hurt?"

"But…" A cold rush spread from my head to my feet, draining all feeling of relief from me. I pushed away, legs wobbling as I tried to put space between us. "*How* are you here, Tarron?"

The side of his lip pulled up, not a single speck of worry upon his handsome face. "Because I knew where to look. No matter the space between us, I believe I will always find my way back to you."

I pushed at his chest, palms dusting across the soft velvet of the jacket he wore. But Tarron gripped hard onto my upper arms, making me cringe with pain.

"You are hurting me."

"Oh, I am sorry," he said, but his grip did not lessen. "It could have been far worse, you know. I hope the time you have had makes you understand that."

The truth settled over me as clear as day.

"You…" I hated myself for not understanding sooner. Not once did his name come to mind, as I listed the potential people that could have paid Briar to do this. "Erix was right."

"Luckily, he is not here… his ego would inflate if he heard you admit that. Now stop struggling. It is better for us both if you calm down."

"You wanted me dead!"

"Wanted, yes. That all changed for me though. Your death is the furthest from where I see your future." He tugged me harshly, slamming my chest into his frame and holding me prisoner as his arm snaked around my back. There was no fighting it. There was no strength left in me. No fight. Only fear. "I have great plans for you. For us. But first, we must get this day over with. I would have waited until after the Passing to see you, but I could not keep myself away. It was a risk to come here. Farrador is crawling with people who wish to see you return. But it was a risk I was willing to take."

With weak arms, I pushed out, wanting nothing more than to cause him pain. "I hate you."

Tarron frowned, slick brows tugging downwards. "You might hate me today, but I can promise you those feelings will change, just as mine have for you. The moment I heard of what you did at the Hunter's camp and what that meant for our kind, I wished to see you gutted from here to here." His finger sliced upwards from my lower stomach to beneath my chin. His nail held my head up to face him. "But then I saw a potential that I had never contemplated. It was always the hope that the Oakstorm Court's power would be the only way to control the storm that we readied to unleash on Durmain. But with you by my side, it will be far easier to regain control... and that is exactly what I require when we are ready for domination tomorrow."

The Passing. It was today.

Even in my weakened state, I felt a spark of hope return.

"I would rather die than help you." I gathered the little spit I could muster and gobbed it at Tarron. The pathetic splatter landed on his cheek. I revelled in the surprise as Tarron let go of me to deal with it.

"Do not say that, Robin." Tarron pulled a square piece of material from the breast pocket of his jacket and used it to clear the spittle as it dripped down his sharp cheek. "I have not long grown used to the idea of you living. It is imperative to my family's plan."

I seethed, speaking through gritted teeth. "I will do everything in my power never to help with whatever your deluded mind has conjured."

"You are forgetting one very important fact. So, allow me to remind you that your father currently dwells in my court. Do not make me use him as a reason for you to comply. Truly, I really do not want to have to go to such lengths."

"If you hurt him..."

Tarron threw his hands up in surrender. "No point telling me that. It is my father you should warn. Imagine how thrilled he was when I presented him with the man who aided in my own mother and brother's abduction. You are going to have to convince him to hold back years of anguish and hate when you finally get the chance to meet him. For now, though... you are going to just have to wait."

"What are you talking about?" I had heard him but struggled to make sense of what he had said.

"Your dear father was involved with transporting my family

to the Hand. Whereas your mother was able to return, mine never made it back. My family were not deemed *lucky* like your mother had been."

I shook my head. "That's a wild guess. You have no reason to believe that."

"It was a hunch at first, but my father has been able to get out lots of interesting answers from your father during his short stay. I still can't understand how your father was able to decide that Julianne's life was more important than my mother's. My baby brother's. That is an answer we are yet to obtain. But time will tell. Just imagine what else he is going to reveal over the coming days. He feels as though he has nothing to live for now. With everyone believing the gryvern have killed you, just as they killed your mother, he is just revealing anything and everything. Amazing what you can get out of a person who believes they have no purpose to live."

"The gryvern... that was your doing?"

"Hard to control, but not impossible. You just have to know what motivates them. My father has a *very* close bond with them."

"But the humans..." My brain felt as though it would implode in my skull. "They control them. The humans killed my mother, the Icethorn Court."

"And that is exactly what we wanted the world to believe. Do you really believe the humans have power over such creatures? Powerless as they are themselves, they can hardly control their own selves. No, the gryvern are the Oakstorm's pets. King Doran's pets, to be exact. They do as he commands."

My eyes widened, a burning hate filling every inch of my aching, tired body. I felt a power return, clenching my fists to my sides until my nails threatened to draw blood from my palms. "You killed them. You did it, not the humans. My mother is dead because of you!"

"Well." Tarron began to pace, hand tracing his sharp jaw as he spoke. "It was actually my father who gave the command. But of course, I was well aware of the plan. Destroy the Icethorn Court, blame the humans and start a war. It was like killing two birds with one stone. Father dealt with a dark jealously that Julianne returned, whereas his wife did not. Then he wanted to cause the humans pain too. Share what he and I felt. Kill the Icethorns, let their power break through to Durmain and allow us to finally receive retribution. Revenge for what the humans do to our kind. Bring pain to their door, just as they brought it to ours. Then you got in the way. Threatened our plans. My father wished to see you dead and wanted me to ensure that was seen through. Yet here we are. Here *you* are. Still living, breathing. Father is not too happy with my change of heart, but we will prove to him that you can be most helpful. Together. You see that I care for you, don't you? Just as I do not blame you for what your mother did to my family, you cannot blame me for my father's actions."

I could see from his gaze that Tarron longed for me to smile at him. To tell him that I didn't hate him, and I wanted nothing more than to help him in his quest.

But in truth, I wanted to wrap my hands around his throat and squeeze the air from his lungs. My fingers itched at the tight iron bracelet, thoughts of what my power would do to him right here, right now.

But I had to be clever. Just as Briar had explained, slow and steady.

Only the hand of the person the iron band belonged to could remove it. Although Briar had done it, it was because of Tarron. I had to put faith that he was the one who had the iron spelled.

I stumbled a step towards Tarron, forcing a placid expression onto my face. The tears that pooled in my eyes told him one story, but it was not sadness. It was hot, overwhelming and horrific anger that caused my eyes to fill.

Tarron welcomed me into his arms. I ran my hands up his chest, noticing the imprint left on his jacket as the material shifted beneath my touch. I kept my gaze soft, wide and blinking. I took my time to speak, careful not to reveal the demon that longed to strike out and rip his beautiful blue eyes from his face.

"I... understand now," I told him, without explaining what part of his story I connected with. He was right. I couldn't blame him for his father's actions. His father's commands. But I didn't need to blame Tarron to know I required him to escape this place, if I wanted any chance to stop all of this. "Take me with you. I will help you."

Tarron's hands rubbed my arms, breathing through a smile as he tilted his head like a confused puppy. "As much as I wish to believe you, trust is earned, and I am not blind; I know your mind has not been changed. Not yet. But once you see the damage your family's power does to Durmain, you will then accept it, blood for magic."

I was so close, his fingers grasping my wrists, the tips of them brushing just shy of the iron band.

"No." I could not stop my lips from pulling tight or my body from shaking with the desire to lash out, to cause pain. "I do not want to help. You are right–"

Tarron silenced me with a kiss. My entire body tensed, unable to move, as his face smashed into mine. His lips were cold and unwanted. I felt his tongue try to encourage my own mouth to part, but disgust was impossible to ignore. I bit down hard, drawing blood from his lower lip. Tarron's muffled scream was music to my ears as my teeth cut into his skin.

He pulled back sharply. All I could taste was copper, as though my mouth was full of coin.

"Bastard!" he screamed, skin glowing bright as he covered his bloodied mouth. Before he could do anything else, I grabbed his shoulders, pulled back my head and snapped my skull into the bridge of his nose. The room was bathed in darkness for a split moment. I thought it was my own mind losing consciousness as the pain of the connection overwhelmed me, but then light soon returned, revealing the dishevelled and twisted face of Tarron.

"Like I said," I growled, trying to steady my stance as adrenaline masked the weakness that actually gripped my body. "I will never help you. Keep me alive, and I will stop you, after the Passing or before. As long as I live, I will see that you fail."

"You will change your mind in time. Kindness is not my only way of making you comply," Tarron said, spitting blood as he screamed at me. "Do not force me to make you do as I need."

"Make me?" I pulled my hand from behind my back, revealing the grip on the dagger. Tarron's face paled, looking down to the empty sheath that was hidden beneath his jacket. I had felt it when he first held me as it dug into my chest. "I'm not one to do anything I'm told to do."

Tarron couldn't stop me as I slipped *his* dagger between the iron bracelet and my skin. It was a risk. But fey were tricksters, as was their magic. I put trust that the spell on the band was no different.

I cared little for the pain as the sharp edge cut into my flesh, not as I tugged hard with as much force as I could muster.

I had learned quickly upon my imprisonment that the bracelet wouldn't be removed except by the person it belonged to. And using Tarron's dagger, his presence smudged all over it, I tricked that fucking band off.

This was a risk, but one that finally paid off.

The snap of the bracelet was a beautiful sound. It was louder than the small gasp that Tarron made. He stepped back, slicing the air to create his portal of light to escape. But my magic was back and with it, a rush of energy and strength that me gasping for breath.

I ran for him, just as the slip of light closed. My shoulder connected with his waist, knocking out his breath as we passed together through the portal.

As our bodies connected with the hard, unforgiving floor beyond, I felt the light, cold kiss of magic swell in my chest.

It was time to fight for my life.

CHAPTER 36

I scratched at Tarron's body as he tried to push himself from the floor and out of my grasp. I could hardly make sense of where we'd travelled to. And I didn't care either. All I needed to know was the pain I caused Tarron as my fingers left vicious ice burns across his skin. Magic flowed from my touch, tainting the air and dropping the temperature, so our forced, heavy breaths came out in white puffs.

"Enough," he warned, hissing as my fingers wrapped around his wrist to stop the slap he threw towards me. "This does not need to play out this way."

"I will... never stop," I replied through a growl, trying to make sense of the place around me, whilst not taking my full attention off Tarron. Deep within, I felt a kernel of relief to be in a room full of natural light, not in the box of never-ending darkness. But that feeling was short-lived as Tarron changed his tactic from defence to attack.

Tarron hoisted his legs between us and kicked out like a bucking horse. The wind was knocked from my stomach as I fell back. There was nothing I could do to stop the back of my skull from colliding with the floor.

Ignoring the pain and the taste of blood across my tongue, I pushed myself up to see Tarron heaving laboured breaths. We were in his chamber in Farrador. I had longed to return to this city over the past days, and now, seeing the familiar walls and floors, it was jarring, a dream brought to life.

But the fight was not over yet.

Tarron sliced two fingers down the air between us.

"Your attempt, though valiant, is wasted. You will not ruin this for me. For my family. Back to your box until I am ready to forgive you." The portal conjured into existence inches before me. "In. Now."

"You really don't know me well at all. Not that it matters now, but you really should have gotten to know me better if you hoped to blindly woo me into doing as you please." I wanted to laugh at him as the portal showed me a vision of the dark room we'd only just left.

Dread crept into the corners of my mind, but the storm of frozen winds kept it at bay. Slowly, I pushed myself to stand, looking to the portal, then to Tarron and then to the closed-door; beyond it must have been guards, someone to come in and stop this. I could shout, give my return away, but then I wouldn't get the chance to unleash my wrath upon him.

"I never do as I am told," I said, fuelled by the uncontrolled storm inside of me.

The spindle of light slammed closed, sealing off the dark room. Tarron studied me, hands ready by his sides, fingers twitching with anticipation. I did the same, allowing the magic inside of me to grow until my ribs felt as though they would explode. The pressure was painful but oddly welcoming, as though the days I'd been disconnected from it caused the magic to have a sense of urgency. What discomfort it provided me was only a promise of what it could do to Tarron.

"What are you going to do?" he asked, tilting his head with a smile so ominous it made the shape of his face change for a moment. "Kill me? Doing so would start a civil war. And unlike you, my father has the power and numbers ready for just that. All you have is empty lands. You have nothing. No mother. No siblings. No followers. And soon enough, no father."

"I could hurt you," I answered, trying to ignore his threat to my father's life. "Until you wish you were dead."

Tarron shook his head, tangles of long, brown curls shifting dramatically across his shoulders. "Untrained as a fawn. I have been patient and held back for your sake. For *our* sake. But I understand now that you leave me with no choice but to end this, just as my court attempted all those years ago."

I could taste the honesty in his promise. It should've made me reconsider my rushed plan, but instead, it only urged me to see it through with even more desperation.

"As much as I wish to see you dead," I said, lip curling, "I'm not stupid enough to see it through."

Tarron risked a step forward, a glow of golden light starting to twist around his hands. "If not stupid, then what are you?"

"Robin Icethorn," I answered, grinning as he flinched at the announcement of my name. "Sincerest apologies for ruining all your hard work, Tarron. But all good things come to those who deserve them, and you deserve fuck all."

Tarron pounced forward, a beam of light splitting from his hands until it solidified into a blade. I couldn't control my power as he did, call upon it in ways that would counter his attack. So, I did the only thing I knew I could do with my magic.

Let go.

Throwing my arms wide, I released the magic within me. My feral scream mixed with the sudden rush of frozen winds that exploded from me in a circlet of mist and wind.

Tarron was torn from his feet by the blast, alongside furniture which had been picked up in the winds. As one, they crashed into walls, the sound of cracking wood mixed with something that tore a scream of agony from the princeling.

The windows rattled beneath the pressure until they couldn't withstand it.

I threw my hands above my head as the glass shattered, each window exploding and raining shards beyond the room. Onward my power pushed, past the limitations of the room, until I filled the air beyond the castle.

This was my signal. My cry for aid. If Erix, or Althea, or anyone who cared for my disappearance wanted to find me, I was now a beacon of winter, begging to be found.

The winds calmed, and with that, I felt exhaustion take hold. I would've dropped to my knees if I didn't see Tarron clambering to his feet once again. He was like a bug, flipped upon its back but always trying to right himself.

He just kept coming.

Tarron's eyes were wide, and his lips moved frantically, but I couldn't hear him over the cold winds that poured from my skin.

He raised a hand, catching my attention for a moment. A burst of sudden, bright light blinded me. I stumbled back, eyes stinging from the flash. Then hands were on me, reaching for my neck with a sure grip.

I couldn't open my eyes to see him, for the darkness of my mind was a safe place. But I didn't need my sight to fight back. I slapped and scratched at his hold, trying to stop him from squeezing tighter.

"You will die, and I will be blamed. But still, it's no crime besides a simple, mundane fey dying by my hands. You are not an Icethorn, not yet, and I won't allow that to ever happen." I could not breathe, not as his thumbs pushed into my windpipe until his nails cut into the skin. "I will go on trial and face punishment, but that will pass quickly, and my army will march long before your body is buried. Die knowing you had the choice to live by my grace. Die knowing that I chose peace with you, and you chose *this*."

Opening my eyes when the blinding light was gone, I kicked out, but my energy was dwindling. Each blink was heavier... slower. His grip tightened more than I believed possible, but still, I would look towards the door of his room, wishing, waiting for someone to come through.

I kept the cold magic alive, forcing it through my weakening touch as I left marks of ice down his cheeks, his dishevelled curls crisping as my chill cascaded over him.

Tarron never faltered. He hardly cared as his skin turned a dark red, to an almost black from frostbite. In the reflection of his large, frantic, azure gaze, I saw my own self looking back, hopelessly giving in to the death he wished so greatly for me to succumb to.

A tear slipped down his cheek. It was an odd thing to witness of one's self. As I watched it slither down his skin, I forgot the need for air in my lungs.

I crumpled to the floor, retching as air flooded back into my lungs. Although the phantom of his touch still lingered over the skin across my neck, the pressure was gone.

Tarron had let go of me.

I heard someone say his name. Gulping for air, I looked up to see a figure standing in the open doorway. My vision was doubled and fuzzy. I squinted, trying to make out details but could only see that Tarron stood before me, facing whoever had entered.

"Here comes the hero," Tarron shouted, deep voice breaking with panic. "What are you going to do? Stop me?"

The figure stepped forward, silhouette blurred by shadows. Although my hearing rang as if bells tolled within them, I began to recognise the rumbling feminine voice of the speaker. "Step away from him. Let it end without any more unnecessary pain."

Sharp, bright blades of light conjured back into Tarron's hands as he readied himself into a fighting stance before me. His body was a shield, keeping the second visitor from reaching me.

"Lay another finger on his head, and I will destroy you. It is over.""

I didn't need to question who just threatened Tarron.

"You forget who you speak to, berserker. This is far from over. It has only just begun."

Berserker – that nickname alone revealed to me who was here.

Erix had found me.

"The room will soon be swarmed–"

"And I will welcome them all!" Tarron spat. "You can all watch as I end his life and allow the war we have planned to proceed. I do this for us. I do this for you."

My sight steadied with each long blink. Soon enough, I could see the figure for who she was. Gyah. Dressed in her guard uniform, decorated with weapons at her waist that she didn't reach for, not as she negotiated calmly for my life to be spared. Gyah stared at me with concern, then back to Tarron, where her gaze changed to controlled hate.

"This has gone on long enough," Gyah scorned, as though she spoke to a child.

Shouts reached us from the open doorway. Tarron noticed, releasing a grunt of annoyance as he frantically looked between Gyah and the door. "And what, dear girl, are you going to do about it?"

He levelled his blade of light towards Gyah, looking down the sharpened edge through narrowed eyes. I wanted to reach for him, but my arms were heavy and unmoving. Still, my lungs clawed for breath as though his hands still gripped my throat.

She didn't flinch as he presented the blade between them. Instead, the outline of her frame wavered, and she spoke as though two voices dwelled within her. "I admit, I have always wondered what an Oakstorm tasted like…"

Gyah shifted before our eyes, skin melting to shadow and returning in the leathery, scaled body of her Eldrae form. But it was what Tarron required, a moment to move without the threat of her pouncing.

In the seconds it took for her skin to become scales, Tarron turned on me, gripped me by the scruff of my shirt and hoisted me from the floor.

"They want a show." He split the air, conjuring a portal. This time I was powerless to stop it. "Then that is what I shall give them."

Gyah stretched her wings, releasing a terrifying roar that rocked the ice-covered room. She was quick, but Tarron was quicker. He yanked me towards the portal as her talon-tipped wings gorged into stone. With a blade of hot, burning light pressing to my back, I could do nothing but allow myself to be taken.

The wide, spit-covered jaws flashed before us for a moment, then the portal closed, and the vision of the creature vanished.

I readied myself to be welcomed by the darkness of my prison, but I was quickly proven otherwise. Noise greeted us as Tarron dragged me through his spindle of light, into a large room bustling with life.

Voices of chatter and chaos silenced as we suddenly stood among them. A crowd, faces of wealth and power adorned with crowns and garbed in gowns and uniforms, stood back from us until we were circled by all of them.

I looked over their faces of disbelief and horror, searching for someone, anyone who would help. But the glowing blade was now inches beneath my chin. One sure swipe, and my skin would meet its edge.

"Tarron Oakstorm. You dare bring violence into my court? Against an Icethorn on the day of the Passing." Queen Lyra pushed herself through the crowd, eyes aglow with an inner fire. Her auburn hair spilt over her brass-toned gown, held back from her face by the circlet of golden thorns and vines upon her head, metal shaped into leaves that glittered with gems of amber and ruby. "Under the nature and rule of these lands, I command you to let him go."

"I am your equal. You do not control me," Tarron shouted back, nails digging into my shoulder. "One step closer, and this will end before you all."

"Do you need a reminder as to whose court you reside in?" Her voice was full of fury, so much so that the many flames alight across the grand chandelier above flickered. The crowd reacted audibly, shying away from the reaching flames.

"I am doing this for *us*. What is one life if it means our future is secured? You all knew nothing of this boy before. He is as unimportant as he was when you did not know of his existence. Stopping me would be a far greater crime than the loss of his life." As he spoke over the crowd, we watched as decorated fey guards pushed through their ranks, forming a barrier of blades and shields between the fey and us. Queen Lyra refused to be pushed behind their lines. Slowly, other crowned figures stepped through to join her side. Fey who I'd not seen before but I could understand the power they held. I recognised it, like for like.

There were three of them. Two tall men with dark bronze skin and strong facial features holding hands; both wore circlets of what looked to be droplets of static rain made from azure crystals. And the third, his features swollen but familiar, long curling dark hair, except thin and tangled, unlike his son's. It was Tarron's father. Doran Oakstorm. It had to be, without question.

His stomach pushed out at his shirt and jacket, pulling buttons apart from one another as though they would split. His crown was worn and dull, as though the gold had been mistreated over years, forgotten. And unlike the others around him, his stare was hungry and full of disgust whilst he regarded me.

"Release him, Tarron Oakstorm," one of the other men said, letting go of his hold on the man at his side. Slowly, he moved a hand for a curved blade at his hip. "This is not the place for such discord. Do not defile the Passing, doing so will only offend Altar."

"Silence yourself, Peta." The gruff voice of Tarron's father stammered awkwardly. He spoke as though he needed to cough years of grime and dirt from his throat. The sound scratched at my ears. "You have petitioned for the war to proceed, let my son ensure that nothing threatens those plans again."

"The death of an Icethorn is not required. There are other ways—"

"Always with your search for peace!" Tarron called out, screaming like a petulant child. "I gave Robin that choice, and he decided to refuse it. You want this war as much as the next."

All eyes fell upon me where I squirmed weakly in Tarron's hold.

Peta squared his shoulders at the short, round frame of the Oakstorm King. "Not at the sake of his life. I would prefer order and balance given the chance, and you currently are holding that outcome in your hands."

"Are you all forgetting the lives the humans have taken? The many who have been slain and taken. Loved ones separated. What they did to the Icethorn–"

"The humans didn't kill my mother–" I was silenced by the hissing of my own skin as Tarron's blade pressed into me, with the edge so close I feared to swallow.

"Let him speak," Queen Lyra growled deeply.

Tarron didn't listen. Instead, his lips pressed close to my ears, tickling the soft skin as he whispered. "You brought this upon yourself, Robin. As your life spills before them all, know that this is your doing. It could've been different. So different. But you chose not to comply."

As Tarron spoke, his hand released my shoulder and moved flat down my back. His touch made me want to cringe away, but the blade at my throat kept me in place. I tried to call upon my magic, but it was too weak to aid me.

"Finish it," Doran Oakstorm commanded his son.

"Stop this now!" Queen Lyra said, voice pinched in worry as she predicted what was to follow.

Then a new shout joined, just as a flash of heat spread from my back and through my stomach before me. I looked down, suddenly uncaring for the blade at my throat. It didn't matter as I inspected the bloodied tip of the new bright, glowing sword of light that exposed itself through my centre. In a flash, it was gone, my hands left in the space where it had been to catch the droplets of blood that began to spill from the wound.

Tarron's presence was ripped away, at least that was what I thought. I couldn't move to see what had happened, not as the numbness spread from my stomach outwards across my body.

I fell before Queen Lyra could reach me, knees clattering to the ground. Where I should have felt pain at the connection of bone against the stone floor, I felt nothing.

"I have got you, dear boy." Queen Lyra guided me into her arms, holding my head up with hands covered in blood. My blood. Her lips were moving, but it sounded as if my head was kept underwater.

Guards rushed forward in a wave, and my head slowly turned to follow them.

Tarron was splayed across the floor, feet twitching but the rest of him oddly still. Was it the person straddling his waist that kept him immobile? Or was it the raining of fists, crashing down without break or rhythm, into Tarron's face, that had that effect? The slamming of fists thudded through the very ground with each connection. Blood sprayed, spoiling into the air and filling it with a copper tang. I could taste Tarron's blood alongside my own. And I was choking on it, spluttering gore out my mouth as my lungs filled and I coughed.

The attacker above Tarron turned to me as guards reached for his board shoulders and hauled him off. Eyes of silver stood out against the dark, unforgiving shadows around them, a face of tension pinched in horror as he looked at me.

Erix.

I mouthed his name, wondering why I couldn't hear myself. I tried to lift a hand to reach for him, but I dared not remove it from the pumping wound on my stomach.

Erix fought free of the guards, fists slick with dark blood. He was shouting, but I couldn't grasp a sound. I focused on his lips, the edges of my gaze closing in with shadows. It took countless guards to hold Erix at bay. I tried to keep my focus on him, but each blink was becoming longer. I was beginning to believe I'd never open my eyes again.

This time the darkness wouldn't relent.

I heard it echoing in my mind softly. It welcomed me, luring me into the peace that could only be death. My name spoken by a symphony of voices. It was my mother, her light voice urging me towards her, calling me to join. Flashes of her dark hair blew across her hidden face, but I knew she was smiling, welcoming me into her arms once again.

"Robin, Robin, Robin."

CHAPTER 37

My body was alive with searing pain, a feeling so intense it had me gasping for air. The muscles in my stomach spasmed, causing me to bolt upright until hands pushed me back down.

I screamed, but the roll of material in my mouth stifled the sound. As my consciousness came around, it was that gag that prevented me from holding breath.

Althea was before me, red hair swept from her face. Lines creased across her freckled forehead as she focused on the source of my agony. If it was not for Queen Lyra and her arms, which wrapped around me in a vice of flesh, I would've struck out to push Althea away.

"Bite down through the pain," Queen Lyra commanded.

I could hardly register what was happening from the shock of being dragged out from the darkness. But soon enough, I looked down to a pale hand, covered in flame and the sour scent of burning skin. Althea swept her fire over the wound Tarron had left me. It was quick. When Althea peeled her hand off my stomach, flames extinguishing in a blink, I could see smoke drifting from the angry handprint left in her wake.

She had scorched my skin, mutilating the place the stab wound had been. Stanching the flow of blood with fire.

"Now his back!" Althea reached around me, voice quivering with frantic worry. I could do nothing to stop her from touching the weeping wound at my back. Queen Lyra pushed me forward until I was doubled over. Without Althea blocking the view, I could still see the chaos of the room. Not much time must've passed since I gave in to the darkness. The room was still alive with guards and fey entrapped in the horror of the scene.

Erix was on his knees, his fellow guards holding him down with arms pinned behind his back. Between us lay Tarron, his father blocking the view of his bloodied and broken face. The Oakstorm King screamed and shouted, hands desperately racing across his son's body. I would've tried harder to make sense of what he said, but my own muffled scream blocked out the sound.

The swab of material fell from my mouth as the searing heat of burning flesh greeted me again. I cringed away, howling as Althea's fire felt as though it devoured the entire length of skin across my back.

Erix fought in response, trying to pull out of the four guards' hold. He didn't stop even as they pointed the sharp ends of swords towards him. One wrong move, and he would be skewered on the ends of steel.

Tears poured down the cold skin of my cheeks long after Althea peeled her hand from me once again. I half expected her to move to another part of my body, but instead, she rocked back onto her heels until her face was all I could see.

"I have stopped the external bleeding but can do nothing for the damage inside of you."

I panted, unable to catch my breath, for each inhale was full of agony. Looking down once again, I saw the outline of her hand across my stomach and the oozing red and black marks of her burn; no longer could I see the wound beneath, but I still felt it. Each slight move felt as though I was being tortured with agony.

"Doran Oakstorm," Queen Lyra shouted above the chaos. "I beg that you heal Robin."

Tarron's father turned, face as pale as fresh snow. Spittle and tears mixed together, dribbling from his many chins as he glowered at the queen who commanded him. "My son is dead. And yet you see it fit to make commands of me?"

I could see Queen Lyra swallow, even hearing the gulp as she kept me in her arms. "And Robin will die if you do nothing. Only you may have the power to heal him. Right the wrongs your son has made."

"I will not…" His voice was rough and full of hysterical emotion. His large body shifted to the side, enough for me to catch a glimpse of what used to be a face. Tarron's face. Now it was a caved-in shell, exposed gore and bone holding a pool of blood which seeped across the floor beneath him. Tarron was dead. Erix had killed him. Even now, Tarron's blood dripped from Erix's fists as he tugged and fought against the fey guards.

I should've looked away from the horror of the prince, but I almost couldn't. Because my mind couldn't fathom how such destruction had been caused by one man. By Erix.

Queen Lyra's voice shook as she forced out another plea. "You stubborn mule! This could end. You have the power to put an end to this. And it *should* end. Heal him, Doran, do not make me beg."

All around us, people moved. Noble fey were herded like cattle from the scene. I could hardly focus on them, nor care, as my gaze moved from Erix to Tarron and back.

"We will get you help," Althea said, gentle fingers brushing the trail of tears from my face. "I promise we will not let you die like this."

"Where is she?" I managed, wincing as I gripped Althea's wrist. "Briar?"

Confusion rattled her expression, tugging her brows into a frown. "Briar is fine. What matters is getting you help."

"No." My voice was hoarse as though my lungs were full of liquid I could not remove. "Briar, she… she helped him. It was she who helped him take me. Althea… Althea, I am sorry."

Althea rocked back, but I refused to let go of her wrist. I could see in her wide, green-brown eyes that she attempted to make sense of what I'd revealed. To her, my words were a puzzle with pieces missing. One that finally made sense.

Althea stood, looking over the crowd with lips pulled taut. I knew she searched for Briar before she came back to my level and spoke.

"If she is smart, then she will have fled." Althea masked clear sadness with a face of thunderous anger.

"My son is dead!" King Doran shrieked, skin flashing bright with golden light as he demanded our attention. Those nearest to him shied away; even my own eyes flicked shut against the sudden light. As the glow dimmed, we all witnessed as King Doran looked over his own power with disbelief. I wondered if Queen Lyra and Althea felt how strong his magic was. How his power filled the air with a crisp scent of summer meadows and fresh, warmed grass. With Tarron dead, King Doran was the second-last of his court. His power was… overwhelming.

"And another child will die, if you do not save him," Althea spat fire as she spoke.

"Ask me to heal that boy one more time, and you will see what happens."

"Stand down." Queen Lyra put herself between her daughter and Doran. The brass-toned gown she wore was not made for battle, even though the bone-like shards poked up around the collar of the dress with tips that gleamed like blades. The Cedarfall guards turned on King Doran like the unpredictable threat he had become. "Leave, Doran. Before I make you."

"Insolent woman," Doran spat. "My own child lies dead on the floor at my feet, killed by one of your own. And yet you treat me as a threat? His head will be mine. Or I will take vengeance from your own child, Lyra. This one will do just fine."

Doran pointed to Althea who never wavered in standing her ground.

But as though Althea had become a delicate flower, the guards holding Erix let him go and sprang forward to stand by her side. She didn't need their assistance. Even against a man as powerful and mad as Doran Oakstorm, Althea was prepared to hold her own.

Finally free, Erix threw himself towards me. His armour crashed against the ground as he knelt, reaching for my face with shaking, warm hands. He cared little for the powerful king who demanded Erix's life as payment. All his focus was on me, hands cradling my cheeks as his silver gaze looked over me without blinking. "Little bird, I never stopped looking for you."

His words shot through my heart, piercing deeper than any blade. "I should have believed you…"

"Not now. When you are better, you can tell me that you were wrong, and I was right. For now, you just need to survive."

I didn't have the strength to tell him how he was wrong. I felt myself bleeding out from within, even beneath the still agonising pain of Althea's touch across my skin. I hardly had the energy to reach for his hands as they held me, even though I desired to.

"You killed Tarron."

Erix's expression pained, his hold of my gaze wavering. "I did. And I'd do it over, if given the choice."

"Now Doran… he wants your life in exchange."

They argued about it now. King Doran demanding Erix's life for his son's. For Erix to be handed over, taken from me. If not Erix, one of Lyra's many children.

"I am your guard, little bird. My duty is to protect you and stop anyone who is a threat." Erix's voice was a whisper, so much so that it was hard to hear him above the chaos. "I was simply doing as I was required."

Erix drew me into his arms whilst the room sparked in a war of words and threats.

"I think I'm dying, Erix." I winced as I tried to sit up. It was impossible to move, my insides felt as though they'd been flayed open.

"I will not let you. In fact, I forbid you to even speak those words aloud." I saw his turmoil a beat before Erix pressed his forehead into mine. The darkness I'd not long been pulled from lulled me to return. I felt it creeping in, a predator ready to devour me. Part of me longed to just give in. At least I'd no longer feel pain. No longer suffer. My mother would be waiting just as she had before.

It was the easier choice.

But nothing worth anything in life was ever easy.

"Not even your stubbornness can keep me alive, Erix." I scoffed a laugh, followed by a hiss as a wave of pain flowed over me.

"Don't you dare give up on me, Robin."

"Robin?" I laughed weakly. "I know I'm in trouble... when you use my *actual* name."

"If you die, so do the hopes of your people. Hold on to that."

Once again, I envisioned the devouring storm of winter. "It's too late."

"You are wrong. It is never too late."

"I can't, Erix, I can't do it now."

He pulled back from me, lips pursed and eyes brimming with tears that darkened his eyes as though they reflected the grey storm that was close to breaking across the world. "Are you admitting that you don't even want to try? We could sit here and wait for you to fade, or we can leave for Icethorn now. Get to the border. You told me what you need to do. The man I have come to care for is not the giving up kind."

"Erix, you need to get out of here." It was Althea speaking to him now. A line of guards now stood between King Doran and us. I even saw the backs of the two Elmdew royals on either side of Queen Lyra as they faced him down. "You are under our protection, but we will not be able to stop Doran if he truly wants to take you."

Even with the threat plain as day, Erix didn't remove his attention from me. "Robin, tell me you want to try, and we will go together. We do this together, just as I promised."

Althea didn't need to question what we spoke of. She simply knew. "Gyah can take you. But you need to leave, Erix, now."

"Robin... say the words."

"He will not–" Althea began, but I silenced her with my response.

Perhaps it was Erix's true belief in me that helped me hold onto this last chance, or the reality of what was to come for the world if I died. But I looked up at him, gritting my teeth through the pain as I finally sat up unaided.

"Okay," I said, forcing as much strength into my voice as I could. "I will try. For you."

Erix released a sigh, smiling through his anguish. "That is all I could have ever asked for."

King Doran's cry followed us through the skies of Farrador and beyond. I looked back over the screaming winds as Gyah flew us from the castle, witnessing flashes of bright, unyielding light as a battle occurred within the polished stone walls.

Gyah had been ready, just as Althea had said. One moment we were on the floor behind a wall of powerful fey, the next upon Gyah's scaled back as she flew up from the room, breaking through a tall, glass window and flying east towards the Icethorn Court. If it was not for Erix holding me steady, I would've tumbled from her side. My grip was weak, my hands hardly able to hold myself up as my energy melted away from me with each passing moment.

Gyah flew with speed I'd not known possible, or at least it seemed as such, for every time I opened my eyes, the scene below was different. Was I losing time? Unable to keep myself conscious as the internal bleeding lulled me closer to death's door?

First, the ground below was the outstretched camp of warriors. The next, it was open fields. Then a sea of forest and woodland. We passed over small hamlets of buildings, the outstretched shadow of Gyah's wings splayed across the ground far below.

Soon enough, the air grew colder, and the sky thickened with dense clouds. My first breath of the fresh, freezing air filled me with energy that I believed to be long lost. I held my eyes open for longer now, witnessing the blanket of snow that spread across the ground below.

"The Icethorn power is spreading," Erix muttered above the screaming winds. He was shivering as he held onto me, hunching in as the barrelling of sudden snow pelted down upon us. "The Passing of seasons is almost upon us."

The scene suddenly changed. As the snow fell heavier and the sky became thick and grey, we could no longer see before us. The magic here *was* heavier than it had been during my last visit.

It filled my soul and made my mind alert. A rush of pure adrenaline, offering me moments to spare, fending off death.

"I can feel it." The newfound energy masked the pain within me. I was able to grip onto Gyah's powerful neck to keep myself steady. The tugging I felt in my chest intensified, confirming we were headed in the right direction. I gave in to it, opening myself up to the welcoming power without fear or trepidation. It felt natural to lift a hand towards the dense fog we flew through, as though it too reached for me.

My stomach jolted as Gyah suddenly dropped her height. Erix's arm wrapped tighter around my middle, brushing over the burn marks, which should have caused me discomfort.

But I felt nothing.

Nothing but the cold. Nothing but the eternal winter that greeted us.

We fell beneath the pregnant clouds of snow until we could see the ground once again. The dark, still surface of The Sleeping Depths was beneath us. We then flew over the bank, bodies of forgotten gryvern now buried beneath piles of snow.

It made sense that I felt the magic of the court, because we were within its boundaries. Minutes passed and Berrow was suddenly beneath us – the ruined town no more than a blur as Gyah kept flying. Not once did she slow. The beat of her wings writhed with unrelenting power, as urgent as the beating of my heart as we passed over the edge of the town that Erix and I had looked over together days ago.

Beneath us was the chasm of mountains. I saw the valley far below, and the dark mass of buildings that lay empty and abandoned, and ahead of us was the reason why. Far larger than I'd last seen it, was the bundle of power that raced through the skies of Icethorn like a horde of silver dragons.

It moved with frantic, unpredictable speed as it thrashed and crashed through the sky. Into the sides of mountains, it smashed, causing an avalanche of snow and stone to race towards the valley far below.

"There," I called out, the pain within me a distant memory. The sky had darkened, signalling the end of the day. The Passing was almost over, but still, we had time. "We need to reach it. Get me as close as you can."

The blood within me hummed at the promise of power.

Gyah released a deep, guttural roar and pumped her wings faster, stronger. The pressure from the incoming wind intensified. I had to lean close to her slick body, urging Erix to do the same.

But then I saw them. Flying around the bundle of untamed, unclaimed power in a herd of their own, were the gryvern.

"Higher!" I screamed, the cold winds echoing my urgency. Gyah's body curved upwards, climbing the sky as the gryvern reached us with speed. The song of steel against leather sung behind me as Erix levelled his sword. He thrust it through the air as the first reached us, slicing skin as Gyah kept climbing higher and higher into the sky.

The storm of magic was beneath us now, growing further away. I could feel its panic as clear as my own. My chest tugged as the cord tightened, returning the weakness back to my body as we put distance between us and the power.

This was the gryvern's command – Doran's last-ditch effort to stop me from claiming my future. Even in death, Tarron's command lingered, his hope for me to fail.

I longed for Gyah to slow and return to my power, but words wouldn't form. The air was growing thinner the higher we flew, but still, the gryvern chased beneath us, snapping teeth and snatching at Gyah with pointed claws.

This was it. The end. Gyah released a horrific screech as gryvern flew to our side, knocking into her body. Erix's sword cut so close to my back as his body was thrown forward.

He released me, unable to hold on as he tried to slice out at yet another gryvern. I felt the burn wounds tear open at my chest and my back. Warm blood greeted the cold of my skin, and I knew that this was the end.

But with my blood came the chance I required.

I closed my eyes and released my hold of Gyah. Erix shouted my name, fingers gripping onto the back of my ripped, dirtied tunic, but his attempt to stop me was in vain.

We'd come this far with the power I finally longed to claim below me. If we were going to fail, I wasn't going to do so without trying one last time. All I could think of would be the disappointment on my mother's face when she finally greeted me in death.

When I finally slipped down Gyah's scaled side, it was because I wanted to. I pulled free from Erix's grasp with ease, his attention focused on the onslaught of gryvern. He noticed the lack of my presence a beat too late.

Then I fell

Like a stone through the air, I tumbled, eyes pinched closed as I passed the reaching, grasping claws of the gryvern.

Through screaming winter winds, there was nothing to stop me. If I had opened my eyes, I would've seen the ground beneath me grow closer and closer. There was no reason to watch it now. All there was room for was hope and the will that the power, my deserved power, would embrace me as I fell.

CHAPTER 38

"Robin." Julianne Icethorn was before me, her face covered by the billowing of dark hair. "You've found your way home."

I stood before the phantom of my mother, the comfort of cold snow seeping into the skin of my feet. All around us was the blanket of white, never-ending winter. The stark beauty of the sky blended so seamlessly with the ground that it felt as though the view had no beginning and no end.

"Am I dead?" I asked my mother, voice echoing whereas hers didn't.

"No, my dear boy. It is not your time to pass from one realm to the next. There is much for you to do for the realms before your time is upon you."

I thought I'd feel relief, but instead, I felt a stabbing sadness as I looked upon my mother. "Then what punishment do I face? To see you without *seeing* you." I wanted to reach for her but hesitated. She was so close, all I had to do was push the hair from her face and look at her features.

Somehow I knew my hand would pass through her body like fingers through mist.

"One day, we will be reunited, but your story is far from over. I need you to live. To thrive. You have an important choice before you, and I know in my heart that you are ready to make it."

"So, it worked?" I asked her, blinking as if I could see Gyah and Erix growing smaller the further I fell to the waiting ground.

"It did." Her voice crackled like the thawing of ice. "The power we left behind is yours now. I am proud of you for what you have achieved."

My heart swelled at hearing her say those words, but beneath it all, I still could not shake the deep sadness. "I forgive you. For leaving me. I blamed you for so long, but now I understand."

I didn't know why I said it, but I felt as though she needed to hear the words, just as much as I needed to say them.

The invisible winds that caused her hair to flow wildly, calmed for a moment. I caught the brief glance of obsidian eyes, darker than the night itself. Everyone was right. I was a mirror image of my mother.

"It was not an easy decision to make," Julianne Icethorn said. "I had heard whispers of the plans against the Icethorn Court's lives and felt it safer to keep you far away from me. I planned to come for you and your father, but fate found me quicker. I was coming for you, Robin. You must understand that. In another world, in another time, you would have been by my side for as long as fate allowed. You and your father. But you were my future, and to ensure you had one, I had to walk away."

"I know." A tear slipped free, cascading down my cheek. "Is this all in my head?"

"It is, but it is as real as you are. I have waited for years to see you again. Although my body is gone, perished in the ground, my soul has been waiting, longing for you to come to me. And you have. Now my soul, my power, is yours as it should have been from the beginning." Mother reached out a hand, fingers outstretched for me. "Will you claim the legacy for yourself?"

I hesitated but then reached for her. "I just wish this was different. That it happened... not like this."

"As do I, my darling boy." Her fingers wrapped around mine. The reality of her touch – the impossibility of it, had me gasping for breath. "But know that I will always be with you. Just as you have always been with me."

Another tear spilt, followed by another and another. It was how real her touch felt that brought a deep sadness to mix with the sudden happiness. Touching my mother's hand was like holding snow in my palm, waiting for it to melt away.

"Mother..."

"Yes?" Her fingers tightened, squeezing me as I, too, held onto her as if my life depended on it.

"What next? Where do I go from here?"

The wind calmed, allowing the strands of her hair to fall around her shoulders. For a brief moment, I saw her bright, red lips smiling and deep, black eyes full of pride. Then she spoke, squeezing my hand and spreading a fresh chill throughout the veins, bones and skin of my body.

"You live."

CHAPTER 39

I stood before the faded mirror, fingers tracing the pink, puckered scar of Althea's handprint upon my stomach. Every day I found myself looking for the scar Tarron had left me when his blade of light cut clean through me, but that was gone now, only the harsh memory of it a scar in my mind.

They offered to remove it, but I chose to keep it. As a reminder, more than anything else, that trust always came with a price.

Erix stepped behind me, hands reaching around my side for the shirt that was left unbuttoned. "Tell me what is bothering you, little bird."

I let him do the buttons up, fingers moving with ease as he started at my collar and moved down towards the waistband of the dark trousers I wore. "Even now, I feel like an imposter. About to face down a crowd of people, half of whom look at me with hate and the rest with an admiration I don't feel as though I deserve."

"You should care little for what they think of you." My skin shivered as his knuckles brushed the firmness of my stomach. "They will come to see you for what you are. They do not have a choice whether they accept you as the king you are now, for there is nothing more certain than that fact."

A *king*. He'd come to remind me daily, interchanging my nickname as frequently as he did his underwear. *Little bird. King.* I hadn't decided on which one made my skin shiver more.

"I might've stopped the ruination they had planned, but it is clear the tension has not dissipated as we hoped for. King Daron has made that obvious." I turned to face Erix without breaking the band of his arms. Once again, my mind went to my father, and I felt as though I had been stabbed all over again.

Erix looked down upon me with the same expression he'd given me when he found me standing, numb but alive, in the expanse of snow days ago, with an expression of relief and disbelief. It was as though he'd expected to find my broken, dead body against the ground. He never admitted it, but I knew he looked at me as though I was made from glass and would break at any given moment. In truth, I wasn't the delicate one. Not anymore. I could feel a power far greater than what I'd previously experienced. It lingered within my blood, my bones, every morsel of my being. I was winter, and it was me. Cold, unrelenting and never-ending. The power, although welcome, was frightening. But its presence ensured that I could keep myself safe.

A power I needed now. For my father. To get him back.

Erix, on the other hand, was unsafe. King Daron's petition for his head intensified with each passing day. It would only be a matter of time for that to be forced in some manner or another.

"Daron –" Erix never provided the man a title "– can waste his breath with his wants and requirements. I told you, and the Cedarfall Court has made it clear that I'm not to be tried for Tarron's death."

"You were merely doing what a personal guard is required to do," I repeated the same statement he'd told me over and over. My fear was for him to be taken, but I felt guilty for making Erix feel the need to settle my nerves even though the Oakstorm Court, or what was left of it, wanted to see him dead.

"Precisely." He pressed a kiss upon my forehead. I allowed myself a moment to think of nothing but his touch. "Now, as your personal guard, I suggest you finish getting changed quickly before the wrath of Althea is put upon us for being late."

I slipped from his hold, tucking the shirt into my trousers as Erix reached for the cloaked jacket that waited for me to put it on. "What if that's the whole point?"

"You cannot hide from them forever." Erix beckoned for me to extend my arms so he could thread them through the jacket.

"Not even for one more night?"

Looking back into the mirror, I watched as Erix brushed his hands down the material of the jacket. His touch was caring. His focus was entirely on making sure I looked the part that I was now required to play.

King Robin Icethorn.

"It will be a quick evening. The Passing was rather interrupted, and it is tradition for the court to acknowledge the handing over of control to the following season. It's a bunch of pointless conversations with food and drink, but tradition is tradition, and soon enough, it will be you needing to host the same festivities as the cycle proceeds anew."

"I'm out of my depth," I admitted, admiring the stunning craftsmanship of the outfit Eroan had made for me. The trousers were dark black, matching the colouring of my hair and eyes. The jacket was light and allowed movement. Silver and white threading twisted across the deep navy of the material, the imagery of mountains hidden among the design. All that was missing was the final decoration that I'd put off wearing for as long as I could.

"Then allow me to keep you afloat," Erix said. "No one expects you to proceed through your future blindly. Eroan is not the only member of your court who survived. Soon enough, you will have a court full of those willing to help, urging to see you succeed."

"And an equal number of people who still wish me dead."

Briar hadn't returned since Althea had last seen her. I'd come to learn that the threat of the Children of the Asp was as real as the human Hunters who'd still been seen sweeping through the Wychwood border.

Issues for tomorrow. But issues nevertheless.

A knock at the door surprised us before a freckled face peeped around it with a smile so wide it brought one of my own. "I do hope I'm not interrupting anything... *again*."

My cheeks warmed as I greeted Althea. Gyah followed into the room after her, unleashing a string of apologies. "Believe me, I tried to keep her out. There is only so much I can do to stop a Cedarfall."

Althea threw her hands up in defeat. "I would have left you to it, but there is a room full of important people waiting for you to arrive. The longer you make them wait, the more I have to have silly conversations to inflate the egos of those who crave it."

"I told you..." Erix muttered out the corner of his mouth.

Althea brushed past Erix, providing him with a friendly snarl which spurred a laugh from all of us. "I admit, I am both jealous and apologetic that you have to wear this thing."

I watched as she moved to the side dresser, reaching for the large square box that waited. It had been left closed since Eroan brought it to me. He'd been rather emotional, thanking me for the opportunity and expressing how he tried to keep the likeness to the one Mother had worn.

Althea reached for the lid and carefully lifted it open. Part of me wanted to ask her to stop, as if it was her pulling the crown free from the velvet-lined box that would make this all real, not the unimaginable power rushing through me or knowing that I would soon leave for the Icethorn Court once again. No, it was the crown I was to wear that solidified this all into reality.

"Is it really necessary for me to wear it?" It *was* beautiful. Seeing it in her hands, besides the small glimpse I'd stolen when Eroan gave it to me, was breathtaking. The crown was crafted on a band of white gold. All around the circlet were tall, sharp spikes reminiscent of the frozen tops of mountains. It glowed like icicles capturing the first light of morning. It could've been wielded as a weapon itself, the tips of each spike so sharp even Althea carried it to me with care.

"May I?" she asked softly, standing before me. The room was silent, albeit the thudding of my heart in my chest was loud enough for them all to hear.

"If you have to," I replied, rolling my eyes as small nervous laughter escaped me.

Althea nodded, lifting her hands above my head. Slowly, she lowered the crown upon my head, pushing the dark wisps of my hair flat to my head and keeping them in place. I expected it to be heavy but was surprised to see Althea's hands back by her side. Carefully I reached up to feel the cold metal, just to confirm it was sitting upon my head.

"So," I asked, aware of Gyah, Althea and Erix all staring at me with wide, unblinking eyes. "How do I look?"

It was Erix who replied, clearing his throat as though he had removed himself from a trance. "You look as you should."

"Just like a king," Althea said.

"An Icethorn," Gyah confirmed, bowing her head first, and then the rest of them following.

"Exactly," Erix added, drinking me in with his full attention. "But more importantly, you look like Robin."

It was impossible to ignore the tension during the evening's festivities. My suspicions were right. Whereas many greeted me in the throne room with kindness and acceptance, there were fey who kept their distance. Queen Lyra and King Thallan didn't stray far from my side. King Peta Elmdew and his husband, consort Dai, showed me kindness but still whispered quietly between themselves whilst watching my every move.

The room was split on their opinion of me, but the more I drank the wine, the less I cared. Even the fear of poison in the food was a distant memory. If Briar or the Children of the Asp would come for me again, I couldn't imagine they'd resort to old ways. Tarron was their benefactor and he was dead. Unless someone else offered up the funds, they'd leave me alone.

I had something else to worry about. My father. The thought of him, as it always did, spurred a violent sickness in my gut.

My cheeks hurt from forcing a smile, but I didn't give up, for the encouraging looks from Althea and Gyah kept me going.

It was the constant touch of Erix's hand upon my back that steadied my mind more than anything. It was as if he could read my mind, knowing when I needed him to distract me from the evening.

I was never more thankful than when Queen Lyra announced the end of the night. But the happiness and relief lasted only a moment.

The door to the throne room slammed open, disrupting the crowd and bathing it in silence. We all watched as three guards pushed through the bodies of fey, straight towards the table where we were situated at the room's head.

Queen Lyra stood, readying herself for the report the guards had to share. Something had happened, and the room waited with bated breath to find out what it was.

They spoke privately with their queen quickly before she dismissed them with a wave of her hand, looking at me for a moment before addressing the table. Queen Lyra's face drained of all colour. "A human has been found at Farrador's city walls."

The table erupted in whispered disbelief.

Althea stood beside me, addressing her mother. "The Mist of Deyalnar should keep them out. Are they certain it's a human?"

She gave one sharp nod.

"Is it a Hunter?" someone asked, spurring worried murmurs from the crowd.

Queen Lyra ignored the question, instead calling for a crowd of guards we had not noticed hovering beyond the now open doors. "Bring him in."

All heads turned towards the entrance to the throne room as the guards pushed a hooded figure forward. Chains were wrapped around his ankles and wrists, keeping both hands tied behind his back; they rattled with each step, the only noise that dared fill the crowded room.

Only when they came to a stop before the table did Queen Lyra speak again. "Remove his hood. If he has a message, he is welcome to share it before us all."

I watched, blood humming in my ears, as the guards surrounding the human pulled free the hood obscuring his face. The first thing I saw was the rounded edge of human ears. His clothing was worn, dirtied and old as though it had been the only material to grace his skin in many years. Only the black, splashed mark of the Hand across his clothing looked new.

"Human," Queen Lyra commanded. "You have come an awfully long way. Please, share what it is you have come to say."

The man raised his face towards her, a grin cut across his dirtied and marked face. He was old, perhaps Father's age. His light, mousy hair was thin, giving view to the pockmarked scalp beneath. When he finally spoke, his words made no sense. He bowed dramatically, as much as the chains at his wrists and ankles allowed. "I am a gift."

"From whom?"

"The Hand." The man began to laugh, spit falling from his lips which gave view to a toothless mouth. "He wishes you to meet him. He didn't believe you'd want to see him personally, but maybe you'll change your mind, once you see what I have to show you."

"Seize him," Queen Lyra snapped, panic filling her voice with urgency. But the man carried on, unbothered by the many hands that reached for him.

"He wants you to know that it'd been impossible without your aid, no matter how unwilling it has been."

"I have heard enough. Take him away."

The human didn't struggle as hands grasped him. His gaze swept across the table, landing on each of us for a paused moment. When his stare reached me, my insides prickled with discomfort as though he recognised a part of me that was like him.

Human.

"The Hand looks forward to finally meeting you in person. Meeting you all. But for now, here is your gift."

The fey guards around him stopped moving, each stiffening in place like stone. It took a moment to make sense of what we witnessed as the human broke free from the chains and lifted his hands like claws at his sides. "Feast your eyes upon what *he* has made."

The fey guards screamed but made no sound. Each one of them lifted from the ground as though unseen strings pulled them into the air. But that was not what we witnessed. No. This was different. Wrong.

The human lifted his hands higher, and with his motion, the guards' bodies rose from the ground.

When the human stopped, so did the fey – hanging like puppets without string in mid-air.

It only stopped when he lowered his arms. The guards tumbled back to the ground in a symphony of cracking as bone met the stone floor.

My chair fell back as I stood abruptly, looking at the iron-tipped arrow which protruded from the human's neck. All eyes fell to Gyah, who still held her bow as though it was ready to fire yet another arrow.

The human coughed, spluttering blood down his chin. He blinked, hands reaching up towards the arrow as though he would simply pull it free. But then he fell forward, face smashing into the slabbed floor with a sickening crunch.

No one spoke. Only the fey who'd not long since been held aloft in the air by unnatural means dared make a sound as they struggled where they lay – broken and bleeding.

"Erix," I said, reaching for him. I could see him struggle as he peeled his fingers away from the hilt of his sword as though he expected the human to reanimate and attack once again. He took my hand, pulling me to his side where he held me, still without taking his eyes off the body below us. "It can't be right. That was some trick... it had to be."

Erix didn't reply. Instead, he looked to Althea, whose fingers still tickled with flame, ready to attack if she needed.

"Humans are powerless. It has always been that way," Althea said, trying to convince herself or the crowd that listened in. But it was pointless. We had all witnessed it. Not only should his presence be impossible, but what he did... what he could do.

Yet the truth was bleeding out on the floor before us. Humans had access to magic that our histories only tied to the fey. But that had changed now, and it was all linked to the mysterious figure behind the Hunters. The Hand.

"It would seem that the humans were prepared for the war," Queen Lyra confirmed our darkest thoughts. "This *Hand*, the power behind the Hunters and the missing fey, has finally decided to make himself known to us."

"Tarron was right," I whispered beneath Queen Lyra's voice. "I didn't stop a war, but only delayed it."

"It is too early to know what this means," Erix replied, voice a rumble of his own haunting terror. "It could be trick. A ploy from Doran to make us act."

I shook my head, looking back towards the human with magic that should not belong to him. "The Hand wanted the fey for a reason. It's not the blood he is harvesting, but the power inside of it. And it would seem now we may know why."

Keep reading for an exclusive
bonus chapter for
A Betrayal of Storms,
told from Erix's point of view...

BONUS CHAPTER

Robin Icethorn was the most beautiful man I had ever laid my eyes upon. That fact had not wavered since I'd first met him all those days ago. Strange how short the time had been since he entered my orbit, and yet I felt as though he had been a part of my life for years. If he was not the missing part, he filled the Robin-shaped hole within me with ease.

I should have been reading the books supplied by Queen Lyra's scholars, but I could not take my eyes off him. How he nibbled his lower lip when he focused, the way in which his finger brushed the page and the concentration etched into the lines across his brow. There was not a single detail I wished to miss.

Occasionally he would look up at me, almost catching me in my pure fascination. Although those moments were fleeting, I was desperate for him to look away again, just so I could continue studying him.

Truthfully, I wanted to do so much more. But since we had arrived in Farrador, Robin had been distracted, his mind elsewhere. I dared not speak it aloud for fear my insecurities would be confirmed, but I felt as though his distance had everything to do with Tarron Oakstorm.

Just thinking about him soured my insides, and made the beast that had been lurking all my life stir to the surface.

But I had to keep control. For myself, for Robin. He was my focus.

Robin yawned for the fifth time since starting the page he had turned to.

"If you are tired, little bird, might I suggest a break?"

I noticed that every time I used the nickname I gave him, Robin would bristle as though a cool breath had brushed the back of his neck. Knowing I had such a physical effect on him with just my words gave me a sense of satisfaction that I craved. That was *exactly* why I fit those two sweet words in, whenever I could.

"To be honest, the words are all blending into one at this point," Robin replied, narrowing his eyes on the page as if that would stop the script from rolling like waves of water. "But I worry that if I give up now, I'll miss the chance to find answers."

"A few moments to rest your eyes and stretch will do you good," I said, closing the book I held but had not started. "Perhaps a walk around the battlements?"

Robin winced, a shiver coursing across his skin. "I'd rather not. Just looking out the window makes me sick."

I did not need to question why. Even with the thick stone walls, the sound of the army beyond the tower was enough to unsettle anyone's stomach. Let alone the man who balanced on the knife-edge of either starting a war or stopping it.

"Then some food," I suggested.

"I ate so many sticky buns at breakfast, if I put one more thing in my body, I'll be sick."

My brows raised into my hairline. Robin noticed my reaction a second after realising how his reply could be misconstrued. I adored the way his midnight eyes glistened, windows to the most emotive soul I had ever met. The right side of his mouth would quirk upwards whenever Robin's thoughts turned to naughtier topics. What I would give to close the space between us and put those rose-red lips against my own. To taste him, to make him scream my name.

There was nothing more beautiful than my name occupying his mouth… as well as other, more tangible things.

"Don't say it," Robin warned, obsidian eyes alight with mischief.

I lifted my arms in surrender, catching the way Robin's attention flickered to the muscles: something he always seemed occupied with. "My lips are sealed, and the precarious thoughts dissipating as I speak."

Robin pouted.

"Oh, did I say something to displease you, little bird?"

There it was again, that shiver, making the faint hairs on his arms raise to standing. I strained on the edge of my seat, aware of the hardening happening beneath my undershorts.

"Well," Robin drawled whilst placing the tome on the floor by his feet. "There *is* one thing you could do for me."

Saliva prickled inside my cheeks, filling my mouth, proving just how physically I starved for Robin. "Anything you need, it is my duty to provide."

I saw the word form on his lips before he spoke it. "Distraction."

I leaned forwards, flexing every muscle in my taut body as I drew closer to him. "When are you going to stop referring to it as a distraction, and simply ask me to fuck you?"

Robin gasped, eyes going straight for the door as if someone would come barrelling in. It was not exactly a wasted concern, considering Althea Cedarfall had last walked in on us. Any earlier and she would have seen me with my mouth full of the Icethorn heir.

"Language, Erix. What *has* gotten into you?"

"Oh, I don't know," I replied, finally standing, not caring to hide the obvious bulge in my leather breeches. Robin noticed too, his lips parting on a muted exhale. His focus was stuck to my groin as I sauntered over to him, nudged his knees apart with my hand and stepped in between them. "*You* have gotten into me. You've burrowed so deep inside of me, that I fear nothing will ever get you out."

"Like a thorn?"

My lips turned upwards as I reached for Robin's jaw. He didn't stop me. Instead, he arched in his seat, nails digging into the armrest as I placed my thumb on his lower lip. I tugged it carefully, not wanting to hurt him, whilst so desperately needing to feel the softness of his tongue.

"Like an arrow. Something piercing. A thorn can be removed and the wound healed. The arrow, though, leaves damage after removal, even if the person struck survives. *That* is what you are to me. A lasting wound. A scar to be proud of."

Robin could not respond with my thumb in his mouth. I almost removed it so I could hear his sultry voice, but I didn't act quickly enough. With wide eyes looking up at me through dark lashes, Robin wrapped that pretty fucking tongue around my digit.

A groan escaped the deepest parts of me. It encouraged Robin, who deliberately scored his teeth against my skin.

"So, I shall reiterate your options." My mouth was parched, my body desperate for him. "A walk, some food or–"

Robin pulled back and answered before I could finish. "I'll go with option number three."

"For being royalty, you really have no manners."

He fluttered his lashes, almost destroying me. "Pretty please."

"That's better," I said, before turning for the door. "Much, much better."

I checked the door was locked two times, just to be sure. By the time I turned back around, Robin was already undressing.

"Wait a moment," I said, sauntering back over to him. "What's the rush?"

He narrowed his eyes on me, scrutinising as he unbuttoned his tunic. "Silly question, Erix. You know *exactly* what the rush is about."

I had a feeling Robin was *not* talking about continuing his research. From the way he looked up at me, there was only one desire on his mind.

Me.

And that made me feel powerful.

"It's rather refreshing when someone else gives the commands," Robin admitted, tongue lacing his lower lip, enticing me to snatch it between my teeth.

"Is that so?" I asked, arching to reach beneath the waistband of my trousers to grip my straining cock.

He tipped his head in agreement, fluttering those fucking eyes at me. Another second and I would break beneath his gaze, shattered into a million pieces, never with the desire to be fixed by hands other than his.

"Well," I breathed, feeling the strings of control snap one by one. "If that is the case, get on your knees."

"Look whose forgotten his manners now," Robin chirped before sinking his teeth into his lower lip.

"Knees, little bird."

He did not need to be told a third time. Robin dropped to the ground beneath me, hands reaching desperately for my belt. It was undone in a blink, pulled out of the loops around my waist and then dumped to the floor.

"Look at you," I sang, heart beating like the flock of a thousand birds. "You really were in need of a distraction, weren't you?"

Either Robin didn't hear me, or just didn't have the care to reply, because another handful of seconds and my cock was gripped in his hand and guided inside of his mouth. The second his lips brushed the curve of my tip, my world came apart at the seams.

My fingers tangled in the back of his hair as my roar of pleasure echoed around the room. Robin fought against the thickness of my thighs as one hand tugged my trousers down to my ankles. Perhaps I should have helped him, but alas, my body was no longer my own. It belonged to him entirely.

I moved when he wanted me to.

As much as I longed to be strong for him, I was reduced to a pathetic excuse for a man, with no control. Because it had not been but three minutes with my cock enjoying the pleasure of his mouth, and I'd nearly finished.

I tore him off me, and I swore the glistening spit across his parted mouth made controlling myself close to impossible.

"Normally I would complain if the man I laid with could barely last a few minutes, but then again, no man has ever tasted as sweet as you," Robin said, blinking up at me, eyes watering from taking me deep into the back of his throat.

"In your mouth, I'm far more than a man," I said, breathless and yet I had done nothing but stand there and let him rule me.

"Then what are you, Erix?"

Robin's questions settled over my skin like the first snowfall of winter. Chilling to the bone, yet as pleasant as a hundred kisses from soft lips. And my answer, enticed by his siren call, fell out of me with ease. "Yours. If you would have me."

Robin paused, and for a brief moment I almost regretted my answer. Then he blinked, returning from whatever thoughts he harboured, re-joining me in this reality. "I think you took that role the moment you stepped into my line of sight."

My heart leaped in my throat. Deep down, where the beast hid, I knew I didn't deserve him. Not until he understood my secrets, my past, and the way they would affect my future. But until then, I could pretend. Because he needed me just as badly as I needed him.

What came next was a shifting in tides, slow and steady. Robin allowed me to pick him up from the floor. I carried him over the four-poster bed, laying him gently on his back. Not once did he take his eyes off me. Not as I finished undressing him, leaving his naked body nestled amongst the rumpled gold silk sheets.

What I would give for the time to touch every inch of his skin. To leave my imprint on him, just as he had with my spirit.

Between kisses and touches, I raised Robin's back and slipped a pillow beneath the bottom of his spine. His legs found their way over my shoulders, whilst I kissed the inside of his calves, brushing my fingers up and over his thighs to his exposed arse.

I reminded myself to thank Althea for the vial of lubrication which had been left in the bedside drawer. Clearly it was some twisted inside joke after she'd walked in on us the last time. But either way, it would come in handy.

Whilst Robin watched, I emptied the vial onto my length, massaging it in, using some on the tip of two fingers to prepare him for me. His whispered gasp made the fire inside of me burn wilder – hotter. Blistering to the point that I was desperate to take him.

I positioned myself at his entrance and, careful not to hurt him, I leaned into him. This time, when Robin moaned through the feeling of us joining as one, I caught it with my mouth pressed over his.

My tongue explored his until I had sheathed myself inside of him all the way to the hilt. Robin arched his back off the sheets, enough for me to slip a hand beneath and add pressure to the bottom of his spine. His thighs tightened, his nails sinking into my back. And slowly, ever so slowly, I began to move.

The feeling was bliss. It was everything and more. I had craved the pressure of his arse since the first time I had experienced it, but this was different. All touches, silence, and eye contact. Robin existed in a place where he had no room for worries. I recognised it in the way his forehead smoothed, his eyes widening and the tension in his brow lessened.

I would offer him this peace, over and over, if given the chance.

And I felt no need to rush myself, but to enjoy the few minutes I would last.

"You are the most beautiful creature I have ever laid my eyes on," I said, drawing my hips back before thrusting forwards. A bead of sweat trickled down my temple, leaving a trail all the way down the curves of my hardened chest. "Looking down at you is a blessing. Seeing you look up at me is something I do not feel as though I deserve."

Robin reached for me, laying a cool hand on my cheek. A storm lingered beneath his skin, with the power to turn flesh to glass. And yet I never feared him, never believed he had it in him to hurt me.

If only that feeling was mutual.

"Erix," Robin exhaled.

There it was. The sound that I put above anything else in the world. My name coming from his lips.

"Say it again," I said, unable to keep the pleading from my tone. "I want to hear you scream my name. I want no other name to ever grace your tongue."

Robin swallowed hard, eyes rolling back into his head as I picked up in my pace. "Erix," he whined, nails sinking deeper into me, power rolling from him in undulant waves. "Erix. Erix. Er–ix!"

"Gods," I groaned, feeling the pressure build. It was becoming impossible to hold back. I wanted to give it to him and more – so much more.

When our eyes locked again, I knew I was done for. Robin drew me down to his mouth, stopping as our lips brushed. Then he whispered my name so quietly even I believed it was a trick of some kind.

"Cum for me, Erix."

My pace quickened, my thrusts shortening as the pleasure built to new heights. I was never one to disappoint, and surely not for Robin. All I needed was his confirmation, and I released the little control I had over myself.

I laid my forehead against his, enjoying the cold kiss of his skin against the damp heat of mine. The wave of pleasure captured me, sweeping me away into the devouring feeling that was Robin Icethorn.

We laid amongst crumpled sheets for what could've been hours. I gathered Robin up in my arms, tickling fingers down his back, all whilst my body still quivered with the aftereffects of orgasm. After a while, I gently pulled myself from beneath him and climbed off the bed.

"No," Robin called out. "I'm not ready for this to end. Come back to me."

"And I thought you said you were enjoying not being the one to give orders," I said, shooting him a look.

"That's right, but–"

"But as much as I could waste weeks lying beside you, we have a task at hand, and reality to face."

"Killjoy," Robin complained, spreading out on the bed and refusing to move.

"Perhaps, but there will be plenty of time for moments like this when we find what we are looking for. Until then, I'm going to request that a bath is drawn up for you," I said, buttoning up my shirt whilst Robin just lay there, skin flushed and chest heaving.

"But what about the books?" he asked, not that either of us truly cared about them now.

"I will read them to you," I said.

"You will?" Robin leaned up on his elbows.

I nodded. "It would be my pleasure."

Turning my back on him, Robin took the moment before I slipped out of the room to call something out. "*You* are my pleasure, Erix. A distraction, yes. But also someone I really enjoy being around. I hope you know that."

He could not see my face, or the smile that broke across it. But I felt weightless as I took the step forwards. "And you are mine, Robin Icethorn. My duty *and* my pleasure."

ACKNOWLEDGEMENTS

Thank you to all those readers and supports who have followed the *A Betrayal of Storms* journey since it began in 2021. I am so excited that we made it this far. My Patreon family: Lupe, Binnie A, Booknerd_Charlie, Tally, Megan B, Autumn. Thank you for supporting this journey of mine. You are the best.

Laura R. Samotin. Thank you for putting me on this path. Without you guiding me, holding my hand, this dream of mine would never have been possible. Hannah, my amazing agent. Firstly, thank you for even listening to Laura and being open to talk to me. Then, and more importantly, thank you for all your hard work, tireless effort and enthusiasm, and thank you for coping with all those messages I send you.

Eleanor, Desola, Caroline, Amy, Lauren and all the incredible Angry Robot team – thank you for taking a chance on me! I am so happy to have found a home with you, and for my books. It feels really nice being in the Robot family. This first novel feels like the building block in a really incredible relationship we have started. I look forwards to all the adventures to come – including that world-wide book tour followed by the movie deal where I get us all parts as fey royalty in the background. Manifest with me.

Beth, Jasmine, Lola and Millie. Thank you for those tireless gaming sessions of Dead by Deadlight, where you listen to me waffle about my books. You are the best cheerleaders around.

Harry, my darling husband, who has been with me from the beginning of my author journey, and will hopefully be with me long after it ends. Every story I tell, every character I make, I plant a little seed of your inside of them. Love you.

And to that little gay Ben who grew up watching Disney films, wishing the princess didn't always get to steal the hot prince. This story it for you, by you, and also a gift to every other little boy who dreamed the same dreams as me.

We are Angry Robot, your favourite independent, genre-fluid publisher, bringing you the very best in sci-fi, fantasy, horror and everything in between!

Check out our website at www.angryrobotbooks. com to see our entire catalogue.

Follow us on social media:
Twitter @angryrobotbooks
Instagram @angryrobotbooks
TikTok @angryrobotbooks

Sign up to our mailing list now: